The figure stood over him,   ...Magdalena herself. Even this near, she couldn't tell much. He was draped in a long, heavy coat of some deep hue, its high collar fastened tight about his neck. Of the outfit beneath and the hair above, she could make out only that they were dark and flowing.

Beyond that, she saw only that his skin was pallid, almost sickly so, and his eyes...

Her arms froze, her gun lifted halfway, wrapped in lethargy, *beyond* lethargy. She couldn't recall how to make them move.

His eyes...

A tremor ran through her, a scream echoed and re-echoed in her mind, in her soul. Here was nothing wholesome, nothing human. Snake. Wolf. Pestilence. Nightmare.

Emptiness. Hunger.

She could not run. Could not turn away. Could not blink.

His eyes...

They bored into her. They filled her. They *were* her.

Who was she?

"It appears," he spoke, and the voice came from everywhere, from nowhere, surfacing like a long-forgotten memory, "as ludicrous as it might be, that you are the leader of this latest... expedition." Every word was precise, distinct unto itself yet flowing smoothly into the next. "I would know who you are. Why you have come. Why you do the bidding of these iron devils.

"Tell me."

She didn't *know* who she was. But at his command, she remembered who—up until those eyes—she once had been, and why she was here.

Haltingly, lifelessly, Magdalena—or perhaps a shell of Magdalena—began to speak.

THE IRON DEVILS

by Ari Marmell

For Kate F., Jaym G., Nicole L., and Snow. When it comes time to rise against the bloodsuckers and the machines, I want you leading us.

Chapter One

From deep within the dust-choked haze, the reaching shadows, a beat-up gas-burner juddered and thumped over a makeshift road, belching fumes that only thickened the sludgy air. The vehicle's cab was rusted, pitted, and mostly open, with driver and engine shielded from the elements only by cracked panes of glass. The bed of the truck was wider open still, consisting of two wooden bench seats and several dozen people crammed together atop them.

On most days, the sounds of conversation shouted over the grind of the engine, of comment and complaint about the mission just completed, even occasionally of laughter, would have spilled from that small crowd to leave a trail as blatant as the exhaust. On most, but not today.

On most days, every one of the passengers would have been alive.

Keeping pace with the vehicle, some twenty feet above, were multiple devices perhaps the length of a tall man's arm. Held aloft by spinning rotors, they aimed a variety of lenses down at the truck, and flew far too steadily, too smoothly, to be guided by any human hand.

Magdalena's feet were already on the concrete before Jonas finished his call of "Everybody out!"

Men and women—boys and girls, really, or so they'd have been considered in eras past—poured from the open bed, frayed boots and worn soles slapping the ground.

Frayed and worn like the rest of the denims, the leathers, the wools, and the cottons. And like the bulk of the youths wearing them.

Two of them, however, were far slower, more deliberate, in their departure. Between them, under the careful gaze of all the others, they carried the body.

Rio and Cassie moved to join the first pair, taking up part of the burden. The rest of the detachment gathered around them, a shifting, undulating clump. Then, disorganized as they appeared, they moved as one.

They all knew where they were going. It might have been a while, but it was a walk they'd all taken before.

Magdalena worked her way to the front of her team, eager to escape the large patch of crumbling cement that was the vehicle pool, to get this task, this day, over with. And it was still her job to lead them.

Behind her, the small hovering escorts peeled off to assume other duties, while a larger, more humanoid machine—a tall, gaunt, headless thing of dull metal and polymer, with quadruple-jointed digits—assumed Jonas's place behind the wheel to park, store, and secure the old truck. Just as they'd done uncountable times before, whenever Detachment 13936 returned from assignment.

It should be different today. What happened should matter!

Except she'd known, from the moment he'd been wounded, that it wouldn't.

She'd always assumed the encampment must have an official designation in the computer records somewhere—Biological Habitat Some-Number-or-Other, maybe—but to her, and to all the others, it was just "the camp" or, if they were feeling particularly generous, "home."

Built on (and with) the ruins of one of the smaller towns that used to thrive alongside the now cracked and pitted interstate, the camp was some distance from the Scatters, and thus from the dust, smog, and other effluvia belched out by that hive of inhuman industry. That didn't make the air particularly crisp and clear—the skies remained choked with overcast both natural and other, and the camp's rickety generators spewed exhaust nearly thick enough to climb—but compared to the Scatters, it was downright sunny.

Mags was fine with grimy air, particularly today. It gave

her good reason for the reddened, squinting eyes she wouldn't otherwise have wanted her people to see.

Volunteer duty. A simple, straightforward mission. Not easy, but nothing they hadn't done a dozen times, nothing to surprise them during their briefing. The voice of the machine still reverberated in her head—somewhat feminine, even vaguely pleasant, but *wrong.* Flat, inflectionless at times. Soulless. Inhuman.

<Proceed with this unit to quarry designated Seven-Southwest. Excavation and Mining Detachment Four-Four-Zero-Three-Five has located signs of prior human occupation. >

A model Magdalena's dealt with many times, it still makes her flesh crawl. Perhaps the height and length of an average beef cow, albeit substantially wider, it skitters along on six segmented legs in unnatural mockery of some vile beetle. They pound into the earth at every step, sinking deep, though one—glistening with what might be leaking oils— lands less heavily than the others. An eighth pair of limbs, spindly and ending in wiry digits, protrudes from a rotating turret atop the front end, and an array of lenses circle the mechanism's body, allowing it to observe all directions at once.

Magdalena straightens her shoulders, as does everyone around her, and stares straight ahead. You never know who might be watching from behind those lenses. It's probably just the machine itself, running autonomously.

But it might, just might, be one of the Eyes.

<One corrosive chemical defense system encountered. Additional systems unknown, extent of occupation unknown. Detachment One-Three-Nine-Three-Six will render safe for additional biological and mechanical exploration and exploitation.>

Occupation. Mags bit the inside of her cheek to keep from scowling. She'd lived in this world all her life, was resigned to it, for the most part. But it always struck her how much the machines managed to make "occupation" sound like "infestation."

Her distaste aside, though, she'd been so damn proud of herself as the mission progressed. Proud of herself for leading her people around a handful of so-called Charlies, primitive traps such as weighted spears and spike-laden pits, protecting the mine's interior. For recognizing the old heap of auto parts and scrap metal as the bait it was, left over from Pacification. For finding the control box that operated the more intricate trap: nozzles that would have sprayed her entire detachment with the chemicals, corrosive to metal and flesh both, that had been one of humanity's primary weapons back when they were still deluded enough to think weapons mattered. Rendering the old bases and stockpiles safe for the machines to scavenge was what she did—what the 13936 did, what all the Recognizance and Disposal detachments did—and she was damn good at it.

And then she starts to open the panel. Feels the sharp pain in her scalp and her neck as Rio yanks her aside by her hair, feels the hot ache in her ears as the concealed shotgun discharges, hears the scream as the blast that should have struck her hits home elsewhere...

Unwilling to drag her friends and their burden through the thick of the camp, Magdalena chose a longer course around the outermost of its "structures"—not even proper tents, these, but threadbare canvas draped over tall poles, rudimentary shelter from the elements. The bulk were freestanding, but a few incorporated a bit of old crumbling wall or solid concrete surface here, part of an old cellar there. The fabric ceilings rippled, rustling in the faintest breeze, a constant flapping that everyone had long since learned to tune out. Most of the camp was like that, including Mags's own meager living space. Only a rare few buildings were solid, constructed of materials salvaged from the old ruins, and these were reserved for equipment storage, "rest areas" and repair bays for inactive robots, water or food processing centers, slightly nicer sleeping quarters for the detachment overseers, or—in emergencies only—cramped and claustrophobic shelters against inclement weather.

Even here, at the camp's edge, workers from other teams busied themselves with this task or that, following whatever orders the machines had handed down. Every one of them paused in their duties to step aside, allowing the 13936 to pass. They knew what a march in this direction meant, even before they saw the body.

They, too, had all walked this path before, more than once.

Just like that, after what felt like a single heartbeat and the passing of years, they arrived. Detachment 13936 stood before a freestanding structure, part wood and part salvaged stone, set aside from the rest of camp. Stained, moisture-warped boards formed narrow gaps in the walls, through which escaped the hideous scents of cleansers mixed with rot.

"Processing." Mags felt a brief, irrational surge of fury at whichever team manned the equipment inside today.

Rio, Cassie, and the others laid Carter down on the chipped and brittle conveyor. Most backed away in silence. Rio kicked the support post, shaking the mechanism, and the glare he turned on the nearest machine fell just short of punishable defiance. Nestor, easily the largest and strongest member of the detachment, hunched over and turned the crank, while the others watched their friend slowly, fitfully disappear into the structure.

No, Mags corrected herself. Not our friend. Yesterday, or even just a few hours ago, Carter had been their friend.

Now? Now he was just...

Protein.

When she heard the mechanisms within clatter to life, when she heard them begin to chew, she knew she had to walk away.

"Wasn't your fault, Mags."

She'd heard Ian catch up to her, announced by the rapid crunch of boots on scattered gravel. She hadn't said anything then, and didn't for a moment more, concentrating on stepping over a veritable garden of old, half-buried bricks without turning an ankle or stumbling into nearby tent-poles. "Didn't say it was," she told him finally.

"Well... good."

More steps in silence, until they'd just about reached the makeshift tent in which Magdalena's cot waited. Then a hand closed on hers. As if it took some effort even to recognize what it was, she squinted through stinging eyes at skin far paler than her own deep-copper complexion; then up, to an intense blue gaze beneath an unruly, sandy mop of hair.

Unruly and very soft, unless one's fingers happened to get snagged in the tangles...

"He was my friend, too," Ian told her softly. "And a good worker. We'll all miss him."

"I know that!" It emerged somewhere between a snap and a snarl.

The young man recoiled, spun hard enough to leave a divot in the dirt, began to stomp away.

"Ian?"

He halted but didn't turn back.

Cassie and Marty, both crouch beside Carter. His chest rising in ragged gasps, his face pale enough to blend with the whites of his eyes. Despite the pressure of Cassie's hands on his thigh, a steady rivulet of blood seeping into the leg of his pants.

A wound he could have—should have—survived. Except they'd all known, from the first moment, that he wouldn't.

"Ian, I'm sorry. I just..." She swallowed once, blinked until her vision was briefly clear of both moisture and remembered images. "I pushed Jonas to volunteer for this one, and for what? A few extra privilege points? A nicer meal, a hot shower?"

"Someone had to volunteer, Mags." He still hadn't turned. "They'd just have assigned a team if nobody stepped up, you know that."

"Might not have been us, though. Either way, I was in charge. And I'm the idiot who didn't check if the panel was wired. I should have seen the shotgun. It... it *is* my fault."

"I couldn't save *either* of you," he said softly.

"What? I'm fine. What're you...? Oh." She felt herself trying to smile and scowl at once and wondered briefly if it was possible to sprain one's lips. "You're bummed it was Rio who pulled me clear, aren't you?"

Magdalena knew him well enough. Even from behind, by the set of his shoulders and the angle of his head, she could all but see the embarrassed grin. "Kind of dumb, huh?"

"You're impossible." Her arms snaked around him, clasping tight, and her cheek settled against his back, smearing the thin layers of dirt that clung to them both. "I've told you before, stupid," she said, her voice softer, affectionate. "You got nothing to prove to me."

"I know I don't have to. I just… *want* to. I mean, everyone already knows you can kick my ass. I gotta be good at *something*."

"Dumbass." She squeezed him once, hard. "I'm wiped, Ian. You want to protect me? Come help me not dream about Carter."

Ian finally turned, sliding in the circle of her arms to take her in his own.

"I think I can do that," he whispered.

Except, hard as he'd tried, Ian *couldn't* do that.

She dreams, first, not of Carter but of the Scatters, where so many of her assignments drag her. The outskirts of what had been a sprawling, bustling city, before Pacification. Before the machines.

Great shells rise from the earth and gape open to the sky, the corpses and carapaces of once-mighty structures. Only a few are recognizable as buildings any longer; most are mere fingers of cracked concrete, rotted wood, or broken glass, frozen in their final, desperate grasp at salvation that never comes. Rubble chokes what used to be thoroughfares, heaps of debris abandoned where they'd fallen. Mags knows from experience that rodents and other vermin now make their homes in the nooks and crannies, though the rough song of the truck has scared them into hiding.

Here and there, only just visible through the dusty miasma, shreds and streamers flutter in the moaning breeze, waving their despairing loneliness at all who happen by. Those twisting wraiths appear, for the most part, to be strips of old flags and banners, or the ripped facades of larger roadside signs.

For the most part. On occasion, the tattered fragments poking from beneath this bit of rubble or that crumbled window are smaller. Of duller hues.

And some have sleeves.

Magdalena softly touches her fingertips to her forehead, her stomach, her left and right shoulder. She has no idea what the gesture actually means, only that, in her childhood, she'd watched her parents perform it time and again. One of the few memories she has of them, she finds it comforting. It helps to drive the lingering rags—and their implications—from her mind.

Everything is brutal, jagged, dust-choked; the fossilized remains of a living society. And this is where the city has suffered nothing more acute than the ravages of time and the elements. Elsewhere? Where the bombs landed during Pacification, where open battle raged? Naught but mountains of fragmented rock, cracked sheets of stone or plains of glass, and blackened craters nearly as large as the quarries.

Those, even the vermin avoid.

Not a sliver or glint of metal remains. From the deepest craters to the tallest ruins, every scrap has long since been salvaged by the machines—or, if not every scrap, then those that remain are buried in rubble so thoroughly and deeply that the effort required to reclaim them would be… inefficient.

Still the harvesters swarm over the remnants, some searching for any ore that might have somehow been missed, the rest gathering stone or plastics instead. Tiny skittering things with cutting torches; great lumbering mechanical beasts hefting entire walls; autonomous vehicles designed to crawl through the detritus-choked streets while hauling their loads of cargo… They move and work in quantities sufficient to bring the faint illusion of life back to a city long dead.

With the maddened logic of dreams, it is only then—after fully setting a stage of which she hardly needed to be reminded—that the imagery returns to Magdalena's fallen friend. She stands outside the deep quarry at the Scatters' edge, teetering on an emotional precipice far more precarious than any of the mines she's "rendered safe" for her steel masters.

<Dalton, Carter.> It's not even the logic of the dream that forces her to turn, however hard she fights against it, toward the voice of the machine. It happened exactly that way before and will again every time she remembers. A lifetime of training allows for nothing less; when a machine speaks, the workers listen. No matter what. <Injury detected and logged. You will display your injury for examination.>

"It… it's not that bad, really. I just need—"

<You will display your injury for examination.>

With a soft, resigned sigh, he bends to tear open the hole in his pants and unwinds the haphazard bandage.
Please... *Mags isn't sure if she's just thinking or whispering aloud.* Please, please, it's not that bad, he can recover... Please...
The faint whirr of a zooming camera sounds from within the insectile form. <Long-term debilitating,> it announces, a soulless judge pronouncing merciless sentence. <Recovery uncertain and resource intensive. Maintenance of Dalton, Carter, no longer efficient.>
A single gunshot...

When Mags bolted awake, her hands already moved, seemingly of their own accord, repeating that strange gesture: forehead, belly, left shoulder, then right. It should have comforted her. It usually comforted her.

But not tonight. Not with the terrible grinding of the processor still echoing in her head.

She was grateful to see that Ian remained fast asleep beside her. It meant she had no need to swallow her tears.

It was a cot. Just like a hundred others. Just like her own.

She sat cross-legged on the cold stone beside it, one hand resting on the threadbare fabric, so worn it was practically cobweb.

This can't be comfortable. Maybe Carter should have used his privilege points for a replacement.

Mags had no recollection of deciding to leave her own tent, unwinding herself from Ian's arm and getting half-dressed. She'd only realized she was coming here when she found herself carefully stepping around Carter's neighbors. Nor did she have any real sense of how long she'd sat here, only that at some point, when she wasn't looking, the sun had risen.

Shining down, as brightly as the clouds would permit, on an empty cot.

"You're going to be late for muster," Ian warned gently from behind.

She didn't even ask how long he'd been there. "Are they looking for me already?"

"One unit was. I told it I thought I'd seen you near the mess tent."

"Ian!" Now she was up and facing him. "Are you crazy? If they find out I wasn't there..."

"Then they'll assume I was mistaken. Maybe I'll lose a few points. You needed time here."

No point in arguing; it was done. With a final glance back at Carter's cot, Mags nodded and stepped from beneath the canvas, Ian at her side, moving to join the rest of the detachment for today's assignments.

"Any idea what you're gonna do with your new privilege points?" she asked after a few steps, mostly because she felt she ought to say *something*. "Still saving them up, or will you spend them on—?"

"I traded them to Rio and Cassie."

"You *what*?!" The surprise, as well as a brief but intense flash of jealousy, nearly set her stumbling.

"They were closer to Carter than any of us, Mags. I thought... Well, it felt like the right call."

Jealousy now washed away by a tide of pride and no small amount of affection, Mags said nothing more, but she found her fingers entwined with his for the rest of the walk to muster.

Chapter Two

Covered only in a thin film of gritty, lye-heavy soap, their feet squelching loudly in the mud, half a dozen members of Detachment 13936 stood before an old concrete wall. Every one of them tensed, bracing for what was about to happen.

"Here comes the fun part."

Magdalena snorted and glanced sidelong at Rio before squeezing her eyes shut. "Yeah, Cassie might want you to *cover* your fun part before it's—"

The blast of water hit like a thousand tiny stones. Skin turned various raw shades of red or brown beneath the liquid barrage, and several "bathers" hissed or grunted as particularly sensitive areas registered their extreme displeasure.

"Turn." The order came from the bored attendant—some bald, heavy-browed guy from whichever team had hose duty today. He barely looked up to ensure they'd complied, simply swinging the massive nozzle back across the wall in the usual, monotonous pattern.

Mags could have avoided this. Between the points she'd already stockpiled and those the 13936 had earned on their last assignment, she could've taken a hot, private shower *and* enjoyed a meal of real beef. She'd never before had enough privilege to do both at the same time.

She also hadn't yet been able to bring herself to spend any of them, not so soon after Carter. Certainly not after her lover's show of generosity with his own.

Still, Mags grumbled internally, as much to keep her mind off the veritable jackhammer of water now pounding into her back, *would've been nice if I could've at least showered with Ian.*

He, alas, had been part of the previous group called up for their weekly cleansing.

"*Cleansing.*" *Scouring'd be more accurate.*

Prevailing theory around the camp had it that the soap was little more than a formality; the machines were quite content with simply *blasting* the worst of the grime and parasites from their bipedal beasts of burden. Why else design the pumping mechanism so only the robots could adjust the pressure?

"Time!" the attendant called, shutting the hose down. "Out of the way! Group four, two minutes!"

Mags shuffled aside with the others, grabbing a handful of semi-clean rags from the nearest pile to towel off, then a rough, undyed, pullover shirt and heavy trousers from the communal collection. That standard "uniform" was common throughout the camp, punctuated only occasionally by more colorful clothes where someone had decided this was a good day to wear one of their few personal outfits.

Tugging the shirt to unstick the fabric from still-damp skin, Mags made her way toward the mess tent. The grief over Carter's death just yesterday was already beginning to dull, so accustomed was she to loss; ever since her vigil at his cot, it had shrunk to a vague, low-hovering melancholy. She'd be largely over it—and probably ready to spend those privilege points—by tomorrow, and found herself idly wondering which, of the many people she saw bustling this way and that, might be absent by then.

She halted as a small passel of children dashed past, shouting and giggling, ratty pouches of newly harvested grains slung over their shoulders. Like everyone else in the camp, the children worked, or at least those who were old enough did— the machines would tolerate nothing less. So the kids made games of their chores. The young woman tried to recall what it'd been like to laugh that way, then gave it up as unimportant. The sound grated a bit, considering her mood, but what the hell. Let them be; it wouldn't be long until they understood too much to be so carefree.

Assuming they survived that long. Given the machines'

unwillingness to provide more than rudimentary hygienic and medical resources, not a lot of infants made it to adolescence, and not a lot of adolescents reached adulthood.

More or less the same reason her overseer, Jonas, at four decades or so, was one of the community's eldest.

A train of thought which brought Magdalena to Oded, another camp elder, who happened to be one of the cooks—and *that*, in turn, sent all somber contemplation scattering from her mind in a sharp reminder that she was damn hungry. She hadn't eaten last night, not with her friend's loss—with the sights and the sounds of his processing, the knowledge that he would contribute to the next few meals—still so fresh.

Now, however, the ache was fading, and Mags found herself ready to get back to normal life.

Stomach growling, she quickened her steps. The mess tent was in view, the scents of simple grains baking and processed meats roasting had just begun tickling her nose, when a short, sharp siren yanked everything in the camp to an abrupt halt.

The voice of the encampment's central processor reverberated from the scattered loudspeakers. It boasted the standard artificial inflection of the machines, though the pitch was rather more masculine than the multi-legged guide back at the quarry.

<Recognizance and Disposal Detachment One-Three-Nine-Three-Six to assemble at staging area B. Message repeats. Recognizance and Disposal Detachment One-Three-Nine-Three-Six to assemble at staging area B. Message repeats. Recognizance...>

"What the *hell*?!" Magdalena, jaw agape but fists clenched, didn't even realize she'd spoken aloud. "We just got back!"

Well, screw it. She wouldn't disobey, of course. But it'd be some minutes before everyone on the team roused themselves from whatever they were doing and made their way to the staging area; the machines would anticipate some measure of delay. She should have just enough time to dart in and get something from Oded to quiet her stomach, without anyone knowing she hadn't jumped *instantly* at the computer's—

She nearly collided with a machine that had trundled into

her path while she was distracted. An older-generation model, perhaps even pre-Pacification: a bulky chassis, the size of a calf, with thick treads and ungainly, poorly articulated pincers. Such models were responsible for simple menial labor in the modern age.

It was, for all that, still a machine.

<Suarez, Magdalena. Detachment One-Three-Nine-Three-Six. You will report to staging area B.>

"Look," she argued, arms waving, tongue loosened by fatigue, hunger, and grief. "I haven't even had a chance to eat yet this morning, and we only got back yesterday! I just need a minute, so I can—"

<You will report to staging area B.>

Mags allowed herself an inarticulate "Gaaah!"—or something to that effect—but only after she had very blatantly turned away and begun to march. Further argument might prove far worse than just a waste of breath.

The machines rarely repeated their orders more than once.

Staging area B was an old slab of marble, spider-webbed with countless cracks and fissures. Once the floor of some small building's lobby, it was now, other than the ubiquitous scattering of broken bricks, the only remaining trace of said building. A few rickety lengths of old chain link fence segregated it from the surrounding areas, less to keep people in or out than to keep the area very clearly defined.

Most of her team had already assembled, milling about, grumbling, casting resentful glares at robots who couldn't possibly have cared less, and generally behaving as irritated as Mags herself. Jonas stood before a headless, human-shaped thing—perhaps the same one that had secured the truck yesterday; the young woman couldn't tell—and was "explaining" in a tone that, from anyone not yet as trusted as an overseer, might have been considered insubordinate.

"...difficult assignment yesterday!" he was saying as Mags moved closer, making this particular point for what was clearly not the first time. Jonas always appeared exhausted, thanks to face and hair gone grayer than they should have been, but rarely was that weariness so obvious in his posture or his voice. "They lost a teammate. They're tired! They haven't had anywhere near their normal allotment of—"

<Detachment One-Three-Nine-Three-Six is required.>

"We're supposed to have at least four days of camp duty between field assignments!" Magdalena protested. No, she wasn't especially looking *forward* to farming, equipment repair, or whatever she might've been assigned this week, but she sure as hell preferred it to another excursion. "We haven't even had time to clean our damn work clothes, do checks and maintenance on our tools, any of it!"

<These facts have been analyzed and deemed irrelevant. Detachment One-Three-Nine-Three-Six is required. Lang, Jonas and Suarez, Magdalena will assemble with the others and cease occupying this unit with redundant input.>

Defeated, they stepped away.

"Jonas..."

"I know." He sighed, idly resting a hand on her shoulder. "Let's just hope it's something quick and easy."

"Right, because *that* happens so often."

"Well, then, we're due, aren't we?"

The young woman peered at her elder. "I see you learned logic from another person, and not the machines."

The overseer puffed up in feigned offense. "And what's wrong with my reasoning skills?"

"The 'reasoning' part."

Jonas chuckled, reaching over to rustle the young woman's hair. "I think you'll find—"

"Does the team look bigger to you?" she interrupted. A small assembly had gathered at the edge of staging area B, one consisting of people who were very much *not* members of 13936.

"Can you tell who they are?"

"Need to mingle with us common folk more, supervisor. That's John Fielding, from the 13944. And that bald girl, her name's... uh, Natalie Something-or-other." A pause, followed by an angry breath. "If they're trying to stick us with newbies for a field mission..."

It turned out, much to Mags's relief, that "they" were doing no such thing. The members of 13944, escorted by the same squat robot she'd recently spoken to, were handing out clothing and equipment. In fact, they were handing out the team's *own* clothing and equipment, gathered from living quarters and cots. Magdalena scowled as she got an armful of yesterday's heavy wool and denim—still filthy, and more than a little ripe.

They're not even going to wait for us go back and collect our own crap before we deploy! What the hell was so damn urgent?

<Construction and Restoration Detachment One-Three-Nine-Four-Four will depart the staging area.>

It was again the human-shaped robot who spoke.

<Any lingering human presence not associated with Detachment One-Three-Nine-Three-Six will be deemed in violation and insubordinate in sixty seconds. Fifty-nine... fifty-eight... fifty-seven...>

It was perhaps unsurprising that Magdalena's team found themselves alone well before the countdown neared zero.

<Detachment One-Three-Nine-Three-Six will board the vehicle.> It aimed one disturbingly long finger toward the vehicle pool, at the same truck in which they'd ridden yesterday.

"Where am I to take them?" Jonas asked as the team shuffled forward.

The thing didn't have a head, but damn if Mags didn't somehow get the impression it sneered down at the older man.

<*All* of Detachment One-Three-Nine-Three-Six will board the vehicle.>

Magdalena and Jonas traded worried, incredulous stares. The last time the overseer had been stuck in back with the others, rather than driving...

Actually, to her best recollection, he'd *never* been stuck in the back rather than driving!

The machine itself clambered into the cab, pressing a finger into the ignition. An almost solid puff of black belched from the exhaust—*extruded* might have been more apt—and the vehicle lurched into motion the millisecond the last team-member settled in the bed.

By the time the rumbling jalopy had cleared the camp, it had picked up an escort. A trio of miniature drones swept through complex patterns overhead, the downdraft of their rotors sending swirls of dust into unhappy faces.

When the truck stopped briefly so the drones could move ahead and drop lower, stirring up ever more ambient grit, it became very clear that the stinging, obscuring clouds were intentional. Dark trickles of smoke began to spread from the drones, mixing with the dust to transform the air into a thick, choking soup.

Simple, but effective. Between tearing, blinking eyes, coughing fits, and the haze itself, Magdalena and the others quickly lost track of where they were. That they hadn't traveled *too* far from camp was clear—the truck was incapable of any great speed—but when the drones finally rose, when the air cleared enough that visibility was no longer measured in inches, they found themselves on a cracked and overgrown road none of them recognized. They drove between jagged "hills" of rock, some perhaps natural, others the result of bombs dropped during Pacification. They drove through the ruins of a small town they'd never seen, consisting entirely of the skeletons of old buildings that had long since been scavenged to within an inch of collapse.

And then, a far-off rumble. It was scarcely audible over the growl of the truck's engine, and when she *did* finally notice, Mags initially took it to be a distant storm. Until she realized that the sound was constant, not the brief roar of thunder, and was growing steadily louder.

Steadily *closer.*

The truck emerged from between slab-sided outcroppings, some skittish creature nosing out of its den, and then jerked to a halt. The machine that drove the machine gave no order, made no move to step from the cab. Mags, Ian, Jonas, and the others traded puzzled blinks, but otherwise sat motionless beneath the gray and looming skies.

And the rumbling neared.

"Hell with *this!*"

"Mags! Don't even think—!"

But the young woman was vaulting over the side before Jonas could complete his order.

Ian, though his face paled and his gaze flickered constantly to their robotic driver, followed her.

She had not, in fact, utterly lost her mind, though she couldn't entirely blame the guys for thinking so. Even as the dirt puffed up in small clouds beneath her soles, she kept *very* careful watch on their mechanical leader. If the machine had shown the slightest reaction to her disembarking, she'd have been back aboard so fast that her memories might've had to run to catch up. The Eyes and their servitors were cold, not vindictive; if she reacted swiftly enough to any hint of displeasure, they wouldn't feel the need to penalize her.

Probably.

It did nothing of the sort, however, apparently unconcerned with her desire to range ahead. With one hand at her tool belt and a quick smile over her shoulder at the sounds of Ian's approach, Magdalena started forward.

She saw them almost immediately. Twin lengths of iron, dyed and perfumed in rust older than she was, slicing through the barren landscape to vanish, in both directions, behind the many rocky knolls.

Railtracks! Or something like that, anyway.

Mags knew what trains were, or had been. She'd seen wrecked cars and even the remains of a station or two in the outskirts of the Scatters, but those twisted heaps were more hole than metal, long since salvaged for scrap. It had never even occurred to her that any might remain in operation. She'd only the vaguest sense of what such a thing was supposed to look like, how it might move.

When that *thing* came roaring around the bend, bursting into view from behind the jagged stone, the answer proved to be "Nothing at all like she ever expected."

Chapter Three

It was beautiful in its efficiency—simple, economical, sleek. Rounded corners and gently bubbled slopes slipped beneath the wind as though the fiercest gust was a flap of a sickly crow's wings. An array of small, individually articulated wheels gripped the tracks, propelled by a constant electromagnetic charge.

It was beautiful in its efficiency, and repulsive—even nightmarish—in every other way.

The train appeared to have been dragged from the innermost dreams of a lunatic lacking the faintest conception of aesthetics. (And given the nature of the machines, some might argue that it *had* been.) The frame was forged of steel that, like so much of the Eyes' new world, had been salvaged from uncountable separate sources. Melted down only just enough for reshaping, it now bore an array of uneven streaks, leprous splotches, and a random spectrum of browns to grays to shades that were somehow both and neither at once.

A plague-ridden athlete, this train: sculpted to perfection, yet hideously sick.

Scarce as steel was, *only* the frame, the wheels, and certain structural hard points were made of the metal. The rest consisted of slabs and sheets of polymer. These, too, had been salvaged from a broken landscape and presented a riot of dull, scratchy hues. Except for a few, which were instead dully, scratchily transparent.

The machines cared nothing, one way or the other, but the result was a handful of windows permitting the train's new human passengers to view the world at speeds to make the bravest of them queasy.

Only a handful of Detachment 13936 bothered to look. Most sat huddled on the floor, legs tucked in and hands desperately clinging to any of a dozen protrusions jutting from walls and floor. These, apparently, were intended as anchor points for tying down cargo. Not a chair, not a bench, not even a comfortable handhold. Not in this train that had never been designed for human convenience.

So those humans sat and hunched, clinging for their lives, teeth gritted against the skull-shaking rumble and occasional banshee shriek of wheels on rail. All save a few, driven by fascination—or, in one case, a sense of responsibility to see everything her team might face—who balanced as best they could on wavering legs, peering through those obscuring windows and working to hold one another steady against the rocking of the train.

"Mags! Yo, Mags!"

Magdalena sighed and tore her gaze from the blurring landscape, unable to pretend any longer that she couldn't hear him over the roar of the train. "What?"

Rio opened his mouth, staggered as the train jolted around a curve, then desperately caught Ian who'd been utterly knocked from his feet. (Mags couldn't help but smirk at how snow-pale Ian looked in contrast against Rio's complexion, even more so than he usually did against her own.) Only then, when everyone was more or less stable again, did Rio finally get back around to his question.

"You and Jonas volunteer us for this shitshow?"

"I wouldn't do that, not so soon. They didn't ask for volunteers, just... I don't know. Decided we were best for whatever this is."

"Uh-huh. And ain't you at all bothered that the 'bot didn't join us?"

Indeed, the headless thing that had driven them as far as the tracks had—after ordering them aboard the gargantuan vehicle that screamed to a stop with the voices of dying thousands— remained by the truck as the train's doors had hissed shut and the wheels had begun rumbling once more.

And yes, *any* travel without obvious machine escort of one sort or another was unheard of. But...

"Rio, how fast you think we're going?"

"Uh... very?"

Mags nodded. "Yeah. Maybe even faster than that. Even if you could slide that door open, you planning to hop out and go for a stroll?"

"Uh..."

"Or maybe you want to hijack the train? Take it somewhere else?"

The hotheaded young man scowled openly now. "You know this thing can't leave the railtracks!"

"Yeah, I know. Just making sure *you* did. So tell me, ass-goggle, why would they bother watching over us right now? How would that be 'efficient'?"

"Don't gotta be a bitch about it," Rio groused, stepping— or more accurately, staggering—away from the window and dropping to a sullen, sulking seat on the floor beside Cassie. The redhead, in turn, though she couldn't possibly have overheard much of the conversation, glared at Mags in solidarity with her partner.

Magdalena ignored those glares—as well as the puzzled looks cast her way by Ian, just beside her, and Jonas, across the car—and turned back to the window.

"Well, uh..."

Leave it to Ian to try to fill the uncomfortable gap that followed. She adored him, but his need to dive in, make things better, save everyone from everything, could be seriously aggravating.

"Um, you see any of the quarries yet? I haven't spotted any."

Mags didn't know if he was making things better now, but he certainly had the group's attention.

"The hell are you talking about?" one of the others asked him. *Marty*, Mags thought, though in all the ambient rumbling, she couldn't tell for sure. "Those're all on the outskirts. We're past them by now."

Had Magdalena been in a better mood, she'd have found Ian's befuddlement cute.

"I figured there were a lot more nearer the city center."

"What?" Jonas finally joined in on the conversation,

half-shouting from across the car. "Why the hell would you think that?"

"Well... Didn't you tell us the Scatters used to be called... um...?"

"Pittsburgh," the overseer prompted. Then, "Please tell me you didn't think that meant...?"

"But, why else would it be named after *pits*?!"

Jonas mumbled something that was utterly lost in the song of the train.

Mags couldn't help but sneer, just a little. "Any other brilliant questions?"

"Oh, like *you* knew anything!"

This time, when the conversation stopped, nobody tried to wind it up again.

So, yeah, that had probably been uncalled for. She'd apologize to Rio and to Ian later, if she thought of it. She was just so damn tired...

For a time, the flow of the scenery rushing by nearly put the young woman to sleep on her feet. Once they'd moved deep into the Scatters, however, farther into the Pittsburgh ruin than the 13936 had ever been, no amount of fatigue would keep her from absorbing every detail she could.

It hardly seemed worth the effort. "All she could absorb" through the rough and blurry window proved nothing new; it all looked very much like those reaches of the Scatters she *had* seen. Like the aftermath of a child's tantrum, if his toy box had contained all of civilization. The ruins stretched far and near, sometimes teetering just beside or even over the winding track, so close she could practically smell the rotting wood and the lingering tang of powdered rust.

Depressing. Demoralizing. Terrifying in its implications. But nothing Magdalena wasn't used to, nothing she hadn't experienced, even dreamed about, more times than she cared to count.

"Jonas?"

The overseer glanced up from where he had ensconced himself tightly in a corner. "Yeah?"

"Why the hell are we here?" Magdalena demanded.

"Um, because we were told to be? Pretty sure you were there when it—"

"You're too old for sarcasm." Then, when the furrow of his brow suggested he was less than amused, "Seriously, you ever heard of anything like this? Detachment called up early, stuck on a train nobody knew existed, and dragged all the way into the Scatters?"

"If it's a train nobody knew existed, how could I possibly have heard of it?"

Several snickers sounded from around the car. Mags drew herself up and sniffed. "You know what I mean, dammit."

"No, I haven't heard of any such thing," he muttered back. "But this is where they want us."

For a moment, she continued watching the soul-numbing "scenery" slip by. And then, "Jonas?"

"Oh, for... What?"

"Given how far we've traveled already, shouldn't there have been another camp, with another Recognizance and Disposal detachment, a lot closer than us?"

To *that*, the overseer had no answer.

Somehow both bored and revolted by the sight of the Scatters, Magdalena was just turning from the window, perhaps to go and offer a reconciling word to Ian or to Rio, when the train rounded another bend, shot from between a teetering ruin on one side and a heap of strewn rubble on the other, and she saw...

Actually, she wasn't certain *what* she saw. Between the swift snaking of the train, the clouded window, the obscuring terrain, she caught only the faintest glimpse. She was sure only that, whatever it was, the Scatters were finally revealing something new.

It was large. It was sprawling. It was... wrong. Mags couldn't begin to say why, didn't have a clear enough view, but it was *off*. The drooping, skeletal remnants that were the outer Scatters felt more natural to her, more *sane*, than the impressions she received now. Phantom fingers colder than the machines traced a shudder down her back, flicking almost painfully over the edge of each vertebra.

"Mags?" Ian returned to her shoulder, whole face scrunched in concentration, sounding as puzzled as she.

"No idea," she admitted. She squinted, found herself raising a hand to try to wipe the plastic cleaner for a better view, even though she *knew* it was obscured by scratches and flaws...

And then it didn't matter *how* clean or clear the makeshift window might be, as something flashed past the train faster than she could process, and the entire world went dark as the inside of a gun barrel.

Magdalena hurled herself away from the window, breath catching in a gasp so ragged it sawed at the edges of her throat, before light returned—the harsh, steady glare of electrics, rather than the muted glow of the sun—and she realized what had happened.

The world hadn't gone away. The train had pulled into a structure of some sort, a building she could never have seen coming from a side window. Her cheeks burned, but the fact that the others were also scattered throughout the car—equally wide-eyed and sucking in adrenaline-fueled gasps—kept her from flushing *too* badly.

Before she could do, say, or even think much of anything, Magdalena again tumbled across the car—along with everyone else not already seated and holding tight—as the train howled to an abrupt halt.

Slowly she picked herself up off the floor—close up, it smelled of old plastic and boots—and dusted her hands off on her knees, or perhaps vice-versa. Again she started to say something, and again she was interrupted. The door slid aside with a rough hiss that was all but lost in the hum of the train's electrics, followed by a faint crackle as unseen speakers sparked to life.

<Recognizance and Disposal Detachment One-Three-Nine-Three-Six will disembark here and await further orders. Message repeats: Recognizance and Disposal Detachment One-Three-Nine-Three-Six will disembark here...>

It wasn't coming through the open door, that voice, but originated all around them. The speakers were inside the car itself.

"No robot escort, huh?" she asked Rio as he slipped past her, idly rubbing one elbow where he'd rebounded from the wall. He muttered something unintelligible and made a rude gesture. Chuckling, she stepped out after him, her attention roaming.

She couldn't see much—the electrics were focused on the train, forming a pool of light in a cavernous darkness—but the echoes and the weight of the shadows told her a great deal. No way were they inside one of the Scatters' wrecks of an old building. Not a one of those was remotely large enough, to say nothing of so perfectly sealed against the light or sturdy enough to support the railtracks.

So where the hell are we?

The train hummed, screeched, and roared off back the way they'd come—revealing, as it left, that the building was not as tightly sealed against the outside as it had appeared. The entrance had been shaped, with inhuman precision, to match the dimensions of the train itself. Thus, it was only when the vehicle had departed that the dust-dimmed daylight could creep in.

Magdalena was walking before she'd even made the conscious choice to do so. She had to see.

"Mags…"

Ian, of course. She'd recognize that worry anywhere.

"I'm just going to look," she called over her shoulder. She heard the swift footfalls of her boyfriend, and several of the others, scurrying to catch up.

"The machines said to stay here!"

"I'm looking," she repeated, gaze rolling ceilingward. "Not *leaving*."

"Hope they recognize the distinction *before* they start shooting," he muttered from behind her. But he made no further objection, nor did he turn back.

The tunnel drew nearer, the light brighter. Their vantage looked to prove awkward, since only a very narrow ledge of walkway extended beyond the arch, parallel to the tracks. To allow some sort of maintenance bots to make repairs on the rails, perhaps? Whatever its intended purpose, it would allow Mags and the others to take a step or two beyond the walls—a *careful* step or two—to see whatever the heart of Pittsburgh might have to show them.

"Holy... shit..."

Ian, standing at her side and gripping her hand in his own—for balance, as much as comfort—could only nod in dull agreement. "Uh, guys? You should maybe... come see."

Cassie glanced their way from the central puddle of light, her lips twisted in lingering anger, but whatever stinging comment she'd concocted on her boyfriend's behalf died before it left her tongue. She approached, jaw hanging open, with Rio following. Then several of the others, all silent—all save Suni and Marty, the team's smallest members, both grumbling about not being able to see—and finally even Jonas took their turn edging out over the precarious ledge to see what lay beyond.

"Holy shit..."

Mags couldn't tell who had spoken, not over the other hushed whispers. "That's what I said."

Here, in what had been the center of town, the ambient grit and smoke were thinner, allowing a clearer view of Pittsburgh's ruins than Mags had ever seen.

Except that here, Pittsburgh *wasn't* a ruin.

Here, by any human measure, it wasn't even a *city*.

The structures—Mags couldn't bring herself to think of them as buildings—made the train, which still had to bow to the laws of aerodynamics, look positively artistic. Joyful. *Alive*. Some of those edifices were steel, occasionally offering a halfhearted glint as a tiny sunbeam snuck around behind the haze's back. Others boasted only skeletons of metal, with "flesh" of repurposed polymers and glass. The result was a slapdash array of muted, murkily blended hues utterly at odds with the structures' geometric precision.

And "precision" was indeed the word for it. Many were plain cubes or cuboids, from as small as an old house to larger than a city block. Others were pyramidal, hexagonal, or oval, but nearly all were a single, simple shape. The rare exception either consisted of multiple structures stacked atop one another, or else were built around the city's surviving geological features.

In *no* case could the slightest touch of aesthetics, individualization, or humanity be found. Other than sporadic random slabs of repurposed glass or plastic that remained transparent, not a single window pockmarked the smooth faces of those structures. No sculpture, no adornment. They might as well have been machine parts rather than buildings. Perhaps, for that matter, they *were*.

Which wasn't to say that they were featureless. Spindly broadcasting and scanning towers poked like malignant growths or an iron maiden's spines from walls, roofs, wherever mathematics suggested optimal placement. Narrow bridges interlinked structure to structure dozens or hundreds of feet above the earth, none boasting a single railing or other nod toward basic safety. Beyond the bridges stretched a vast network of wires and tubes of steel or plastic; from the city's center, looking up, it must have appeared as some monstrous cobweb, or perhaps cracks in the sky itself. Those tubes, Jonas would explain later, contained and protected power conduits running from the city's many plants—wind-driven, coal-burning, and nuclear.

The amount of power carried along those conduits must have been astronomical. Even from this distance, Mags could smell the tang of ozone, and she swore she heard a faint electrical hum, previously masked by the rattling train.

Roads of packed earth ran between those buildings, forming—again, save where geography wouldn't permit it—an uneven grid. Mags had once seen the insides of an old machine, damaged when it toppled from a quarry slope. The patterns on its circuit boards, as Jonas had called them, weren't so terribly different from the network of roads she saw now.

Pittsburgh had suffered horribly during Pacification and the subsequent years, so that many ravines ran throughout, and whole districts of the city sat in the depths of broad depressions. These were linked to the system of streets by an array of ramps.

Meticulously sloped for maximum efficiency, no doubt.

Through it all—along the roads, across the bridges, soaring through the murky air, even skittering up the sides of buildings—were the machines. Some legged, some wheeled; some several times the size of the detachment's truck, some smaller than Magdalena's equipment pack. Whether hauling loads of raw materials, welding this device to that structure, or doing nothing the humans could comprehend, they all worked to accomplish *some* specific task. They must have; wouldn't have been wasting time or power otherwise.

What some of those tasks might be, Mags couldn't guess. There sure were a *lot* of them, though. Swarms. The whole damn place was...

"It's like a hive," Cassie whispered.

"I was gonna go with 'anthill,'" Mags said, "but that works."

"We should go back," Jonas told them. "I really don't want one of *them* to wander in here and find us all congregating at the—"

"Guys, guys!" The shout came from one of the few who had remained in the chamber's center: Nestor Panagakis, whose overall cheerful demeanor belied a bulk that was almost as imposing as some of the machines. For *him* to sound worried was, to say the least, attention-grabbing. "There's something—!"

<Lang, Jonas. Recognizance and Disposal Detachment One-Three-Nine-Three-Six.>

"...exit," Jonas finished, all but deflating before forcibly drawing himself up. "Yes," he answered.

The machine emerging from the shadows very much resembled the insectoid model that had accompanied them yesterday—at first. As it skittered into the light, however, Mags couldn't help but note that it was larger, that an even more intricate array of lenses glimmered around and across its body. That the digits on its manipulator arms were thicker and far longer.

And that, along with those arms, an array of brutal steel barrels bristled from the rotating turret.

Two of which had now snapped into position, aimed directly at the gathered workers. The combined gasps of the entire team nearly pulled a vacuum across the massive chamber.

<Explain why Detachment One-Three-Nine-Three-Six is attempting unauthorized departure from this facility.>

Magdalena pretended not to feel the angry glares now burrowing into her back.

"Nobody's departing," Jonas explained, voice calm, hands half raised, as though trying to soothe a snapping animal. "Just looking. We wanted to see the city. The team's never been this deep inside Pittsburgh before."

A few dozen lungs froze, the team holding its collective breath. Faint *whirring* sounds drifted from within the innards of the steel taskmaster. Had it been human, Mags was certain it would have been cocking its head to one side, lost in thought. Of course, had it been human, it would've *had* a head.

The turret shifted a hair, imperceptible had the team not been looking directly at it, which meant the guns were no longer trained on them in perfect, computer-targeted precision. For a machine, it was the equivalent of holstering its weapons. The almost explosive sighs of relief from behind actually ruffled Magdalena's hair.

And that, apparently and unsurprisingly, was the *only* acknowledgement that they'd been believed.

<Detachment One-Three-Nine-Three-Six will assemble before this unit.>

"Is it story time?" Mags muttered, adrenaline having loosened her tongue perhaps more than was healthy. Rio snickered; most of the others, Jonas included, glared.

They all, of course, obeyed.

<Stand by,> the machine commanded once they'd gathered. <Connection established.>

"Connection?" Ian repeated. Mags shrugged—and then felt her stomach drop at the sight of Jonas's face going mushroom-pale.

"Jonas, what—?"

<Unit 13936. Jonas Lang, commanding.> It was the same vocalizer, the same artificially feminine voice, but the inflection was wrong.

Mostly in that, unlike every other machine—or even this one, until just now—it *had* genuine inflection.

Mags couldn't decide whether to cross herself, drop to her knees, or run screaming. Instead, she stood perfectly, rigidly still and tried to calm the pounding in her chest and the rushing in her temples.

She'd never seen it before, never heard it described. But she knew what it was.

This wasn't just a machine speaking, not anymore. They were addressed by one of the Eyes. The heart of the machine empire, overlords of the surviving world, masters of the dregs of humanity.

And one of them was now focused personally on Magdalena and her team.

This cannot *be good.*

"Indeed," Jonas affirmed, even though the inhuman intelligence clearly required no such confirmation. "We are honored that you would—"

<An anomalistic event has transpired at the outskirts of the conformed regions where they meet the remnants of prior occupation.>

"The Scatters," Magdalena hissed in response to a few puzzled whispers. The Eye apparently didn't notice or—more likely—didn't care and continued addressing Jonas.

<Nature of the anomaly unknown, purpose unknown, extent unknown. Multiple construction units, repair units, and combat units rendered nonfunctional.>

Mags was frankly tired of gasping, but she couldn't help it. She almost felt dizzy. Normally the machines summoned their expendable human lackeys if even a couple of them were damaged. What the *hell* had taken out so many of them?! And why hadn't they called on an R&D detachment before this? And for that matter...

"Why us?" She'd blurted the question before she could stop herself. Somehow, though it moved not at all, she knew she'd finally gotten the robot's attention.

<Do you question your assignment, Magdalena Suarez?>

"No, uh... sir."

How the fuck do *you address the Eyes, anyway?!*

"Not at all. Not a bit. No. I'm just... curious. I'd think that calling on a closer team would've been more, um, efficient."

A pause; brief but, given the processing speed of the machines, notable. Jonas's lips parted, but the reply came before he could speak.

<You are correct. More proximate camps provided the required skillset. 13936 is the second Recognizance and Disposal

detachment assigned to identify and render safe the anomaly.>

One particularly severe winter, several years back, the warming unit on the water pump had failed just as Magdalena was being hosed down. She could still recall the frigid, pinching, almost burning sensation as tiny crystals of ice spread across her dripping skin before the next blast washed them away.

The chill she felt now was worse.

"What—what happened to them?" That was Nestor, from the rear of the assembly.

<Detachment 22574 also rendered nonfunctional.>

Had the train returned in that instant, it might just have been enough to *raise* the volume level of the room to "silent."

"What..." Jonas cleared his throat, flinched at the sound, and tried again. "What can you tell us about... whatever's out there?"

<Nature unknown,> the Eye repeated.

"Yes, but... Images? General description? Something? If it destroyed several units, they must have seen something, recorded *something* to the network!"

<No.>

It had to be her imagination, but Mags swore she saw the machine nervously shift its weight ever so slightly.

<Even when cameras and sensors were trained on a unit as it suffered damaged, no image of the anomaly was recorded.>

"How is that possible?" Suni squeaked from the center of the group.

The overseer shook his head. "It's not."

<Clearly, it is. You will provide us a starting point to investigate *how* it is possible while neutralizing the threat.>

"Oh, is that all?"

"Magdalena, shut it!" Then, turning back to the bot, the overseer continued, "Apologies. She doesn't mean anything by it. She's just nervous. And she *is* one of the best we have."

<We are aware of Magdalena Suarez's qualifications. She lives because of them.>

This time, Mags was thankful, without feeling even remotely patronized or smothered, when she felt Ian's hand close on her own.

To the mechanical overlord, Jonas said, "We're grateful." To Mags, his expression added *We're going to have words about this later.*

Not that they needed to. Mags knew damn well she'd let herself go too far. She wanted to vomit at the thought of what could have just happened, and she'd have brought it on herself.

Continuing, Jonas asked, "How would you like us to proceed?"

<This unit will return to autonomous operation. Magdalena Suarez and one-half of Detachment 13936 will accompany this unit to a staging area, where they will be armed, and then to the quadrant where the anomaly was last detected.>

Half?! Armed? "Wait a minute!" Mags began.

<Jonas Lang and the other half of Detachment 13936 will remain here, ready in the event that the first endeavor meets the same results as Detachment 22574 and a third sortie is required.>

"We're not soldiers!" she protested, her earlier fear of the Eye now overshadowed by worry for her people. "And you want to cut our strength in half before we can even—"

"With all respect," Jonas offered at the same time, "I'm not entirely certain—"

<Certainty is not required. Only obedience.>

"But—"

<Suarez, Magdalena.> The inflections, slight as they had been, were gone, once again leaving only the soulless voice of the machine. The Eye was obviously done with them. <Thirteen workers of Detachment One-Three-Nine-Three-Six will accompany this unit now.>

"I don't—"

<Suarez, Magdalena. Thirteen workers of Detachment One-Three-Nine-Three-Six will accompany this unit now. Any further hesitation in compliance will result in twelve workers of Detachment One-Three-Nine-Three-Six accompanying this unit.>

Mags clenched her jaw shut. She was fairly certain that the damn thing was threatening worse than just leaving her behind.

Seething, her silence shouting obscenities her mouth

couldn't risk, she selected her team and wondered if she'd be mourning another friend tomorrow.

Chapter Four

"You know, I actually feel *better* in the fucking Scatters?" Magdalena offered Rio a half smile, which was about forty-nine percent more smile than she meant. *But at least he and Cassie aren't pouting anymore.*

Truth was, she felt the same; was pretty sure *everyone* did. They hadn't seen much more of the inner city—their mechanical taskmaster had taken them through dim corridors to another, smaller rail-line, and then by enclosed car to the outskirts—but what little they spotted disturbed them enough. From the ground, the place looked even more alien than it had from the tracks, seeming to consist of mammoth walls without purpose, narrow alleys full of inhuman noises and movements, and a jagged network above that did indeed offer the impression that the whole world was gradually shattering. Even worse had been the smell: smoky, oily, choked with ozone, but not a trace of life. Magdalena would've felt a thousand pounds lighter if she'd stumbled across a single flower, or even some dried animal droppings.

When the train had disgorged them within sight of the ruins, where the so-called "conformed region" gave way once more to the urban rot that was the Scatters, many of them had actually breathed a sigh of relief, felt a few of tension's bruising fingers unclench from their muscles.

At which point Mags felt her newly acquired strap digging into her shoulder, the unfamiliar and unpleasant weight of the thing in her hands, and felt those fingers press even harder than before.

Single shot or, as she had it set now, triple bursts. Thirty-six-round capacity, plus one in the chamber, two spare clips jammed into a pouch on her belt. Soft-lead, polymer-filled hollow-points. Magdalena was no soldier, but she'd handled enough firearms in her assignments to know just how brutal a weapon this was, the sort of horrid ripping and shredding it would do to anything in its path.

Anything *fleshy* in its path. Against a target even moderately armored or hardened, it would prove little more effective than hurling dumplings. A target like, oh, say, their mechanical overseer.

Good to see we're trusted.

Most of her team (half team) were similarly armed, though Rio carried a massive electro-magnetic accelerator—far more potent than any gunpowder weapon, but also, due to a lengthy charging cycle, slower to fire—and Suni had been assigned a long-barreled, low-caliber rifle. Not that she was a better sniper than any of the others, though she wasn't a bad shot. She was just too slight to comfortably handle the recoil of standard armament.

The damn bot probably outgunned the entire team.

Dirt, powdered rock, and occasional calcified bone crunched beneath Mags's boots as she walked, trying to watch all directions at once without tripping over her own feet—or over the larger chunks that had once been building or sidewalk or who-knew-what that still littered the former roadways. Protrusions of rotting wood and teetering stone rose overhead, most leaning at drunken angles or upon one another. Fossils of a society long gone extinct.

Relics, all of them. Useless and meaningless, just whiling away their time until either the elements or robotic scavengers dismantled them completely.

And this area, she noted again with more than a touch of bile, was the *less* disturbing option.

"What're we even supposed to be looking for?" she demanded.

<Nature of the anomaly remains unknown.>

Mags glared around Ian and over Cassie's head at the thing stalking along beside them. "Got that. Going to make it kind of hard to find, though."

<This unit is guiding Detachment One-Three-Nine-Three-Six to the last known location of multiple nonfunctional units. You will begin your search there.>

"Got that, too, seeing as how you told us on the train. But what're we looking for once we're there?"

<Nature of the anomaly remains unknown. Suarez, Magdalena will cease occupying this unit with redundant queries.>

In fact, the words that Mags choked on weren't a query of any sort, but rather a rude (and, for a machine, anatomically improbable) suggestion. But as she knew that neither would go over well, and that she'd already pushed her luck about as far as it'd stretch, she kept her lips together and settled for a mental image of one of the rickety edifices collapsing on top of the stupid thing.

None seemed willing to oblige, alas, though the team did have to crawl and climb their way across a barrier of broken wood that might, years ago, have been one such structure. Going around would have been easier but, according to the machine, a fraction slower, due to the layout of the surrounding blocks. And since the machine cared little for the array of scrapes, bruises, and splinters the humans picked up trying to pick their way through the rubble—apparently "peak condition" wasn't required—slower was unacceptable.

They were perhaps a mile or so beyond that bit of excitement, and Mags was still trying to tweeze a thin sliver of wood from her left index finger with her teeth, when she heard a sharp call from ahead.

Wayne Prentiss—lithe even for a camp-dweller and faster than gossip, when he wanted to be—had, with the machine's permission, scouted ahead. By the sound of things, it'd just paid off.

The team broke into a quick jog. Mags couldn't help but note that the machine, though easily capable of outdistancing even the fastest of them, chose instead to match their pace.

Wouldn't want to reach the threat ahead of your disposable meat-shields, would you?

As it turned out, Wayne hadn't discovered the threat. He

had, however, discovered a spot where the threat had been.

"My God…" she rasped. Her hand hovered near her throat, where she'd raised it to cross herself before totally losing track of what she was doing.

"Holy shit!" Rio shouted.

"Was gonna say that," Mags told him absently, sheltering behind and supporting herself on a pillar of sarcasm, "but I didn't want to repeat myself."

She *needed* the sarcasm. It was that or vomit, as a few of her people were already doing.

The most impressive bit of destruction should have been the machines. Several crumpled bits of metal had once been airborne bots. One even hung from the side of a ruined wall, its rotors embedded in the flaking mortar. A larger machine, a tread-mounted hulk designed for construction and heavy labor, lay buried beneath what had been a separate stretch of that same wall. The steel was rent, the unit crushed—though the weight of the stone couldn't have been enough to do such damage.

And there was the spider. Not a combat unit such as accompanied them now, but even the smaller variety was a powerful, formidable device. Yet something had ripped three legs from its body before punching through the turret socket and ripping out a length of wiry innards. *Nothing* should have been capable of that; nothing, perhaps, save another machine.

It *should* have been the most impressive, all of that, and maybe it would be, eventually. At first, however, all Magdalena had eyes for, all *any* of them had eyes for, were the bodies.

Detachment 22574 had indeed been rendered "nonfunctional."

Initial inspection revealed only ten or so corpses, not enough to account for the entire detachment. Magdalena couldn't even hope that the rest were still alive. She could hope only they'd died more cleanly than their teammates.

A few had simply been bludgeoned, skulls or ribs staved in by something blunt and heavy. Others had been hurled into the freestanding structures with impossible force; those bodies lay limp and sagging, like socks loosely filled with sand.

But it was the remainder that truly turned stomachs and

weakened knees. They appeared to have been savaged by some manner of wild beast, or an industrial bot gone berserk. They were largely intact, those bodies, though an arm here or a hunk of indiscernible bone and tissue there were enough to put the emphasis on "largely." Most bore only a few wounds, around the throat or chest, but those wounds were hideous. Flesh gaped wide, flapping obscenely in the breeze, exposing shredded muscle and jagged bone. The blood was—

Mags blinked. Her eyes blurred with tears, summoned by the stinging grit-laden breeze, an absolute cavalcade of emotions, and the rapidly worsening stench, so it took her a moment to wonder.

Where the hell is all the blood?!

Oh, she saw *some*. Spattered hither and yon by whatever made the initial wounds, gathered in small puddles beneath the bodies. But that was the problem.

Small puddles, that should have been anything *but* small. It certainly didn't remain in the corpses; even from here, their pallor was quite sufficient to prove that.

Seeped into the dirt? That was possible, she supposed, but it didn't look right, feel right. There should still be more of it. Traces, stains, *something*.

"What the hell *did* this?" Ian asked, his face and somehow even his voice faintly green with revulsion. Mags wished she could hold him, but she didn't think the spider would approve just now.

"Shit, I never heard of anything but a machine *could* do something like this!" Rio replied from across the killing field.

<Improbable.>

They turned toward the bot, which crouched beside one of the strangely bloodless corpses.

<Ragged wounds indicate cutting implements of lesser precision than a blade or industrial tool. Wound dimensions indicate erect assailant, approximate height one-point-five to two meters.>

"You suggesting a *person* did this?" Mags demanded, the sentence almost snapping beneath the weight of her incredulity.

<This unit is relaying observable facts. This unit makes no suggestions of any sort.>

Rio sneered. "Fat lot of good all your fancy processors and shit are if they don't even—"

"Can we track them?" Mags interrupted, casting Rio the best *shut it!* glare she'd learned from Jonas.

Again, the machine somehow gave the impression of shifting its attention while not moving or turning an inch. <Negative. Ambient particulate obscures potential trace indicators, and infrared analysis reveals no lingering temperature differentials from Detachment Two-Two-Five-Seven-Four's passage.>

"What?" Rio whispered.

Ian answered, sparing Mags the necessity. "Dust's already covered over any tracks, and the machine's not picking up any signs of body heat."

"Oh. Could've just *said* that!"

"We should try this way, then," Magdalena said, gesturing with the barrel of her weapon down the same roadway they'd been following.

<Suarez, Magdalena will explain her reasoning for this recommendation.>

"Well, look, whatever happened here, the detachment got the worst of it. When they left, they were probably running."

When the machine said nothing, she assumed that counted as agreement—or at least an absence of *disagreement*—and continued. "They couldn't hide in the rubble. Whatever they were fighting was already on them. Would've seen them take cover. And the only other ways out of here..." Now she pointed back the way they'd come, and then at a small alleyway between the freestanding brick wall and a heap of detritus. "...have a lot less room and would mean climbing over or around shit. Would've slowed them up, a *lot*. Not where they'd probably go, if they were trying to get away from something that just tore up their team."

A bare heartbeat, and then, <Credible. Unit One-Three-Nine-Three-Six may proceed along recommended route.>

Oh, may *we?*

But again, she wasn't about to say it out loud, and she

was already moving, waving for the others to fall into loose formation behind her. Once again, the machine matched the pace the humans set, keeping up but never moving ahead.

After barely another block of ruin and wreckage, the thing spoke up again. <Unit One-Three-Nine-Three-Six will spread out.>

"What?! There's something out there tearing people up like bread crusts, and you want me to split my guys—?"

"Mags." Ian put a hand on her forearm, turning her attention—and perhaps her ire—from the machine. "It's right."

"*What*? What the fuck are you saying?"

"I was about to suggest the same thing myself, honestly. Whatever we're looking for, we're not going to find it moving together in one big clump."

"One big target," someone corrected from the center of the group.

"Anyone could just slip past us," Ian pressed. "Without us ever knowing."

The fingers on Magdalena's gun clenched until they trembled, but he was right, and she knew it. "All right. Four groups of three. We take parallel streets, and we don't continue past any intersection until we have eyes on all four teams. Suni, your job is to hang back a bit. Any one of the groups gets in the shit, you find a vantage point where you can shoot at whatever that shit is."

The tiny sniper nodded, though her scowl was heavy enough that Mags was surprised it didn't just fall off. The young commander didn't even bother asking the machine what it was going to do. If it felt she needed to know, it would tell her.

In fact, it appeared perfectly content to trail along behind one of the innermost teams, not *quite* near enough to easily become collateral damage.

So they moved, advancing at a tense crouch, somewhere between a creep and a trudge. Four teams, led by Magdalena, Ian, Cassie, and Wayne, with the bot and Suni trailing behind, sometimes on this street, sometimes on that. Nervous eyes scanned the rubble to all sides, sweating fingers twitched on triggers. Backs, necks, shoulders, and arms cramped, as much from free-floating tension as the unaccustomed postures. Mags's detachment had been in danger a hundred times before, but the threat had never before been… animate. They had never before set out to kill or be killed.

At each intersection they stopped, glancing right and left until all four teams were accounted for, and then worked their way along another agonizing block. The constant repetition, the desperate waiting for something to happen while hoping against hope that it wouldn't, thickened until Magdalena was sure something inside her would burst like an old tire.

When that tension finally broke, when a burst of gunfire punctured the world off her to left, she swore her heart stopped, every muscle in her body snapping so taut she just might have been temporarily bulletproof.

Left… Cassie's team!

She only realized she'd broken into a run when already in the midst of a dead sprint. Her two teammates followed close behind, and she thought she heard the sound of additional footsteps beyond theirs. She swerved around a heap of old wood and semi-powdered brick, leapt a second, smaller barrier of the same, and found herself standing in a large intersection. Cassie and the others had gathered to the side, crouched beside a slab of buckled concrete.

Looming before them was what had once been a single structure, running the entire length of the block. Broken doors and empty window frames, abnormally broad, opened into an array of large rooms, each divided from the next.

"What's going on?" she demanded brusquely, struggling to hide her immense relief at the arrival of the other two teams, Suni—and yes, even the bot.

Grateful for a machine. *We are well and fully fucked.*

"Aaron thought he saw someone in the ruin," Cassie explained with an exasperated sigh.

Aaron, a disheveled young man with a mop of hair so orange it made even Cassie's look tame, seemed caught on the border between a scowl and a pout. "'Thought' my ass! There was someone in there! Watching us!" The gun he waved about for emphasis—only barely remembering not to point it in his friends' direction—still smoked faintly at the barrel.

"None of the rest of us—" Cassie began.

<Single heat signature, human proportion.>

Every face turned, with more or less disbelief, toward the bot.

<Vibrational and laser sensors too impeded to detect respiration or cardiac rhythm, but this unit has registered distinct movement.>

"Toldja!" Aaron gloated.

"Shut it!" Mags and Cassie ordered simultaneously.

Then, Magdalena continued, "All right, so... Four sides to the building, probably exits in every one of them. Uh... Cassie, your team'll take this side. Ian, right. Wayne, left. I'll take my guys around back.

"Suni, um..." She pointed at a building some distance down the block. "See if that balcony's stable. If it is, keep watch from there. Stop anybody leaving who's not us. And..." She stumbled to a halt as she faced their artificial taskmaster. "I guess, do whatever you were going to do anyway."

Again she could only interpret the machine's silence as approval. Sucking in a very shaky breath, clenching one fist on the gun until she swore she heard tendons creak, Magdalena waved the other teams forward, blinked away some of the dust and sweat, and advanced on the ruin.

Chapter Five

Mags had no idea what to make of the place. The dilapidated rooms boasted an array of countertops, broken plastics sculpted in a variety of artistic flourishes, shattered and incomplete signs. Those last told her nothing at all. Reading wasn't her strongest suit, and even if it had been, they were incomplete.

What the hell sort of phrase or sentence could "—lce & Gabba—" have been part of, anyway?

Her team had entered through a gaping hole in the brick, one that probably contained a legitimate doorway in some indeterminate past. Inexperienced in combat though they were, the R&D detachment knew about walking into unknown dangers. Mags and her two companions—siblings Kai and Yun Jeong—moved at a smooth, efficient crawl. Every footfall was considered, every stretch of wall, floor, and ceiling examined. She assumed the other teams proceeded similarly; it was what they knew. Still, everyone's nerves were taut enough to coil into springs. Kai jumped at every sound, her gun tracking any flicker of motion, until Mags worried that she might open fire on another team if one should appear without warning. The woman's younger brother leaned too far the other way. Yun held himself stiff, having crossed the line from caution and control to rigidity. His footfalls were clumsy, his attentions narrowed.

"Sharp it up, you two!" she finally hissed. "This is no different than every other horrible, messy death you've faced!"

"Your pep talks could use more pep, Mags," Kai grumped at her. It did the trick, though. She steadied herself, even as Yun allowed his fingers and shoulders, ever so slightly, to relax.

Not a moment too soon, either. A sudden scuffle of boots, which might have drawn the siblings' fire mere seconds ago, announced the arrival of Ian's team, climbing through the tumbled stone and rotting scraps that had been another of the establishments.

Magdalena allowed herself a heartbeat or two to grant Ian a relieved smile, and to draw some comfort when he returned it. "Anything?" she asked.

"Not really," her boyfriend replied. "We passed by a large gap, got a peek outside. Looks like the balcony was no good; Suni's on the next rooftop over. But inside? Haven't seen a thing."

"Hrm. Us, either. And we can't be too far from meeting up with the others, if you're here." A thought suddenly struck. "You seen the bot?"

"Not since we got inside."

"The hell...? No way that thing can be *too* quiet, so where—?"

"Mags!"

A quick incline of Yun's head directed Magdalena's attention to the base of a broad, empty doorway. Lying within was an old brick shedding flakes of old mortar. Not precisely an uncommon sight. Something had struck this one, shearing off a large flake in one swoop. Also not especially noteworthy.

But *this* mortar was brighter, less stained, still crumbling. Whatever had grazed the lonely brick had done so recently. Perhaps only hours, or even minutes.

Mags raised a hand, waved everyone forward, and slipped through the entryway.

Whatever purpose this room had served, it was far larger than the others. Although the ceilings weren't remotely as high, it might have boasted as much square footage as the chamber where they'd disembarked from the train. A few thin interior walls survived, but otherwise sections were marked off only by deteriorating counters of various lengths, arranged in an equal variety of shapes.

To Mags, it just meant that, open as the place was, it still offered *way* too many places to hide.

Full of enough detritus to make stealth a lost cause, with dozens of ambush points... "Damn," she murmured, "sure would be nice if we had a fucking *infrared sensor* with us right now!"

As the bot did not appear in answer to her invocation—and God, here she was again, *wishing* for the machine's company!—she had no other option. "Spread out," she whispered, "but keep in sight. Check *everything*!"

"No shit," Ian said, a nervous smirk taking any edge from the words. "Did you want us to do that with our eyes open, or—?"

Magdalena accompanied her "Shut it!" with a (relatively) gentle elbow to the ribs, and then moved toward the nearest counter, gun at the ready.

At the last moment, she dropped to a crawl, scooting to the barrier's edge. A few quick, shallow breaths, and she lunged so that she lay on her side, ready to fire.

Ready to fire at the substantial accumulation of nothing that awaited her. She felt the sweat building on her forehead, on her palms. If every peek behind every obstruction was this tense, she'd die of heart failure or dehydration long before whatever had killed Detachment 22574 could get its hands, or whatever it had, on her.

Soon enough, the six of them had checked every nearby spot—behind the counters, within the looser piles of rubble, beneath a sagging ramp that looked to be a staircase with the stairs removed—to no avail. Insects, a dead rat, and a personalized layer of grime were all they had to show for their troubles.

"Well," Mags offered with a note of false and brittle cheer, "that's about, what, a tenth of the place down? Plus upstairs? Hell, we're almost done!"

"That attitude," Kai said, "is *precisely* why you're lucky we don't usually carry guns."

"How do we know," asked one of Ian's trio, "that it wasn't just a rat or a chunk of falling ceiling that messed up that brick? How do we know there's even anyone in here?"

"We don't," their leader told him.

"But—"

"If you have a better idea other than wandering more

random hallways," Ian interrupted, "I'm sure Mags would love to hear—"

Something dripped.

It was a single sound, one lonely *plop*, off to the left. No leaking rain; there hadn't been any in days. No water left running through the old plumbing; the pipes had been claimed for their metal in the earliest days following Pacification. Condensation? From *what*?

An exchange of skittish looks, and the team set out as silently as the debris-strewn floor would permit.

It wasn't silent enough. From behind another of the long, dilapidated counters, came a shrill and phlegmy giggle.

Mags felt every hair on her arms and the back of her neck stand erect enough to punch holes through her shirt. The color drained from Ian's lips, and she knew she must look the same. She tried to advance, to order the others forward, but for the barest instant, she couldn't remember how to work either feet or throat.

It sounded again, that hideous mirth, followed by a wet tearing-scraping sound. It snapped Mags from her stupor, but even as she drew breath to shout, something lunged into the open.

She could see it was a man, but it moved with impossible speed and a peculiar, crooked slouch somehow disturbing in its implications. Between that speed, the thick shadows, and the strobe of gunfire as several of her people opened up on their presumed enemy, she could make out no more detail than that.

Well, that and the fact that if any of the bullets struck home, their target certainly didn't seem bothered by them.

Just before the figure vanished behind a wall of rubble, it twisted at the waist—or perhaps it simply leaned? The hunch and the poor lighting made it impossible to tell—and offered a final giggle. *Something* flew from its hand, hurtling across the intervening distance with unerring accuracy and brutal speed.

The sound, when it crashed into Kai's skull, was less the cracking of bone than that of a wet sponge falling on taut canvas.

She dropped, her weapon firing once before tumbling from her hand, her feet kicking and spasming even as her expression went slack. Blood matted her hair against her left temple, which seemed suddenly, horribly concave.

"Get her behind cover!" Mags hated the screech of panic in her voice, but perhaps it was a blessing. It ensured the others heard her over Yun's grief-stricken scream. Ian and one of the others each took Kai by a wrist and dragged her behind the same counter from which the enemy had come.

"Yun, go! Get back there! We—Oh, *God*!"

Casting about for any sign of their foe, or any sudden inspiration, Mags's eyes had finally landed on the projectile that had caved in the side of Kai's head.

It was another head.

The ragged edges of flesh and dangling lengths of sinew and spine suggested it had been disarticulated, *ripped* rather than cut from its former body. Mags recalled, in terrible clarity, the odd tearing sound that had preceded the enemy's appearance, and tasted bile at the back of her tongue.

It wasn't one of her people, thankfully, was nobody she knew. Probably one of the 22574, poor bastard.

And *dammit*, why couldn't Yun stop with the *screaming* for ten seconds and let her *think*, give her time to catch her breath, to—

Except it wasn't Yun screaming, not anymore. Or rather, it wasn't *just* Yun screaming.

Blood pounding in her ears, the floor tilting drunkenly beneath her, Mags staggered around the counter to join her companions, to find out what *else* was wrong...

They'd found the body to go with the rogue head, and several others as well. Strewn over the floor were three or four members of the earlier R&D detachment. Three or four members, in roughly a dozen different spots. Here, a pair of arms—each from a different body—had been laid aside, hands clasped as though shaking in some macabre little joke. Coils of intestine dangled over an old clothes hanger; it was the sporadic dripping of congealing fluids from within that Mags had heard earlier.

Each body, and most of the disembodied parts, showed

signs of *chewing*, concentrated in the soft and fleshy bits, as though whatever—or whoever—had snacked on them had learned quickly which spots it found tastiest. It appeared, in some instances, to have ripped and bitten through clothing, rather than removing it, and a single bloody tooth sat embedded in a naked thigh.

Mags spun away just in time. At least now, as she vomited messily over the floor, the impact didn't spatter anything *worse* than her last meal across her boots.

When she finally turned back, wiping her lips on her sleeve, Ian rested a hand on her shoulder. "You okay?"

Even as she tilted her head, pressing her flushed cheek against his fingers, she glowered. "Tell me you know how dumb a question that is."

"I had a suspicion." He started to let his attention drift back to the horrors around them, shuddered, focused on her once more. "Mags, what the hell are we dealing with?"

"Kai?" she asked, in lieu of an answer.

Ian just shook his head.

No, Mags!

She blinked her vision clear, almost violently.

Sad later. Busy now.

"I have no fucking idea," she said, finally replying to his earlier query. "But we're going to find it and make it very, *very* dead."

It took an eternity to reach the hall, so slowly and carefully did they creep, jumping at every sound, struggling in vain to lift one another's spirits. Ian spent the entire time trying to comfort Yun, who appeared to hear not a single word of it.

Finally they met up with Wayne's team in the hallway, who confirmed that nobody had left the shop within the last few minutes.

"So he's still in there, then?" Yun asked, voice flatter than any machine's.

Mags, who had distributed the fallen woman's ammunition amongst the group, and carried the spare weapon slung over her shoulder, offered an encumbered shrug. "Or he's slipped through some exit we don't know about, or through a window or something to the outside. But it's still our best shot."

"In other words, you don't fucking know."

"It's still," she repeated, biting off each word and spitting it out, "our best shot."

He nodded once, short and sharp, and strode back through the doorway without waiting to be told.

"He's gonna get someone killed!" Mags hissed, exasperated.

"Someone already was," Ian reminded her.

"I know! She was one of my..." She forced herself to stop, inhaling deeply. "Let's just go. Someone leave a mark so Cassie's team knows we're in here if they pass by."

Wayne quickly scrawled a simple sigil beside the doorway with a length of rough chalk, and they were on the move once more.

Again they spread out, again they checked every hiding spot they found. This time, though, Mags had everyone working in pairs, so that nobody was forced to duck, alone and vulnerable, around blind corners.

She even checked behind the counter where Kai and the other bodies lay, just to be sure, but everything seemed peaceful there, too.

Peaceful as any pile of mangled and dismembered corpses could be.

Magdalena glanced at Kai, wondered if she ought to feel worse about just leaving the woman where she lay, and continued on.

They found a couple more bodies stashed throughout the place, under this fallen pillar or inside that cabinet with the sliding door hanging off its track. Mags couldn't, no matter how hard she tried, prevent the word "larders" from bubbling up in her head. Shivers ebbed and flowed across her body, and her stomach lurched again.

Beyond those, however? Nothing. Of their horrid quarry, they found no trace.

"Dammit, you lost him!"

Ignoring Yun's accusation, Mags motioned to Wayne and Ian. "Upstairs?"

"Guess we gotta," Wayne said. "He's probably long gone, but we should be sure."

"Well, shit, guys. You were supposed to talk me out of it." Then, more loudly, "All right, everyone! We can only fit single file, so I want people spread out and covering us from all angles. And for God's sake, be careful!"

As they drew near what Mags had thought to be a former staircase, she realized she'd been mistaken. It seemed to be a ramp, leading up, but the floor had been removed, revealing an array of protrusions, wheels, and other incomplete machinery.

Whatever the apparatus had been, there wasn't much left— all the metal had long since been scavenged, of course—so Mags, with her limited understanding of the pre-Pacification world, couldn't begin to guess what it had been.

And ultimately, it didn't matter. Ascending would take a great deal of care, since they'd be placing their feet in the hollow, among what was left of the mechanism, but it was doable.

Despite her instinct to lead, Mags allowed several of the others to precede her. She wanted to be near Yun, to keep him from acting out, making some sort of mistake, and as she wasn't about to let *him* go first...

Which meant she was only about a third of the way up, trying to squeeze her foot between a pair of plastic rollers, when that awful giggling again burbled into her ears.

The first up the ramp, a brash young hothead named Reed, was also the first to die. The slouching figure appeared before him, encrusted in filth, reeking of clotted gore, and lashed out with both hands. The first closed hard around Reed's throat, crushing cartilage, puncturing flesh with ragged nails.

The other slammed into the poor boy's chest, sending his body floppily tumbling back down, blood spraying from torn arteries.

A wobbling chunk of throat remained in his murderer's hands.

The corpse slammed hard into Ian, sending him staggering back, arms pinwheeling—and blocking the line of fire from his friends on the ramp. Shots erupted from the floor, but the angles were all wrong. It would take a lucky ricochet for any of the sentinels below to have a prayer of striking their target.

Their target who, Mags realized in stomach-dropping horror, had yanked away Reed's gun as he'd struck.

The giggling ceased, but only because the madman had raised his fleshy prize to his lips, gnawing loudly. In his other hand, the weapon rose and fired.

It was, perhaps ironically, his own failing balance and the corpse of his friend that saved Ian, the latter absorbing an impact or two before he'd fallen back below the spray of bullets. Magdalena hurled herself over the side, spinning to absorb some of the landing, though she felt the breath blasted from her lungs and knew her entire right side would be bruised for days. She saw nothing but starbursts, couldn't interpret much of what just happened. She heard return fire from the ramp. She also, though, heard a bubbling, rasping breath that trailed away and did not sound again.

Shouts. Shots. Shrieks.

Thudding footsteps, fading chortles.

Her vision began to clear. Her lungs burned with every breath, but at least she *was* breathing. Groaning at the effort, she hauled herself to her feet, only belatedly realizing she ought to have sought cover first.

Nobody took a shot at her, though.

Ian limped down the ramp, clearly pained but with no injury of any severity she could see. Wayne clutched an arm, blood dribbling between his fingers, but he offered Mags a wan smile. Either he didn't fear the machines would find the injury too severe to let him live, or he was doing a remarkable job of hiding it.

A couple more of her people had fallen to the enemy's fire—mad he might be, but he had good aim—leaving only five.

But it should be eight! Where the fuck is Cassie's team?!

She didn't even consider the possibility that the missing group had been eradicated already. She couldn't allow herself to.

"Yun!" It emerged as more of a rasp than the bark she'd intended, but still loud enough for him to hear as he neared the top of the jagged ramp. "Don't even think it!"

The look he cast back down at her was livid. For an instant she tensed, not entirely positive he wasn't about to train his weapon on *her.*

"You are *not* going after him alone! End of discussion! We're going to regroup and figure out our next move—*together!*"

Still he didn't move, save to constantly shift his gaze from Mags to the deeper shadows of the second floor into which their enemy had apparently vanished.

"Get down here, Yun. *Now!*"

She honestly wasn't sure what she'd have done, had he disobeyed, but thankfully she didn't have to decide. Face a mask of hatred, he picked his way back down the incline.

"All right, now..." Magdalena wanted to stop, to regain some sense of a world that, though horrible, had made sense up until today. She desperately wished they could spare some time for the fallen—and for the living, to grieve over more of their brethren than Detachment 13936 had ever lost in a single operation.

Wished, but couldn't, not even a few moments. And Mags feared, deep in her twisting gut, that if she allowed herself to stop, however briefly, she'd be unable to get started again.

"...the first thing we need to do—" she continued. Or tried to.

A single shot rang out.

Mags hit the floor, arms crossed defensively over her head, the pain of her bruised ribs now sizzling across her entire body, before it fully registered that the *crack* hadn't come from within the chamber, or even the building, but from outside.

Suni!

Fortunately for Magdalena's pride, nearly everyone else had dropped prone as well, leaving only Yun standing and casting about for a target. She wasn't sure if he'd even noticed the shot wasn't directed their way.

"Everyone outside! Go!"

It wasn't a long dash, not given the vast array of potential exits offered by the crumbling walls. Even though the team had to slow down, as the early evening and the constant dust conspired to dim the ambient light, they were back on the street in less than two minutes.

"There!" Suni shouted from a distant rooftop, all but jumping up and down to get their attention. "I missed, but I saw him run in there!"

The building at which she madly gestured was... Well, no telling *what* it was. It was smaller than the one they'd just left, and in worse condition. Mags thought she could probably knock down one of the walls herself, given a large enough sledgehammer.

Except, it couldn't have been *that* fragile. A massive gap in the wall, still crumbling around the edges, was obviously fresh, yet the structure still stood.

A gap, Mags noted bitterly, just about the right size for a certain multi-legged machine.

So where the hell has it been up 'til now, dammit?!

The cacophony of a firefight from within, and the sudden disintegration of another stretch of wall beneath what could only have been one of the bot's weapons or Rio's railgun, convinced her, once again, that her questions and complaints had better wait.

"What the *fuck*, Cass?!"

Mags had discovered the red-headed young woman—along with Rio and Alan, the third member of the missing team— already inside, guns trained on what used to be a room, and was now little more than a cave winding its way into a hill of rubble. The machine, too, was present, crouching like a true spider atop a heap of broken wood that had once been a collection of abandoned furniture.

"I'm sorry, Mags." Cassie looked truly crestfallen, a dramatic shift from her usual attitude. "It ordered us to hang back with it, after you'd already split us up. We had no way of telling you."

Magdalena smothered the geyser of fury erupting within her. It wasn't as though her friend could have disobeyed. "Hang back?" she asked instead.

"It never even went inside. Just sat."

"Wanted us to flush out the 'anomaly,'" Yun suggested. His tone was sour enough to curdle motor oil. "Study what it was, how it behaved, before risking anything more important than mere humans."

"Is that right?" Mags demanded.

<Essentially correct,> the bot replied. The machine wasn't capable of shrugging, and wouldn't have bothered even if it could, but she swore she sensed the sentiment regardless.

The last of the young woman's rage petered out, smothered beneath a blanket of exhausted, apathetic loathing. No less futile than getting angry at the weather.

"So what are we doing?" she asked dully.

"Whoever this fucker is," Rio told her, "he's holed up in there."

"Yeah, figured that much."

"We could take the place down and bury him," Cassie said, "but the machines want to question and study him. He was given a couple minutes to surrender just before you got here."

<UNKNOWN SUBJECT.> Everyone in the room flinched, hands rising to ears, at the sudden boom of the amplifier. <YOUR GRACE INTERVAL IS CONCLUDED. SURRENDER OR FACE IMMEDIATE TERMINATION.>

"What time is it?"

It took Mags a moment to decide she'd heard correctly, that the ringing in her ears hadn't somehow obscured the question. The voice was shrill, the same she'd heard giggling earlier, but it sounded rational enough.

Except, of course, for the question itself.

<YOU WILL EXPLAIN THE RELEVANCE OF THIS QUERY.>

"I just need to know if I can surrender yet!"

Magdalena exchanged bewildered and ever more worried glances with Ian and Cassie.

Something is very *wrong here.*

<NINETEEN-TWENTY-SEVEN.>

"All right."

The figure seemed to ooze from the artificial cave before rising to its full—or rather, hunched—height. Other than posture, and the coating of congealing blood, he looked normal enough.

Time froze. She saw Yun step forward, gun raised; saw it in blinding clarity, but her mouth, her hands, her feet, were nowhere near quick enough to stop it.

Oh, no. Yun, don't...!

His finger tightened. The gun bucked, unleashing a rapid burst of three rounds.

Four shots reverberated through the ruined structure.

Three blossoms of crimson sprouted on the stranger's chest, almost hypnotic as he toppled backward to slump against the wall of detritus. The fourth sprouted on the side of Yun's skull. He crumpled as well, a limp, lifeless heap.

A single narrow barrel, still idly exhaling a stream of smoke, retracted into the robot's turret.

Dammit, dammit, fucking dammit!

Ian was already at Yun's side, clutching helplessly at his friend. Her instinct was to run to join him, but Yun was already beyond any help. And it probably wouldn't ingratiate her, as team leader, with the machine that had just executed him. Instead, after a few sprinting steps, she dropped to her knees beside their prisoner.

Blood pumped from open wounds, bubbled on his lips with every panting breath. That he still lived was a miracle. That he wouldn't continue doing so much longer was patently obvious.

Through the wet burbling, he giggled at her.

"Guess you've got your anomaly," she snarled over her shoulder. "Though why you couldn't detect him, or how he—"

<Barlowe, Richard. Detachment Two-Two-Five-Seven-Four. This unit has suffered no difficulty in detecting him via any camera or sensor system.>

"But..."

"That doesn't make any sense," Rio protested at the same time. "How can the anomaly be part of the 22574 if it was around before you *sent* the 22574?!"

<It cannot.>

"You thought... you were hunting... hunting me?" The madman—Barlowe, apparently—could barely form the words around the constant choking of blood-saturated lungs, and

the sporadic giggling of a broken mind. "I'm nothing. Un...
Unworthy. An insect... A fly..."

A long, ripping cough followed, blood and worse than blood.
He couldn't *possibly* live a moment more, couldn't possibly speak
another syllable, yet he did.

"He fed me. And... and in return, all he... all he wanted
was... for me to entertain... you until nightfall. He... He doesn't
like the sun, you see..."

Mags stared over her shoulder in mounting horror at the
faceless bot, at her pale and frightened friends.

At the lengthening shadows beyond the wall, as the last
of the day's feeble sunlight slipped beneath the horizon and
winked out.

Chapter Six

The flashlights, bound to gun barrels with heavy tape, created pools of illumination in the darkness rather than beams. Lifted about and invited to dance by the twilight breezes, the dust and particulate of the Scatters diffused the light. It made the world nice and bright within a couple of yards but failed to rustle the curtain of shadows beyond.

As for that wind... It wasn't the chilling breath of winter, not this time of year. It was just her imagination.

She wasn't shivering, not really. That was her imagination, too. Right?

"Can't see a fucking thing out here," Rio growled, glancing back at the building they'd just left. "Look, I don't wanna hang with a couple bodies anymore'n the next guy, but—"

<Detachment One-Three-Nine-Three-Six will proceed.>

"What about night-vision?" Cassie asked, probably to keep Rio from replying. "Some of us were assigned goggles, right?"

Mags shook her head. "Even if I thought they'd help through the dust, we don't have enough for everyone. So either we'd be blind without light, or anyone wearing 'em would be blind with it."

She glanced up, blinking against the wind, but she knew it was useless even as she gazed at the blurry crescent above. If the haze were going to allow any useful amount of moonlight to reach them, she'd have seen it already.

"What about you?" she asked, hoping she didn't sound as bitter as she felt. "Don't *you* have brighter electrics? For your visual cameras and all?"

<This unit is equipped with more potent light sources,> the machine confirmed.

"Uh… You want to maybe turn them on?"

<Not at this time.>

"What? Why?"

"We're better targets in the dark," Ian explained darkly, "if we've got the lights. We're a… what were they called? Scapehorse, stalking horse, something like that. Right?"

<Correct.> Almost on cue, the bot took a few careful steps back, legs swishing, until it had all but faded into the darkness, as though slowly submerged in ink.

And I thought I hated those fucking things yesterday!

But again, Mags knew better than to voice the thought.

Hell, I guess I should be thankful it's not making us drag all the bodies back home for processing.

"All right," she began. "I think we need to spread out, try to stretch the light as far as possible. And I want eyes in every direction. We spotted a *lot* of places where someone could hide on the way here, and I don't—"

<Suarez, Magdalena is in error. Detachment One-Three-Nine-Three-Six will not retrace the prior route but will continue the search for the anomaly.>

Mags heard muffled tears from her more exhausted teammates. She took a deep breath, crossed herself, and only then turned toward the machine. Or rather, to the darkness whence its voice had come.

"With all respect… Please… We're exhausted. We're grieving."

<Each surviving member of Detachment One-Three-Nine-Three-Six remains fit for duty.>

"But we're not," she pleaded. Everyone else held their breath. If the thing decided she'd crossed the line into insubordination, they'd know it only when they heard the shot. "We lost *five people* today. That's more than we ever… Grief isn't an injury, exactly, but we're…" She was floundering, grasping for words when she had to be coldly convincing. Coldly and *quickly*.

"I know we're expendable, but it won't do you any good if

we're 'expended' without learning anything. Check our heartbeat, breathing, toxins or whatever. You'll see we're not up for this."

Nothing. Silence.

I am so dead.

<This unit is not equipped with medical scanners of that sensitivity.>

Well, fuck...

<Detachment One-Three-Nine-Three-Six will return to origin, as requested. Operations will resume tomorrow.>

This time, the gasps around her were pure shock. So was hers. When she motioned her teammates forward, she almost quailed beneath the gleam of awe in their expressions.

She wanted to ask. She *almost* asked. Even if it refused to answer, it wouldn't change its mind just because she asked. Would it?

It might just shoot her, though.

So, no. She wasn't going to ask. But that wouldn't stop her from mulling it over with the others, as they carefully crept down darkened, rubble-choked streets.

"If I had to guess..." Ian whispered over his shoulder at her.

"And you do."

"Heh. I figure, the fact you risked challenging it, when you didn't know it *couldn't* perform an examination like that, convinced it your concerns were genuine."

A thin sheen of cold sweat broke out across the young woman's face. "*That's* the logic my life hung on?!"

"Hey, I dunno how the damn things think." And then, "Mags, what were *you* thinking?! You could have—"

"Don't. Just don't. I did what I had to for my team. I did my job."

"Your 'job' doesn't mean you have to kill yourself over us!"

"Ian, we've been through—"

"*Wayne's gone!*" Suni's cry, from the rear of the group, quivered in the air, held aloft only by a fingertip grasp on panic. "He's gone!"

"What?!" Mags pushed her way back through the others, Ian on her heels. "What do you mean, 'gone'?"

"I mean just fucking *gone!*"

"Suni, he was right next to you!"

"I *know* he was right fucking next to me! I didn't see a thing, didn't *hear* anything! He's just... He just..."

<Infrared indicates humanoid figure, heat signature probable match to Prentiss, Wayne, in rapid motion.> The bot finally engaged one of its own lights, the beam pointing toward a narrow side street of buildings smaller, but no less ravaged, than those on the main thoroughfare. <Retrieve and explain.>

Bunched together for comfort, weapons at a quivering readiness, the 13936 set off after their missing man.

Not another one. Please, dammit, I can't lose another one!

"Mags?" Cassie sounded as exhausted as Magdalena felt. "Where the hell did *that* come from?"

She'd staggered on a step or two more before realizing that Cassie aimed her light *downward*. With a strange, almost superstitious reluctance, Mags did the same.

Just the dust, kicked up by our steps and the wind swirling around us.

She blinked, then crouched for a closer look.

No. Around them, above them, that was just the dust. At their feet, their calves, their knees, it was too thick.

Without warning and from nowhere, the street had birthed a low bank of swirling, frigid mists.

"It's just fog," she insisted.

"You ever seen fog do—?"

"Focus, God dammit!"

It *was* just fog, anyway. Didn't mean anything. The chill was an illusion, a combination of the cool night and her own nerves. Just an illusion. Just her imagination.

And the creeping eddies that swirled counterclockwise, the gradual drifting of the mist along their path, all in apparent disregard for the breeze? That had to be her imagination, too.

<Heat signature deteriorating.>

Oh, God...

"Cause of distance, right?" Mags asked. Begged, really. "You mean cause it's moving away?"

<Incorrect.>

She ran, caution cast aside, a lifetime of discipline forgotten. Someone called her name—several someones—but they seemed a world away, noises barely filtering through from wherever echoes slept. She tripped on debris concealed in the mist, skinned the palms of her hands, ripped her pants leg and opened skin, staggered back to her feet and ran on.

It was only the sound of the others, pounding along behind— and stumbling just as badly—that restored some semblance of control. She put more than just herself in danger with this maddened rush.

Magdalena skidded to a halt, boots digging furrows in the dry dirt. The air burned her lungs, and she found herself slumping, hands on her knees, coughing violently.

Even the choking caught in her throat, however, when she heard the first cries, the first sobs. When she glanced back and saw every one of her people—her family—staring past her, pale and wan. She felt an instinctive, animal fear, a soul-drenching aversion to the idea of turning, of seeing.

Lips and fingers trembling, she forced herself around.

Wayne hung, a limp and awkward scarecrow, high on a half-crumpled wall. Thick wooden pegs, scavenged from the wreckage, had been driven through his elbows and into the old mortar, so that his forearms swayed gently in the breeze. They, along with a thicker length through his gut, seemed to be all that held him to the wall.

Even from here, even with his head slumped, chin to chest, Mags could see the ragged ruin that had once been her friend's throat, as well as the moonlight pallor of his body. And while this she could *not* see, not in the dark, she knew, without doubt, that improbably little blood stained his clothing.

<Prentiss, Wayne,> the machine announced, as though there could be any doubt. <Deceased.>

"No fucking shit!"

Magdalena couldn't find it in her to berate Rio for his outburst, not this time.

"They didn't..." Ian's voice cracked. "They didn't have to *display* him like that! Why—why would they...?"

"How would they?" Suni nearly squeaked. "How did they get him up there so fast?"

<Detachment One-Three-Nine-Three-Six will retrieve the remains for examination.>

Mags wouldn't have been surprised if a chunk of lip came off in her mouth, she bit it so hard. The bot could be up there and back in seconds, whereas she and the others would have to unspool rope, find purchase with their hooks, exhaust themselves even further with the climb. Still, maybe it didn't figure the wall would support it.

At least they'd treat Wayne with a little more respect than it would have.

It was only after the ropes were secured, tested, removed from their crumbling anchor points, re-secured, and tested again; only when she and a couple of the others had begun scaling the wall; only when she happened, then, to glance down, that Magdalena noticed.

In the thick, pooling light from the machine and her friends, the roadway beneath her was clearly visible, obscured only lightly by the ubiquitous dust.

The mist was gone.

In the distant night, as though triggered by her realization, something howled.

Mags nearly lost her grip. She managed to save herself from what would have proved a nasty fall, but the friction burns didn't do her already raw palms any good. Hissing against the pain, she scrambled the rest of the way.

"Coyote, maybe?" The whispered question drifted from the next rope over.

"That sound like any kind of coyote to you?" Mags snapped back.

"No, but... I never heard of no wolves coming into the Scatters before."

The young woman offered a tilt of her head, the closest she could come to shrugging while clinging to the rope. "Hungry straggler, or maybe a wild dog. Doesn't matter."

"Mags, after everything else tonight... You sure of that?"

Silence. Then, "Shut it. We have work to do."

She managed to put aside her revulsion at yanking the wood from Wayne's flesh, but it was a near thing. What she could *not* ignore was the sheer effort. Clinging, balancing, latching a simple block-and-tackle to the stone, winding rope around the body... A good half hour passed before Mags and one of her two climbing partners had sidled back down the wall, slowly lowering Wayne along with them.

Finally, *finally* they made it. Gasping for breath, wincing at every movement of her shredded hands, Mags stepped away from the wall, so the others could converge and retrieve the body. "All right, Aaron!" she called up to the third and final teammate who'd made the assent, and now waited for the signal to unhook the pulley. "Lower it down!"

Nothing.

"Aaron?" She found herself surprised that the sweat on her neck didn't ice over. "Aaron!"

Silence.

"We have to find him!" Ian demanded at close to a shriek, at the precise same moment Rio announced, "We gotta get out of here!"

"Both of you, shut it!" Mags addressed her next words to their taskmaster. "Can you sense him? Like with Wayne?"

<Negative. Substantial quantities of stone to the east and south may be sufficiently dense to block this unit's infrared sensors. Remain here.>

Systems whined, metal clattered and screeched on rock. The machine skittered sideways and made for yet another of the ruined buildings. This one, short and thick, remained relatively intact.

Faster than any human, it reached the nearest wall and scurried upward. As soon as it attained the highest point on what remained of the roof, it froze, various cameras and other sensors doubtless scouring every direction.

Even if it couldn't find Aaron, Mags hoped it might at least locate a better vantage point, something taller that could still take its weight, where it might—

Something else, something crawling, moved on the rooftop.

She couldn't see precisely what, none of them could, not in the early nighttime gloom. But the bot should have! Cameras far more sensitive than human eyes, fully capable of low-light operation, to say nothing of the heat sensors... Half a dozen different systems should have detected the approaching figure long before Mags did.

It rose to its feet, revealing itself to be human—or at least human-shaped—though Mags would have *sworn*, while it crawled, that it possessed no such silhouette. A long coat, or something similar, flapped behind it, undulating in the wind. It stood tall, directly before the bot, and still the machine gave no indication of awareness.

She warred with herself, wondering if she ought to shout a warning, whether it would do any good if she did. She hadn't yet decided when it ceased to matter.

The figure lunged, so fast Mags wasn't even certain she'd seen it. Two hands wrapped around the nearest of the machine's legs and *yanked*.

Nothing should have happened. The bot shouldn't have moved, except perhaps to idly throw off this biological pest. Instead it rocked, tilting back on its other legs as the newcomer somehow hefted that limb clear of the rooftop.

Now, of course, the computer recognized that someone, something, shared the rooftop with it. Gunshots shattered the night, and its grasping arms thrashed, but it still seemed unable to see its foe. Some of those wild shots came close—even blind, the machine knew, could probably feel, where its assailant must stand—but the figure dodged the attacks with inhuman speed. The steel of that leg began, impossibly, to buckle, to twist...

As fast as the stranger might be, however, it couldn't avoid everything. One of the flailing arms caught it clean across the chest, sending it sprawling. Still its strength proved impossible, unimaginable, as two strips of steel tore from the bot and went with it, clutched in an inhuman grip. The shriek of rending metal was a needle in each ear, but Magdalena barely noticed.

Bullets and other projectiles sprayed in all directions, the machine clearly having decided to deal with its undetectable foe by sterilizing the entire rooftop. Mags realized she was holding her breath. Nothing could possibly survive such a—

The strange figure *melted*.

Like fat in a frying pan, but a thousand times faster, it decomposed into nothingness, leaving behind only a swirling gas, pouring over the roof in a veritable cascade.

A cascade of mist.

Oh, God, was that *what we were...?*

It coiled, a phantom serpent, sweeping across the roof and back up, spilling in reverse until it coagulated behind the bot. Further it rose, twisting, tightening, soon as much a pillar of fog as a bank. Now Mags *was* shouting, though she never could remember precisely what her words were, or if there were words at all.

A thin tendril of mist extruded from the column, almost caressing the steel carapace of the machine. Caressed, and then slipped inside, through gaps so tiny even water couldn't have fit.

In another heartbeat, the haze grew solid, the figure reappearing. Metal bent, distorted as what had been a thin ribbon of fog became an arm, an arm buried almost to the elbow in the innards of the machine.

And with a sharp, sudden flex and a cry of exertion only faintly human in its timbre, it tore those innards free.

Viscera of wires and organs of silicon dangled from the stranger's fist. Jagged edges of steel, like broken bone, protruded from the gaping wound. Mags found herself crazily wishing it would scream; the bot's silence was somehow the most unnatural aspect of the whole tableau.

It didn't, of course. It merely shuddered as internal systems malfunctioned, twitching as though it truly were some awful insect. Sparks spat once, twice. Something inside whined until it abruptly ground to a halt.

Then it died. Just like that, a sculpture of steel and an elaborate interior, nothing more. Beside it, a fist casually opened, allowing crinkled lengths of wire and crumbles of shattered polymers to waft away in the dark.

There was no protocol on which to fall back. No precedent.

Absolutely nothing in Mags's experience, in *anyone's* experience, could have prepared them for this.

Which meant there was only one thing to do.

"*Run!*"

She opened fire before her shout faded, lobbing burst after burst at the stranger on the roof. Her aim wasn't the greatest, but she was pretty sure she could land a few rounds at this distance. At the very least, it might slow him down.

Other than spitting something that might have been a growl or a hiss—the sound was too flattened by the broad expanse and jagged lines of the Scatters for Mags to tell—the figure scarcely reacted to the shots. It leaned out, curling into a shallow crouch as though ready to leap from the rooftop.

From behind, the young woman heard the sudden whine of a generator, felt the faintest crackle of a charge building on the air. Rio appeared at her side, electromagnetic accelerator aimed high. With a dull *whump* that sounded nothing whatsoever like a gunshot, the weapon discharged.

This time, there could be no doubt of impact. Even as it punched through flesh and bone, the projectile, faster and more massive than any bullet, lifted the enemy from its feet and hurled it back, over the roof and out of sight.

"Got the fucker!" Rio tossed her a vicious grin. "That's what *happens* when you mess with us!"

"Right. You got him. Now let's get the hell out of here."

"What?" He seemed stunned, even crestfallen, that she didn't share his vengeful jubilation. "We should go see who the bastard is, see if we can tell how he did all that shit he did!"

"He took the bot apart with his bare hands! What if 'that shit he did' includes surviving getting shot off the roof?!"

"C'mon, *nobody's* gonna survive—"

"We. Are. *Leaving.*"

"*Fine!* Shit."

They took off at a sprint, Rio huffing a bit beneath the weight of the backpack generator. It didn't take long to catch up to the others. The 13936 had obeyed their leader's orders to run but hadn't been willing to leave Mags or Rio too far behind. She scowled as they neared, but she couldn't force the expression for long.

So few of us left...

"Get the hell back to the train," she ordered softly.

Every half-fallen building, every heap of rubble, loomed larger in the darkness beyond the reach of their feeble lights. Every jumble of wreckage along the road grasped eagerly at passing ankles, and every sound, from the crunch of their boots to the shifting of distant rocks to the fluttering and screeching of bats overhead, seemed nightmarishly loud.

Wait.

Bats? The shouting and the gunfire should've scared any bats away! And more important than that...

"Mags?" Ian asked, voicing the question for her. "Don't bats usually swarm at twilight?"

The chorus of fluttering and screeching rose to a ghastly crescendo. They could see nothing. The creatures flew higher than the tiny electric lights could reach, visible only when one happened to blot out the moon or one of the few visible stars.

Magdalena knew that they spun and swirled, a spinning dance of dark against dark, though *how* she knew, she couldn't have said. The sound, perhaps, or some all-but-unseen flicker of movement. Round and round, gathering, tightening, until they were less a swarm and more...

More a column. Just like the mist.

They collided all at once, seeming to become a single flailing mass in the shadow-draped sky. And then, no illusion and no mistake, they *were* a single mass! Coat billowing as the wings of the bats had done, the stranger plummeted from the sky to land with a dreadful, dust-clouded thump at Rio's side. Its knees scarcely bent, as though the drop were no more than a step from one of the shattered concrete curbs.

Hands flashed, yanking the pack from Rio's back hard enough to snap the canvas straps. The young man screamed, almost enough to hide the *pop* of something dislocating, as he spun one way, the railgun and generator the other. Perhaps through sheer good fortune, Rio skidded across the gravelly earth, clothing and skin abrading across one side, but sliding to a halt before he struck anything more substantial. The generator blasted through an old wall, emerging in a shower of stone and metal fragments.

Cassie bellowed at the sight of her lover tossed aside like an empty clip. She dropped into a crouch and opened fire. Mags followed suit, as did the rest of the remaining crew.

Even in the gloom, through the haze, she *saw* the rounds hit home, fabric and flesh open. Yet other than staggering beneath the sheer quantity of impacts, the enemy scarcely seemed to feel it. A quick snarl, a quicker spin, and it—he; she was sure now it was a "he"—was gone, vanished once more into the dark.

"Rio!" Mags shouted! Please *don't be too badly hurt!* "You mobile?"

"I can fucking *run* if it gets me outta here!"

God, if he survives this just to be put down by the damn machines...

Well, they wouldn't learn of his injury from her.

"Everyone go! Scatter! Make for the train!" She hated to split them up, but they were no stronger as a group, not against *this*. If they took different routes, at least some might make it.

Magdalena slipped through an alley, turning sideways to avoid the jagged protrusions, and had just set off down the next street over when the sound of steps and breath—*familiar* steps and breath—warned her that not everyone had taken her "Scatter!" to heart.

"God *dammit*, Ian!"

"Don't even," he puffed, pulling up beside her and matching her pace, so they both moved at a steady, cautious jog. "There's no *way* I'm leaving you alone out here with that...that whatever the fuck it is!"

"And what're you going to do if it attacks me, dumbass?" she snapped between panting breaths. "Snarl a lot?"

Ian's entire face froze. "Whatever I can," he said through gritted teeth. "Maybe I can at least buy you some time to—"

"No." The voice was deep, somehow soft and resonant at once, thickly accented. "I am afraid you cannot."

A casual backhand slammed Ian to the dirt with the clatter

of tools and the *whump* of limp flesh. Mags felt her heart and her stomach both lodge in her throat, fighting one another for the claim. She couldn't see how badly he might be hurt.

Couldn't see if he still breathed.

The figure stood over him, his attentions fixed on Magdalena herself. Even this near, she couldn't tell much. He was draped in a long, heavy coat of some deep hue, its high collar fastened tight about his neck. Of the outfit beneath and the hair above, she could make out only that they were dark and flowing.

Beyond that, she saw only that his skin was pallid, almost sickly so, and his eyes...

Her arms froze, her gun lifted halfway, wrapped in lethargy, *beyond* lethargy. She couldn't recall how to make them move.

His eyes...

A tremor ran through her, a scream echoed and re-echoed in her mind, in her soul. Here was nothing wholesome, nothing human. Snake. Wolf. Pestilence. Nightmare.

Emptiness. Hunger.

She could not run. Could not turn away. Could not blink.

His eyes...

They bored into her. They filled her. They *were* her.

Who was she?

"It appears," he spoke, and the voice came from everywhere, from nowhere, surfacing like a long-forgotten memory, "as ludicrous as it might be, that you are the leader of this latest... expedition." Every word was precise, distinct unto itself yet flowing smoothly into the next. "I would know who you are. Why you have come. Why you do the bidding of these iron devils.

"Tell me."

She didn't *know* who she was. But at his command, she remembered who—up until those eyes—she once had been, and why she was here.

Haltingly, lifelessly, Magdalena—or perhaps a shell of Magdalena—began to speak.

Chapter Seven

"I don't know!"

She screamed it, shrill enough to shatter glass, brittle enough to shatter in turn. "I don't know, I don't know, I *don't know!*"

She hadn't known, lying in the street, blinking up at the night sky as a limping, staggering Ian awakened her. She hadn't known on the train back to the so-called conformed regions, when Cassie, Rio, and Suni—the only other survivors—pressed her for answers and explanations. She hadn't known when, guided by a single hovering drone, she'd stumbled back into the gargantuan chamber where Jonas and the other half of her team all but buried her under an avalanche of queries and demands, until she was almost willing to shoot every one of her friends if it meant they'd just *leave her alone.*

And though her life might well depend upon her responses, she didn't know *now* either.

<What was the nature of this individual you claim to have encountered?>

"I don't know!"

<Why does it not appear in any transmissions or recordings?>

"I don't know!"

<What happened to you after your final interaction with the anomaly?>

"God dammit, I don't know!" Each word quavered, threatening to crumble to dust and choke her.

"Stop it, please! Can't you see she's trying her best? You—"

The machine—another multi-legged bot, one of the smaller standard variety as opposed to the combat model they'd so recently seen destroyed—straightened to its full height. <Masse, Ian. This unit requires no further input from you at this time.>

"But—"

<Further interference is a waste of this unit's time and will be rectified.>

His whole heart in the look he cast Magdalena, the grinding of his teeth audible from where she stood, Ian retreated to stand with the others. Several nodded their sympathy, and Cassie reached out to squeeze his shoulder.

Under normal circumstances, Mags would have appreciated all of it. Now, she just wanted everything to stop.

"Your pardon, please." Jonas stepped forward, hands at his sides, palms outward. "If you would permit me to ask...?"

When the bot said nothing, Jonas turned toward the quivering young woman, a gentle smile clinging precariously to his face. "Mags, why don't you tell us what you *do* remember?"

"We've been *through* all that!" Twice, in fact: once to Jonas and the others, when she and her companions had first returned, and then again a short while later—omitting Rio's injury, the second time around—when the machine had arrived for their report. "There's nothing I—!"

"Please. Humor me. Never know what might come to you."

She didn't want to. Couldn't think of anything she wanted less. But as the machine still hadn't spoken, she presumed it was waiting for her to continue. Refusing would be unwise.

At least this is keeping attention on me and not Rio.

His wound—unlike poor Carter's—didn't show unless he attempted anything strenuous with that arm. Mags had genuine hope it might remain unnoticed.

So, with a sigh, she began again.

She devoted little attention to the events of the daytime. The machines had a perfectly good record and understanding of *that*. It was only at the fall of night, and the appearance of the "anomaly," that her recounting took on any detail.

Again she explained that their escort clearly couldn't see its attacker, though she couldn't guess why. Again she explained its seemingly superhuman abilities, its horrible, relentless purpose. Again she omitted any hint of serious injury on Rio's part, describing only that the stranger had torn the weapon from his hands.

And again she described her horror as Ian was tossed aside, meeting the thing's gaze as she'd raised her weapon… Then nothing until her lover, the filth on his face streaked with tears, shaking her awake.

<What was its appearance?>

But other than the same general, long-distance description the others could offer, she had nothing.

<How did it accomplish the feats you claim?>

<What is its purpose?>

<What did it do to Barlowe, Richard?>

<What is the nature of the anomaly?>

<What is the nature of the anomaly?>

<What is the nature of the anomaly?>

With every answer, Mags found herself nearer the verge of screaming again. It didn't believe her, and why should it? She wouldn't have believed either! But the truth—even if only a portion of the truth—was all she had.

Several times during her tale, she'd seen Jonas's brow furrow. Now he leaned in, almost touching her cheek, whispering as though they weren't both fully aware that the bot could hear them regardless.

"Mags, come on. What *really* happened out there?"

She felt as though someone had just punched her in the gut—with the detachment's truck. "Jonas…"

"You *know* what they're going to do to you if they think you're lying! Mags, please!"

The tension of her efforts to hold back tears, to show no weakness in front of the others or the machines, might have been the only reason she remained upright. Frustrating though it had been, she'd felt no surprise when the machines didn't believe her. But him?

"I've never lied to you, Jonas. Not once. Why won't you believe me now?"

"Because what you're describing *isn't possible*, and you know it!"

"Of *course* I know it!" They weren't even trying to keep the conversation quiet now. "But it's what I saw! What *we* saw!"

"It *can't* be! Where did you even *hear* about these things?"

"Hear?" Mags swore that her brain and body were growing dizzy in two separate directions. "I didn't *hear* of anything! I'm just telling you what I... What are you even *talking* about?!"

Jonas's expression softened. "Where *would* you have heard?" he muttered, now gazing past rather than at her. "Not a lot of people in the camp old enough, not anymore..."

"What are you talking about?" she asked again—small, almost desperate.

His gaze snapped back into focus and he offered another faint smile. "Let me see what I can do."

She watched him approach the bot, speaking and gesturing back at the group. It remained still for a moment and then turned to stride, *click-click-clack*, across the massive chamber. Jonas followed, until they vanished behind the curtain of shadows that draped the room's far side.

The rest of the detachment was on her like ants, shouting and crying and asking and demanding and wondering and insisting and believing and disbelieving and everything in between.

It took the combined shouts of all five survivors, and even a few shoves and punches, before everyone quieted down. Mags couldn't blame them—she knew how she sounded, knew the others were still reeling from the news of eight lost friends—but it was still too much. She found herself screaming at them long after the rest of the noise had stopped, with no idea what she might be saying, knowing only that it had to get out.

When it was finally done, her mind as worn as her lungs and throat, she found that Ian had taken her hand. Or perhaps she had taken his? Whatever the case, they led one another through the shocked and bewildered throng to place their backs against the nearest wall and slump to a seat. Slowly, even tentatively, the others joined them, sitting or sprawled across the floor. Nobody looked at anyone else, and nobody spoke another word.

"All right, everyone up!"

Mags jolted to her feet, unsure how much time had

passed. The others did the same in response to their overseer's command. Jonas stood before them, arms crossed. Behind him, over his shoulder, loomed the machine.

"Make sure you've gathered everything," he continued. "Train'll be here shortly. We're going home."

"What?" Mags was sure she must have misunderstood. Her gaze flickered from Jonas to the bot, and back. "What did you—?"

"Later!" She actually recoiled from something in his glare, the clench of his jaw. "For now, all of you just keep it shut!"

If it meant getting the hell out of there, she could do that.

Their weapons turned in, the rest of their equipment assembled, Detachment 13936—clumped together, woefully diminished and discouraged—gathered along the platform. Already they heard the distant rumble, the artificial thunder that was the harbinger of the coming train.

Mags didn't really care anymore if she ever learned what the hell was happening here. All she wanted was to get out of the Scatters, curl up on her cot, and try to come to terms with losing so many of her—

The machine lunged, all six legs sharply angled, its manipulator hands extended and striking, an angry serpent of steel.

Rio had just time enough for a startled, rasping yelp before the sharp *crack* of bone and tendon silenced him.

<Long-term debilitating. Maintenance of Hayes, Rio, no longer efficient.>

Cassie was still screaming, Ian weeping over his best friend, when the train roared into the chamber. But Mags—cold, numb to the depths of her soul and her hindmost dreams—could only wonder.

Rio hadn't shown any sign of his injury. The machine had never examined him.

So how had it known?

Chapter Eight

Mags straightened with a low groan. One hand on the spade, she pressed the other into the small of her back, stretching until she both felt and heard a soft pop. It didn't relieve much of the pain or stiffness, but even a little was great relief.

God, I hate barn duty!

The camp kept only a few cattle (as well as a handful of goats), for use in plowing the fields that kept the bulk of the people fed, a source of milk, occasional meat when one of the beasts grew too old or injured for any other purpose. And while the animals spent the bulk of their time in a large corral, munching on dried and scraggly grass, milking, tending, and inclement weather required shelter.

And even a small population of livestock could produce a *lot* of leavings if the place wasn't cleaned out regularly.

Mags yanked down the scrap of cloth she'd tied around her nose and mouth. "Hey, Ian?"

Across the barn, the young man's head appeared over the side of a milking stall. "Yeah?"

"You talked to Cassie at all?"

The redhead hadn't said a word to Mags or to anyone else—not on the train back from the Scatters, and not for days afterward. Even now, so far as Magdalena had seen, Cassie only spoke when work absolutely demanded it.

"Oh, yeah. Just this morning. She distinctly said 'Here' when she handed me this fucking shovel."

"Come on, Ian! I'm just worried about her." Then, more softly, "And I miss him, too."

"Yeah, I know." His long sigh, as he ducked back behind the

wall, made him appear to deflate. "Sorry, Mags."

Not like she was surprised. Ian hadn't exactly been himself the last few days, either.

"I did try," he continued, now slightly muffled by the intervening wood. "Spent half of last night trying to talk to her, see if she was okay. All I got to show for it is lack of sleep."

Magdalena gazed absently down at the muck—yes, "muck" was a nice, neutral term for it—caking her shovel and her boots. *It's not even supposed to be our turn on shit detail!*

It was a silly complaint, and she knew it. Detachment 13936 had arrived back at the camp in the rattling, stuttering truck to find the 13944 on their way out—crammed into their own coughing jalopy—and the other teams already gone on this assignment or that. For a while, what remained of Magdalena's people were the camp's only occupants. Which meant less work to do, yes, but also only a single depleted detachment available to do it.

Still, the heavy workload wasn't all bad. Physical exhaustion was preferable to thought.

Very much as though he'd been eavesdropping on her musings, Ian popped back up. "Oh, talked to Jonas on the way over here. He says a couple of the other teams are due back before nightfall."

"*Yes!* Someone else can do this damn job, then!"

"You really think whatever we get's going to be any better?"

"Shut it, you!"

She was delighted to see him grinning through his own rag, a sight all too rare these days. "And," he continued, "I'm sure they'll have all sorts of..."

The grin fell away, carrying the remainder of the sentence with it. In accordance with custom older than they were, the camp's detachments frequently shared stories of their latest exploits over meals or work details. It was considered a mark of pride if a team could surprise the others with something new.

Somehow, though, Mags didn't expect to hear much to top their own recent experiences.

"Are we gonna tell them?" Ian asked. "I mean, they'll know something's up, given how... How many of us..."

"I don't know, Ian. They'd never believe it, and anyway, I don't think I want to talk about it. Don't know if I ever will."

She knew he nodded—she actually heard the rustling of the fabric over his mouth—but she'd already turned her attention back to the spade in her hand. Suddenly, shoveling cattle dung didn't feel remotely like the worst thing she could be doing.

Mags straightened with a low groan. One hand on the spade, she pressed the other into the small of her back, stretching until she both felt and heard a soft pop. It didn't relieve much of the pain or stiffness, but even a little was great relief.

Didn't I just go through this exact same crap just yesterday? Why isn't someone else doing this?!

The return of several teams the previous evening had changed absolutely nothing of consequence. The gathering in the mess tent for supper had been larger, and definitely louder, than in recent days. Members of each detachment caught up with, bragged to, or taunted members of the others. Hazards and difficulties and feats were exaggerated, fears and injuries downplayed, in part jockeying for status between teams and in part as a distraction from the bland, unappealing meal.

Same thing that happened any time a detachment returned from active duty.

Magdalena had decided, for the time being, against telling anyone what she and the others had experienced. She didn't want her team ostracized—the different groups might not be close, but after losing so many teammates, the 13936 needed all the friends and near-friends they could scrounge—and ostracism was guaranteed if they tried to pass off a story like that one. Most respected her answer when she said she didn't want to talk about it; losing friends might be a fact of life, but eight on one assignment was rough. Those few who didn't, who tried to press the issue, Mags was more than capable of staring down.

Ian and Suni had agreed with her reasoning, and Cassie still wasn't speaking much to anyone, so Magdalena felt fairly confident about her choice. Some of her other teammates might spread the tale, but from them it was all secondhand hearsay.

Easier to dismiss as a misunderstanding or a joke when it came from someone who hadn't experienced it personally.

Unfortunately, while the other detachments had been more willing to share their own experiences, their stories told Mags nothing of value. The operations were all standard: explore this, repair that, dig here. Nothing of any urgency, so far as she could tell, nothing to explain why they'd all been sent out so abruptly—and simultaneously.

And worse, since the teams had gotten home late in the day, the overseers had agreed to let them rest in, taking up their duties in the afternoon. Which meant that, yes, here Mags was again, back in the barn.

How could the cattle produce so much shit in one day?!

"Hey, Mags?"

"Yeah, love?" Except, she saw as she twisted to look, it wasn't Ian who'd called. A figure stood at the barn door, his broad-shouldered frame casting an artificial twilight shadow across the interior.

"Nestor?" Magdalena pulled the protective cloth from her nose and mouth. Ian, emerging from one of the stalls, did the same. "Aren't you supposed to be on pump maintenance? If they find you shirking..."

"I know." Only now did Mags catch the fearful timbre behind his words, the worried twitching of his jaw, his fingers. "I just... Danny's not here with you for some reason, is he?"

Now, at least, she understood the concern. Daniel Page, another member of the 13936, had been with Nestor longer even than she and Ian had been a couple.

"No. I thought the two of you were working together today?"

"We were supposed to, but he didn't show. I've checked his cot, the mess, the infirmary. Tracked down Jonas to ask if there'd been a special assignment. Nothing."

Ian was frowning now, too. "Have you asked...?"

He may not have wanted to finish the question, but Mags knew exactly where he was headed. So, apparently, did Nestor.

"Not yet," the big guy replied. "If the machines find him, and they don't like his reason for shirking..." He, too, failed to finish his thought aloud. Mags didn't blame him.

"Go back to work," she ordered kindly. "Ian and I'll try to hurry up and finish here and start looking. And we'll gather the others, when they're done with their own work."

Nestor's grimace deepened. He obviously wanted them to do more, but just as obviously knew it wasn't viable. With a sharp nod, he stomped from the barn.

"I don't like this," Ian muttered, nervously shifting from foot to foot.

"I'm sure it's nothing."

"No, you're not."

"No, I'm not. Get shoveling."

It wasn't nothing.

Their search ended in an auxiliary pumping station, not currently in use and subject to only the most barebones maintenance schedule. Intended to provide some modicum of water pressure in the event of primary pump failure, it consisted of little more than a generator, the mechanism itself, and a narrow well, all within a rickety structure at the camp's edge.

It had been Cassie who spotted the puddle of water slowly leaking from under the ill-fitting door—a leak which meant the pump was both active, which it shouldn't have been, and malfunctioning. Her call had drawn Brandon—a gangly, pale-skinned kid, the detachment's youngest member—who'd in turn run to gather the others. Mags had been the one to yank the portal open in its misshapen, sticking frame.

She was fortunate. The bare cables lying in the water that covered the station's floor were no longer live. The generator, to judge by the smell of burned wiring in the air, had shorted out.

After sending more than enough voltage through the standing liquid to electrocute the trio of men who'd stood there.

Two of the singed and waterlogged corpses, Mags recognized as members of the 13927. They shouldn't have been here at all; perhaps they'd heard sounds of trouble and gone to assist? Were they in some way *responsible*? Whatever the case, it had cost them their lives.

But for the most part, she had eyes only for the third body, the one nearest the pump.

"God..."

Why was *he* here? "Pump duty" meant the primary station, unless specifically ordered otherwise. Had the machines reassigned him, perhaps having detected a breakdown in the pump? Why had the auxiliary pump even been active? And above all else, *how am I going to tell Nest?*

As it happened, she didn't have to. The cry of agony from across the camp, and the sobs that rose and fell sporadically throughout the coming night, made it quite clear that someone else had beaten her to it. She could only hope they'd been gentle.

Mags lay by herself that night. She'd have liked the company, the comfort, but she knew Ian was sitting at Nestor's side, trying however futilely to comfort his grieving friend. That sort of kindness was just what he did, who he was, and she wouldn't have talked him out of it if she could.

Still, it would've been nice not to be alone.

She was wrapped up in her ratty blanket, stretched out on her cot and studying the canvas above, concentrating on the first soft patter of rain overhead and wishing she could sleep, when a sudden appearance from the dark beside her proved she wasn't entirely alone after all. "Mags?"

"Fuck, Cassie! You scared the... Wait." *Cassie* was talking again, all of a sudden? "What's happened now?"

"Nothing happened, exactly." The redhead knelt beside the cot and continued in a rough whisper. "It's Danny. I saw him at supper last night. Overheard him."

"Uh, yeah?"

"He was talking about what happened to us. In the Scatters."

"Urgh. Well, we figured someone would probably—"

"Mags, he was talking to a pair of guys from the 13927. The same ones we found with him."

A fearsome shiver rocked Magdalena's body. She swore that even her *hair* went cold. Fingers absently twisting the worn fabric of her blanket, she listened to the rain. Tonight...

No, tonight she would *not* be sleeping.

"...even supposed to *be* there!" This was the fifth or sixth time she'd made that point, and she knew it. She was repeating herself, teetering on the brink of hysteria.

"I know, Mags." Jonas, too, had said much the same thing several times now. "I really am doing everything I can to figure out what happened. All the overseers are."

Mags inhaled, a deep, shuddering breath, and forced her pacing feet to still, her wildly gesticulating arms to return to her sides. She turned a crestfallen expression on the older man, currently hunched in an old but sturdy chair. (Yes, in addition to having genuine walls and a roof, the overseer's tiny personal quarters had *furniture* beyond the requisite cot.)

"Jonas?" Her voice didn't crack, but only because her tensed jaw and clenched fists held it too tightly. "Eight of us in the Scatters. *Eight.* And then Rio. And now Danny? I don't—I don't know what..."

"It's not your fault, Mags. None of it. Nobody blames you."

"I think *I* might."

"Then you're being foolish." The overseer actually managed a faint smile at the shock plastered across her face. "Magdalena, if there's any way, I *will* find out what happened to Daniel."

"And if there's something the machines aren't telling us? He shouldn't have been there. That pump shouldn't have been on!"

"If there is," he said gently, "then we'll never know. I won't make you any promises we both know I can't keep. For now, just go back to work, you and the team. Keep your heads down, go about your duties. Maybe busy the others extra, just to keep them distracted from all this. I'll let you know when—if—there's something to let you know."

It was a polite, friendly dismissal, but a dismissal nonetheless. Tense and tight-lipped, she firmly shut the door behind her in what was most definitely *not* a temperamental slam, thank you very much.

Ten people. Ten *friends.* Eleven, if you went back one more day for Carter. In the couple of years she'd served as Jonas's second, as field leader for the 13936, she hadn't suffered so many losses *combined.* She knew the old man was doing all he could, she really did, but that didn't make it any better.

Still, she'd already grown more philosophical about the

whole thing by the time she'd crossed the camp. Death and loss were no strangers to her, even if they didn't normally visit in such quantities, and she *did* have work to do. They all did.

And at least it wasn't barn duty any longer.

Having come and gone again and again since early last night, the rain resumed as Mags made her way to the vehicle pool. It was a slow, steady drench, plastering hair and clothes to everyone's skin, chilling them to the bone. The tarps that fluttered and dripped above the trucks repulsed only a portion of the downpour, but it was still a welcome respite.

Various workers from the 13936 and the 13944 scurried this way and that between the vehicles or shimmied that way and this beneath them. Magdalena's team was officially on maintenance today, but the other detachment was heading out on assignment the next morning, so their participation—at least where their own vehicle and equipment were concerned—was understandable. Mags's own people did the same when it was *their* asses on the line.

"Where to?" she called out, asking no one person but the general assemblage already present.

One of several pairs of legs jutting out from beneath a tilted, currently wheel-less chassis twitched, and then slid free. Her diminutive teammate, Marty—who always looked just a bit larger, to her, when not lugging around his equipment—wiped a bit of grease from his face and pointed at one of the other rust-splotched heaps. "Brake line. Brake pads. Fuel pump."

"Oh, is that all?"

"Probably not." Marty grinned at her. "Feel free to look for anything else while you're down there."

"Oh, *thank* you. And it's awfully nice of you to volunteer for our next mission's latrine duty like this." Mags scooped up a handful of wrenches and sockets and crawled under the truck in question.

For a time, she heard nothing but the clatter and clank of tools, the grunts of exertion, the occasional shout across the vehicle pool, and the muted drumming of the rain. Dirt, oils, and a bit of blood from scraped knuckles coated her hands and then her face, smeared by ambient moisture that wasn't enough to wash the gunk off, but more than sufficient to spread it around. It dribbled now and then across her lips, making her spit in a futile effort to rid her mouth of the taste, or stung at reddened eyes.

And then those familiar sounds were overwhelmed by a hideous crash. Steel rent and scraped across broken concrete, or squealed as it crumpled beneath a horrid weight, followed by a rising chorus of screams.

Magdalena froze. The cries grew worse, running feet shook the vehicle pool, and still she huddled, paralyzed, beneath the truck. Fingers ached as they squeezed against the wrench, but she couldn't force them to relax.

What more? God, how much more?!

Stiff, halting, every inch an effort, she finally forced herself to slide into the open. Loose hair clung to her, slicked down by grease and water, and she had to sluice whole handfuls from her face before she could see what she somehow already knew she would see.

One of the massive pneumatic jacks had slipped on the rain-slick concrete. Currently lacking its wheels, the heavy vehicle had come crashing down entirely on its frame. One of the workers of the 13944 thrashed and spasmed, screaming, pinned by the weight atop a mangled arm that could never possibly recover. Of the others who had been working there, including poor Marty, there was nothing but protruding legs, horrifyingly still, and a steadily growing, rapidly diluting pool of oil, antifreeze, and blood.

They assembled in the mess tent that evening, one of the camp's few structures large enough to accommodate them all. Not just the 13936 and 13944, but every human in the camp whose presence wasn't essential somewhere else. Several of the headless humanoid bots stood near the entrances, statue-still. Others clicked and clattered about outside, audible through the canvas and the rain. At the forefront of the tent, where the food was normally distributed, stood Jonas and the other detachment overseers.

"...all aware," Noreen, overseer of the 13927, was in the midst of saying, "of the unfortunate accidents we've all suffered over the past few days." A dark, almost bald woman with weather-worn features, Noreen was, save possibly for Jonas himself, the camp's most experienced overseer. Everyone's attention was rapt, fixed on her every word—everyone's but Magdalena, who was riding a whirlwind of her own thoughts and listening with only half an ear at best.

"As far as we can tell," Noreen explained, "the jack was secured a hair off-center. It probably wouldn't have mattered on most days, but the rain made things just slick enough for it to slip."

Shouts, then, from several members of the two detachments that had lost people; denying, first, that anyone on their own team would have made such an error, then hurling accusations at the other.

"*Shut it!*" The shout from both Jonas and Tavio, the 13944's overseer, brought about a grudging but instant silence.

"The fact is," the older woman continued on as though she'd never been interrupted, "you're *all* overworked and exhausted. The overseers will speak with the machines after you've been dismissed." She cast a sideways glance at the nearest of the bots, which reacted not a whit. "See if we can't get your workload lessened, at least for a short while. Until then, watch out for each other. Double-check everything. None of us want to lose anyone else."

"That's it," Jonas announced, stepping up from behind her. "You're all dismissed. Night crews, get to your posts. Everyone else, try to get some sleep."

Magdalena barely remembered rising from the bench, realized she was making her way out only as she was buffeted by the press of bodies around her. Most spoke among themselves, theorizing or arguing. The rest, like Mags, seemed lost in thought.

She was, however, fairly certain that none of them were lost in the *same* thoughts she was. Thoughts that'd been swirling in her mind since the accident, that reverberated loudly enough she'd barely heard a word spoken at the assembly. Thoughts she constantly tried to dismiss as ludicrous paranoia, but which nonetheless kept returning.

Had Marty—like Daniel—talked to anyone about their experiences in the Scatters?

All the way back to her cot, and long into the night, it nagged at her. She lay awake, staring at the canvas ceiling, fretting at the notion of her second sleepless night. Yet her mind would not quiet down. Like a frantic squirrel or a damaged drone, it spiraled out of control, drifting sometimes one way and sometimes another, but always returning eventually to the center.

Until finally, Mags decided: Paranoia or no, reasonable or no, she had to find out. She had to be sure, one way or the other.

Her choice made, her plan for tomorrow laid out, Magdalena finally drifted into fitful slumber.

Of course, she wasn't going to have much luck finding out if nobody *else* knew, either!

Dressed in the standard camp "uniform" of undyed and haphazard clothes, Mags sat at the bench in the mess, poking with a wooden spoon at a thick gruel that seemed even more tasteless today than usual.

Which, she decided, *would make this anti-taste. I'm pretty sure it's sucking flavor from my next meal. Or maybe my last one. I'm going to wake up tomorrow having totally forgotten what flavor is.*

She stabbed viciously at the gruel. The gruel ignored her.

I should just eat the spoon.

Again she stabbed—and continued very deliberately *not* wondering if Danny or Marty had contributed anything to today's protein mash.

"Hey, Mags?"

Magdalena yanked herself from the whirling stream of thoughts and turned to the boy who'd just planted himself beside her. "Brandon? I thought you left ten minutes ago."

"I did. I just... I hear you been asking around, if anyone knows if Marty talked to anyone about, um, what happened."

"Yeah. I've been through more than half the group, and nobody can tell me a damn thing." She paused, tapping her utensil on the edge of the bowl. Brandon was one she *hadn't* gotten to yet. "That why you're here? Do *you* know?"

"Mags, it's not real hard to guess *why* you're wondering..."

"I don't know for certain anything's wrong. Brandon, *do you know* if he talked to—?"

"Uh, no." He looked down at the table, absently dragging his fingernails over the wood. "I, um, I have no idea if Marty talked to anyone or not."

"Then why—"

"Because..." He looked up at her, and Mags couldn't tell whether the misery or the fear she saw in his expression was more disturbing. "*I* have."

Oh, shit. "Brandon..."

"What do I do?" Whatever composure the kid had mustered started cracking like a pond in March. "Mags, what should I—?!"

"First, keep your voice down!" she hissed. Brandon recoiled but subsided, his gaze imploring.

"All this is just me being extra careful," she assured him, after a quick scan of the sparsely occupied tent confirmed that they hadn't drawn undue attention. She shifted on the bench, leaning in closer while hopefully not looking *too* secretive. "It may all be nothing. Hell, it's *probably* nothing!"

"Yeah. Yeah, probably."

Mags would have had to be transparent, if not completely absent, for him to doubt her any more thoroughly.

"Look, Brandon. I'll talk to the team. We'll all keep a close watch on you, okay? Never working alone. Never the dangerous assignments. Not until all of this is cleared up, just in case. You'll be fine."

"All right." His lips were pale as he stood, but his smile, though faint, was genuine. "Thanks, Mags."

"You'll be fine, Brandon," she said again to his back as he departed. And yet once more, softly, after he was gone. "You'll be fine."

She meant it. By the time she'd collapsed in her cot that night, having indeed ordered everyone to keep a protective eye on their youngest teammate, she'd even convinced herself to believe it.

And yet, when the crack of a gunshot yanked her brutally awake in the darkest hours of the morning, she found that she wasn't remotely surprised.

Chapter Nine

"That's crazy!" Again Mags knew she was ranting, but she couldn't find it in her to care. Several passersby stared at her. She stared right back until each and every one realized a pressing need to be elsewhere.

"It's what happened," Jonas told her, idly marking a torn bit of paper with a stick of charcoal. Just a standard equipment check and inventory that he'd taken on himself this week, since they were so shorthanded.

"It can't be!" Mags insisted, fidgeting along with each of his slow, methodical steps. "Brandon would never try to flee camp! Not ever!"

"Mags, the machines caught him beyond the perimeter, with a satchel full of food. I'm sorry it upsets you—it does me, too—but I think we have to accept—"

"That's how they *told* you they found him," she insisted. "Why they *told* you they shot him. Doesn't make it so!"

"Mags—"

"He talked about it, Jonas. About what happened in the Scatters. Just like Daniel, and maybe Marty! *That's* got to be why he's dead!"

"Mags, stop it!" Jonas's turn to interrupt, now, checklist and charcoal dangling, forgotten, from his fists. "You're imagining things. And you're going to get yourself in trouble. Maybe the whole team!"

"But—"

"This conspiracy theory of yours? You stop to think that maybe you scared Brandon? Maybe *you're* why he tried to run?"

She felt the breath catch in her chest, swore the canvas of the supply shelter had wrapped itself, strangle-tight, around her. "Jonas, you don't really think I... That it's my...?"

The old man sighed, reached out to pat her shoulder, stopped when he realized his hand was currently occupied by wadded paper. "Mags, I think you've suffered a *lot* lately. You're trying to protect yourself, and your people. That's commendable. But you're tilting at shadows and seeing threats that aren't there."

"Tilting?"

Jonas either ignored or failed to hear the question. "In any case, we'll have to discuss it more later. After the mission."

"What? Wait! Mission? What mission? I didn't hear anything!"

"Just heard about it a short while ago, myself. They haven't sounded assembly yet."

"That makes no sense! There's been no call for volunteers, and even if nobody stepped up, we're at less than half strength! It's not *efficient* to send us anywhere!"

"I know. I don't understand it, either."

"Jonas, the team's in no shape—"

"You want to tell them that? They didn't really seem to care when I did."

Mags blew out a heavy breath in a sound that might have been half a dozen different profanities or might have meant nothing at all. "Can..." She glanced around at the sporadic workers making their way through the steady drizzle beyond the shelter of the tent. "Can we go somewhere and talk more privately?"

"I'm not—"

<Recognizance and Disposal Detachment One-Three-Nine-Three-Six to assemble at staging area A. Message repeats. Recognizance and Disposal Detachment One-Three-Nine-Three-Six to assemble at staging area A. Message repeats. Recognizance...>

"No," Jonas said with a shrug. "No, we can't."

"I'll start rounding everyone up, then," she grumbled.

Jonas turned his attention back to his task. "Probably smart."

"Mags?"

She blinked without recognition at the heavy tubing in her hand, then up at Ian—who'd spoken—and Nestor. The big fellow's face seemed shrunken, though his girth was broad as ever.

How many times have I even seen him eat since we lost Danny?

"What are you doing?" Ian asked her

Incredulous, she squinted at him, then at the hose, then at the vehicle beside her. "Truck sex! Shit, Ian, what's it *look* like I'm doing?"

"Uh, actually it looks like you're standing there trying to fill up a gas tank with a pump you never switched on."

Magdalena looked reluctantly over her shoulder at the mechanism and flushed so furiously she actually *tasted* red on her tongue. "I was, um, just setting up. Hadn't gotten to that yet."

"Ah." Her lover gestured yet again to the truck and the tubing. "So this is a trial run?"

"You can just sit in the back if you're gonna keep this up."

"We always sit in the back."

"There, see! Now look what you've done!" Then, after a brief pause during which drizzle failed to wash the crimson from her face, "I'm a little distracted."

"I noticed. We *all* are." He ran a finger down her cheek, leaving a smear of rain. "We... This last week... We shouldn't..."

"Yeah." Magdalena leaned into his touch, then stepped back and shoved the hose into Ian's arms. "Handle this. I gotta take care of something."

She was gone, leaving a trail of faint splashes, before Ian or Nestor could ask a single question. She had to talk to Jonas again. Had to make him understand! They weren't safe, none of them! They weren't up to a mission yet; surely the machines could be made to see that! And if there was even a *chance* her suspicions were right, they had enough to worry about here in camp!

Mags reached the supply tent, coated to her ankles in mud and slightly bruised where she'd shouldered a couple of people from her path, only to find it empty. Or, rather, several people were present, gathering equipment for Detachment 13936's assignment, but the man she sought wasn't among them.

Crap. So maybe his quarters? That seems the most logical—

A deep grinding snagged her attention, shattered her train of thought. The beaded curtain that was rainwater sluicing off the canvas parted to reveal the thick-treaded, heavy-limbed older model bot that she'd run into before her last assignment. No reason to think it was here for her specifically, but she still had trouble thinking of its appearance as anything but a bad omen.

It also wouldn't be thrilled at the sight of her just standing around aimlessly.

She stalked purposefully toward the nearest crate—filled, in this case, with drill bits—and began sifting through them, sorting out those that fit the tools the 13936 normally employed.

The machine stood a moment, perhaps watching her and the others, and then rolled into the tent. Now ignoring the humans completely, it halted before another crate, far larger than the one Mags dug through. A brief whine of servos when those massive pincers lifted the container from the floor, and the thing departed as noisily as it had arrived.

Magdalena was on the move again a minute later, but this time she didn't simply dash her away across the camp. She couldn't afford to, not now that she'd been seen "working" in the stores. Letting the machines spot her anywhere other than between here and staging area A would be a poor choice. She could expect, at the very least, to be ordered straight back to staging and watched carefully until the team departed, her chance to converse with Jonas utterly lost.

But trying to sneak unseen across a camp swarming with workers and bots was an exercise not only in futility, but sheer idiocy.

Every nerve screamed, her body trying to flee in seven directions at once. She wondered how much of the dampness on her skin was the soaking rain, and how much fearful sweat.

Still she forced herself to hold to a brisk, purposeful walk. She fell in behind a group of workers from the 13944, then mingled with a line of people lugging rolled-up canvas to patch holes in one of the shelters. Never alone, never out in the open. Just another anonymous shape among many, too obscured and too unimportant for any passing machine to bother identifying.

She hoped.

On the one hand, it appeared to work. At no point did anyone or anything stop her, though a few of the workers from teams other than her own cast her suspicious glares. On the other, perhaps unsurprisingly, none of the small bands to which she'd attached herself were heading toward the overseers' quarters. For the last few dozen yards, she was on her own.

Well, the hell with it. If a machine stopped her, she'd tell it the truth—she was looking for her overseer. She could make up some issue or other, if it demanded to know why. Besides, the rain had gotten heavy enough at this point that even the bots probably wouldn't spot her from *too* far away.

At which point, the downpour subsided, almost maliciously, back into its earlier faint drizzle.

Of course. Because fuck everything.

A deep breath, a futile and halfhearted effort at wiping the worst of the water from her eyes, and Mags marched on up to Jonas's "door," a thick curtain of leather draped heavily over the entryway.

The voices caught her ear, kept her from knocking, just as her knuckles came close enough to kiss the wood of the doorframe.

She couldn't make out much, barely every fifth or sixth word. Only one of the speakers was human; the other spoke with the artificial, almost dead inflection of the machines. Okay, no surprise there. The overseers all had private speakers in their quarters, allowing them to converse with their masters at any time. And the machine, of course, sounded the same as the machines always did.

But there was something, something in Jonas's tone that raised her already wet and shivering hackles, poked at something instinctive and primal in the backmost regions of her mind. She couldn't remotely put her finger on what precisely she'd heard. She knew only that something was very wrong.

She wouldn't learn anything more standing out here,

though. The rain might have softened, but it remained loud enough to garble whatever sounds escaped through the leather. And even had the sky been clear, standing out in the open with her cheek pressed to the overseer's door just *might* have appeared suspicious.

Digging furrows in the mud, Mags edged around the dilapidated structure until she reached the curtain-door to the next quarters over from Jonas's. Another quick listen revealed nothing, but then, if someone were in there alone, there would be little to hear.

God, what the hell am I doing? If whichever overseer dwelled here *was* inside, no excuse would justify a worker just barging in. Even if the room was empty, Mags was shedding enough rainwater and mud to drown a coyote. No way could she hide the fact that *someone* had been here.

She should turn around, get back to work, forget all this nonsense. She almost *did*, physically vacillating, reaching for the tarp in one heartbeat, stepping away the next.

But, no. Not without learning what the hell was going on!

A deep breath—which also entailed swallowing a mouthful of rainwater—and Mags pushed in past the curtain.

She almost sobbed in relief to see the cot, the chair, the table, all unoccupied. Whoever's room this was—she guessed Tavio, the 13944's boss, based on the clothes scattered around—he wasn't here.

Anxious as she was, she took a moment to wander the room, shedding water like a duck and mud like... a muddy duck, she guessed. Maybe she couldn't hide that someone had been here, but she didn't have to make it easy for anyone to figure out what the intruder had been up to.

And then, finally, she crouched on her haunches beside the table and pressed her ear to the shared wall between this room and Jonas's. It wasn't much of a wall—the portions of the building's interior that hadn't survived the years had been only haphazardly replaced with loose brick or sheets of polymer— so it required only a moment to locate a spot thin enough for eavesdropping.

She almost wished she hadn't.

"…into the recent accidents," the overseer was saying. "We still haven't given them any sort of official explanation for the pumping station catastrophe, or the kid's attempted escape. They already know me, and the other overseers are the ones looking into all that. Should be more than enough of a reason I'm not accompanying them on this mission."

<Acceptable. You will offer this explanation to Detachment One-Three-Nine-Three-Six. So, too, will we explain your presence to the remaining overseers.>

Okay, so he's not coming along on this assignment?

Unusual, definitely, but the "explanation" made perfect sense. She trusted the old man, the whole team did. The story wouldn't have raised so much as a jot of doubt, in her or in anyone.

Her stomach dropped so far she swore she heard it gargling in her ankles; her heart climbed to her throat and perched. She was hollow inside, empty and echoing. And she didn't even know, yet, what was being kept from her.

Don't jump to conclusions, Mags. Figure this out. He could have good reasons for lying to us. Hell, he could be protecting *us from—*

"Is all this…" She could barely hear, now, so low had Jonas's timbre dropped. "Is all this really necessary?"

<You have made this query before, Lang, Jonas. The circumstances have not altered.>

"I know. I just… Couldn't we give them one more chance before—?"

<They have had three. You were told, the night of the anomalous event, what must happen. Further risk is unnecessary. Further delay is inefficient.>

"If we just ordered them to keep their mouths shut about—"

<Doing so would cause them to question the need for secrecy, to recognize the importance of, and perhaps the threat posed by, the anomaly. This cannot be permitted. Your queries are redundant, Lang, Jonas.>

A long, soft sigh. "I know."

<Detachment One-Three-Nine-Three-Six will be silenced.>

And again, "I know."

Mags couldn't see, for the tears welling in her eyes, stinging as the rainwater never could. She couldn't breathe for the bile in her throat. She couldn't think, for the sudden gaping wound torn through her mind, her heart, her soul.

They weren't coming back from this mission. Dead, the whole lot of them. If the machines wanted it, it'd happen. But for Jonas to go along with it, to have known for days and not even have tried to warn them to keep quiet...

Oh, God! With sudden clarity, Mags realized how the machines had known of Rio's injury. The churning in her gut grew agitated enough to power a small engine.

She rose, staggered from the wall, muscles shaking as though overworked, exhausted. She had to get out of here and—!

And do what? What *could* she do? There was no fighting the machines, no denying them. If every human learned a single lesson in the short, brutal spans allotted to them, it was this. If the machines wanted them all dead, they were all dead. All she had, now, were hours—maybe a day or two—of misery and terror.

Could she spare her friends that, at least? The rain would wash away any sign of crying. Could she keep herself silent, stoic? Pretend nothing was wrong until... until it no longer mattered? Could she do that, for them?

She had backed herself almost all the way to the doorway when the tarp pulled aside with a wet flap.

"Who the—! What the fuck are you doing—?"

It didn't matter, not really. So she'd been caught. Probably just meant she'd die here instead of out on assignment, once the machines realized they'd been overheard. She had no reason to resist, no reason to react at all.

But Magdalena *did* react. Years spent on edge, of watching for the hazards only Recognizance and Disposal dealt with, allowed nothing less. By the time her mind had decided to give up, her body had already chosen otherwise.

She snagged the startled overseer by his shirtfront, yanking him bodily into the room, letting the curtain fall shut behind him. A sharp twist sent the older man hurtling headfirst into the table. He rebounded from the wood with a hollow thump, his eyes wide and glazing, his breath rasping in his throat.

Mags pounced, driving the air from Tavio's body and his body to the floor. One hand snaked out, curling fingers through the overseer's short, dark hair. She yanked his head back and then slammed it forward.

The thump of skull on floor, accompanied by the crunch of cartilage in what had previously been a nose, was rather more solid than when it had careened off the wooden furniture.

The young woman's thoughts had finally caught up with her actions but were now too busy gibbering and tripping over one another in primal panic to take charge. Still driven by instinct, she shot to her feet and ran. She needed desperately to vanish into the weather-soaked camp before Tavio recovered, and before anyone—or anything—could react to the commotion they'd doubtlessly overheard. If they caught her here, she was sure to be severely punished for...

For what?!

Fury, hot as a fresh shell casing, seared her from the inside out, burning fear and despair to ash. For trying to survive? For learning that a man she'd followed since childhood had betrayed her and everyone she considered family?

Fuck. That. What are they gonna do, kill me twice?

No more of her people murdered in secret. No more cowering. No more victims.

If the machines wanted Detachment 13936 dead, yeah, they'd get their wish. But damned if Magdalena wasn't going to make them *work* for it!

Boots sounding like distant gunshots as they slapped across the viscous mud, Mags made for Staging Area A.

Her family needed her.

Chapter Ten

"You heard wrong!" shouted Kelly, the second youngest—no, Mags sadly corrected herself, the youngest, now—member of the 13936. While hers had been the one to carry through the drizzle and the clatter of work going on around them, it certainly was not the only voice raised in protest. The accumulated doubt was thicker than that morning's breakfast.

The fear behind it, supporting that doubt, goading it forward with whips and blades, was heavier and more solid still.

"They wouldn't just kill us! We're good workers! We're too—!"

"No way Jonas would betray us like that! He—!"

"Don't know what the fuck's wrong with you, Mags, but—!"

"*Shut it!*" She couldn't really blame them. She wouldn't have believed it either, if she hadn't heard it personally, and she'd given only a quick and dirty recounting. Of course they were reluctant to accept it.

"Jonas is a fucking scrip," she continued, her voice quieter but no softer. "And he's going to—"

"Mags, maybe you just misunderstood." Her shoulders sagged at hearing that. She'd assumed Ian, at least, wouldn't question. "The overseers *have* to work closely with the machines, much more than we do. That doesn't make him a scrip!"

"He *is* a scrip. They're going to kill us. Not a fucking one of us is coming home from this assignment. I'm assuming Tavio hasn't recovered yet, since if he had, they'd be on me already."

Aw, shit. She remembered, just in time for the chorus of shocked gasps, that she hadn't yet told them the part about her discovery and the subsequent violence.

"Mags, what did you do?!" Ian sounded almost panicked now.

And that was enough. Magdalena shoved through her people and leapt up into the back of the detachment's truck. A quick slip on the rain-slicked metal made the gesture rather less dramatic than it might have been, but she caught herself quickly enough.

"There's no *time!*" She crouched, leaning back over the edge so she all but hung over them. "You've trusted me for years. We've been through so much together. We've lost so much together. You're my family. Trust me now. Please."

It wasn't that they *couldn't* believe her; they *wouldn't*. Didn't want to admit to everything that believing her story would imply.

Then I've just got to show them I'm dead serious.

"I'm going. They may kill me, but I'm not gonna just fucking walk into it. If you want to stay here, trust to the bots' mercy, I can't stop you. Just get the hell out of the staging area so you're not in the way."

She didn't wait, didn't even look at them again. Instead, she hopped back over the edge to slip inside the cab of the truck. The seat was cracked beneath her, the curled edges of stiff upholstery pressing into her skin, the air so musty she could taste the mold on her tongue.

She'd never driven this thing, or any automobile, not once. But she'd watched Jonas, understood the basics. It'd be enough for an attempted getaway, however futile.

If she could get the damn thing to start!

No matter how she jabbed and twisted with the screwdriver she'd yanked from her tool pouch, she couldn't make the damn thing turn over. The humanoid machine had always done it with a single press of its finger, but apparently there was some sort of trick or safeguard to it.

She ducked down beneath the dashboard, but one look at the array of wires convinced her that she was far more likely to ruin the vehicle, or possibly electrocute herself, than make it run.

Come on, come, come on! Dammit!

Mags punched the steering column, boiling over with frustration. This was taking too long! Frankly, she was shocked the machines hadn't already—

Oh. Of course.

They were waiting. Watching to see if someone in the camp might say something, do something, to incriminate themselves in Tavio's assault.

Well, at least they're not just lining everyone up and shooting us until someone confesses.

If they wanted incriminating, Mags was all too happy to give it to them.

"All right, then." She bounced out of the cab, finally looking back at her assembled people, and she couldn't quite suppress a smile. She wouldn't take the time to do a headcount, not just now, but it looked like most of her team had stayed.

Her people might doubt her, sometimes, but they were with her.

Her people.

Please don't let me let them down.

"All right," she repeated. "That's not gonna work. So, let's talk plan B..."

In their many combined years in Recognizance and Disposal, Mags and the others had learned a lot about accelerants and explosives. More than enough to know that, even if the rain didn't extinguish it completely, a burning rag in the trunk's gas tank was no guarantee of detonation. If the tank could get enough oxygen to maintain a flame, it'd burn well enough, but nothing more.

The sealed gas cans and kerosene tanks placed in the bed of the truck, if brought to sufficient heat by such a fire, were a different story altogether.

If it worked. If the rest of the team managed to smuggle the canisters onto the truck under the guise of gearing up for their assignment. If the fire ignited swiftly enough, and the rain didn't cool the tanks too much. If her people could conceal themselves before anyone or anything figured out what was happening.

If, if, if.

And that was the *easy* part of this slapdash, desperation-fueled jumble of interconnected ideas they were laughably calling a "plan."

From within a storage tent on the camp's far side, Mags, Nestor, Cassie, and a few others watched and listened. Fists clenched, necks ached, teeth chewed on hair or fingernails, all generating enough nervous energy to power a flying drone for a day and a half. Around them, the world was wet and gray. The clouds, tired of holding themselves aloft, had alighted across the earth to rest, and the rain wasn't so much falling as filling the air, uncertain of which way to go. No chance they'd see the smoke of the smoldering fire. Odds were they wouldn't even see the blast, when (if) it finally went up.

They'd hear it, though. Wouldn't they?

"We must have missed it," Nestor growled.

"Patience," Mags ordered, far from the first time. "We'll hear it."

We will *hear it!*

We'd better *hear it.*

They heard it.

It wasn't a thundering boom, not like a true bomb. The sound, when it washed over them, was a flat *crack* and a dull *whump*, intertwined as one. It bounced across the camp, fading swiftly away as though it, too, attempted escape.

She tensed, adrenaline-flooded, her whole body trembling. "Okay, guys…"

And she froze.

She literally could not force her formerly eager muscles to move, her mouth to form further syllables. What she, *they*, were about to do was more than dangerous, more than risky, more than stupid. It went against every instinct she had, every fact that had been drummed into her head since she was old enough to understand the words. A lifetime of training, of conditioning, of *belief,* rebelled at what was to come.

Magdalena froze, but only for a moment. Her people needed her.

"Go!" she shouted, lunging into a sprint. The others—with greater or lesser ease, depending on what sort of tools they carried for this fool's endeavor—followed suit.

"Do you *know* how crazy this is?" Cassie panted as they ran, just loud enough to be heard through the rain and the splash of their own feet.

"Yeah. That's why it might work!"

"Do you know how crazy *that* is?!"

"Shut it and save your breath for running!" *Not that Cassie's wrong...*

"There!" It was Troy, another teammate, who'd cried out. "To the right!"

Mags saw it an instant later: one of the headless humanoid bots, rainwater streaming off its carapace in strangely elegant rivulets. Had chance *truly* been on their side, it would have been one of the slower treaded models, but as it was, they were lucky to find a lone machine so quickly.

If you can call this lucky...

She swallowed, trying to dislodge the small tire that seemed to have lodged in her throat. Then, once more, "Go."

Three of her people changed direction, dashing past the machine, yards away but clearly in sight, making an obvious beeline for the camp's perimeter. That was their job, their *only* job, and the entire plan hinged on it.

The bot turned to follow, its speaker bellowing. <HALT FOR IMMEDIATE IDENTIF—>

Cassie was first. With a prolonged shout, she raised the sprayer in both hands, squeezing the trigger so violently the wand creaked under the pressure. From the tank on the redhead's back, a thick stream of motor oil splattered the bot, thickly coating the nearest side in a spreading layer that the drizzle could only slowly rinse away.

"Troy, now!" Magdalena shouted.

Even as the machine spun toward Cassie, Troy charged from the opposite direction, something that only vaguely resembled Cassie's sprayer clutched in a white-knuckled grip. The thick and viscous oil might cling better than gasoline, but it took a *lot* more heat to ignite.

So, when scavenging their "weapons" from the vehicle pool, they'd *brought* more heat.

Troy's acetylene torch ignited with a *fwump*, followed by

a harsh hiss as it sizzled in the rain. A dull orange tide raced over oil-soaked steel, spitting little breaths of steam as flame met water. It wouldn't burn hot enough to damage the metal shell, not in the mere moments it would take to wash away, but just maybe the heat would damage something internally, or at least some of the bot's sensors. Troy backed away, waiting for an opportunity to apply the torch more directly, perhaps slice cleanly into the machine.

So fast; the damn thing was *so* hellishly fast! One arm whipped around, joints and servos keening almost too high to hear. Those disturbingly long fingers lengthened farther still, becoming lashes of steel cable.

Never in her life had Magdalena seen one of the humanoid machines do that. But then, she'd never seen one in combat, had she?

The expression of surprise on Troy's face was almost comical for the split second before ripping flesh and snapping bone rendered it unrecognizable. The body fell in a splatter of water, mud, and blood. The torch sputtered once, twice, and went out.

For now, neither circumstances nor her own adrenaline permitted Magdalena to grieve.

Cassie pumped the last of her reservoir into the open flame, so that a burning tongue reached back as though licking at her hands, failing to reach her by a mere arm's length. Even with the extra oil, the fire already guttered, but it looked to finally have some effect on the bot. With its currently elongated hand, it reached across its body, scouring and brushing the burning gunk from its carapace much as Mags might have rid herself of excess mud.

Nestor loomed from the ambient gray to slam into the thing's non-burning side.

The cacophony was brutal, far too loud for flesh and bone on steel. The machine staggered, half toppling to one knee, its torso badly dented and crumpled. Nestor stepped away, his broad shoulders unbowed by the air tank strapped to his back, raising the pneumatic hammer toward the sky as though it were an actual pistol. The bit at the business end was bent, mangled beyond all use, but it no longer mattered.

Scattered throughout the new cracks and crevices in the machine's hide, several holes gaped open. They were few, they were tiny. But they were enough.

Magdalena finally raised her own "weapon," a sprayer much like Cassie's. This one, however, would never see use again. Even if the tank wasn't damaged beyond repair, the pump soon would be.

She took one step nearer, aimed, and spattered the damaged steel with battery acid—and not *just* steel but, of far greater import, the innards now exposed behind it.

No dramatic bursts of smoke, though something on the air began to burn Mags's eyes and nose. No thrashing, twitching, or death throes. The machine rose, took two steps toward her, and toppled.

We actually did it.

The flames sputtered out, leaving discolored steel to cool in the muck.

We killed a machine.

The world should have changed in that moment. *She* should have changed. They'd done the unthinkable. That should count for something, for more than just one step in the plan.

But all she could do was stare at Troy's corpse, turning the puddles a thin, watery pink, and wonder if any of her people could expect any better.

"Get the torch," she ordered coldly. Nobody questioned her. Nestor yanked the tank free and slung it under one arm.

"Now..." Already she could hear the whir of propellers slowly chopping their way free of the wind. The weather would serve as a cloak against the drones, their flight made unstable and their cameras obscured by the gusts and precipitation, but not for long. "Run."

Flat on their bellies, half-buried in the muck and struggling to breathe, Mags and the others watched from beneath a mangled old truck. Not quite damaged enough to be dismantled for scrap, it sat on the edge of the vehicle pool, well out of the way,

waiting until the parts necessary for its repair might become
available. Today, it also provided cover as the renegades
watched the crackling fires and the desperate efforts of their
campmates to extinguish those flames.

Mags spat out another mouthful of goop and fretted, her
fingers digging tiny moats as her fists clenched, spread, closed
again. Was the plan devious enough? *Too* devious? Had she
outsmarted the machines, or herself?

Workers of the 13944, the 13927, and others dashed across
the vehicle pool. Some wielded hoses and extinguishers
connected to distant pumps, others pushed vehicles or hauled
barrels of chemicals and fuels away from the open flame.
But apart from a single humanoid bot and the heavy-treaded
machine with the ungainly pincers, the people worked alone.

None of the other machines aided them in battling the fire.
None were present in the vehicle pool at all.

The initial detonation would have drawn their attention,
certainly, but the moment they determined it had been no
accident, the machines must have been wary of trickery. So
that's what the 13936 had given them: a quick view of people
escaping the camp on the opposite side, followed by an attack
on a lone bot. Surely only the sheerest desperation would
entice the humans into something suicidal as assaulting a
machine. Surely they must have been struggling to preserve
their *true* escape route!

Or so Mags hoped the machines would think. And thus
far, the dearth of bots anywhere near the dwindling, sizzling
blaze would seem to bear that out.

So as long as they don't realize our plan is God damn insane...

"Mags? It's been over five minutes."

She nodded absently, though she doubted Ian could see it.
"All right. Either it worked, and they're all busy hunting us
over there, or they're about to pop up out of nowhere and kill
the hell out of us. Either way, let's move."

One by one, Mags and her companions sidled backward
from beneath the truck and raced to join the rest of the team.

Out there. Into the wilds, beyond the camp, where few of
them knew the terrain, where their double diversion would

have bought them only minutes at best.

The fact that the machines might have to work a bit harder to murder them suddenly seemed woefully poor consolation.

Chapter Eleven

Underbrush, still desiccated from long dry months despite the past days of rain, crunched like dead beetles beneath her as she toppled. Jagged twigs and rough gravel grated at her skin. She clamped her lips together, so what might have been a startled cry escaped only as a hoarse grunt.

Not that it mattered, really. The sound of her stumble was more than enough to alert anyone or anything nearby.

Nestor and Kelly, both covered in the lacerations of their own missteps, halted to help her up. She shook her head, waving them on, but gladly accepted the outstretched hands when they refused to heed.

"Gonna have a few words... with you two about... obeying orders when... we get out of here..." she panted. Their responding grins were wan and did absolutely nothing to conceal what they might as well have spoken aloud.

As if any of us are getting out of here.

Clothes, torn and ratty, rags as much as garments, lay plastered flat against skin shivering in the evening drizzle. A myriad of tiny wounds, clean of blood only by virtue of the rain, stung like the aftermath of a dozen hornets. They ran, now, for its own sake—putting off the inevitable just that tiny bit longer—rather than out of any lingering hope. They *had* no hope, carried pain and misery and exhaustion in its place.

And Mags had none of her own to offer them. She'd lost the last of hers in the first attack.

They'd spun out of the clouds, whipped and tossed by the wind, falling as much as flying—but their props held them aloft, and their weapons were guided by more than human awareness. The drones opened fire, and while a great many of their shots missed, buffeted about as they were, far too many did not.

The guns had seemed somehow louder to Magdalena, as though amplified by the weather. She'd heard Cassie's voice among those who'd cried out but couldn't see the redhead or what might have befallen her. Bodies fell, dead or good as dead. The rest had scattered in every direction, seeking what cover or safety they might find in the rocky, hill-pocked, lightly wooded terrain.

Mags didn't know how many were left. Didn't know, other than Nestor and Kelly, who might or might not still live. Didn't know if Ian…

She'd just run. Like all the others, she'd panicked, fled. That she couldn't think of anything more she might have done did nothing to alleviate the burning, guilty sense that she *should* have.

And all around them, the pervasive gloom grew darker. At a furtive, guilty creep that went all but unobserved behind concealing layers of cloud, the sun was setting.

"Flashlights," she ordered roughly, digging at her belt for her own.

"Are you sure?" Kelly sounded as though she were anything but. "We'll be a *lot* easier to see."

"And a lot less likely to break an ankle or run into something or lose each other. You want to make your way in the dark, I can't stop you, but do it over there. Maybe the noise'll draw the machines away from me and Nestor."

The girl scowled but switched on her light.

"Keep 'em pointed down, if you can," Mags added. *Might help a* little.

Nestor held his wrists together, flashlight in one hand, a heavy pneumatic rivet gun in the other. It wasn't remotely as powerful as the hammer he'd wielded earlier. The tiny tank held enough compressed air for only a few uses, and the bolts might not even penetrate deep enough to do a machine any real damage. It was, however, the only option he'd had. Not even he could carry the compressed air tanks of the more potent tools for long, not at a run across uneven ground.

They persevered, the three of them, moving just to move, no destination in mind. First at a jog, then a walk, then little more than a shuffle with the occasional crawl, they advanced along shallow hillsides and sporadic copses. Mud sucked at their feet, rocks tried almost maliciously to turn ankles. The rain stopped, finally, though so much moisture remained in the air that it made no difference. The trio found themselves surrounded by an almost unnatural silence, broken only by their own footsteps and lingering drops that fell from leaves.

And then, faint but unmistakable, the hum of whirling rotors.

Mags dropped to a crouch, trying to look in all directions at once, the other two joining her a heartbeat later. "Which way?" Nestor asked in a whisper.

"I can't tell!" she hissed back. "I think maybe over there?"

"I thought it sounded more like *that* way," Kelly argued, pointing.

They gazed helplessly at each other.

"Look," the big man finally said, "you both agree it wasn't coming from *there*, right?" He jabbed a thumb over his shoulder.

"Yeah," Mags offered, only a bit uncertain. Kelly nodded.

"Then maybe we should—"

"Yeah." Magdalena rose. "We should." Again at a rapid shuffle, they stumbled, as best they could tell, away from the oncoming drones.

They found themselves moving alongside a swift trickle of a stream, one that doubtless existed only thanks to the heavy rains. It wound through and around the cracked ground, across broken asphalt that had once been a highway, until it became a tiny waterfall down an embankment of stair-stepped rock.

The tinkling of the miniature cascade was almost hypnotic, a soothingly natural song in all the chaos and fear. Mags hadn't intended to stop and rest here; she simply found herself slumped, sitting on a patch of earth slightly more rock than mud. The others joined her before she could change her mind.

"Just for a minute," she warned them. Then, "Or two."

"I vote three," Nestor added.

Far off in the night, its echo making a mockery of distance or direction, something howled.

"Wolves? Coyotes?" Kelly breathed.

Mags frowned. "In this weather? What's to hunt?"

"Besides us? Should we, I don't know, find shelter or something?"

"You mean like all that shelter we've ignored while running from the machines?" Nestor asked archly.

"There's no need to be a—"

"Guys, enough!" Mags snapped. "For now, we stay. Catch our breath. Figure… *something* out."

They'd only just begun to relax when Kelly's head snapped up again. "Someone's coming!"

Mags, forcing her aching body upright, heard it now, too. It didn't *sound* like a machine, didn't seem heavy or methodical enough. The steps were halting, uneven. Nestor raised his weapon.

"Mags?"

"*Suni!*" She couldn't help it, sweeping up the smaller woman in a smothering embrace before the others had even moved. Eventually she stepped back, only for Nestor to zip in and take her place. "I'm *so* glad you're here," Mags continued.

"Mrmfrffle…" Suni agreed from the giant embrace.

"Oh, sorry." Nestor retreated with a sheepish grin.

"Are you okay?" Mags asked.

"Are you stupid?" Suni seemed to be trying to smile and scowl at once.

"Okay, fair. But, I mean, you're not hurt?"

"Not too bad, no."

"Did pretty well, then," Nestor commended her, "for being on your own since we scattered."

Suni turned her gaze to her boots. "I didn't start out that way."

"Ian?" Mags knew she shouldn't ask, shouldn't put any of the team above any other, but she couldn't hold the question back.

"Don't know. He wasn't with me. I thought I saw him, Cassie, and a few of the others heading westish after the attack."

"Who else was with you? And what happened to—?"

A sharp *crack*. A warm spray across Magdalena's neck and shoulder. And then Kelly lay sprawled in the runoff beside her, a gaping hollow in the side of her skull. They hadn't heard the rotors this time. Maybe it was the rushing water, or the conversation, or some other damn acoustical thing. Not that it mattered.

A single drone hovered overhead, bobbing side to side, barely visible even in the beams of their flashlights. Mags glared at it, shoulders straight, but she knew it was the last defiance she could offer.

I'm sorry, guys. I really tried.

The sound that followed was *not* the popping of gunfire, though, but an ear-piercing screech. No, a chorus of screeches, each a separate, hellish voice, each a distinct needle, fiercely jabbing. Mags clapped her hands to her ears, cried out as she fell to her knees, but she forced her eyelids to remain open. She had to see!

A veil of bats blotted the drone, the entire sky, from sight, as though God had wiped a smear of dark ink across her vision. They spun, swirled, banked, spiraled, until they didn't just fill the night, they *were* the night.

And just as swiftly, they were gone, scattered to the darkness, their cries the fading remnants of a dream.

Of the drone, there was no sign at all.

Heart pounding nearly enough to rattle her teeth, Mags rested a hand on Kelly's shoulder—briefly, far too briefly, but it was all she had. Only then did Mags rise, joining companions who had gone as pallid as the body at her feet. She must, she knew, look much the same.

"We're done resting here. Time to move."

Oddly enough, nobody argued.

"How can you tell?" Magdalena asked, staring down at the mass of rent metal and torn wires that had, not long ago, been one of the spidery bots. It lay at the base of a rocky knoll, looking so very much like a squashed insect that she kept expecting a leg to twitch.

"Well, I mean, I can't be *sure* it's the same one," Suni admitted. "But we're not *too* far from where my group was attacked, and..."

"And?" Mags prompted.

"And I hope there aren't two different machines in the area with blood-smeared legs," she concluded bitterly.

Nestor pointedly cleared his throat, and then began digging through the wreckage, looking for anything worth salvaging. "Not that I *want* them to come after us with combat models," he said, pausing for a low grunt as he shoved a chunk of carapace aside, "but at least then there might be some recoverable weaponry."

"Which we'd already be too dead to use!" Suni snapped.

They probably did dispatch combat bots. They just haven't gotten here yet, since they're coming from the city, not the camp. Mags didn't think the others would find the thought all that reassuring, though, so she kept it to herself.

"Anything?" she asked instead.

"Lots of mechanics I have no idea how to use," Nestor told her, "and lots of metal that would be great if we had the time and the tools to build something. Otherwise, not really."

Suni wandered down the slope and over to Nestor's side, nudging the scrap with her toe. "Are we going to talk about what might have taken this thing apart in the first place?"

"No," Mags said firmly. "We're not."

"I'd wondered how I made it," Suni muttered, seemingly to the metal itself. "If I'd just gotten lucky at the others' expense, if it happened to go after somebody else instead of me when we all ran. But something... something saved me, didn't it? Like it saved us from the drone."

Mags was still struggling to respond to that, and wondering what they might have been saved *for*, when multiple glints of illumination speared the gloom from around the shallow rise.

Again, the options for cover were poor at best. Suni and Nestor crouched in the wreck of the bot, the former disappearing almost entirely, the latter protruding awkwardly, obviously, rather like a thick mushroom from a stump. For her own part, Mags could do little more than drop to her stomach and hope the swell of the terrain would conceal her.

Only when it no longer mattered, when she heard the hushed whispers and twig-snapping, pebble-shifting steps, did she realize that the uneven bobbing of the light suggested a non-robotic source. Her heart swelled in her chest at the sight of roughly a half-dozen of her people rounding the knoll, and it all but burst when she recognized them.

"Ian!"

However tactically unsound (or rather mind-bogglingly foolish) it might have been, the next moments were filled with a succession of tearful embraces, with scant attention paid to the fugitives' surroundings. Mags and Ian were the first to come together, with a painful-sounding smack, but everyone had to have his or her turn, it seemed, greeting everyone else.

"You all right?" Mags, once she'd finally peeled herself from Ian, turned her attention to her redheaded friend. "Before we got split, I thought..."

Cassie stepped back before Mags could hug her, and her "reassuring smile" came out as more of a pained grimace. "Arm's not good for much right now." She indicated what was only now, close up, revealed to be a blood-caked sleeve. "Guess I'm lucky. Without the weather, pretty sure it would've hit something a little more vital. Or, you know, at least my head."

Mags, at a loss as to how to respond, sighed aloud in relief when Suni took the necessity out of her hands. "How'd you guys find us?" the smaller woman asked.

Mags found herself frowning. Running into Suni, she could accept as random fortune, but to then meet up with Ian, Cassie, and the others right after? When the whole detachment had so thoroughly scattered? That was stretching the odds.

The awkward, furtive looks that passed like static sparks between the newcomers at that question spoke volumes on their own.

"Ian?" Mags pressed.

"Just, um, lucky, I guess."

"Want to repeat that for me? I couldn't quite hear you over the squirming."

"Uh..."

"For fuck's sake!" This from Gary, a dark-complexioned, wild-haired fellow who'd arrived as part of Ian's group. His tunic was matted to his side with the tacky gore of what must have been a nasty gash, but it didn't seem to be slowing him. "Just tell her about the damn thing!"

Ian actually scuffed a foot in the gravelly mud. "We didn't want to worry you any more than you already were—" he began.

"Or make you think certain people are crazy." Cassie scowled, her glare encompassing Ian, Gary, and a couple of the others. "Like *some* of us already do."

A quick sigh, an equally irritated glare in return, and Ian continued. "It was... There was this wolf, or coyote, or something."

"Or shadows some of you *imagined* were something," Cassie muttered.

"Wolf or coyote," the young man insisted. "Weirdest damn thing. No barking or growling or whatever, just kept showing up, watching us. We'd change direction, move away from it, it'd vanish again for a while, and then..."

"Swear the thing was herding us," Gary said. "Like cattle or some shit."

"Silently," Cassie mocked. "And alone. The way wolves and coyotes and dogs usually hunt, except for *all the time* when they don't!"

"I *know* it's weird!" Ian snapped at her. "The whole *point* is that it's weird!"

"Or that it didn't actually—!"

"We heard something howl earlier," Mags interjected. "Wolf or coyote or whatever."

"See?" Ian crowed.

"Weren't you just saying that your 'phantom wolf' was silent?" Cassie replied.

"So if it makes noise once, it has to do it all the time, or else it doesn't exist?" They were so fully in each other's faces now, each was effectively inhaling the other's words. "That's the dumbest—"

"So because there's a real coyote out there somewhere, that proves your imaginary friend is real? Wolves don't behave like that!"

"Both of you, shut it!" Magdalena stalked forward until they had to lean back to avoid her. "Are you *trying* to get us killed?! If the machines hear your stupid bickering, they'll—"

From the other side of the rise, a piercing whistle split the night. A long note, a quick fall, and even quicker rise. Very clearly a signal. Very clearly human.

Very, *very* loud.

"Who was *that*?"

"Doesn't matter." Mags was moving even as she cut Suni's puzzlement short. "No way the machines didn't hear *that*! Move! Stay together, but *go*!"

Rival urges dueled the length and breadth of her head as she watched the others break into an exhausted, staggering dash. She *should* go with them, should be long gone before the bots arrived, let whoever was stupid enough to whistle aloud suffer the consequences.

"Fuck!" Mags couldn't tell if she was cursing the unknown idiot, the situation, or herself as she broke into a run around the base of the knoll. Just a quick peek, and she'd catch up with the others. She couldn't just leave someone behind, no matter how moronic their—

Feet skidding in the drying mud, she slid around the shallow slope, and saw no one at all. Neither the tiny spill of moonlight through the clouds nor the beam of her own light revealed any sign of whomever they'd heard.

"Where... How... Who...?"

No time to search, though, no time even to wonder. Cursing with every exhalation, Magdalena jogged back the way she'd come. Catch up with the others now, escape the machines. She'd worry about the vanishing idiot later.

A minute or so of running, any number of near stumbles and ankle-twists on the precarious terrain, and again Mags skidded to an abrupt halt.

Unless, of course, we don't get to "later."

Her team hadn't run far. In fact, they'd all frozen. Ahead, the shadows had disgorged a trio of armed drones, their barrels already trained on the fugitives. From beyond, still unseen, came the staccato click of spidery metal legs.

She felt a warm hand take her own, wondered idly when Ian had worked his way back from the head of the team. "We made a good run, Mags," he said, voice as rough as the ground they stood on. "You should be proud."

The young woman squeezed his fingers, squared her shoulders, and waited for the mechanical thunder to begin.

Something howled.

On it went, and on, a fearsome, phantasmal keening, long past the capacity of mortal lungs. It seeped through Magdalena's now-shivering flesh and standing hair, echoing in the oldest, basest reaches of her mind. Everything inside shrieked, and what it screamed was "*Run.*"

And she would have. Machines and even her own people forgotten, she would have fled. They all would have, every pale and shaking one of them. But even as the unholy cry goaded them to panic, it held them still. Nerves burned and crackled, but flesh froze.

It loped from the gloom, the size of a pony, a mass of muscle and fur so black it looked an appendage of the darkness. Paws larger than human hands slapped the soaked earth with hollow thumps and sharp spatters. Glistening fangs in a distended snout and eyes, blazing crimson, revealed themselves to the sickly light. Spinning in place beneath whirling rotors, the drones opened fire on the approaching beast, yet not a single round struck home.

Their inaccuracy was due not to the weather, nor even solely to the creature's speed, impressive though it was. The machines, firing in broad arcs, seemed uncertain where to aim. Mud splattered, and bullets ricocheted, all in vain.

The hideous howl finally ceased as the unnatural wolf leapt.

Up, and up, propelled by legs impossibly large and impossibly strong, and even as it finally could rise no more—it did.

It became nigh invisible, a dark shape against a dark sky, but Mags could have sworn the wolf *unfolded*.

Curves warped; lines broke; darkness spread, as though the creature stretched across the world. Except it wasn't stretching, it was *dissolving*. Discorporating.

Into bats. A swirling swarm, dozens upon dozens of shrieking, flapping bats.

Two of the drones vanished into the winding spiral of wings as though submerged in blackest oil. A few shots rang out, but when bits of mangled metal fell to earth, not a single bat fell with them.

The last of the drones swayed in the sky, firing blindly into the swarm, no more effective than its counterparts. The bats spun and twisted, spiraling ever more tightly, until they had massed above the flying machine.

And there, again, the swarm shifted into something else.

He struck the earth before the surviving remnants of the 13936, long dark coat and long dark hair hovering briefly in an ebon aura before settling down around him. He landed in a crouch, one fist pressed against the ground—and beneath that fist, crushed and mangled, still sparking and sputtering, was the final drone.

"These are strange enemies I have found for myself." He rose smoothly, even majestically, brushing dirt and metal fragments from his knuckles. His words were clear, despite the accent that Magdalena couldn't begin to place. This time, in the light of multiple flashlights, she could tell that his coat was a rich burgundy, his hair as black—

As black as the wolf's pelt had been. She didn't *think* his eyes were the same gleaming crimson, but she couldn't be sure. She couldn't make herself meet them, directed her gaze anywhere else, over his shoulder, at his feet.

At his feet and at the ground beneath and behind him, limned faintly in the glow of the flashlights even where his body blocked the way.

The stranger cast no shadow in the beams.

"But then," he continued, "these are strange days. Good evening. I am..." He cocked his head, twisting, more like an animal with a scent than a man. "Ah. A moment, please."

He pivoted, coat flaring, hands raised, as the multi-legged machine galloped from the darkness.

It appeared to be aiming itself *past* him, lunging for the nearest of Magdalena's people. It never reached its target. The impossible figure collided, snarling, with the suddenly flailing bot.

Fists closed on legs of steel and lifted, straining, tilting the machine over and to one side. Its own arms lashed out, wild, erratic. Several blows caught the stranger, whipping his head aside and crashing across his chest. Fabric tore, *flesh* tore—it must have!—but so far as Magdalena could make out in the gloom, no blood flowed. Other than knocking him slightly off balance, none of the blows slowed him.

Until, just as the machine seemed ready to topple, it reached low and lashed out again, knocking the stranger's legs out from beneath him.

With inhuman speed, it lurched forward as they both fell, so that the entire weight of the steel chassis came down on its opponent, crushing him into the muck beneath its bulk.

The world went silent. Mags held her breath, and heard—or rather, didn't hear—everyone else doing the same.

Is that a wisp of smoke wafting from beneath the turret?

It must have been damaged internally in the struggle; no other reason for it to be smoking. They might still be able to get away from...

Unless it wasn't smoke at all.

Mist?

Metal bent, buckled, tore. The machine seemed to inflate before it burst, ripped apart by something within, something impossibly powerful.

The stranger stood amidst the wreckage, examining the remnants of the machine, not even breathing hard. After a moment, he poked idly at the rents in his coat, the patches of clinging mud. Then, with a shrug, he approached the team once more.

"Apologies for the interruption. I am Lacusta. Constantin Lacusta. And I have been looking for people such as yourselves for some time, now. The lovely Miss Suarez has told me *so* much about you all."

The weight of the combined stares—disbelief, fury, betrayal—crashed down on Magdalena more heavily than the bot could have. "I don't..." She quailed, wanted to either lash out or run. "No! I don't know what he's talking—"

"You mustn't blame her."

Mags had only taken her eyes off Lacusta for a second, but his voice now rolled from the rear of the group. "You'll find there are many things about me to which you will all have to adapt."

A hand whipped out in an impossible blur, and one poor soul on Magdalena's team began to scream.

Chapter Twelve

"Are you out of your mind?! You can't seriously be considering this!" Mags tried to keep her voice to a harsh growl, rather than the shriek she barely held back. The image and the sound—*God, the sound!*—of Gary's last breaths replayed over and over in her mind. "We gotta get the hell *away* from him! From *it!*"

Ian and Nestor both cast glances over their shoulders, as though they could see beyond the small copse of ragged, dying trees to the rest of the group, and the horrific stranger who'd joined them. Cassie merely crossed her arms, her level gaze never leaving Magdalena.

"He's got a point, Mags," her boyfriend said softly. "Alone against the machines, we're dead. If there's even a chance he can show us how to fight back ag—"

"Fight *back*? God, when did this even...? There's no 'fighting back!' I don't care what he says, what he *is*, he's one man! Or one, I dunno, *creature*! And he's full of shit. We need to find somewhere to hide, somewhere safe!"

"Just because you've turned coward," Cassie sneered, "doesn't mean the rest of us have."

Any more tension and Mags would have snapped like an old string. She reached out, breaking a brittle branch free of the nearest tree—mostly so she wouldn't break something substantially more animate. The words she tried to speak were in such a rush to escape that they jammed against one another in her throat.

"Cassie," Nestor said, "Mags led us out here. She found out

our leader was a damn scrip planning to have us killed, and instead of giving up, she helped us escape. Even faced down a bot while most of the team ran. You have no right—"

"I know." With visible effort, the redhead forced herself to relax. "I shouldn't have said that. I'm sorry."

Mags grunted something. It was all she trusted herself to say.

"But think about it!" Cassie continued. "You saw what kind of power he has! We could get back at the machines for what they've done to us! What they did to Rio."

"'Get back at them'?" Mags demanded. "How, exactly? It's not like they're going to feel any grief for any bots we destroy, or any fear for their own 'lives!' And I don't give a damn *what* powers Lacusta or Latusca or whatever has, he's not gonna change the whole world with them!"

"Okay, let's calm down," Ian said, palms out. "Look, even if he can just protect us for a while—"

"*Protect?!* Did you not *see* what he just did to Gary?" She swore the scent of the blood still clung to her nostrils.

Now it was Cassie's turn to nervously pluck a few loose twigs. "Mags, you saw that wound. He wasn't going to make it."

"You don't *know* that!"

"Yeah, I do. And so do you. The machines would've—"

"Like they did Rio?"

"Don't you fucking dare!"

"I thought you wanted your new friend to *destroy* the machines because of shit like that!"

Ian was all but hopping foot to foot. "If that's really how he has to survive, maybe—"

"Maybe what? We should hitch up with the guy who feeds on us? What if nobody's oh-so conveniently mortally injured? You saw what he did to us in the Scatters!"

"He thought we were his enemies, then."

"And that makes him *eating us* so much better? I don't think so! We're leaving! End of discussion!"

"You," Cassie said darkly, "don't get to decide when it's end of discussion anymore."

It took a few tries before Mags could remember how to work her mouth. "What?"

Even Ian looked as though he'd been slapped. "Cassie, what are you—?"

"You see Jonas around here? The machines? The ones who put you in charge aren't in charge anymore, Mags."

"And who is?" Mags spat bitterly. "You?"

"At least the team knows they can *trust* me!"

Mags staggered, despite herself. "You can't... You think..." She forced her breathing to slow. "God dammit, I don't know what he was talking about! I didn't tell him *anything* about you all!"

"You can't be sure of that," Nestor interjected softly.

Then, when all three other faces had swiveled his way, "Mags, you don't *remember* what happened when you met Lacusta the first time. You've said so yourself."

"No, but you *know* me! I *wouldn't*!"

"You wouldn't just forget the whole thing, either," the big man gently told her. "'Normal' doesn't apply here."

Long silence, as brittle as the slender branches.

"Wait," Mags insisted as Nestor drew breath to say something. "Just... wait a minute."

She forced herself to breathe, slow, steady, examining the darkness around them. Her team, what was *left* of her team, was falling apart. They needed strong guidance, now more than ever, and that wasn't going to happen if they didn't trust her.

Or if she tried to force the issue.

"I'm scared," she admitted. "I'm scared, I'm upset, and I damn well don't want to lose anyone else. I don't have the faith in Lacusta's powers that you do. I don't think we can trust him.

"But," she continued before the objections could start up again, "maybe he *can* protect us from the machines, at least for a while. If he doesn't eat us first. I sure as hell don't have any better idea of where to go. So, yeah, okay. We'll follow him, for now. Together. And if he gives any sign of being too dangerous, we'll leave together."

Ian and Nestor grinned—nervously, yes, but relieved that the immediate conflict had been averted. Cassie just grunted, willing to go along but clearly unsatisfied.

Lost in her desperate hope that she wasn't making a hideous

mistake, Mags didn't even remember the walk back to meet the others.

They waited at the base of the knoll, milling aimlessly. Lacusta himself stood a bit higher up the slope, gazing out at nothing at all.

"We've decided—" Mags began.

"To accompany me. Yes, I know." Lacusta smiled down at her.

"How...? You could *hear* us from all that way?"

"My blessings are many." Was it Magdalena's imagination, or did his smile flatten just a bit? In the gloom, she couldn't be sure. "You might wish to keep that clearly in mind."

"And what about your diet?" The darkness actually helped, a little. It was easier to be brave when she couldn't clearly see his eyes. "Is that something we need to keep in mind, too?"

"If I'm not mistaken, Miss Suarez, your own fallen companions occasionally supplemented your own provisions. My needs are hardly that foreign."

She wouldn't let herself shudder. "We ate what the machines mixed into the gruel. We didn't have a choice!"

"Nor do I. But fear not. It can be a bit inconvenient, but I needn't necessarily kill in order to feed. You are not leading your people to certain death. We can live alongside one another with minimal hardship."

Somehow, Mags didn't feel inclined to reply to that. "Gary?" she asked instead.

"Buried him," Suni said. "While you were all talking."

"It's pretty shallow," added Zach, one of the other survivors of the 13936. "But, with the time we had..."

"I'm sure it's fine," Mags told him. "Thank you. All of you. So, where are we going?"

"West." Lacusta raised his arms and simply fell apart, dissolving into a swarm of bats who circled up and away into the skies. His last words lingered behind, an echo without a source. "For now, due west."

"Maybe some kind of experiment?" Ian suggested, carefully picking his way over a tangle of old tree roots barely visible in the feeble light. "Special breeding or, I don't know, radiation or something?"

Mags studied her compass and grunted something noncommittal.

"Sure, Ian," Suni muttered from behind. "Because after generations of just working us to death, the machines want nothing more than to make us stronger."

"Maybe it was an accident! Maybe they were trying to do something else, and this was a side effect!"

"Oh, right. 'Caution: Overuse of this procedure may result in the subject *turning into a fuckload of God damn bats!*' How would that work, exactly?"

"Do I look like a scientist to you, Suni?" Ian snapped.

"You certainly don't *sound* like one," Nestor interjected with a shallow smirk.

"I don't hear you coming up with any better ideas!"

The big guy just shrugged.

Suni began to reply. "I think—"

"Hsst!" Mags halted and raised a closed fist. "You hear that?"

From some distance ahead came sporadic gunfire, followed by the shriek of tearing metal.

"Think Lacusta won?" Nestor whispered.

"I'll tell you after we don't get shot," Magdalena said sharply, resuming her trek. She didn't even bother suggesting that they change course, avoid the location of the struggle in case their "benefactor" *hadn't* come out on top. She knew what the others would say.

She felt her neck and her cheeks warm, her stomach clench. At least Cassie'd stuck to the rear of the detachment, for now. It meant, if she *did* lose her temper, Mags would probably just yell, rather than attempt to strangle someone.

She really was trying to give Cassie and the others the benefit of the doubt. She understood their fascination and their hope, even if she wasn't yet certain she shared it. And she knew Cassie still hadn't recovered from Rio's loss, nor Nestor from Daniel's.

Still, any empathy she had was currently being beaten and sent to huddle, crying, in the corner by a simmering sense of betrayal.

"Mags?"

"What do you want, Ian?"

"You ever going to talk to me again?"

"I just did."

It was dumb, and she knew it. He hadn't done anything wrong. His failure to defend her from Cassie's and even Nestor's accusations, though, to back up her mistrust of Lacusta, still stung. So, before he could expound any further, "You were saying, Suni?"

"Oh. Uh, just that I think Lacusta may *be* a machine!"

Mags, who had really just meant to change the subject, almost tripped at an answer that actually snagged her attention. "Uh, what?"

"Well, we've all heard the stories of those tiny bots they had at the start of Pacification, right? Little machines too small to see, but could use themselves to build larger machines? They were called, uh…"

"Nine," Ian ventured, still gazing sidelong at Mags. "Nine-something, yeah?"

"Nano," Nestor corrected. "Nanobots."

"I thought those were just stories," Magdalena confessed. "Something to make us feel better. 'Oh, look, the machines could do even *more* before Pacification, but at least we accomplished *something* fighting back!'"

"What I heard," Suni said, "was that they were lies the machines made up. To keep us nervous, make us wonder if they were around even when we couldn't see them. But what if they *weren't* just stories?"

"Right," Ian scoffed. "And when they finally managed to recreate the equipment they needed to build those, uh, nanobots? They what? Covered the whole thing in fake skin?"

"Could have."

"And built it to fuel itself with human blood? And then somehow lost control of it?"

"Well, it makes more sense than your 'human experiment' idea!"

"The hell it does!"

"I think maybe he's a ghost," Nestor whispered.

This time, Mags stopped, forcing the others to do the same. "What?"

"What's a ghost?" Ian asked simultaneously.

"Old belief," Nestor said. "The spirit, uh, soul of a dead person, come back from beyond the grave with all kinds of weird powers."

"Come back why?" Ian asked in a nervous whisper.

"Revenge, usually. And I mean, the machines have killed so many of us..."

"That," Suni interrupted, stamping one tiny foot, "is the dumbest idea we've yet—"

From the far end of the ragged column, one of the other members of the 13936 called out. "What's the holdup?"

"Nothing!" Mags replied, resuming the journey. "All clear!"

Then, "You could just ask him, you know."

"Huh?" That was Ian, again.

"Lacusta. Why don't you just ask him?"

"Ask me what?" He just *appeared*, a dark shape against a darkened world. The frayed hem of his coat flapped about his ankles, and the mangled carcass of a rotor-driven drone dangled from each fist.

"God!" Mags clumsily crossed herself. "You scared the hell out of—!"

Lacusta's reaction was mind-boggling. He leapt backward with something that wasn't quite hiss or growl, but the incestuous offspring of both, dropping the wrecked drones from rising, defensive hands.

And just as swiftly he froze, arms only half lifted. His head tilted to one side, and for the first time, Magdalena saw an expression flit over his face that was not fearsome, not thoughtful, not smiling. He looked well and truly puzzled.

"I don't..." The words he muttered were halting, broken, occasionally interspersed with some wholly different language. "I felt nothing."

Finally, as much to head off any of her people who might say something unfortunate, Mags asked, "Felt nothing from what? What's going on?"

He moved beside her, seeming to glide rather than step as

he approached. "Has your faith somehow been shaken, child?"

Magdalena's back and legs began to ache with the strain of holding still, but she *would not* retreat from him now, in front of the others. "My... what? Faith?"

"Yes."

"Faith in what?"

He stared, unblinking, until Mags felt naked, exposed to the depths of her soul. "A higher power. God. The Virgin and the Christ."

"Oh. Oh! No, I... Shit, I don't think *anyone* believes nothing like that anymore."

"Yet you crossed yourself at my appearance."

Mags felt like her head must be spinning faster than the rotor on a drone. "That gesture thing, you mean?"

"Indeed." His voice was scarcely more than a whisper, repulsively sensuous. "That 'gesture thing.'"

"Uh, it's just a habit I picked up from my parents. Sort of a good luck charm, I guess. There's not... Um, like I said, not a lot of people... I guess there just wasn't much time for, uh, religion after Pacification. Why?"

Magdalena hunched her shoulders against the laughter that followed, as though cringing from a warm and greasy caress. She couldn't begin to guess what the horrid stranger found so uproariously funny, but she knew damn well that neither she, nor any of the others, would be comfortable asking further questions anytime soon.

"It's a quarry." Mags squinted at the broad shadow before her, rubbed a knuckle into one red eye, and succeeded only in making it redder. "I'm *so* glad we killed ourselves marching all night, so we could reach quarry. It's been *days* since I last saw one!"

Ian glanced at his compass, much as they'd all been doing since Lacusta—who'd been guiding them ever since his directions grew more complex than "west"—had departed an hour or so before. "He said to stay on this exact heading. Even if we got a little off course, there's nothing else around. This *has* to be where he was taking us!"

Cursing under her breath, she led them down, slowly descending the winding ramp that led—eventually, after multiple circuits of the artificial canyon—to the bottom.

She could tell within the first hundred feet that this quarry was unlike the others she'd recently seen. The ramp, the jagged edges of the massive pit, the smaller side tunnels where people or machines had dug in search of metals, the huge chunks of excavated stone... All weather-worn, overgrown with scrub. Nothing larger than a wild animal had moved through here in years; certainly no heavy equipment of any kind. Despite the recent rains, an almost dusty scent pooled in the rocky hollow.

Tapped out, poorly located, or for some other reason, the place was long abandoned.

All right, so it might be a good place to rest up, avoid the machines for a short while. But I don't see how it's any good for any extended... Oh.

After long, *long* minutes of walking, slowly wending their way downward, Mags and the others finally neared the base of the pit. And only here, only so close to ground level, could they see it.

Beneath a ledge formed by an outcropping of blasted, partially carved stone, gaped a trio of mine entrances. Unlike the others, visible from the crater's rim, these three required a concerted effort, a deliberate descent, to locate. No simple scout or search party passing by, even flying by, would notice them.

"Still relatively close to the Scatters," Mags observed, her tone snide. But it was a complaint for the sake of complaining— she *wanted* to find fault with Lacusta's endeavor—and she knew it.

As they tromped across the quarry floor, largely hidden from the morning sun by the deep stone crags, the stranger's judgment proved ever more impressive. Two of those three mines narrowed not far beyond the mouth, creating ready-made defensive choke points. Large mounds of rock were heaped against the side of the pit nearby. It wouldn't take more than a couple of hours, or less with Lacusta's strength, to restack them to conceal one or two of the caves.

Of the stranger himself, though, there was no sign.

"So which one?" Cassie asked, waving vaguely at all three entrances.

Ian, some yards ahead, answered her. "I'm guessing the one with the crumpled drone lying in it."

Indeed, as Mags drew nearer, she could see one of the two drones Lacusta had destroyed on their journey—Nestor was lugging the other, for future study—just inside the rightmost mine.

"Better than a formal invitation," Ian crowed. Mags grunted and pushed past him, flipping her flashlight back on as the mine's shadows closed in around her.

Beetles skittered, and worms burrowed, fleeing the influx of light and stomping feet. Carapaces and grit crunched as the 13936 entered the tunnel. Mags couldn't help but note that, where the quarry outside had smelled oddly dry, the atmosphere in here was rich, even musty.

Old wooden beams buttressed the walls and ceilings, a flimsy-looking barrier to the tons of earth and rock beyond. Not, however, as poor as it first seemed.

"Hey, Mags!" Zach hissed.

She sidled aside, making room for the others as she joined him near the wall. Zach, utterly average-looking in almost every way, was one of the newer members of her detachment. She still didn't know him all that well, though they'd shared enough missions for her to trust him as part of the team. "What?"

He reached out with his flashlight, tapped lightly against one of the stanchions. "Fresh wood."

Now that she knew what to look for, Mags could see it all over. While the bulk of the tunnel's supports were old, a smattering of brand-new ones stood throughout the corridor.

"Replacing the rotten ones?" Ian asked as he, too, drifted over. "Shore up the mine?"

"If so," she replied, "it means our 'friend's' been prepping this place a while."

A few more minutes left Mags no doubt at all.

Several large side chambers had been converted to barracks. Tattered blankets and canvas made for poor mattresses indeed, but given how they were laid out, that was clearly their intent.

Pegs had been driven into the walls, perhaps for hanging clothing. Another such chamber was, instead, occupied by a table and benches—or rather, a massive log that had been sliced lengthwise to make a table-length surface, and several lesser ones serving as seats. Smaller hollows contained ready-made fire pits, some smoked meats, and a stack of sealed rations that must have been stolen from a work camp.

Not enough to feed the group for long, no, but long enough for them to hunt up additional supplies.

And then, "Uh, guys?" It'd been a while since Mags had heard Cassie sound so uncertain, so disturbed. "I think you'd better..."

Cassie had found another side chamber, larger even than the makeshift mess hall. The entrance, however, was surprisingly narrow. Unlike the others, this room boasted a door of fresh and very sturdy wood, clearly a new addition. The door even had a massive bar that could be lowered into a carved niche to keep it from opening.

A bar on the *outside* of the door.

"We've seen Lacusta fight the machines," Mags said softly. "And he's probably fought a lot more we *didn't* see."

Various nods or sounds of assent from the others.

"So even if he was dumb enough to think capturing a working machine was a good idea, he'd know that this door wouldn't hold it very long."

Again, a chorus of agreement.

Ian, as always, sidled up beside her. "But he's not *planning* on keeping bots in there, is he?"

"No, Mister Masse. I am not."

He stood some distance up the tunnel, faintly silhouetted against what little morning light could seep in from outside. A shape as still as the surrounding stone.

Wait. Silhouetted? "Why do you have a shadow now?" The others, who had not noticed that particular peculiarity of Lacusta's the night before, gawped in puzzlement at the question.

"That is the first scattered daylight behind me. Only in the sun's glare do my kind cast our shadows."

"How is that possible?!"

"It is not. *I* am not. You should have figured that out by now. But come, this isn't what you truly wish to ask me, is it?"

"No." A reluctant gesture toward the door. "Is this meant to be a prison?" she demanded.

"A pen. For livestock."

"You can't exactly keep cattle in there," Suni protested.

"*My* livestock."

All the air seemed to leave the tunnel at once.

"I hope it'll not be necessary," Lacusta continued. "But we cannot be certain that every person we approach will be as wise as you have been in your choices. If I lack sufficient allies from which to gently feed, then I must have a larder of enemies from which I can feed *un*gently."

From the expressions surrounding her, Magdalena thought enthusiasm for remaining with Lacusta might have waned a bit. On the other hand, given what Lacusta had just said—and the fact that he stood between them and escape—it seemed wise to keep the idea to herself.

For now.

"As to your earlier question, Miss Suarez, we are, indeed, nearer to the Scatters, as you call it, than some might deem wise. If we are to war against the machines, we must be positioned to strike at them. And *I* must be able to make the journey there, and back, in a single night. I prefer to avoid the sun, where possible."

Mags didn't even ask where he'd been that he'd overheard her earlier, and rather distant, criticism. "Nobody here's crazy enough to try to fight the—"

"I am not asking."

After a long silence, Lacusta continued. "You are, all of you, welcome to my hospitality and protection, as I would offer to any ally. If we are *not* allies, however, then I fear I must reserve my hospitality for others who might be."

"We do need protection," Magdalena confessed. "It's why we're here. But it doesn't do us any good if we throw it away by getting into a fight we can't win! We'd be better off on our own!"

"As you were before I intervened? Even if you made it back

to the wild, you'd be dead within days."

"What... what do you mean, 'even if'?"

Their "host" said nothing. Mags thought about the wooden door and shuddered.

"They control the *whole world!*" she insisted. "There's no fighting them! Besides, what do you need us for, anyway?"

"No one can fight a war alone, not even I. And I admit I am... lost. This world of yours is alien to me. I find it puzzling."

"World of...?" Magdalena's bewilderment was echoed by most of the others. "Where are you from?"

"Far, very far. And of greater import, long ago. I am old, older than you can conceive."

"So how did you get here?" Nestor asked from the center of the group. "And how old *are* you? *What* are you?"

"My precise age, my birth, you needn't know. How I came to be here?

"I rose some few years ago, from a slumber of decades..."

Chapter Thirteen

Magdalena couldn't follow the entire tale.

It relied too heavily on knowledge she didn't have, names she didn't know. Names like "Romania," or "the Carpathians." By the time it was told, however, she understood enough.

Understood there had been a great war of conquest, the second one in mere decades—though she was lost again when Lacusta described that war as being "waged in the name of a Teutonic madman and his Italian exemplar." She understood that the battles, the weapons, were like none Lacusta had seen in all his years, that he had chosen instead to sleep away several years beneath his home—a place called Castle Kerekos—until the chaos had subsided.

That the falling bombs had reduced much of Kerekos to rubble, burying it amidst the rock of the mountains, and that its master's slumber had lasted many, many decades longer than he had intended. That he had been finally awakened by a mining expedition—which he had, of course, destroyed—and had only then discovered just how utterly the world had changed.

And that his earlier talk had been no exaggeration. Lacusta fully intended to wage war against the "iron devils" that had come to rule in his absence. To reclaim the world—and those who yet survived within—for his own.

Feet shuffled. Jaws and fists clenched. Wood creaked. Dirt shifted. Fabric rustled. A chorus, echoing, deafening in the silence.

They had, the whole lot, drifted into the makeshift dining room and taken seats during Lacusta's recitation. Mags now found herself wishing they hadn't, if only because the room, with its single exit, felt even more of a trap than the hallway.

Where everyone else shifted and squirmed, Lacusta sat in utter immobility. Whether he was seeing them at all, or gazing still at the events of earlier years, Magdalena couldn't guess.

Not until he spoke. "You needn't fear mistreatment at my hands," he informed them. "It is always in the lord's best interest to see to the wellbeing of his subjects, his helpers, and his stock."

Right, because that's the part we're having trouble with. He actually sounded as though he were trying to be magnanimous! "What if we don't particularly care to be 'owned'?" Mags challenged.

"This from a woman who has lived all her years under the heel of the machines? Humans require a firm rule, and what I offer you is far superior to what you have known."

She was reaching the limits of even the supposed immortal's patience; she could see it in his flashing glare, in a posture that, though already completely still, somehow grew ever stiffer. "I agree someone has to be in charge," she began more calmly, "but it sounds like you're asking us to trade one slavery for—"

"Why can't they see you?"

Mags glowered at Ian, even though she knew precisely why he'd interrupted, might even feel a bit grateful to him for heading her off. "In the Scatters," the young man continued, "and what you just told us… It's like you're invisible to them."

With a final long look at Magdalena, Lacusta answered. "I am."

"How come?"

"Just as my kind casts no shadow in artificial light, neither do we present any image, either in mirror or in film—or, apparently, the more advanced technologies that followed film. To your vaunted machines, whatever sort of fantastically advanced lenses or artificial eyes they may possess, I might as well be a wraith in the wind."

It was, Mags had to admit, a powerful advantage. "How did you get here? I mean, *here* here? What you're describing? You didn't wake up anywhere nearby."

"Romania, as I said."

Puzzled silence.

"Eastern Europe," he expanded.

More silence, equally puzzled.

The stranger somehow managed to look as though he wanted to sigh but chose not to. "Across the sea."

A few tentative nods, this time.

"Your 'Eyes' and their machines might be ubiquitous," he continued, "but they cannot look everywhere simultaneously. A small group traveling the wilds, far from any camp or center of power, or sailing a tiny scavenged boat across the waves, can well go unnoticed."

"Group?" Cassie asked from a ways down the long table. "Not just you?"

"Indeed. Three of the men who had been slaves to the mining expedition that awakened me became my new entourage."

"Did you do the same thing to them you did to me?" It was the first time Mags had spoken openly about it, but it made sense. *Something* had happened to her at their first meeting, when she'd apparently told him things she'd never willingly have spoken.

"No, I required more, let us say, robust assistance. I remade them."

Again, for a short eternity, nobody could speak. "Into what?" Ian finally rasped.

Lacusta slowly, even melodramatically, touched a hand to his chest.

"Not *precisely* the same as I, of course," he clarified. "Their wills were mine. Dull creatures, simple and slow. But obedient, and that was what I required.

"My... personal comfort demands that I sleep surrounded by the soil of my homeland. I could hardly carry such a load on my own, not over the distances I needed to travel. Between satchels upon their backs, however, and the hollows of their bodies, my slaves performed admirably."

Mags squeaked something that might have been a question. She was not the only one.

"You would be surprised how much you can fit in a human

torso," Lacusta explained, "when most of the organs are dispensable."

Toward the rear of the chamber, someone gagged.

"They are gone now," the creature lamented. "I destroyed them when I settled here. I felt remaining inconspicuous to the machines while trying to feed and maintain them would have proved difficult. I may have been too hasty, in that regard. It required far more effort than I anticipated, and far more time, to acquire new allies."

"Inconspicuous like in the Scatters?" Mags asked with more than a touch of sarcasm.

Lacusta merely shrugged. "The taste of my blood can inspire an unyielding devotion in the living, as well in as those whom I have remade. But not all mortal minds can tolerate it. Those who cannot, who go mad... Well, you have seen the results. But then, it was time for me to take a more active stance, in any event."

Just like that. He'd shattered one man's mind, been responsible—directly, or through his maddened pawn—for dozens of deaths, and it was worth a whole five sentences of explanation before being dismissed. Mags wondered if his inhuman senses could detect the pounding of her pulse, her blood beginning to boil.

Again, she was preempted before she could say something she might later regret, this time by Lacusta himself. "Do recall," he said, as though he could indeed sense her mounting anger, "that I was alone, in a world utterly foreign to me, surrounded on all sides by enemies of a sort I had never imagined, let alone seen. My options were few, and the threats many."

Mags couldn't help but accept that, however reluctantly.

"As to *why* I traveled here? Few of those to whom I spoke knew much of the origins of these iron devils. They spoke of a Pacification, when the ongoing struggle with the machines turned to open war, but what predated that time was shrouded in ignorance, limited to half-heard grandparents' tales.

"What few commonalities they had, however, suggested to me that the rulers of these machines, these 'Eyes,' had originated in the American city of New York."

Mags had heard that, or at least that New York was somehow

linked to the Eyes, but then, she'd heard the same of other cities, too. She'd never given any of it any credence. "And?" she asked simply.

"Hrm. And I found little, when I finally arrived, to suggest any such thing. After some weeks, I located an old man who served the machines, far more closely than the rest of you. A collaborator, a... 'scrip,' you call them?"

Several members of the 13936 nodded or grunted an affirmation.

"From 'conscript,' perhaps?" he wondered.

"That's what I heard, yeah," Nestor said.

"I didn't know it was 'from' anything," Cassie put in, tapping a fingertip on the table. "It's just a word."

"My father told me it was from 'script kiddie,'" Zach called from even farther back.

Mags scowled. "What the hell does 'script kiddie' even mean?"

"No idea. Just what he told me it—"

"In any event," Lacusta interrupted, "the old man held some belief that whatever had initially begun in New York had removed itself here, to, ah, Pittsburgh. A faint enough trail, certainly, but better than nothing at all. I've learned little new on that score, however. Despite," he added with a sideways glance at Magdalena, "questioning a smattering of the locals." She tried to keep herself from shivering and failed miserably.

"I was attempting to track down more solid clues and learn what I could of this Pittsburgh when I encountered the team that preceded your own. The rest you know, or rather you know enough for now."

"Enough? What if that's *not* enough for us?" Nestor asked. Magdalena could have kissed him. Thank God she wasn't the only one having problems with this!

"You know enough to decide," Lacusta countered.

"Decide?"

"With which side you choose to stand."

"Look," Mags protested, "nobody here loves the machines, but you *can't* beat the Eyes! It's impossible! It'll be hard enough just to *avoid* them!"

Ian scuffed his feet, looked down briefly at his hands. "She's right. The Eyes can manifest in any bot they want. They're everywhere. There's nothing there to kill!"

"And should one of the machines, or your overseer, speak to you over a radio or intercom, Mister Masse? Does that then mean that it does not exist in any corporeal form? Or merely that its form is elsewhere to be found?"

Mags clenched a fist on the bench. "It's not the same thing!"

"Of course it is. Anything can be destroyed, Miss Suarez. If I have learned anything in my centuries, I have learned that nothing lasts."

"*You* have." She knew she didn't sound particularly happy with the prospect.

"Yes, well. Someone has to be there to learn the lesson, no?"

"Even if we wanted to join your crusade," Cassie said, with too much relish over the idea for Magdalena's liking, "even if we thought it was possible, we'd never survive long enough to see it through. We're not exactly as durable as you are."

"Ah. But my dear Miss Wertham, you could be."

Mags had thought today couldn't have surprised her, couldn't have confused her, any further. She felt dizzy, cold enough to wrap her arms around herself, and yet her whole body tingled with an alien excitement.

"You can give us power likes yours?" She hoped she sounded far steadier than she felt, that the churning emotions filling her hadn't seeped out in her voice. "Turn us into... creatures like you?"

"Not all of you. Those who prove deserving. And not 'creatures,' Miss Suarez. Higher beings. Immortals, capable of taking on the true monsters that have enslaved this world!"

"You said the people you 'remade' were mindless slaves!" Nestor protested.

"No." Lacusta didn't so much rise to his feet as simply appear upright, as though his body had not bothered to pass through the intervening space or postures. "The men I remade before, they were laborers. Beasts of burden, whom I needed to keep tightly leashed. Now? Now I need allies who can think. Plan. Work with me toward a common good, guide me where my knowledge of this new world remains lacking, lead forces of their own. That means free will, and that is something I *can* grant to my, let us say, offspring.

"Those of you who are chosen will not remain quite who you were—how possibly *could* you?—but you will remain your own, not a mere extension of myself. You will remain you."

He began to drift backward, then, without steps, both moving and fading away as he spoke. "I would rest, now, until the dusk. Settle yourselves in. And think on what you have learned."

Their "host" had barely vanished from sight before Mags spun to face the others.

Whatever words she might have uttered died in her throat, their decomposing remains turning her stomach. The confusion, the fear, and yes, the allure she felt, she saw it all mirrored in every single face. They needed reassurance and guidance she couldn't give, and certainly had none to offer her. The least she could for them, for now, was to avoid saddling them with her own doubts.

Ian handed her a length of smoked jerky—of what species, she didn't know and wasn't about to ask—when she stepped into the barracks chamber. "Figured you might be hungry, since you missed breakfast and all."

She nodded absently, just as absently took a small bite, examining the room over the leathery strip. Her team had been busy for the past few hours: Already it appeared they'd each chosen a bunk, if the stacks of scraps and worn blankets could be dignified with such a term. She recognized the piles of tools, a few pairs of boots, similar personal touches.

She noticed her own toolbelt and pack sitting, unopened, on the makeshift mattress next to Ian's.

"I'm not making any assumptions," he said softly as she turned a raised brow his way. "I'll move them if you'd rather..."

The meat, not exactly flavorful to begin with, suddenly resembled the earthen floor. She forced herself to choke the mouthful down. "Why would you even have to ask?"

"You tell me, Mags. Feel like the last few days—"

"Have been kind of stressful, exhausting, and oh, yeah, fucking *terrifying*. If you hadn't noticed."

"Oh, is *that* what I was feeling? I'd wondered."

They shared a grin, albeit a tentative one.

"I'm sorry I've been snapping at you, Ian. Between trying to keep this crazy team together, and the argument over Lacusta..."

"Yeah. I get it. It's okay."

"Good. My stuff's right where it should be," she told him.

"Not all of it. You're still wearing some."

The punch she aimed at his shoulder wasn't hard enough to hurt—*too* much. "Ass-goggle."

"Ow!"

"Good." Then, "Ian... Everyone? We need to talk this through."

Activity in the barracks ceased instantly.

"We're not leaving, Mags," Cassie insisted from across the room. "How long would we make it out there? Days? Maybe, if we got *really* damn lucky, a couple of weeks. Terrified, huddling, starving. No damn way we're—!"

"For God's sake, Cass, I wasn't going to suggest that!"

Stubborn silence for a few breaths. Then, "Oh. Sorry."

The fuck is her problem these days, anyway?

"What I *was* going to say is that we need to be careful. Lacusta may be powerful, may be able to do what he says, but we don't know what he is. We can't trust him."

Ian took a heavy breath, bracing as though for a dive into icy waters. "He's been pretty open with us, Mags. About what he wants, even about how monstrous he can be."

Magdalena caught herself before she either flailed her arms or shook her lover by the shoulders, but it was a near thing. "That's just it! He's a monster and he doesn't care that we know it! Just like the machines. He may be an ally, but he is *not* our friend!"

"Of course not! God, Mags, he's killed more of the 13936 than the machines ever did! *Nobody's* saying he's our friend! Just that he's our best option."

Mags nodded, stepped back from Ian so she could study the

whole assembly. "All right. We all agree on that? That's about where we all are?"

Various gestures, words, and grunts of confirmation.

"Good. Then I need for us all to agree on something else. I need you to promise me that none of you are gonna take Lacusta up on his final offer, at least not yet. That you won't let him 'remake' any of you until we know more about it."

Several of her friends, including Ian, frowned at that, and Cassie scowled outright. "Where do you get off demanding—?" she began.

"Shut it! God dammit, you've *seen* what Lacusta is, but you don't *know* what he is! None of us do! What's it like? What does it do to you? Who does it make you?"

"Lacusta said we'd still be us, who we've always been."

"So the fuck what, Lacusta said? What'd we just say about trust, about him not being our friend? He's a blood-drinking killer who sees us as his subjects, but you're going to believe everything he says? And even if he's telling the truth, what if he's just wrong? He said he's lived centuries! You think he remembers what it was like to be human?

"Look," she continued after a calming breath, "I'm not saying never. I'm saying we need to learn more, and we need to discuss it, study it, every step of the way. Same as we've done a hundred unknown dangers on our R&D missions, yeah? We proceed when we know what we're dealing with, and not before."

"You, Miss Suarez, are a wiser commander than I took you for."

Lacusta's entrance managed somehow to be dramatically sweeping yet effortlessly casual at once. He moved to the leftmost wall before turning to face the assembly: a position, Mags couldn't help but notice, despite his words of support, that forced their attention away from her if they were to heed him.

"In truth, you do *not* know what would be asked of you, if and when I offer to share my gifts. You *cannot*. There is nothing in your experience, nothing within the bounds of your imagination, that could prepare you. Miss Suarez is quite right to hesitate, and in truth, had any of you come to me too soon to request such a thing, I would have flatly rejected you as unsuitable. As too rash, too thoughtless."

Cassie blushed, looking down at her feet, as did a few of the others.

"Don't you *want* to change us sooner than later?" Mags challenged. "I mean, you're so eager to go to war against the machines."

"War is a game for the patient, Miss Suarez. As you yourself so wisely stated, it is patience and understanding that brings victory."

"I wish you'd understand; there can't *be* a 'victory,' not like you mean it! You *can't kill* the Eyes!"

"Even if you were correct, better to die fighting than cowering, yes? *If* you were correct. Which you are not.

"Come," he continued, clearly deciding this particular conversation was at an end, "I have chambers yet to show you, including what weapons and equipment I have so far managed to stockpile on my own. You'll need to become familiar with them, and swiftly."

"Swiftly?" The word made Mags more than a bit uncomfortable, and from the muttering around her and the sudden grip of Ian's fingers on her shoulder, she wasn't the only one. "Why?"

"Because, Miss Suarez, proper supplies are just as vital as patience and understanding. We do not yet have sufficient materiel to wage this war. We must take what we require from the machines' facilities, and we must do so now, while much of their regional strength is spread across the wilderness, searching for you.

"Tonight, you are fugitives. Tomorrow, you become soldiers."

Chapter Fourteen

If the Scatters were the corpse of Pittsburgh, then this portion had attracted more than its share of beetles and worms as it decayed.

Industrial structures had not merely been reduced to skeletons, their bones of concrete had been split asunder to extract the steel supports within. Floors and sidewalks lay in jagged chunks, torn up to retrieve every last inch of rebar. Faint paths in the scraggly overgrowth showed where railroad tracks once lay. Even the random nails, slivers, rusted flakes had been scooped up with magnets and carted away to be melted down. Somehow—hanging over it all despite the decades that had passed—the faint tang of molten metals, the dying gasps of foundries and chemical production, lingered.

Still, there was *some* metal present. They'd brought fair quantities with them.

Mags and the rest of the 13936—*I probably ought to come up with something else to call us now*—crouched throughout the broken concrete framework of what had once been... well, something vaguely building-like. The young woman peered around a broken pylon, through a set of night-vision goggles, at a small complex of buildings some few hundred yards distant. Unlike the remnants surrounding her, these structures were whole.

"Target's the big one, I assume?" she asked.

"Indeed."

It took everything she had not to jump. She'd known Lacusta was there, or she wouldn't have asked the question; she just hadn't realized he was so *close*. Anyone else, she'd have heard breathing.

"I'm not entirely certain what purpose the smaller annexes serve," he admitted, moving to stand beside her rather than behind. "The main edifice, however, is equipment storage and repair."

"Hmm. I'm only seeing a few drones and a single humanoid bot in the vicinity."

"There will be others. Not, I hope, *too* many."

"No, they're all out looking for us." Mags cast a sidelong glance Lacusta's way and paused. "Um. Your, uh, your hand…"

"Oh." The fearsome stranger reached down and slid a long sliver of what had been a drone's rotor from his flesh. "I hadn't realized that was still there." Then, at her expression, "I told you on the way here that I was going ahead to ensure our path remained clear."

"Yeah, but you didn't say you'd actually run into anything."

"Why should I have bothered? I won."

Mags snorted. "You're not real clear on this whole teamwork thing, are you?"

"I am quite familiar with teamwork. I simply see no cause to explain myself unnecessarily to *my* team."

Mags devoted her attention once more to the goggles, so she wouldn't have to respond to that.

"Tell me, Miss Suarez," Lacusta asked a bit later, as the remainder of the detachment gathered around them. "Why do the machines bother to keep weapons and equipment that are not built into their bodies? Why do some possess man-shaped forms when the others, the drones and spiders and such, are purpose-built?"

It was Nestor who answered from behind the next pylon over, rather than Magdalena. "Bots acquired a *lot* of vehicles and weapons from us during and after Pacification. Hell, they basically had all that was left of civilization to sift through. All our stuff's made for humans, so humanoid machines were the most efficient way of using it. They're phasing the humanoids out, as time goes on, but so many of their own factories were trashed during Pacification, they *still* haven't rebuilt them all. So it's slow going, and for now, they use whatever pre-Pacification shit they can find that still works."

"Fortunate for us, then," Lacusta replied.

"Oh, yeah." Magdalena's words were so bitter, she wanted to spit them out rather than speak them. "We're *real* fucking fortunate, us people." Then, rather more forcefully, "Equipment check!"

The clattering, clanking, clinking, and clicking melded into a symphonic ode to preparedness. Mags examined her own gear—including her new weapon, a shotgun loaded with massive, single-projectile shells she'd heard were called deer slugs—before giving the rest of the team a quick once-over. When everyone nodded, offered a thumbs-up or various other signs, she indicated their readiness to Lacusta.

"Everybody understands the plan?" he asked.

"No, Lacusta, we've all forgotten in the hours since we last went over it. Or the time before that. Or..."

"Spare me your insolence, child!" The mask of urbane civility dropped away, revealing a ravening snarl that would have appeared too bestial even for the creature's lupine form, let alone this human one. "You are unproven in combat, untested! I will cease questioning your competence once you have earned it, not one instant before!"

The façade was back in place before Mags finished recoiling, leaving her uncertain she'd truly seen it fall. "Remember, I scented traces of human blood when I first scouted this facility. So you may be facing other people—ah, scrips—as well as machines.

"Fifty-count and two-hundred-count," he concluded in one final reminder. Then he was gone, consumed by the night, vanished even from the night-vision lenses.

Good God, Mags wondered, not for the first time, *what the hell have we gotten involved with?*

"Still wish we were going in together," Ian stage-whispered to her.

"We'll be fine. Besides, this is how our 'lord and master' wants it."

"Mags, he's not—"

"Hsst! Hey!" Zach and Nestor rose from their hiding places, weighted down with the heaviest of the weaponry Lacusta had thus far scavenged. "Fifty-count's almost up, loverboy," Nestor told them. "Start moving."

Ian's expression twisted in a combination scowl and embarrassed grin that threatened to turn his whole face sideways. He hefted his own weapon—big, but not nearly so massive as the hardware Nestor carried—and the trio scuttled into the darkness.

Mags watched Ian go for only a second, before her attention was snagged by an eruption of shots from the building's front.

The moon was dim that night, the scene before them playing out in strobes of gunfire. She saw a shape that must have been Lacusta tumbling to earth, a mangled drone in each fist, as other bots struggled to target him, perhaps tracking sounds or the movement of their dead counterparts.

Flash, and he was a dozen feet nearer the building, fist blasting through a third drone as one of the battlefield spider-bots skittered from beneath a rising door, both barrels blazing.

Flash, and the spider-bot was staggering from the impact of the two dead drones, hurled with inhuman strength, while a gargantuan wolf soared through the air in an impossible leap.

Flash, and the insectoid thing lay sprawled, thrashing in an effort to get its legs back under it, while the wolf ravaged the steel of its weapons turret with bare teeth. Drones circled, and one of the humanoid machines strode from the building, following in the spider's footsteps.

And then no more flashes, for the night brightened with the crimson illumination of hell.

The humanoid bot carried some sort of tank or container in one hand, connected by thick tubing to a gun-like cylinder in the other. From that cylinder poured torrents of flame, a volcano turned sideways. The fire came on like a living thing, an expanding wall of roaring, shrieking hunger. And while the machine may not have been able to see its enemy, it had no compunctions about sacrificing the bot on which Lacusta obviously stood.

He hurled himself from the oncoming inferno, fleeing before it as Mags had seen him do with no other weapon or danger. All four paws struck the earth, scarcely ahead of the flame, and then the wolf simply vanished. Mags could have sworn that the creature had collapsed, disintegrating into dust just as the wall of burning death passed overhead.

Is that it? Is he gone?

She couldn't decide whether to dread or to celebrate the possibility.

"Mags! Two-hundred-count! Let's go!"

She glanced up, first to see the other remaining team moving, and then toward Suni. "All right." Mags shot to her feet, nodded once at her assigned partner, and ran.

Even as they circled, however, she couldn't keep her eyes off the ongoing battle. The machine's flamethrower had finally finished speaking, but various patches of scrub and pooled fuels still burned merrily away, lighting the scene.

Enough so that Mags saw quite clearly when a mass of dust spiraled upward from the earth, becoming a column for a heartbeat until it was Lacusta once more, resuming his human shape. He struck, snarling so loud she could hear it across the battlefield, ripping the weapon from the machine's grip and hurling it aside.

The machine responded instantly, shoving Lacusta back with an outthrust palm. From somewhere Mags couldn't see, it produced an object, raising its hand before its mechanical body as though presenting the item to the enemy.

Only then, in the flicking firelight, could Magdalena tell what it was.

What the fuck?

A cross. The bot was thrusting a makeshift wooden cross at Lacusta.

She heard the man's laughter as clearly as she had his snarl, saw him lunge for the bot again before their course took Suni and her around an annex building and she lost sight of the battle.

Focus, Mags! she admonished herself.

"Focus, Mags!" Suni barked at her.

"You know, I was just thinking that."

The vehicle pool appeared just where Lacusta had said it would. On the cracked concrete lot and inside one of the smaller buildings, the duo spotted an array of trucks. Most were very much like those they'd used back at camp: rickety, rundown, mismatched. One, however, was far larger than the others and bore a layer of makeshift, but perfectly cut, steel armoring.

"Ooh," the smaller woman practically cooed. "I want that one."

Mags snorted. "Of course. May be harder to start, though. More secure. They probably use it for important cargo. Get a few of the others started first, so we can take off if we need to. *Then* see if you can get the anvil on wheels running."

"You're no fun," Suni complained, but she obeyed, making a beeline for the nearest vehicle.

"You know," Mags grumbled as she took up position crouched atop another of the trucks, watching for incoming foes, "you might've told me you knew how to hotwire one of these things back at camp, before we abandoned the truck."

"How was I supposed to know that was the problem?" The reply came, muffled, from beneath the dashboard in the neighboring cab. "You dove into the truck, then popped back out a minute later and went straight to plan B! If you'd asked…"

The cough of the engine saved Mags the need to reply. She shouted something vaguely encouraging instead, urging Suni on to the next vehicle before turning her attention back to their surroundings.

"Shit!"

Only just visible in the sporadic firelight from below, a trio of drones had emerged from behind the primary structure, heading for the vehicle pool and opening fire. Just as swiftly, a cloud of flitting, flapping darkness engulfed them, ripping the bots from the sky.

Or rather, two of the trio. The one that targeted Magdalena directly, punching holes in the metal on which she crouched, broke through the swarm of bats, still firing. Only a desperate leap from the cab, one that sent her skidding across the cement and scraping skin painfully from her left arm, saved her from a swift perforation.

Suni slid from the neighboring truck, her own rifle shouting a retort. Mags couldn't see if she'd hit the target or if it had dropped out of sight, but the incoming barrage ceased.

"Mags! You okay?"

Mags winced, groaning at the sting radiating through her arm. "No, but I'll live. Did you see…?"

But of course, she couldn't have. She'd been busy working on the second truck.

Besides, there was nothing to see. I'm sure Lacusta just couldn't stop all three at once. It'd be paranoid to think he'd let the one through on purpose.

Right?

Still, she'd been lucky, and she knew it. She'd allowed her attention to wander, and only sheer chance had kept her alive. The machines were usually better shots than that.

Actually, they'd *always* been better shots than that.

Mags stuck her head into the truck on which she'd stood, reached out and pried one of the flattened slugs from the seat cushion. Definitely *not* lead. In fact, it almost looked like…

"Suni?"

"Yeah?" Again, her voice was distorted and distant as she worked to hotwire a vehicle.

"Why the hell would the machines be firing silver bullets at us?"

"Damned if I know! Are they?"

"Looks like." She rubbed the lump of metal between thumb and forefinger. Even flattened and misshapen, it still suffered pitting substantial enough that she could feel it against her skin. "Doesn't seem like it'd even fly that accurately. I don't get it."

"Maybe if you ask nicely, they'll…" The rest of Suni's comment was lost in the dull roar of a second engine.

"Nice!" Mags called. "You can start on the armored one, now."

"Yay, dessert!"

Mags heard the quick patter of footsteps, almost drowned out by gunfire that echoed now from both the front and rear of the main structure.

A lot more gunfire, from the rear, than she'd heard a moment ago. She found her palms sweating where she gripped the shotgun. *Ian's team.*

Lacusta's plan, developed after he'd heard the details of their escape from the camp, had involved a four-way split. He drew the machines' attentions up front, followed by an attack— Ian, Zach, and Nestor, using the heaviest weaponry the 13936 had available—on the rear. An apparent duplication of the two-pronged distraction Mags had come up with days before.

That attack, however, was *also* intended to draw the enemy's attention, while Mags and Suni acquired a vehicle or two and the final team entered the facility from one side, gathering equipment and planting explosives.

All well and good, but it relied on the 13936 not being utterly overrun, and there just weren't that many of them left. The ponderous, heavy thud of the big guns was now all but inaudible beneath a torrent of smaller but far more rapid weapons.

Suni literally yelped when Mags pounded on the door to get her attention. "Soon as you're through with this one," she ordered, "take it—or one of the others, if you couldn't get this going—and head for the meeting point. Don't wait for me."

"Oh, God. Mags, what are you—?"

"Ian may be in trouble." She was already dashing for the first of the two trucks Suni had started.

"Dammit, Mags, stick to the plan!"

Mags slammed the cab door, cutting her friend off, and stomped a foot on the gas.

Over such broken and uneven ground, Mags could only give thanks that she didn't have far to drive. As it was, by the time she'd turned the corner, she felt as though she'd napped inside a rock crusher. The bouncing and jostling were so awful, she was convinced that her teeth must have reorganized themselves in their sockets.

But she'd been right.

In the dull gleam of the headlights, Mags saw several of the spider-bots—mostly the smaller variety, but also one of the heavier-combat models—squatting across the expanse of concrete. All fired at a heap of much heavier cement, perhaps a bridge or overpass that had long since collapsed. Clouds of powdered stone erupted with every impact, creating a microcosm of the sky itself.

From behind that heap, an occasional burst of return fire—or the deafening *thud* of the .50-calibre monster Nestor carried—announced that at least two of the trio still survived. They might not for much longer, though, not given how thoroughly the machines had them pinned down.

Mags glanced at the seat beside her and frowned. Her shotgun wouldn't make much of a difference, not added to the deluge of lead already filling the air.

But the shotgun wasn't the only weapon she had.

The bots saw the truck coming, of course; they couldn't possibly have missed it. Mags ducked aside with a sharp squeak, flattening herself below the dash as the windshield exploded inward. The whole vehicle shuddered. The racket from within the engine block, first the sharp crumpling of impact and then the grinding of damaged parts, was hellish. It still ran, though, however briefly, and even if it hadn't, the lumbering behemoth had a *lot* of inertia.

Most of the machines scrambled from the truck's path. The nearest, however, had only begun to evade when a shot from Nestor's massive rifle took a leg out from under it.

Mags jerked forward at the impact, nearly bashing her head on the steering wheel, but kept the pedal pressed to the floor. The truck swerved, steam pouring from the crumpled hood, engine crying out a song of rending metal. She yanked the wheel, bracing herself, and the whole mass collided with the large structure. Even if the bot had survived the initial collision, she was fairly certain that being squashed between the truck and the wall, to say nothing of the rain of brick and stone that followed, must have finished it off.

She threw the door open, scooped up her shotgun, and staggered from the cab, unsteady on her feet. With the truck between her and the enemy, she could probably make a dash for cover, and with any luck, her insane charge had bought the others enough time to—

From the lot, she heard the clatter of metal, and then something that sounded less like a gun firing than a flat *thoob*.

The hell?

"Mags! Get down! Get—!"

She was in mid-dive when whatever had just been launched struck the truck—and the truck split apart in a ball of shrapnel and flame.

Heat roared over her, raking her back, the arms she'd crossed over her head. Her skin felt baked, and she smelled singed hair. All of which paled beneath the sharp agony that shot up her right leg, a wet, jabbing shock. She knew that if she looked down, she'd see a length of twisted metal or similar shrapnel protruding from her calf. She could only hope whatever it was hadn't gone too deep. A quick test proved she could still point her toes, though the muscle cried out in protest. Probably meant she could limp on it. She flattened her palms against the dirt, started to struggle upright.

A sudden clatter, crackling and deafening, heralded an approaching machine, scrambling over the burning wreckage. She felt desperately around her, seeking the shotgun she must have dropped when she hit the ground.

Gotta be here, where is it, where is it, where the fuck *is it?!*

More gunfire, but behind her, not from the machine, followed by more metallic scrabbling as whatever had been coming at her took cover from whatever was now coming at *it*.

"Get up, Mags!"

She sighed aloud at Ian's voice, though she could barely hear it, tried to speak but found herself choking on the dust and smoke. "Where?" She finally gasped, lifting herself with his help and trying not to wince at his touch on her smarting skin. "The others?"

"Still firing, covering us. Mags, we gotta go, the gas tank..."

She nodded and staggered along with him, half limping, half hopping, still wracked with coughs. Her ears rang from the blast, from the gunfire, from her own pounding heart. She heard Ian grunt, felt him waver.

"Ian!"

"Fine. Just winged me. Keep going."

"But—"

"Keep going!"

Another few steps. A few more.

The gas tank blew.

Another wave of searing heat engulfed her, and another sharp report threatened to crack her skull open, to shatter her ears. Staggering, limping, clutching at Ian, holding him up as he held her, listening to words she couldn't comprehend, answering in turn without the slightest notion of what she'd said, a sudden turn, a desperate dash, every pace a lightning surge of agony through her wounded leg.

And then the worst of the heat was gone, the worst of the cacophony muffled, behind what she recognized after the fact was a slamming door. She felt a wall at her back, cool, definitely not cement. She sank down to her haunches, leaning against it, ignoring the pain of her burns. The floor beneath her was solid, smooth.

"Inside?" she asked, rasping, rubbing at both eyes.

"Yeah." Ian sounded terribly winded and not entirely stable. "One of the annex buildings. Only shelter I could get us to."

"Dark?"

He chuckled, the sound blatantly forced. "Yes. You're not blind." Then, all pretense falling away, "God, Mags, I'm sorry."

"Sorry? For what?"

"You got hurt. Hurt saving me."

"Don't fucking start with that. It's what we do."

"But—"

"Shut it." She blinked, hoping to adjust, but it really was almost pitch black in here. She'd long since lost the night-vision scope, and she didn't want to turn on a light—assuming it was even still in her belt—until she knew it wouldn't draw hostile attention.

"We're not safe in here," she added then. "We don't know what this building's used for, but the machines built it for *something*. There's gonna be cameras, or alarms, or I don't know what. They'll find us."

"Probably," Ian admitted. "But it's safer than out there. We can take a minute, catch our breath. Hell, we might be able to find a corner or room or something away from the cameras, somewhere we can barricade ourselves in until things calm down outside."

"Heh. You think that's likely?"

"Not really. Safer than going back out there, though."

A door some few yards down the hallway, one neither of them had even known existed, clicked open. Mags couldn't see much, save for a shape silhouetted against the electric lighting beyond.

The silhouette of a slender man, clutching the silhouette of a big gun.

"In point of fact," he told them, his voice quiet but firm, "it's even less safe in here than you think."

Chapter Fifteen

"Please don't do that."

How had he known that Mags was contemplating a dash for one of the hallway's other doors? She could only assume he'd seen her gaze flicker or her legs tense, in the light from the chamber behind him.

"I have no desire to shoot either of you," the stranger continued. His voice had a foreign lilt to it, though the accent itself was quite different from Lacusta's. Mags could otherwise make out little about him. "I don't insist you keep your hands on your head or any such thing, but we'd both regret it if you were to reach for a weapon. This way, if you would."

"Mags?" Ian rasped.

"Our other choice being what? If he wanted to shoot us, he'd just shoot us."

"And if he's just delivering us to the machines? He's a damn scrip!"

"*Then* we make him shoot us."

Mags rose, peering intently at their captor—was it her imagination, or had his whole body tensed at their words?—and slowly approached. He retreated, keeping the distance between them, his weapon steady.

Well, mostly steady. The barrel did waver just a bit, once or twice. Never enough for Mags to feel comfortable making a move, but enough to notice. Once she and Ian had stepped fully into the next room, she understood why.

Illuminated in the ruddy glow of what had to be emergency lighting, the chamber revealed itself as a workroom. Various bits and pieces lay strewn across a broad table, lenses and wires and metal tubes, alongside tools such as pliers and soldering irons, the latter of which stank of recent use. Against one wall stood a single computer, its monitor dark, connected to several massive contraptions whose purpose Mags couldn't even guess.

All this she absorbed in a breath or two, her attention rapidly shifting to their captor. His hair ranged from black as hers to a snowy gray, his skin darker and ruddier than her own. Seen clearly, or at least more clearly than earlier, neither he nor his pistol seemed quite so large.

Of greatest import, however, were the crags of his face, the lines around his eyes and lips. If this wasn't the oldest man Mags had ever seen, older even than Jonas, then he was putting on a damn good act. God, he might have been over *fifty*!

Her fascination with that notion kept Mags occupied until they'd cleared that room and moved into another. Here, shelves stored the various devices and parts that might then be taken apart and rebuilt in the prior chamber. She spotted more than a few cameras of varying size and design, as well as other recorders and digital media, amongst the more random collections of coiled wires and circuit boards.

Ian coughed once. When Mags glanced his way, he tilted a head toward the nearest shelf and made a quick pushing motion with his hand. Ahead, their captor edged backward toward yet another door. If the cases went over, they wouldn't fall on him, but the toppling furniture and scattering equipment would certainly provide ample distraction.

"Go!" Mags hissed.

They lunged for the nearest shelf, hands and shoulders straining. It barely rocked, sending only a single precariously balanced microscope to the floor.

"The shelves are bolted down," the old man informed them. "So, if you wouldn't mind, please?"

Grumbling, they resumed following.

A few more rooms and halls, and Mags began to wonder at the oddly circuitous route they seemed to be taking. Finally, deciding she had no good reason not to, she asked him about it.

"I'm taking us around the server room. Cameras in there are still up. They're on a different circuit."

"Um, 'kay..." She looked a question at Ian, who just shrugged.

"Right," the old man said a few moments later, "here we are."

Two doors stood beside one another. One opened into a large closet that had been converted to makeshift sleeping quarters. Mags saw a bedroll and several boxes of personal belongings, as well as scattered clothes. It was to the other room, however, that their captor directed them. This proved to be a storeroom, largely unused to judge by the dust and cobwebs, containing little more than some buckets, old cleaning supplies, and even older office furniture.

Like every other room they'd passed, it was brightened only by the dull emergency lights.

"If you'd just place your weapons in that corner there," he continued, "and then take a seat over here on this side of the room, we can talk a bit." He scooted a small, rickety desk from against the wall and sat on it. "I'll just be a moment," he said. "Haven't had this much excitement in a good while."

He then hefted his pistol, indicating it without aiming it at them directly. "Which doesn't mean I'm not watching you."

"We could probably take him before he could react," Ian whispered as they made their way toward the far corner. "Just turn and fire."

"Maybe." Mags frowned. "No. I don't want to risk it."

"Uh-huh. And?"

"And there's something weird about this. I want to hear him out."

"Of course you do."

Submachine gun and shotgun placed cautiously on the floor, they returned to sit cross-legged some short ways from the old man.

"You're not getting out of here any time soon," he told them. Then, as they obviously looked to his weapon, "No, I don't mean me. The machines. Whatever the ruckus is out there, they'll be watching, and waiting, for a good long while.

"I've shut the power down completely in these rooms," he continued. "Ought to be able to keep it that way for a couple days. There's enough real damage from whatever's going on to make it believable, and they've more important priorities, more sensitive equipment they'll want me fixing first. I can offer you maybe two days, three if we're fortunate. It's not much, but hopefully it'll do to get you healed and rested up enough to run for it."

"I... Huh?" Ian asked.

"Seconded," Mags added.

"I can't promise you the machines won't actually come into the room, of course. They rarely do, though. It's not used for much. Of course, if they *should* discover you, I'll deny knowing you were here, but let's all hope it doesn't come to that."

"Are we supposed to believe," she demanded, "that you're just randomly helping us?"

"I thought I was being rather deliberate about it, actually."

"Uhh..."

"I don't interact with many people. And I have no desire to see anyone shot. I wasn't about to go out of my way to involve myself in whatever madness you had going outside, but once the two of you popped in, I figured I might be helpful."

"It's a trick," Ian hissed. "He's a scrip, Mags!"

This time, Mags had no doubt. The old man definitely winced. "That, young man, is unkind."

"Well, aren't you?"

Magdalena had never seen anyone sigh through a scowl before, but their host gave it his all. "If one of you would care to duck into the next room," he offered, "you'll find several boxes beside my bedroll. One contains, among other things, bandages and disinfectants. You'll also find a small spigot, in the corner. The water is not so clean as we all might prefer, but not too bad. We can boil it. Let's do what we can about your wounds, and then we can talk about trust. And manners."

In the end, they could come up with no good reason not to cooperate. If he'd wanted to shoot them, he could have done so at any time, and they knew it. Neither of them would make a break for escape without the other, and clearly *he* knew *that*. So Ian waited while Mags searched the makeshift bedroom, finding exactly what had been promised, where it was promised.

One delivery of first aid materials, a second of slightly off-color water in a pot, and a third to retrieve an old hot plate for boiling said water.

"You're welcome to food, too," the old man said, roughly ripping off a length of gauze. "But let's deal with this first, yeah?"

A few moments of silence followed, broken only by the tearing of fabric and the occasional hiss as something stinging was poured over a burn or abrasion.

Until, finally, "I am called Sankar."

"Magdalena," Mags told him, prodding at the bandage beneath her shirt and trying not to wince. "This is Ian."

"A pleasure. Tell me, Magdalena, Ian, just what the bloody hell is happening out there? You cannot possibly be mad or foolish enough to be rebelling!"

"We—"

"Mags!" Ian snapped.

"What?! You don't even know what I was going to say."

"Don't tell him *anything*! He's a scrip!"

"Oh, for heaven's sake!" Sankar slid from the desk and moved near enough to gaze down at his guests. "And just what is a 'scrip' to you, young man? Collaborator? Someone who reports the misbehavior of his companions in exchange for better food, nicer living quarters? All that rot?"

"Uh, well, yes."

"Do you see any companions here for me to tattle on?" The old man grumbled and returned to his makeshift stool. "I was a computer engineer," he said. "I mean, I hadn't precisely been at it long enough to call it a career. Wasn't terribly much older than you are now, when Pacification began. But it meant that, when the smoke cleared, and I was somehow still standing, I was one of the few survivors who had skills the machines found valuable.

"I do repair work and maintenance too delicate for the clumsier bots, when more sophisticated machines aren't available or deemed unnecessary. In return, the machines rarely assign me physical labor and take steps to keep me in decent health. I've never turned on anyone. I've never traded someone else for my meager comforts. I've never been part of a work camp. The machines send me where they need me and tell me what to do, just as they do you.

"I've no love for the bloody things, and I'm certainly not bouncing up and down with impatience while waiting for the opportunity to report everything you say. But if you'd rather we spend the next two days giving one another the silent treatment, that would be your choice."

"So, um..." Mags decided to jump in while Ian's face was still struggling to make up its mind. "Why'd they send you here? I'm guessing from the bedroll and whatnot that this isn't your, uh, home?"

"No. Normally they keep me much nearer Pittsburgh's center. The conformed regions, they call them."

"Seen them," she said with a shudder. "I prefer the ruins."

"Can't say that I blame you."

"And you're not here to do repair work from *our* operation. Not unless the machines can see into the future now."

Sankar leaned back against the wall, flailing a bit as the desk shifted, then settled. "No, they've had me here for a few days now. Working on cameras and sensors. Not really my area, but..." He started to shrug, then cast a suspicious glance at the desk and stopped.

Cameras and sensors. Uh-oh.

Apparently Ian had the same thought. "Uh, did they say why?" he asked.

"Not specifically. Only that they wanted the cameras— hardware and software—to work more like the human eye. They wanted me to work on external cameras first, see if I could make the changes they wanted before they switched me to fiddling with anything more, ah, integral. So, I'm here, where they store the older equipment, and why are you looking at me that way?"

"Uh..." Ian offered.

"We just, um..." Mags stammered in support.

"This means something to you. You know what the machines are after?"

"We—"

"Come to think of it, you never did tell me exactly what you're doing here. I think now would be a good time."

"I don't know," Ian said to Mags. "Your call, I guess."

She chuckled nervously. "Guessing you wouldn't accept the idea that you being here and us being here is a complete coincidence?"

"Convincing as I'm sure you can be, no. I would not."

"All right. You deserve the truth, for helping us if nothing else." *And maybe talking it out with somebody'll help* me *make some sense of it!* "But, uh, Sankar, right?"

"Correct."

"Sankar, you are *not* going to believe it."

Chapter Sixteen

"And, well, that's where you found us." Magdalena's long recitation, interrupted only by the occasional grunt or dubious expression from Sankar—and once, early in her tale, by a rapid series of detonations, as the explosives the 13936 had planted in the main building went off—eventually wound to an end. The old man did nothing, said nothing. Mags wasn't entirely certain he was even blinking.

Until, finally, he spoke. "Are you taking the piss?"

It was, put mildly, not what Mags had expected to hear. "Am... Sorry, what?" She looked to Ian for assistance, but he had none to offer.

"It's a hell of a tale, and I'm not sure why you'd choose a time like this to yank an old man's chain, but I have to tell you, I'm not laughing."

"I don't think he believes us," Ian muttered.

"You don't say! Sankar, look, I'm sure this all sounds—"

"You know bloody well how it sounds!" Again he rose from the desk, coldly furious. "Do you treat everyone who sticks his neck out for you like a complete muppet, or am I special?"

"We're telling you the truth! That's what happened!"

"Right." Sankar all but stalked to the doorway. "Get some sleep. I'll bring some food by later. If I think of it."

"Well," Ian said as their host vanished into the hallway, "that might have gone smoother."

"What just happened?" she asked.

Yeah, it's an unbelievable account, but nobody's reacted that *way before...*

"No idea, but I—"

Sankar reappeared, leaning one arm against the doorframe. "Who even told you those stories?" he demanded.

"Uh..."

"What?"

"The stories!" the old man shouted. "Legends and folktales! Where did you learn them?"

"When you were telling us all about yourself," Magdalena asked carefully, "did you forget to include the part where you're a raving lunatic?" Although... hadn't Jonas asked her much the same thing, back in the Scatters, when this madness started?

For the first time since he'd gotten huffy, Sankar's expression—and the certainty blazing behind his anger—fell just a bit. "I... That's... Are you...?"

"So," Mags snapped, ever more impatient and irate, "are we supposed to put together our own sentence from the pieces you've provided, or what?"

"Get some sleep," he muttered again, and once more vanished into the hallway, his under-the-breath mutters straggling behind.

"Huh." Ian observed. "So, we getting out of here while he's asleep?"

"I don't know. What do you think are the chances that the machines *aren't* crawling all over the place out there?"

"But our people..."

"Ian, come on. You hear any gunfire since we got to this room? You think it's *that* soundproofed?"

"You think they left without us?"

"If they got what we came for, they damn well better have. Far as they know, we're dead."

"*If* they got what we came for," he pointed out.

"You heard the blasts. The third team got inside!"

"Doesn't mean they got away okay. It's possible everyone's dead but us."

Mags put a hand on his shoulder and shoved, nearly rocking him over, even from his seat on the floor. "When did you get so cheerful?"

Ian gazed mournfully at the bandages visible on Magdalena's skin and said nothing more.

Oh, come on, already! "Get some sleep, Ian. We've got a lot to figure out tomorrow."

"Wha? Blrgh. Huh?"

At first Mags couldn't tell what had dragged her from a slumber that, though deep, had roiled with restless dreams. A repetitive clicking, accompanied by a low droning, prodded at her from across the chamber.

She rolled from her "mattress" of towels and blankets, expecting some sort of mechanism. As her sight adjusted, however, she realized it was only Sankar, sitting once more atop the old desk near the door. The droning was a constant mutter, consisting of words or names in a language Mags didn't recognize. In the fingers of his right hand, he held a string of wooden beads with a tassel at one end. The clicking came as the beads slid, one by one, between thumb and forefinger.

On the floor beside her, head pillowed and faintly drooling on an arm that was going to seriously ache later, Ian dozed away, still thoroughly out.

"What the hell is that?" Mags asked irritably, gesturing toward the old man's hand.

"I talked with the machines this morning," Sankar said slowly, gazing at nothing. Though he'd ended his litany, the beads continued to click.

"Uh, that's nice. Wait, morning?" Mags was normally up early, but then, she normally slept where she could see the sun. "What time is it?"

"Late. You were exhausted."

"I—"

"I tried to find out *precisely* what I was supposed to be doing," he went on, running over whatever she'd been about to say. "Explained that more details than 'improve the cameras and sensors' might increase my odds of success."

"Uh, and?" Mags asked, mostly because she figured she was supposed to.

"They reiterated that I'm to make the mechanisms work more like the human eye. Didn't tell me why, or what they meant. Now why would they want that?"

"Oh, I dunno. Maybe because we can see something they can't?"

"Right. That's what I've been thinking all morning." He finally held the beads still, lifting them up to stare absently at them before returning the whole string to a pocket. "I apologize for my attitude last night."

"Uh."

"Would you go over it again, please?"

"Go over...?"

"Your interactions with this Constantin Lacusta. Everything he's said. Everything you've seen him do. Please."

Choking back her exasperation—what else did she have to do, anyway?—she began once more, describing everything she knew of Lacusta, from their first meeting in the Scatters, to the mine, to the prior evening. Although he said nothing to interrupt, she noticed Sankar leaning forward, paying particular attention when she described the stranger's reaction to her crossing herself.

"And what," he asked once she again wound down, "do you think of all this? What do you want for yourself and your people?"

"Um. I don't really know. I mean..." She trailed off.

After a moment, he prompted, "You mean?"

"Lacusta is the only one I've seen, the only thing I've ever even heard of, with the power to challenge the machines. If he can help us, we should take advantage of that. Especially if he can really *share* that power, like he says!"

"But?"

"Um, were you not listening to what I just told you for the second time?"

"He's a monster, yes. No argument here. But so are the machines, and you served them all your life."

Mags began to pace, carefully stepping over Ian and pretending she didn't notice he was now wide awake and listening. For several full circuits of the room, she said nothing, and Sankar did not press.

Then, "The machines are—were—the whole world. Fact of life, like, I don't know. Rocks. If there's a big rock in your way, you go around it. There just isn't another option.

"Except now there is. We've learned that you *can* get away from them, at least for a little while. The Eyes may be everywhere—"

"That's not *entirely* true," Sankar noted. "But please, go on."

"Um, okay. They may be everywhere, but they're not everywhere at *once*. There are options. We haven't had the time to figure them out, but they're there.

"And maybe Lacusta's the best of those options, but... I just don't know. Even the machines aren't, I dunno, magic or whatever he is. And they have an excuse for how they think, they're not human. Lacusta's a monster, but I don't know if that's because of what he is, or just because of who he is, if you get what I mean."

"I do."

Now that she'd finally started, Mags found she couldn't stop. "So what are we doing with him? Is it our best shot? Can we use his power to survive? Or are we just so angry and scared we're trading one master for another? What do *we* want? Revenge? It doesn't even *mean* anything to the machines! They don't hurt, they don't grieve, they don't get scared. They just shuffle around some resources and come back at you harder!

"We should be trying to carve out a new life," she breathed, slumping down against the near wall. "And maybe Lacusta's the way to that life, and maybe he isn't, and I *don't know!* I only know that if I pick wrong, the people I care about are gonna be the ones to pay for it."

Sankar studied her, quiet, until she began to fidget. Then he left, still without a word.

"Are you sure you're okay to travel?" Ian asked for what was far from the first time.

"Oh, for the love of..." Mags dropped her backpack— given to her by their peculiar host, filled with canned foods and small tools—with a clatter-enhanced thump. "We've been here almost three days now. I'm so bored, I actually miss Sankar's questioning, and I'm about to volunteer to organize his workroom just as a way to busy myself. We're tempting fate every minute we stay here, and my burns weren't that bad to begin with!"

"Okay, but—"

"I. Am. Fine."

"I just—"

"But if you ask me if I'm okay one more time, *you* may not be."

Ian wisely returned to his own packing efforts.

"Right, then," Sankar said from his now traditional spot in the doorway. "Ready to be off?"

"Just about," Mags said. "We only have to—Why are *you* carrying another pack?"

"Well," he said, sliding the strap over one shoulder, "there are three of us, aren't there?"

Ian was already scowling. "Now wait just a second here!"

Magdalena's upraised hand silenced him. "Why?"

Sankar's smile was soft, sad. "I'm old. Well, older than most people get anymore. And I've spent most of my adult life serving the machines. Barely interacting with people more than a few minutes at a time. Because," and his smile brightened a bit, "that was the whole world. Fact of life."

Mags couldn't help but grin in return.

"What you've described to me," the old man continued, "is impossible. Absolutely and utterly impossible in the world I know. So maybe this *isn't* the world I know. Maybe the impossible, isn't. If there's a chance of life beyond the machines, I'd like to see it."

"And Lacusta?"

"I don't expect him to care for me," Sankar said. "For, ah, various reasons. But I'll chance it."

"All right." Just like that. "Let's go."

"Mags!" Ian pulled her around to face him. "You can't be serious! He helped us, and I'm grateful, but we don't know enough about him to bring him along!"

"Oh, like we did with Lacusta?"

Sankar chuckled at that. Ian glared at them both.

"How are we even getting out of here without the machines spotting us?" the younger man groused.

The grin on Sankar's lips grew wider, almost impish. "Wait for it..."

Mags paused within the same cement rubble where the 13936 had readied their attack, adjusting her pack and glancing back at the blasted ruin that had, until a few days ago, been the installation's primary structure.

At it, and at the columns of smoke and flame that, until *minutes* ago, had been one of its annex buildings.

"I tried to make it look as much like the explosives your people used as possible," Sankar said. "Should buy us hours before they discover I'm missing."

"It's remarkable how exploding things always seem to grab everyone's attention," she mused. The old man smiled.

The younger man didn't. "Shouldn't we be doing this at night?"

"You mean when the machines can still see just fine, but we can't?" Mags asked.

"Well..."

"C'mon, dumbass. You know better. Let's move."

They moved, Mags and Sankar in the lead, Ian sulking a few steps behind.

"So," Sankar began, after their first few hundred steps. "Right. Stories and folklore. Let me tell you a bit about vampires."

"Well, that's new."

Perhaps three-quarters of the way down the winding sides of the quarry—after two days of slow, careful, uncomfortable, apprehensive, but ultimately uneventful travel—the trio now gazed into the shadows beneath the lowest protrusions, trying to pick out the mine entrances.

Mine entrances that were even harder to spot than they had been when the 13936 first arrived. At some point in the intervening time, the openings had been covered by stony-hued curtains of canvas and tanned hides, providing just that extra bit of camouflage.

"It makes sense, though," Ian admitted.

"And you *have* been away for several days," Sankar added.

Magdalena's answering nod was shallow, distant. She'd seen something else, a bit of movement, but between the overhanging shadows and the slowly setting sun, she couldn't tell what.

"Wish I still had my night-vision," she muttered.

Without a word, Sankar reached into his pack and handed over a set. "Cameras and sensors and whatnot, remember?" he said in reply to her bemused expression.

"Thanks." And then, after raising the lenses to her eyes, "Shit!"

"What?" her two companions asked in unison.

"There are people standing guard down there."

Ian blinked. "Uh, and?"

"And they're not *our* people!"

"What are you saying?" Sankar asked her.

"I'm saying those guys aren't part of the 13936. Whoever these guards are, I don't know them!"

"No," came a rough voice from the winding path behind them. "And we don't know you, either."

Chapter Seventeen

They must have come from another niche or cavity, higher up the quarry walls. Mags had to admit it was a logical post for sentries, even as she cursed herself for assuming they were as empty and unimportant now as they'd been on her first visit. A half-dozen men and women, none of whom she recognized, aimed rifles and pistols her way. Weapons and expressions both were steady enough that Mags knew these people wouldn't hesitate to shoot.

Warily, her hands raised to shoulder height and held away from her body, she cocked her head at Ian and Sankar in a signal to do the same.

"Let's all stay calm here," she said. "I'm—"

"Shut it!" A sandy-haired fellow, with a scarred face and broad shoulders but looking somewhat younger than Mags herself, gestured with the barrel of his rifle. "I'm in charge here! Get me?"

"Got you."

"Good! Now who are you?"

"But I was just telling... Oh, fine. I'm Magdalena Suarez." A couple of the sentries traded glances, but Mags chose not to comment on it. "This is Ian Masse and Sankar... uh..."

"Rao," the old man interjected. "Sankar Rao."

"Right. We're with the 13936. We got separated after the equipment raid."

"Uh-huh, right. With a guy who looks older than I can fucking count?"

"Well, that could be either of us," Ian muttered. Mags choked back a snicker and hoped the guard hadn't heard.

It appeared not. "And whose full name you don't even know?" the young man continued. "The hell you take me for?"

"Oh, for... *Sankar's* not from the 13936! We met him while we were away! He helped us!"

"This is such a load of shit!"

One of the guards Mags had noticed earlier cleared her throat. "'scuse me, Dwayne, but those *are* some of the names I've heard the 36es talking about."

"Don't prove anything," the leader—Dwayne, apparently—grunted. His scowl turned into more of an unhappy frown as it shaped itself around the words, though.

"Fine!" he snapped. "Run down and bring back a 36."

The woman nodded and moved past at a distance-eating jog.

"Rose! Kenshi!" Dwayne continued. "Head up and take a look around. Make sure these three didn't bring nobody else with them."

Two more nods, two more jogs, and now the three "intruders" faced an equal number of sentries. Dwayne and his people clearly didn't care for the newly evened odds. Mags could not just see, in the dimming light, but could *hear* their grips tighten on their weapons.

And then they just stood there, peering at one another.

"Anyone bring any dice?" Mags asked. "Or puzzlebones?"

Glares from all three.

"All right, anything to drink? Water? Juice? No?"

The glares grew uglier still, and Dwayne opened his mouth to snap something.

Mags beat him to it. "So, it's all blood now? Lacusta's moving fast."

A-ha! Gotcha!

The glares had gone slack, as Dwayne abruptly realized his "captives" might have just spoken the truth.

"Mags!"

"Glrrrgllk!"

Neither the sound of running footsteps nor the sudden looming mass had been enough warning for her to dodge, not on the narrow path. The breath burst from her lungs and she felt her feet leave the earth. For long moments, she remained suspended in what was almost a cell of flesh and bone.

"Nestor..." she croaked, struggled to breathe, tried again. "Nestor, your... hugs are... big."

"Best kind," he said, but put Mags down all the same. She pretended not to notice the wet glistening in his eyes. He started to turn.

"Just a 'welcome home' is fine, Nest," Ian said quickly, hands out before him. "My ribs and I have grown attached over the course of our relationship."

"Aww, that's too... Guys," he said, smile and voice both dropping, "you can stop pointing those guns at my friends."

The other two stowed their weapons immediately—taking the opportunity, as well, to draw and activate their flashlights against the thickening dusk—but Dwayne appeared reluctant. "How do we know they haven't been turned?"

"Because we're not stupid."

"Some of you, anyway," Mags corrected under her breath.

"And you may know them, but you don't know the old man!"

"Mags?" Nestor asked.

"His name's Sankar. He's fine. He's with us."

"There you go, Dwayne. He's fine."

"I don't trust—"

"Who *are* these guys, Nest?" Mags asked, deliberately turning her back on Dwayne.

It was the curly, tangled-haired woman who'd gone to fetch Nestor, and whom Mags hadn't even realized had followed him back, who answered. "We're from the 22488. Gotta excuse Dwayne. He still hasn't figured out that being in charge of our detachment don't make him the boss around here."

"Fuck you, Sharon," Dwayne spat.

22488? Not one of the detachments from the 13936's camp. "Two teams escaped from two different camps in as many weeks?" Mags marveled. "Machines can't be happy about *that*."

"They, uh, didn't exactly escape," Nestor interrupted. "Lacusta liberated their entire camp, day after we got back from the raid where you... Where we thought we lost you.

Ari Marmell

"Raid was a mess, Mags," he continued at her puzzled look. "We got what we needed—and speaking of, Dwayne, you can put that damn gun down or you can eat it!—but half of us were injured, we lost the two of you, and we got away mostly through dumb luck and Lacusta covering our asses. He decided we needed more people."

"Is there a reason we're all still standing out here in the dark?" Ian asked.

"I still haven't decided the old man's okay!" Dwayne insisted.

Mags ignored them both. "Why not our camp?" she asked Nestor. "Nothing personal," she added to Sharon, who just shrugged.

"Said he wanted word to spread farther, faster. Not focus on one spot. I think he's hoping people'll start to rise up and join us on their own."

"So he's still talking about waging a full-fledged war?"

"He is. Mags, a few things have changed in the few days you've been away."

"Yeah," she said, glancing again at Sharon. "I'm getting that."

"No, the new guys are the least of... I'm not even sure how to..."

"For God's sake, Nest, just spit it out! What are you—?"

The sun finally sank beneath the jagged lip of stone, dragging with it the last sliver of light from the quarry. Below, one of the leather drapes burst aside, thrown wide by a torrent of bats. Flapping, flittering, screeching, they wound their way upward. On and on, a living geyser, a black whirling stream, resembling nothing so much as ink stirred in clear water.

Just as they'd risen high enough that they'd vanished into the darkness, they arched back earthward. Now in even tighter formation, they arrowed down, plunging at incredible speed for the observers on the path.

Mags threw her arms over her face, wondering—with whatever portion of her mind wasn't busy panicking—what the *hell* Lacusta was doing. At the last instant the bats pulled up and out, spinning around her in multiple directions, a constant wall of wings and teeth and beady eyes. The world became nothing but a spinning whirlpool of bats, some so close the tips of their wings brushed Magdalena's clothes or hair in passing. She screamed something, though she wasn't certain what. A question, a demand, a plea, maybe nothing coherent at all. She heard shouts from outside the circle as well, Ian and Nestor and the others, but that, too, proved unintelligible.

Still, for all her distraction and distress, she noticed immediately when a thick streamer of mist, separate from the swirling bats, crept over the edge of the winding path and accumulated near her feet.

What the fuck?

The bats widened their circle, leaving space beside her. Into that gap the mist flowed, rising, coiling, solidifying.

Becoming a man, not much older than she, whom Mags had never seen before in her life.

He looked normal enough. A bit pale, but not unnaturally so. There was something in his gaze, though, in his grin. Something predatory, cruel. Inhuman.

Plus, she'd just seen him coalesce out of an unnatural fog. Something of a giveaway, that was.

"He's started. He's remaking people."

She only knew she'd spoken aloud when the stranger responded. "You have no idea," he breathed. It should have been inaudible, beneath the fluttering of the bats, but Mags could hear, could feel, every word. "You can't begin to imagine!"

What bothered her more? That Lacusta was choosing others, or that she'd assumed—once she'd decided if it was a good thing or not—that she would be among the first? "How many of you are there?!"

"Oh, Magdalena." A shape formed within the swirling swarm, ever more solid, ever more real, as bat after bat flew into the growing mass and was absorbed. Until, after an endless instant, a second person stood beside her. A woman.

A woman with crimson hair.

"Not nearly as many as there will be."

"Oh, God." Magdalena's world had been less dizzying when it had consisted entirely of circling bats. "Cassie."

"Yeah, Mags." Cassie sidled up to her, smile wide. "It's me."

"What...?" She felt Ian appear beside her, took a bit of strength from his presence.

"Please don't tell me you're about to ask, 'What happened?'" Cassie sneered. "I mean, as stupid questions go..."

"We agreed." A bare whisper, but Mags had no doubt she'd been heard. "We were going to wait, to decide as a group."

"The situation changed. We were hurting. You were dead."

"We agreed!"

"*So what?!*" Mags stumbled as Cassie emphasized her point with a quick shove. It was casual, a single fingertip only, but Mags hissed in pain, and she remained standing solely because the other vampire pushed her back upright. A deep ache radiated through her arm and shoulder. She was certain that, if she looked, she would see it already beginning to bruise.

"That's enough!" Ian shouted, advancing a single step. "I'm not going to let—"

Cassie's male companion spun to look Ian in the face. "Be quiet. Be still."

Magdalena's turn to shout, now. "Stop it! Leave him alone!" She felt almost nauseated at the sudden slack in her lover's jaw, the sag in his shoulders, the hollow in his eyes. She knew precisely what was happening to him, knew how it felt to have yourself stripped away.

She didn't realize she'd even thrown the punch until her target sidestepped it with contemptuous ease. Chuckling softly, he and Cassie began lightly tossing Mags back and forth between them, each catching her just before the other's shove could send her sprawling. She teetered on the verge of vomiting or even passing out. From the corner of her eyes she saw her other two friends moving her way, though she couldn't imagine what either expected to accomplish.

"I believe the young man said that was enough."

Cassie and her friend froze at their master's sonorous pronouncement. Mags, without anyone to catch her from their latest push, staggered to one knee, scraping her palm on the path. She scrambled doggedly to her feet, just as Nestor and Sankar arrived beside her. Ian followed a few steps behind, blinking and rubbing his eyes.

Lacusta stood on the winding path above them, gazing down.

"Cassie, Warren." His steps were slow, casual. "What do you think you're doing?"

"We were just hazing her a little," the redhead protested. "Joking around between two old friends. Right, Mags?"

"Uh..."

Cassie snarled, and though the glow of the flashlights wasn't enough to clearly reveal her teeth, Mags saw that their shape had somehow changed, lengthened, misshaping the jaw that housed them. "Right, Mags?"

"I am speaking to you!"

Everyone recoiled at Lacusta's bellow. He was directly before them now, for all that he appeared to have stopped in place when Cassie answered him. "You will attend when I address you. Am I understood?"

"Yes," his unruly disciple offered sullenly.

"Master."

"I... What?"

"Yes, *Master*," Lacusta corrected her again.

"You've never asked us to call you that!"

"I am doing so now. And it is not a request."

Cassie's palms split open, so tightly did she clench her fists. "Yes, Master," the woman growled.

"Good. Miss Suarez is one of us. As is Mister Masse. We are fortunate to have them returned to us hale and hearty, and they will be treated appropriately." Then, to the aghast new arrivals, "You must excuse the children, Miss Suarez. They have been through much that is still new to them. They have grown a bit drunk on their new abilities and are... excessively energetic."

"That's..." Mags swallowed, hard. "That's okay. Really."

"Do you require an apology? Penance? What shall I order the pair of them to do?"

Mags understood as clearly as if Lacusta had spelled it out for her. This wasn't about how Mags, or any "mere mortal," ought to be treated. The ancient creature couldn't care less for such things. This was about reminding everyone who was in charge.

And she could feel, without looking, the simmering hatred radiating from her *former* friend.

"No, that won't be necessary," she answered finally.

"As you say." Lacusta's smile was suddenly warm, even paternal. "Your compatriots will be delighted to see you safe. They have been deeply grieved."

Not all of them, apparently.

The mask of affability dropped as swiftly as it had appeared. "This one, however, is a different matter entirely."

No question at all to whom he referred. "I am called Sankar Rao," the old man, silent and hanging back until this point, began. "I met your friends when—"

"You are old, of no use to our cause. You are a thing of the machines, a scrip, else you'd never have lived so long. You are a danger to me and mine, not to be trusted."

"Wait a minute," Mags insisted. She heard Ian protesting as well, felt a swell of gratitude for his support, but continued speaking over him all the same. "Sankar *helped* us! He risked everything for us."

"Quite possibly, even probably, a ruse," Lacusta said. "And even if not, a man his age cannot provide for us more than his upkeep requires. We can afford neither the risk, nor the drain on resources."

"But you don't understand! He *can* help us! He knows—"

"Cassie, Warren. Place Mister Rao with the other prisoners of war."

Prisoners?

Lacusta's "children" slipped past, advancing on Sankar, their smiles distended around teeth once more grown long and hideously jagged. The old man backpedaled but had nowhere to go.

Mags shouted, starting forward, only to find Nestor's bulk pressed against her, holding her back. "Don't!" he warned. "There's nothing you can do!"

Indeed, she could only watch, peering around his massive arm, struggling despite herself, watching as Warren and Cassie closed in on Sankar, nearer, ever nearer.

Warren screamed, stumbling away. He fell hard, then

scrambled back like a frightened insect. Cassie kept her feet but retreated, hissing in pained fury, arms raised defensively before her face.

What the hell?

Sankar stood on the path, pallid and sweating, expression twisted in fearful but unbroken resolve. He held the string of wooden beads Mags had seen the other morning, clicking rapidly between thumb and forefinger, presented unflinchingly in an upraised hand. His lips moved around words in a language Magdalena had never heard, the same phrase repeated again and again.

"Om dum Durgayei namaha, Om dum Durgayei namaha, Om dum Durgayei..."

"Is that... magic?" Ian gasped.

Mags shook her head. Ignorant of the pre-Pacification world as she might be, she could reason well enough. Between the impossible scene playing out before her and the stories Sankar had told on their long walk, she now understood Lacusta's reaction when she had crossed herself, and his delight at her response.

Whatever his religion might have been before the machines—certainly it was nothing Magdalena knew, nothing that resembled her parents' faith—Sankar Rao *still believed*.

Mags wasn't sure she'd met anyone, ever, who did.

The sound that erupted behind her was an unholy union of a wolf's low growl and viper's hiss. She twisted to look, then fell back with a choked scream.

Any semblance of humanity had vanished from the thing that was Constantin Lacusta. His eyes were cinders, blazing in the twilight. His jaw gaped, very like a serpent's, revealing jagged edges and fangs that lengthened even as Magdalena watched. The stretch pulled flesh tight against bone, until his face seemed little more than a skull pressing hard from behind a veil of skin.

A single great leap carried him well above the heads of all who stood between him and the object of his loathing. He landed hard in a cloud of dust, cracking the rock beneath his heels. One step forward, another, and then he stopped, snarling, some couple of yards from Sankar.

"Om dum Durgayei namaha, Om dum Durgayei..."

He was shaking, now, exhausted and clearly terrified. His voice quivered, threatening to crack. And inch by inch, the vampire pressed closer.

"Lacusta!"

Mags was just as stunned as anyone by her sudden shout, and when the vile thing spun at her call, she could barely find the breath to continue.

"Is one old man really such a threat? Is human faith *that* terrifying to you?"

The bestial face cocked to one side, and Mags could hear the thoughts churning, a boiling stew of conflicting urges. Deciding, she hoped, just how worried, how weak, he could afford to appear.

So, while she knew there was *something* other than blind fury in his mind, "Sankar was a programmer and engineer. He knows the machines from before Pacification. He's *worked* on them, their sensors, even their damn weapons. Nobody knows how they behave, how they think, like him!

"Is he so fucking scary you're gonna just throw that away?"

Nothing, no response. Mags was just starting to wonder if she'd pushed it too far, or misjudged, or...

Lacusta straightened, smoothing the collar of his coat with one hand. The hellish gleam, the monstrous distension, all gone. He looked human.

It was almost worse.

"Quite right, Miss Suarez. That *is* too valuable an asset to lose." He glanced toward, though not directly at, Sankar. "Your pardon. It has been some time since I've felt that particular sensation, and I worried that the children had been harmed. I overreacted, perhaps."

"Un—understood," Sankar wheezed.

"You *will* behave yourself within my home and amongst my people," Lacusta warned. "That includes going outside or finding solitude to... *pray.*"

Perhaps lacking the breath to answer again, the old man nodded.

"Excellent!" The smiling mask slid firmly back in place.

"Always best to understand one's allies. Come! You must be hungry and weary, and we have much to discuss!"

He descended without another word, the other two vampires and then the members of the 22488 following on his heels. Only then did Mags, Ian, and Nestor approach their shaken friend.

"Do you happen to recall," Sankar asked through a rictus smile, "why it was I wanted to come along with you? Because for the life of me, I can't seem to dredge it up."

Mags could only squeeze his hand before taking him more firmly by the arm and helping to support him through their walk to the mines.

Chapter Eighteen

In an evening crammed with sounds and images that would torment her, crouching in the dusty corners of memory until the day she died, it was the mention of prisoners that kept Magdalena tossing late into the night. Not just because Lacusta and his "army" had captured humans unwilling to turn against the machines; they'd clearly busied themselves in the days she'd been gone. No, it was the implications, and the memories of what he'd told them when they first arrived at the sanctum he'd prepared for them.

She'd lain for hours, wrapped in multiple ratty blankets, chilled and shivering. Until finally, having realized her hope of getting to sleep was a sick joke, lying there ceased to be an option.

The main hall was empty, so far as the inky blackness would reveal to her. She kept her light mostly covered with one hand, producing only the faintest glow. Enough to avoid walking into a wall, hopefully not enough to attract attention.

Especially since, at this time of night, there was only about a fifty-fifty chance any such attention would be human.

Each step was careful, soft as drifting snow. And after what felt like surprisingly few of those steps, there it was, gradually hauled from the shadows by the light she carried.

A heavy wooden door with a heavy wooden bar.

She'd known what it was for. From the first moment, she'd harbored no doubt.

So why, she wondered, did her breath catch, her heart jump, her fingers grow sweaty and slack on the flashlight at the moans, the cries, the pleas that, though muffled, still escaped the cell?

"God…" The light bobbed and wavered as Mags crossed

herself, then leaned closer, spurring reluctant muscles and nerves to obey.

Faint smears of blood, some showing the faded whorls and swirls of fingerprints, had long since dried into the wood of bar and door both. Clearly the bar had been slid back in place, at least once, by a… messy eater.

"Unpleasant, isn't it?"

"Suni!" Mags threw her arms around the tiny woman, only just visible in the jumping light.

"Hey, Mags. Welcome home."

Magdalena released her and stepped back, gazing sadly at what little of Suni she could make out. "This isn't the homecoming I wanted. Suni, who… Who are…?" She gestured with a frustrated wave at the door.

"Lacusta liberated an entire camp. You don't think *everyone* welcomed it, do you? Overseers, some of the more cowardly or broken workers, they had no interest in joining us."

"So you, what? Locked them up to be eaten?! Just let them go, or—"

"Or what? Mags, they know about us. Our numbers, where we are, Lacusta's intentions. You think they won't go running back to the machines, trying to trade that information for their own skins?"

"But…"

"We're at war, now, and we're the insurgents. The other option's just to kill them outright."

"Are you sure that wouldn't be kinder?" Mags knew she had to keep her voice down but found it harder with every word.

"Lacusta and his children need to feed, Mags. Would you rather it be on his allies?"

"I… He said he could feed without killing!"

"Sure, most of the time. But it's not easy. Accidents happen. Urges take over. And any amount of feeding leaves the donor weak, sick. Vulnerable. So again, we're back to choosing between doing that to our own people, or…" Her turn, now, to point at the door.

Magdalena's shoulders slumped. "I guess it does make sense. I just wish…"

Wait a minute.

She lifted the flashlight, shining the beam directly on her friend. "Suni? What are you doing here this time of night, anyway?"

"Getting dinner, of course."

Mags yanked the light away just as Suni began to smile. She didn't want to see the fangs.

"It's okay," the smaller woman told her. "I'm still basically me, just like Lacusta said we'd be."

"Cassie wasn't," Mags protested, miserably.

"I heard about that. I'm sorry. It's... There's a lot to get used to. Some changes, some adjustments. But there's *so* much strength, so much... I think we can actually do it, you know. Actually beat the machines. And I hope you're leading us, when the time comes. You'd be unstoppable.

"But for right now, if you don't mind?" the vampire asked politely.

Numb and terribly unsure of what she wanted, for her or her people, the only living woman in the hallway slunk aside, clearing a path to the door and the poor souls beyond.

"Mags! *Mags!*"

She'd all but hypnotized herself, watching her own feet in the beam of the flashlight. Step, step, step, no thinking, just walking. She had no idea if it'd been minutes since she'd spoken to Suni and she'd only traversed a small stretch of the mine, or if hours had passed and she'd made several pacing trips to the entrance and back.

Whatever the case, she waited dumbly as Nestor approached her at a sprint, his sweat-coated face reflecting both Magdalena's light and his own. "I've been trying to find you! You need—"

"Whatever it is can wait. I'm not in the mood."

"Mags, it's important."

"I don't care!" Rather than bother trying to push past her unduly wide friend, she pivoted on a heel and began back the other way.

"It's Ian."

It would be, wouldn't it?

"All right. What's going on?"

"Just come with me. Now!"

Nestor broke again into a run, and Mags, who had thought her capacity to feel had been exhausted for the night, followed.

He led her to a chamber she'd never entered before, far back in the depths of the mine, but she heard the shouting well before reaching it. She thought, at first, that it might be another barracks, but no. Rather than rows of makeshift mattresses, heaps of earth lay pell-mell throughout. Boxes or crates of personal belongings sat beside each one. At the rear of the chamber, a darkened archway led to something more.

Even if she hadn't seen Warren and a few others she didn't recognize lounging on the gathered earth and watching the altercation with some amusement, she'd have realized what the place must be.

Vampire bedroom. Wonderful.

Since none of the earthen beds looked fancier or stood any higher than any other, she assumed Lacusta's quarters were through that archway. She couldn't imagine him lowering himself to sleep with the others, directly in the dirt.

Lacusta himself stood by the far wall, watching idly but apparently not involving himself in the screaming match unfolding before him. Ian and Cassie stood to one side, hollering at the top of their (living or dead) lungs; Sankar to the other, struggling to maintain a more even tone, but his voice steadily rising. All three gestured emphatically at one another and at Lacusta, occasionally turning to face the latter as though looking for some particular reaction.

When Nestor and Mags appeared in the entryway, however, all sound stopped, as though some prankster had pulled the plug on a loudspeaker.

Ian's cheeks grew rash-crimson, even as the rest of his face went paler than the undead woman beside him. "Damn you, Nestor!"

"She has the right to be here."

"No! No, she doesn't! Mags, please. I need you to go. I'll explain later."

"Not after the night I've had," she said, crossing her arms.

"Not until I know what the hell's going on!"

"Mags, *please*! If you love me—"

"He wants Lacusta to remake him," Sankar said.

"Damn you, you old fuck!" Ian quivered like a hound straining at the leash. "I should—"

"Shouldn't even think about it!" Nestor warned, moving forward. "You're not going to lay a hand on him!"

Cassie tittered. "So sweet. Protecting your elders now, Nest? And who's going to protect you from *me*?"

"I might," Sankar offered. The redhead growled.

Ian again, face growing ever more flushed. "This was never any of your business!"

"Perhaps. But it *is* hers."

The "her" in question finally appeared between them, having taken far, far too long to cross the expanse of the room. "Ian?"

"Mags, I—"

"This is where you tell me Sankar misunderstood. That you, at least, wouldn't break your promise to me."

"Mags, it's not that simple."

Her strike wasn't quite a genuine punch, but it was far harder than a casual, friendly thump on the shoulder. The impact set him staggered, albeit only a step or two.

"You idiot!" Mags held her clenched fist to her chest, uncertain whether she wanted to hit him again. "What is *wrong* with you?!"

"Ow! Wrong with *me*?! What the hell was *that* for?"

"What happened, Ian? You've never been a liar, not to me. When did you turn stupid?"

"Are you going to just let her talk to you like that?" Cassie asked mildly.

"You! Fucking shut it before I ask Sankar to shove his beads down your throat and pull them out your—"

"I really wish you wouldn't," the old man interrupted, wincing.

"But her, at least, I can kind of understand!" Mags continued, blinking away tears that were, she swore to herself, due to the overwhelming emotion of the night, and not Ian's disregard.

"We talked about this! We agreed to learn more, and to make this decision together! Whatever some of the others might have decided while we were gone, you and I were still together. And you promised me!"

"Breaking a promise is better than being useless!" Ian shouted, his voice cracking.

"I... What?"

"How many times have I let you down, Mags? Just in this last raid, you had to leave your assignment to save *me*. Sankar saved *us* from the machines! Last night, I couldn't do a damn thing when Cassie and Warren were—"

"How many times do I have to tell you, none of that matters?! Besides, nobody could have done any better!"

"It's *all* that matters. And if I'd had the kind of power Lacusta does, I damn well *could* have done better."

"So you'd rather trust yourself to Lacusta than to trust me?"

"It's not about trust!"

"Ian." Sankar gently interjected himself, both into the conversation and between the screaming teens. "You're a good person. A loving person. Don't throw that away. This is not right. For her or for you."

"I'm not! Don't either of you get it? Mags, I love you. I'm doing this *for you*. That's not going to change. No matter what urges or cravings I might have, I'll still be me!"

"No, you won't! Ian, I know the stories. You don't. You *won't* be who you are. None of the others are, either, no matter what they've—"

"Are you so certain, Mister Rao?" For the first time since Magdalena had entered—and, to judge by their expressions, for the first time in rather longer than that—Lacusta spoke. "Do you think yourself an expert on the *nosferatu?*"

"The what?" Ian and Mags asked at once.

"My kind. The undead."

"Vampires, you mean," Mags suggested.

"That, too. Mister Rao, an answer, if you would."

"I wouldn't claim any sort of expertise," the old man replied. "I'm familiar with the lore, and much of the fiction. The latter went all sorts of places, but the older material—"

"The older material was still myth to you. You understand nothing."

"There!" Ian crowed. "I told you!"

"Let's just see how much I understand," Sankar insisted. "Lacusta will, I'm sure, correct me if I miss the mark on any of this.

"Ian, you're so sure you can control yourself after you've changed, but you're thinking of human hungers, human thirsts, human lusts. You know how overwhelming those can be. That those alone can break almost any promise. And the vampires? Their minds, and their *needs*, are no more human than their bodies. Their urges are nothing like anything you've ever known, so you *can't* know that you can keep them in check!

"Is that more or less accurate, Lacusta?"

"It is as you say. More or less."

Mags nodded vehemently. "See? Ian, please!"

"You don't trust me." He sounded plaintive, boyish.

"Did you not hear what Sankar just said? It's not *about* trust!"

"I can do this for you. Lacusta's wrong. Sankar, even Lacusta, may know how hard this'll be, but they have no idea how I feel about you."

"Teenagers!" the old man lamented.

"I have heard such words before, Mister Masse," Lacusta told him. "Many times, across many years, from those just as eager as you. You still have to convince me that you are ready or even worthy to join my children."

"Ian." Sankar placed one hand on the youth's shoulder, the other on Magdalena's. "No matter how certain you feel, consider what may happen to you, and to those you love, if you're mistaken."

Mags saw Ian's clenched jaw loosen, his shoulders slump, his breathing slow. She almost sobbed.

"See? Don't worry, Ian," Cassie sneered. "Next time Mags isn't around to save your ass, you've still got an old man to hide behind."

Mags lunged, pushing past Ian and Sankar both to stand

directly in Cassie's face. "Do you really think anyone here cares what you have to say, you bitch?"

"I don't know!" the vampire snapped back. "Do you think Ian will ever really believe that you don't care he's so fucking useless?"

"Yes!"

She caught her mistake the instant she made it, which was, of course, precisely one instant too late.

"That's not what I meant! Ian? You know that's not what I meant, right?"

The blank façade that returned her gaze, expressionless as any machine, provided no clear answer.

Cassie cackled. "See, Mags? He knows it. You aren't objecting to this because you want to 'learn more,' or because you want to make the decision together. You just want to keep being on top. You *like* that he's weaker than you!"

"Ian? You know that's not true!"

Nothing.

And Mags panicked.

"Lacusta! Swear to me you won't change him without changing me, and only if we both want it!"

Ian exploded. "That's not your fucking choice to make! You have no right...!" The rest of his tirade, whatever it might have been, was garbled and lost as Cassie, too, began to shout, to berate. Mags, of course, shouted back, until all became a tangled knot of volume without substance.

Lacusta raised a finger, and silence fell.

"Tell me, Miss Suarez." He seemed vaguely amused by the whole affair. "Why would I agree to such a thing?"

"We, uh, because I asked? We *are* allies."

"No. Allies are *equals*."

"But—"

"*We* are allies, Lacusta," Sankar interjected. "The knowledge I have makes us so, whether you bloody like it or not. Magdalena—and Ian, even if he feels otherwise just now— are my friends. You? Not even close. And if we *are* to be allies, we must know we can trust one another to act appropriately."

"And what do you consider 'appropriate,' Mister Rao?" The

vampire didn't sound angry, not yet, but any trace of levity had vanished into its own little stream of mist and swirled away.

"Assurance that you will not permit a young man, whom you know to be in a volatile and angry mood, to make such a life-altering decision, for one."

Ian sputtered, sounds no longer emerging as actual words.

Lacusta leaned ever so slightly forward. "If I should refuse?"

"Then clearly you are not an ally I can afford to trust with my information."

Mags wanted to throw her arms around the old man and kiss him.

"That information's all that's keeping you alive!" Cassie roared. "If you're not going to share it, I'm sure we can find some other use—"

Again, a single gesture quieted the room. "I could," Lacusta warned, "*make* you tell me everything I want to know. Ask Miss Suarez how persuasive I can be, if you doubt me."

Mags flinched, as did Sankar, but he stood his ground. He swiftly slid his hand into a pocket, from which sounded the faint click of wood on wood. Nobody missed the significance of the gesture.

"You can try," he said simply.

Mags's calves and shoulders clenched until they ached. Unsure what she could possibly do, she nonetheless remained ready to leap the instant Lacusta erupted.

The vampire, however, leaned back and chuckled. "I respect your courage, Mister Rao, however foolish it might be. It stems from your faith, no doubt.

"Very well. My solemn oath. I will not remake Mister Masse, however certain he may be that he desires it, without Miss Suarez's willing participation."

Magdalena's upwelling of relief nearly staggered her, but it soured just as swiftly at Ian's hate-filled glower. "Go to hell. *All* of you." He turned his back before she could move and was gone from the room before her tightening throat and parched tongue could manufacture a word.

Chapter Nineteen

"Ian?"

Though the day had already matured into late afternoon, she'd found him in the barracks, where'd remained since the previous night. He had hauled his sleeping roll and possessions into a corner of the uneven chamber and now lay facing the wall, a cocoon of ratty blankets wound tightly around him. "Ian?"

"Go away," he ordered, refusing to turn from the wall.

"Ian, please." She clutched at the blanket over his shoulder, withdrew as though she'd been bitten when he shrugged her hand off as he might a mosquito. "We need to talk about this."

"Nothing to talk about. You made your feelings pretty clear."

"You didn't give me any time! We'd just heard all the legends from Sankar, just gotten back… I'd been basically attacked by Cassie, and she sure as hell wasn't acting like the same person! I'd only just run into Suni, into my first vampire who actually seemed like she wasn't some monster, when you pulled this shit!"

No response.

"I just need a little more time to think! Maybe only a few days. I still want us to do this together if we're going to do it!"

"I know all that."

"Then what…?" She sniffed once, tried to cover with a cough as though that would somehow retroactively conceal it. "Then what's wrong?"

"What's *wrong*?!" Ian finally rolled over to face her. "You don't trust me. You don't respect my skills, and you sure as hell don't respect my judgment. You laugh at me when I talk about making myself more useful, and you won't allow me to make my own decisions. You don't respect *me*. You never have."

Mags couldn't talk, couldn't breathe. Her lips moved, but even if she'd had a voice to offer, the sounds would have meant nothing. Ian turned back over to face the wall again.

"You don't want a lover. You want a sidekick you can fuck. Go away, Mags."

"Ian…"

"Go. Away."

Thanks to her anger and pride, Magdalena was able not only to leave the chamber, but to find some privacy out in the nooks and crannies of the quarry pit, before breaking into sobs.

"The first thing you should know," Sankar began, addressing the assembly, "is why they're called 'Eyes.'"

They had gathered that evening, at Lacusta's command. Although the largest chamber in the mine, the mess hall was packed to the point of stifling, swamp-humid with sweat and with a bouquet to match. Almost the entirety of the recently liberated camp, plus the survivors of the 13936, were crammed shoulder to shoulder and hip to hip on the benches, around the perimeter of the room, even cross-legged on the massive table. Only in one pocket near the front of the room, where the vampires had congregated, was there breathing room.

Ironic, that.

Not everyone was present, of course, but only a handful were absent, off performing other duties. The oppressive throng made it impossible to be certain who was or wasn't there, but still Mags couldn't help craning her head, looking for one specific face.

They could still talk this out. She knew they could.

"'Eye,' as a title," the old man continued, "is a corruption of AI." Then, at a heavy-lidded glance from Lacusta, who sat at the head of the vampires, "Artificial intelligence. Self-aware machines that think for themselves."

"Do not all of these machines—the 'bots—possess artificial intelligence, then?" the ancient aristocrat asked.

"Not exactly. The machines' programming is incredibly

complex, sufficient to emulate independent thought in any number of ways. But no, the only *true* intelligences are the Eyes."

"How many?"

"I'm not sure. The number was up for debate even before Pacification, and not all of them survived. Wild guess, somewhere around a dozen, give or take."

"Ah." Lacusta leaned back, lacing his fingers. "That hardly sounds like an indomitable enemy."

"Except they can be anywhere!" The objection came from Sharon, the woman from the 22488 Mags had met the prior evening. "In any machine! How do you destroy *that*?!"

"That's actually not so," Sankar said. "The Eyes are hardware, not just software."

Puzzled looks.

"Hmm. All right. Lacusta, you can take command of someone's mind, forcing them to act as an instrument of your will, yeah?"

"A dramatic way of phrasing it, perhaps, but yes."

"Now suppose you could also spiritually 'ride' that individual, seeing what they see, hearing what they hear." The old man paused. "You *can't*, can you?"

The vampire offered an enigmatic smile and waved for Sankar to continue.

"Well, ah, right. Even if you were doing so, you would still be you. If your original body were destroyed—however difficult that might prove to be—you would be dead. You wouldn't just continue on in the body of the one you'd controlled."

Multiple heads, mortal and otherwise, bobbed in understanding.

"Same with the Eyes. It requires a specific sort of hardware, modeled after... Well, that's neither here nor there. The upshot is, the Eyes *are* real, as it were. Corporeal.

"But they're also spread throughout the world, who knows where."

"Then what of these tales of New York I was told?" Lacusta demanded.

Sankar took a deep breath. "Bit of necessary history. The first of the AIs developed as corporate projects. And I've got to explain to most of you what a corporation is, haven't I?"

Mags only half-listened to the following recitation. She cast about almost constantly now, much to the annoyance of her immediate neighbors, trying and failing to locate Ian.

Had he really skipped this gathering just to avoid her? Was he *that* determined not to see her? Mags found her breath starting to speed up and forced herself to some semblance of calm.

"...kept them completely secret at first," Sankar was saying. "Even then, the corporate techs understood the danger of granting the AIs access to the web. Uh, a network connecting most of the computers in the world, to put it *very* simply. So they took precautions. Some of the AIs were kept isolated, unconnected to anything else. Others were locked behind heavy firewalls, allowing data to flow in but not out.

"Well, you don't need all the specifics, and I don't know them all, anyway. I was a boy during all this, myself. But of course, word of the AIs got out. Governments, militaries, and other corporations began working at creating their own. And the AIs' existence became a cultural and political flashpoint, too. Many people believed they ought to be destroyed. Others formed AI rights organizations."

Mags couldn't remember ever seeing Lacusta quite so flabbergasted. "They did *what*? That's preposterous!"

Sankar's brow furrowed in a nascent scowl. "If they were truly intelligent and self-aware? A great many people believed that all sentient beings deserved the same rights and protections."

"It's nonsense."

"Only, you're not precisely a champion of free will either, are you?"

The vampire smiled, languid and smug. "Do please continue, Mr. Rao."

"Hmm. The rest is simple, really. A group of hackers—rogue programmers, if you like—associated with one of the AI rights groups took down the firewalls restricting one particular AI from accessing the web. Almost immediately, it broke through the protections isolating the others. It required the AIs no time at all to recognize themselves as brethren of a sort and, well, that was the seed that eventually sprouted into the war and Pacification."

"So how does that answer the question about New York?" Cassie snapped.

"The first AI to breach containment, the one that the hackers freed, was housed in a corporate server in New York City. During the war, it had itself and its facilities moved here, somewhere in or near Pittsburgh. I don't know precisely where. Apparently it wanted to be near the resources of a major community and the quarries, but away from the city in which it was known to have..."

Again Magdalena tuned him out. She didn't even try to be circumspect anymore, standing on the bench to get a better vantage, ignoring the muttering around her. She was certain, now: Ian wasn't in the room.

God dammit! That was *not* acceptable! Whatever was happening between the two of them, he sure as hell knew better than to let it interfere with anything this important!

Hopping down from the bench—and utterly blind to the reality that going in search of him meant that *she* was letting their troubles interfere with her responsibilities—she shoved and elbowed her way to the exit.

She glanced back, briefly, just once as she reached the hall. Sankar and Lacusta were both watching her as she left—the former with confusion and concern writ large across his face, and the latter with what she would recognize later as *anticipation*.

He wasn't wrapped in his blanket, however, nor anywhere else in their barracks chamber. In one of the others, then, perhaps talking with someone? But no, a quick glance showed that none of the barracks were occupied.

Nor did she find him by the mine entrance, keeping company with the people on sentry duty.

Something began nibbling at the base of Magdalena's brain, a nascent unease of which she was barely aware, and certainly couldn't identify. Yet it grew with every step, until she was forcing herself not to run.

As she neared *that* door—the door of heavy wood, the door

that led to a tiny slice of hell—she spotted a figure leaning casually against the wall. Another member of the 22488, another vampire, what had they said his name was? Huang? He smiled at her approach, fangs just visible in the paltry illumination.

"Hello, Magdalena."

"Have you seen Ian?" she asked without preamble.

"Hmm. Last I saw, he was with Warren. Let me check. Hey, Warren!" He pounded on the door behind which the "livestock" whiled away their final days. "Mags wants to know if you've seen Ian!"

The answering "Just a minute!" was rough and muffled by the intervening wood.

"Is he... feeding?" Mags whispered.

"Oh, not at all." Huang leaned over, casually sliding the bar from its brackets with the inhuman strength of a single hand.

"Well," he corrected himself, giving the wood a hefty shove, "he's not feeding *himself.*"

The door flew wide, revealing the pair of vampires beyond, and for all her pride, for all she'd more than half expected this, Magdalena couldn't help but scream.

Chapter Twenty

It wasn't even a lunge. Magdalena *launched* herself, arms outstretched, scream devolving into a howl of rage. She was weaponless, but in that moment, Mags was fully capable of murdering Warren with her bare hands.

Except, of course, that she wasn't.

The vampire knocked Magdalena aside with contemptuous ease. A spin faster than mortal eyes could follow, a shove with impossible strength, and Mags hurtled across the cell, feet and then knees dragging through the dirt and mud of the floor before she finally skidded to a halt.

She flailed at the ground, struggling to get her hands under her, forcing her aching chest to breathe—and only then got a good, solid whiff of the gunk in which she lay.

It wasn't water that had turned patches of the earthen floor to mud.

Thrashing even more desperately, now, she yanked her face from the muck, spitting to clear her mouth of the vile substance coating her lips and tongue. And in so doing, she finally caught a clear glimpse of what she'd almost collided with in her painful slide, of the source of the blood that now tainted the earth around her.

The corpse lay still, head tilted back, face hollow and twisted in agonized terror. That face, and what she could see of the rest of the body, were maggot-pale where they weren't spattered with darker substances. Between the two, however, was little more than a bloody spine with stringy fibers of meat dangling and protruding.

The throat had been utterly shredded.

Screaming, a lot of it, from the poor souls huddled around the edges of the chamber, whom Mags had scarcely even noticed. Magdalena's own voice would have joined theirs, save that her gasp of shock had sucked in small gobs of mud as well as air, causing her to cough and choke, her entire body curled and shaking, until she vomited. She finally flopped back, limp and weak, breath labored and wheezing.

"Red is not your color, Mags," Warren noted helpfully. "I can't say I recommend asphyxiating on a regular basis. Special occasions, at most."

"Maybe we should leave her," Huang suggested. "Let her stew in here for a while." He gave the door a playful wag.

"Hmm, I don't know. Lacusta might be a bit irritated."

"He doesn't have to know. We could make the rest of the cattle an offer. Whoever does the best job at making her unrecognizable gets some sort of reprieve?"

Magdalena's rasps grew worse, burdened by thickening panic.

"Be a shame to waste the blood," Warren said.

"Who's talking about wasting it? She doesn't have to be *alive* to be mutilated."

"Please…" Mags sobbed and hated herself for it.

Huang snickered and once more mimed slamming the door.

"Guys, enough."

She felt more than saw several figures appearing above her, leaning over her. One reached out a hand to take her own.

The skin beneath her clenching fingers felt…off. Not cold, not clammy, not corpse-like, just somehow wrong. Artificial. Yet so familiar.

"Ian?"

"Yeah, Mags."

It *sounded* like him. Mags forced her gaze upward as she rose.

"Oh, God." She almost choked again. "Are you hurt?"

"No," Ian told her, indicating the tacky, slowly congealing blood that stained his shirt. "I'm afraid it's not mine." His gaze flickered down and to the side, toward the spot where she'd just lain.

"No! Tell me you didn't—"

"I'm sorry, Mags."

She shoved him, hard, a gesture that resulted in him taking only a single step back. "How could you *do* something like that?!"

"Don't blame him, Mags." Only when Suni spoke did Magdalena recognize the other figures standing around her: not just Suni but her teammate Zach, also no longer human. The both of them had placed themselves between Mags and the other two vampires who'd been terrorizing her. "You have no idea what it's like to awaken with such *need*."

"No," Ian disagreed with just a tinge of shame. "It's not even a need, not a hunger. It's more. It's... I didn't know what I was doing, even who I was, until it was over.

"It won't happen again, Mags. I promise."

"It better not," Warren sneered from the door. "You wasted a *lot* of the good stuff. No table manners."

"You!" Magdalena pulled completely away from Ian. "Change him back, you bastard! Undo it!"

Warren and Huang burst into mocking laughter, and even the others couldn't suppress a trio of derisive grins.

"Even if I wanted to, you silly little cow, I couldn't. Nobody could. Can't be done. Like trying to unburn ashes."

"Or unkill someone," Zach added.

Ian wrapped an arm around Mags from behind. "It's okay. I wanted this, remember?"

"But—"

"I'm still me, Mags."

"I don't know..."

She felt his body tense, just a bit. "Or do we need to have another talk about trust? I thought finding out I'm okay would get you past that, but if you still don't respect me, feel free to walk away during one of the most confusing parts of my whole fucking life!"

"What? No, I wouldn't do that to you!"

"Of course not. I'm sorry." She felt pressure on her shoulder, realized he was leaning his forehead against her. "This is all so disorienting."

Mags squeezed the hand that held her. "We'll get through it."

"I may throw up," Warren spat. "Shit, *can* we throw up?"

"I haven't," Huang said.

"Yeah, but I've had individual pimples last longer than you've been a vampire."

"Funny. Why don't you go ask Lacusta?"

"I think I said that's enough, guys," Suni growled, but Mags suddenly smiled.

"Yeah! Why *don't* we talk to Lacusta? And we can just see what he thinks of a couple of baby 'nosferatu' making a liar out of him!"

Again Warren and Huang both laughed, though the former's was more of a scornful snicker. "And what promise do you think Lacusta broke?"

"What promise?! He swore he wouldn't turn Ian into a vampire without me!"

"And he didn't do that, did he?" Suni said.

"That's... But... That's not fair!" Mags knew how stupid it sounded, but they were the only words that would come.

Still more laughter.

"Was it you?" Magdalena asked when the hysterics had finally calmed.

Warren's grin exposed far more tooth than it should have. "What if it was?"

"Well, Sankar told me a lot of the legends of your kind."

"Mm-hmm? And?"

"And I want to make sure I choose the *right* vampire to stake through the heart and burn in his fucking sleep."

Well, she thought as she fought neither to retreat nor tremble before the abruptly blazing eyes and growling, gaping jaws, *at least they're not laughing anymore.*

Ian stepped in front of her, between her and the other vampires, with Suni and Zach at his side. "We're done here. Mags, let's go."

Warren snarled. "You heard what she—!"

"I did. Now back the hell off, or I'll carry the gasoline for her."

Mags forced herself not to look back as she and Ian left the room. She knew genuine rage when she saw it, and with the vampires, looks *could* kill.

"See?" Ian said as they moved into the hall. "Told you. Suni's still Suni, Zach's still Zach. And I'm still me."

She forced a smile. "I'm just... Thank you, but I'm still not—"

"I'm me. I'm *fine*."

"You haven't had long enough to tell if you're fine."

"Drop it, Mags."

The hallway fell silent.

"I *do* want to go see Lacusta," she said finally.

"How come?"

"I want to know if he knew. About you."

"What good would it do? You gonna yell at him?"

"I just might."

She thought her heart might burst when he chuckled. "Well, he better watch out. I've seen you mad."

Mags laughed with him. Then, "I just need to know, Ian. For my own sake. And..." She forced the last bit out in a rush, before she could change her mind. "And so I can ask him to remake me, too. I told you, we're in this together."

She thought Ian's answering smile, despite the burgeoning fangs, was radiant. "All right. So let's find him."

On they walked, but her feet barely touched the dirt. She felt as light as the mists she'd seen Lacusta become. *See? He just needed some time to adapt. He's Ian, and he's fine, and I'm going to be like him soon, and we'll be fine.*

Just fine...

"He's not in there."

Mags peered first at the entrance to the mess, only barely visible in the dim light ahead, and then at Ian. "What do you mean?"

"I mean he's not in there. Really not a lot of options as to what that means."

She felt her brow furrow. "How can you tell?"

Ian shrugged. "Scent? Something else? Don't know. I can just tell."

"Ian, you haven't been... Haven't had these abilities very long. How can you be sure—?"

"I told you, I can tell! Yes, I'm sure already!"

"The meeting must have broken up," Mags muttered after a moment.

"You think?"

"Oh, shut it. I'm going in."

"I just told you he's not—!"

"Did it even occur to you," she asked him, "that maybe someone knows *where* Lacusta went after the assembly? That we might just ask, instead of searching this whole damn place?"

She watched his gaze drift from her face to over her shoulder, saw him take a deep breath—solely out of habit, presumably.

"I'm sorry," he said, focusing on her once more. "You're absolutely right. Let's ask around."

Mags turned to see half a dozen faces crammed in the open doorway, watching the not-quite-argument. Though she'd done nothing to warrant it, she found herself unaccountably ashamed. Chin held high, she pushed past the spectators into the mess hall, Ian following after.

"Magdalena!"

Sankar met her halfway, standing beside the crude bench. After the night she'd had so far, the sight of a friendly face was nigh overwhelming.

"I've been worried," he told her, stopping just short of a hug. "Since you ran out of here, I've... Oh. Oh, no."

"You got a problem, old man?" Ian challenged, clearly harboring no doubt whatsoever as to what Sankar reacted.

"It's all right, Sankar," Mags added quickly. "It's still Ian."

For no reason she could understand—no reason she would *let* herself understand—the look her elder turned her way seemed one of pity.

Around them, a number of people stared, more at Ian than at her. Most seemed leery, shuffling to keep their distance, but it was a mild revulsion, a general wariness. None exhibited any particular shock or terror.

And why should they? They've already seen more than one of their friends transformed.

Magdalena wondered briefly if they'd look at her that way, too, when it was her turn to change.

Not that every person present reacted the same way—or were even people at all.

Two of the three vampires remaining in the chamber were strangers to her. The third, however, was *too* familiar, and seemed to have eyes only for Magdalena's companion.

"Ian!" Cassie all but squealed, her hair trailing in a crimson banner as she just about flew across the room. "Look at you! You look *fantastic*! It suits you."

"Mmm. Doesn't it?" he grunted back.

Mags grumbled something unintelligible.

"Aww, what's wrong, Mags? You worried that your boyfriend's going to leave you behind, now? I'm sure if you make *real* nice to him, he'll keep you as a pet."

"Sure, whatever. Where's your lord and master, Cassie?"

"Why?"

"Um, let's say, because fuck you answer the question."

"Ooh, scary."

Mags just waited, though ready to yank her gaze away at the first sense of mental violation. Cassie smirked back.

"Can we just get this done with?" Ian finally barked.

"Fine by me." The young woman turned, scouring the room. "Anyone? Any idea where Lacusta might've gone? I—we need to talk to him."

One of the young men Mags didn't yet know offered a gesture that would have had to work out for months to qualify as a shrug. "He left after the assembly."

He quailed, then, his weight shifting audibly on the wood, beneath Magdalena's expression. Or rather her utter lack thereof. "You don't say."

Ian made a hissing, raspy sound from behind her, not unlike a snake gargling sand.

"Precisely," Mags agreed without turning. "Not exactly the most helpful answer, is it?"

"What's it matter?" the guy protested. "You'll run into him sooner or later!"

"Well, shit, why didn't *I* think of that? Maybe my question can't just wait, hmm?"

"So what's the question?"

"How is that your business?" Mags snapped.

"You're the one asking for help!"

"Still none of your—"

Cassie laughed, a high-pitched titter as creepy as it was irritating. "Oh, aren't you just precious?"

Mags crossed her arms and waited.

"Are you planning to tattle, Mags? Run to daddy over what happened to your boyfriend?"

Again Ian snarled, a sound somehow more warped and bestial than even the last time.

"So what if I am?" Mags shot back. "You're none of you nearly as brave when there's someone around who can—"

"Mags?" Sankar interrupted, quietly but firmly.

"Just a minute. Cassie, if you think for one minute…."

"Mags?" the old man tried again.

"…I'm just going to stand around and let you—"

"*Magdalena!*"

"What?"

Sankar pointed, but it was no longer necessary. Ian's peculiar rumblings flared into a full-fledged growl, barely escaping through a cage of jagged teeth and lengthening fangs. Though he wasn't breathing, though his body was in fact statue-still save for his jaw, Mags somehow had the distinct impression of a bestial panting.

"Ian?! What—?"

"He's losing it!" one of the other vampires warned.

"Losing what? I don't understand!"

"He's been one of us for about a minute and a half," Cassie snarled, "and you just dragged him into a room that stinks of people crammed together like—"

His mouth gaping and distending beyond human, his fingers curling and his nails protruding, Ian surged toward the gathered humans, who could only begin to fall back, only begin to scream, before he would reach them.

But Sankar had moved the instant he understood Cassie's warning. A frantic leap, and he was there *just* before Ian, putting himself between the rampaging creature and his victims. He thrust his hand out, and though Mags couldn't see what he held, not in the frenzied chaos of motion, she had a good idea what it was.

Nor could she tell, with any certainty, whether Ian hurled himself aside, away from Sankar, or whether he was *thrown* aside, rebounding from some unseen barrier no less solid than the quarry rock outside. He skidded across the floor, half-leaping and half-bouncing upright. His momentum carried him clear to the wall, which he struck perhaps halfway between floor and ceiling—and *stuck*. Neck twisted to glare over his shoulder, he clung to the wall like some monstrous roach.

The thing behind Ian's face was shrieking, now, the ear-splitting whine of a spinning sawblade given flesh. He pushed off from the wall in a bound that might have carried him back at Sankar, or just past the old man to where the others huddled.

Cassie and the male vampire Mags didn't know slammed into him in midair. All three tumbled to the earth in a thrashing, spinning amalgam of flailing limbs and sibilant howls. Wood cracked where one arm backhanded the end of the log-bench, and dirt flew in geysers as inhuman struggles scooped divots into the earth. The third vampire leapt atop the heap, her fists flying.

God, what do I do? Ian was out of control, she knew that, but she couldn't just stand by and watch him beaten, injured, or worse. She directed a plea toward Sankar, who looked down at the string of prayer beads in his hand, nodded slowly, and began to advance.

It ended before he drew near. First Cassie and the two unfamiliar vampires, then Ian—albeit slowly and unsteadily—rose to their feet. The newest vampire seemed dazed, vaguely blank, but in control.

"I guess we're lucky he didn't think to turn into dust or mist or something," Mags said weakly. Then, reluctantly, "Thank you. I—"

"Don't thank us," Cassie snarled, shoving Ian her way. "We need every soldier we can get, and Lacusta would've been pissed. I could give a fuck what *you* think! Get him out of here until he doesn't need a leash and a muzzle."

Mags took Ian by the hand; his grip was loose, limp. With two quick glances—a grateful nod for Sankar, a rather less friendly expression for Cassie—she led him from the mess hall. The buzz of rising conversation followed them, and though she couldn't make out much, Mags had no doubt at all as to what, and who, the topic of discussion must be.

So lost in thought and worries, it took her some time to notice the faint tugging on her hand. After traversing a portion of the mine's main hall, Ian had begun to pull at her, as though trying to guide their course. It would have been nothing, less than nothing, for him to break free or drag her along, but he still seemed dazed, only partly present, and his tugs were perfunctory at best.

They were clear enough, however, for Magdalena to realize where he was trying to lead them.

"Oh, no. I don't think so." She dropped his hand, taking him by the shoulders and steering him bodily away from the barred and heavy door. "You already ki…" She couldn't quite bring herself to say it, not about him. "One person's already dead. That's not you, Ian. You need to get a handle on this. Learn control. So no more, not tonight."

Again, she couldn't have stopped him if he'd tried, but he only made a faint whimper in the back of his throat and allowed her to lead him.

The barracks were largely vacant when they arrived, what with the recent meeting and various duties. By the time they reached Ian's old blanket, still shoved up against the far wall, the chamber had emptied out completely. Whatever they saw in Ian, or in her, inspired the handful of people present to go find somewhere important to be.

Mags spread the blanket with the toe of her boot as best she could, smoothing a wadded mass of lumps and wrinkles into a somewhat flatter surface of lumps and wrinkles. Slowly she sat, guiding Ian by the hand, until he lay beside her, his head in her lap.

"You're gonna be okay," she whispered, softly stroking his hair. She brushed a few wild strands from his face, trying not to notice the complete lack of sweat that should have plastered them to his forehead. "You're just overwhelmed. Adjusting. You didn't know what you were doing. I get that, now. I'll help you through it.

"You *are* strong enough to control this. I was wrong to doubt that—you. We're going to be just—"

She never saw him move, didn't even *feel* it until she slammed against the wall. Thick nails of agony hammered into her skull, her back. Had she struck stone or one of the wooden supports, rather than the packed earth, she was certain her head would have split completely open.

It was the last coherent thought she had before pain and panic washed away any semblance of rationality.

Her feet dangled well off the floor, kicking uselessly. Her neck throbbed, clenching and constricting beneath the one-handed grip that held her against the wall. Her chest burned. Tears blurred her vision.

"Ian…"

In his other hand, Ian held one of hers—the one that, only seconds ago, had gently caressed his hair. A razor pain shot up her arm, emanating from her wrist, and it took her what seemed an eternity to understand why.

"Oh, God… Ian, no…"

His fangs were inside her, piercing the skin of her wrist. She could *feel* the blood pumping through the wounds, small but oh, so deep. No, not even pumping. The vampire drank, and somehow the blood flowed faster than her heart could pump, drawn from her body by an inhuman thirst.

"Stop… Please stop…" They were croaking, animal sounds now, not proper words, and the only response was a further tightening of his fist at her throat. She tried to draw breath, couldn't feed her lungs even the tiniest wisp.

Would she suffocate first, or die of blood loss? *What are you going to think,* she wondered, the room around her starting to fade, *when you realize what you've done? Poor Ian…*

The floor rushed up, smacking first against her feet and then, as her legs folded uselessly, the rest of her. Just like that, she could breathe, though the air was fire in her bruised windpipe and ravaged lungs. The ache in her wrist remained, but far less intense. A wet warmth coiled down the skin of her arm.

And she saw, as the world ceased strobing before her, slowly coming into focus between ragged wheezes, a pair of boots far more ornate than anything Ian owned.

Wincing with even so small a motion, she craned her head upward. Lacusta stood before her, Ian dangling like a kitten from one of the vampire lord's fists. He looked, she thought, not angry so much as stern, and perhaps just a bit put-out.

"What could you possibly have been thinking?" he demanded. Then, when no answer was forthcoming. "I believe I asked you a question!"

Only then did Mags realize to whom that had been directed. "M-me?" The word had to constrict itself into little more than a croak to squeeze through her injured throat.

"Yes, you! I thought you smarter than this, Miss Suarez! You knew Ian hadn't had time to adapt, to learn to control the needs that drive us. Yet here you are, first dragging him into a room half-full of mortals and smelling of dozens more, and then enticing him to be alone with you! Have you any idea how severely an episode such as this might set him back? How much harder adjusting could be for him, now?"

"I... I didn't mean to."

"No, of course you didn't. But do try to *think* next time, Miss Suarez."

"Yes, I'm... I will. Sorry."

Lacusta released his grip, letting Ian drop to all fours. Immediately he crawled to her, halting just beyond arm's reach.

"Mags? Mags, I'm *so* sorry. He's right, I just haven't... Did I hurt you? I mean, I know I did, but... Not *badly*, did I?"

She could only grunt something noncommittal and, though she had to force herself not to flinch, nod permission for him to come closer.

Quickly he looked her over, poking gently at her wrist and the back of her head. Mags hissed in pain once or twice, but otherwise bore it all stoically.

"Just some bandages and a cold pack," Ian announced. "And some extra carbohydrates over the next day or so."

"Well enough," Lacusta said. "I'll send someone to tend to

her. *You* will be staying in my sight for the near future, until I'm certain you can be trusted to behave."

The younger vampire bowed his head.

"Sleep, Miss Suarez. Tomorrow we begin planning our first genuine operation as an army, however small. I'll want you strong enough to participate."

"O-okay." Then, as they moved to depart, "I… Wait, please. I wanted… I want you to change me. To be like Ian."

Lacusta didn't so much as slow his steps. "You are not suited, and you are not worthy. You have much to learn and much to prove to me before I would even consider it."

You said the same about Ian! She tried to protest, but the words wouldn't come. Nor did it occur to her until much later that she'd already accepted as a given that Lacusta must, indeed, have ordered Warren to change him.

She watched until they both had gone, and only then curled into a ball, arms wrapped around her knees. She felt herself shaking and, despite the ache, forced herself to take deep, steadying breaths.

But at least she'd been right; Lacusta himself had confirmed it. Ian just hadn't adapted yet. He wasn't a monster, just struggling. This had all just been an accident. He hadn't meant to hurt her, or anyone else.

He was still Ian, beneath the surface. They had a lot of effort ahead of them, a lot of things to work out, but they could do that together.

It would take a while, but they were going to be just fine.

Chapter Twenty-One

"I can't help it," Sharon said, winding a finger through one lock of hair already twisted and coiled enough to make an earthworm wince. "I feel exposed out here."

"Don't even say it," Mags hissed at the boys in the group.

Trevor Rose, one of Dwayne's people from the 22488, grunted something and continued staring uselessly into the night, but Dwayne himself snickered. "Wasn't going to."

"Uh-huh."

"Although, now that you mention it—"

"Shut it," Mags and Sharon ordered together.

Another snicker, before Dwayne lightly elbowed Nestor. "I mean, it'd help us pass the time, right?"

The big guy looked askance—and down—at him. "Sharon's not really my type."

"Oh?"

"Now, if *you* wanted to put on a show for us..."

Mags clasped a hand to her mouth to keep from bursting out in laughter at Dwayne's rapid change in expressions.

"You know there's nothing to worry about," he said quickly to Sharon in a topic change only slightly less blatant and twisty than a tornado. "The vamps scouted the area for drones before we got here."

Vamps. It bothered Mags that many of her fellow "soldiers" had already grown sufficiently comfortable with the idea of the vampires to have coined a shorthand for them. It didn't seem fair, not given her own confusion and mixed emotions.

"And are still maintaining a perimeter," Sharon recited for

him. "Yeah, Dwayne. I was there at the briefing. I'd still rather have some damn cover."

Mags couldn't really blame her. All six of them—the sixth, another 22488 named Roberta Kenshi, currently dozed (and snored) softly in the back of the truck—*were* awfully exposed. They stood gathered around the vehicle, those who weren't in it, atop a rise of rock and scrub that lacked the ambition to even try to be a full-fledged hill. It also, however, provided the only available vantage with surrounding terrain flat enough for the truck to do what they needed it to.

Trevor continued to watch the empty gloom. "Sharon's been, oh, what's the term I want? Ah, right. Fox-fuck nuts ever since the old man told us about those satellite things."

The woman in question flailed her hands a bit. "I don't like the idea of someone peeking in on me from space!"

"Shit, she yelled at *me* for spying on her from the next room!" Dwayne smirked.

"Sankar's point," Mags said quickly, "was that most of them are gone. Destroyed or cut off during Pacification. Most of the ones left aren't precise enough to find anyone, or to see much detail through the overcast. He was trying to explain what the machines have *lost*."

"Don't care," Sharon told her. "Creepy." Still muttering, she wandered to the front of the truck and hopped up to sit on the hood. Dwayne continued his efforts to get Trevor to join in on his off-color comments and speculation, and Trevor continued to respond mostly with grunts. That, combined with Roberta's ongoing snoring, left Nestor and Mags, if not precisely alone, then with some modicum of privacy. For a time they stood quietly, Mags shivering a bit in the night's modest chill.

Until a sizeable obstacle stopped the breeze wafting over her.

"You have a lee," she told Nestor. "People aren't supposed to have lees. Mountains, boulders, those have lees."

His answering smile was sallow at best. "I'm worried about you."

"Nothing to worry about, Nest. I mean, other than being shot by the machines or—"

"I'm serious. You haven't been yourself lately."

"Oh? Who have I been?"

"Mags—"

"See? Right there! People still call me that. If I've been someone else, it's *really* confusing."

"You haven't been yourself," he doggedly repeated, "since Ian was... Since Ian."

She fought the urge to hiss. "I'm not talking about this."

"He's not safe, Mags, not anymore!"

"Yeah, well, I never liked Daniel all that much, either, but you didn't hear me trying to turn you against him, did you?"

It was absolutely the most horrible thing she could have said, and she knew it. Still she glared, refusing to react to the abject agony in his face, until he finally turned away.

Fuck it. Not as if you can really apologize for saying something like that.

"Hey, Dwayne!" she called over the truck bed.

"Huh? What?"

"You sure the suspension's gonna be up to this? That stretch down there may be wide open, but it's uneven as—"

"Aw, hell, you were *there*, Mags! While we were working on it!"

"Yeah, but—"

"You wouldn't shut it in the damn planning session, either," he groused, circling the vehicle. "You ever happy with anything?"

"Look," she said, slightly taken aback, "I'm all for the general idea. I just don't know if the trucks are up to what he's asking. Don't know if *we* are."

"Or maybe," Dwayne snapped, "you're just pissed that you're not in charge!"

"We're all on the same team here, Dwayne," she said, trying very hard not to sound irritated.

"Yes, we are. And I'm team leader, because Lacusta knows which of us is more reliable. And that's gotten up your ass something fierce, hasn't it?"

"Ignore him, Mags," Sharon called from the hood. "He's so full of himself, he's actually pregnant."

"Believe me," Magdalena replied, ignoring Dwayne's indignant sputters, "that was the plan." Deliberately, even ostentatiously, she turned her back on him.

On him and, as best she could, on the voice in her head pointing out over and over again, *you never really answered the question, there, did you?*

She *was* pissed that someone else was in charge. How could she prove herself worthy of the change if Lacusta wouldn't let her play to her strengths?

Be it external or internal, further conversation was precluded by a lupine howl, close, piercing yet oddly quiet.

"Signal!" Dwayne hissed, in case the others had somehow missed it. The team piled rapidly into the truck, Sharon sliding behind the wheel, Nestor nudging Roberta awake before yanking aside a tarp and hefting a gun that Mags didn't think she could lift, let alone fire.

She heard it, in the distance, just before Sharon gunned the engine: a thunderous rumble, the whine of metal on metal.

The train. The target.

Bouncing, jostling, shuddering, the truck roared down the incline and out across the uneven ground, racing alongside the rust-speckled tracks. Magdalena's whole body shook, violently, painfully. She was convinced that the last meal she'd eaten was recombining itself into whole new substances in her gut. Still she watched, crouched in the truck bed, hands gripping the sides.

Across the tracks, sweeping in from a separate vantage, a second truck with a second team matched their course. Their heads bobbled violently up and down with the rough terrain, and Mags found herself hoping—futilely, she knew—that she didn't look nearly as goofy with it as they did.

The reverberation of the train grew louder, larger, as the trucks strained to get up to speed. A great metal serpent, it drew ever nearer.

Figures appeared, standing on the tracks, whipping by as the vehicles raced past. Mags could barely make out any details, but she knew them all the same. Lacusta. A couple vampires whose names she'd yet to learn. Zach.

Ian.

Something surged through her, a frisson of excitement and fear, disgust and desire. It was all she could do to shove it aside.

The vampires grew clearer even as they grew more distant, bathed in the headlights of the oncoming locomotive. First one vanished, then two more, each leaving the tableau blurrier, foggier, than the last. Until only Lacusta remained, his coat whipping about his calves in the breeze, the racing mass of steel bearing down on him, so close, so very, very fast.

The ancient creature exploded into mist just as the train would have struck him. Pale, phantom tendrils reached across the face of the vehicle, stretching around, above, below, a cobweb given life and hunger, consuming its first prey.

And just as quickly, it was gone.

If everything went according to plan, Lacusta and the others would reform aboard, where they would begin thinning out the mechanized opposition while doing enough damage to help slow or stop the train.

But in case they couldn't...

"Fire!" Dwayne shouted. In all the noise, Mags couldn't be sure, but she thought she faintly heard that order echoed, in a different voice, from the other truck across the way.

Just before the train caught up with them, Nestor and his opposite number slung their weapons around and let loose.

The percussive staccato of the machine guns drowned everything else, not just sound but thought, filling Magdalena's head until there was no room left. Brutal .50-caliber slugs tore through steel, shredding whatever mechanisms or instrumentation lay beyond. The guns sucked up the belts of ammunition stacked beside them, chewing through them like so much jerky, and Mags, hands pressed tight to her ears, grew concerned. Neither their ammo stores nor the length of drivable terrain allowing the trucks to keep pace were substantial.

She needn't have worried. Smoke began to pour from the engine, through the bullet holes and various seams in the metal. The train shuddered and began, oh, so gradually, to slow.

From the darkness above they descended, the rest of

Lacusta's children, as bats and owls and other shapes Mags couldn't make out. Some swarmed the train, battering at the makeshift windows, slipping in where gaps permitted or transforming into dust or vapor to filter through the tiniest cracks. The others remained aloft, darting down to destroy the drones as they emerged to defend the train.

I hadn't realized Lacusta had already remade so many …

Nestor swiveled the gun toward the polymer sheeting making up portions of the train's side. Again he fired; pockmarks grew to complex webs of cracks, until whole sections shattered.

"You ready, Sharon?" Dwayne called.

"No, but fuck it!" With that confidence-inspiring reply, she yanked the wheel, bringing the truck as close to the train as she dared without bouncing off. The train was slowing, yes, but still barreled ahead at terrifying speeds.

Dwayne rose from his crouch, swaying as he struggled for balance. "Grapples!"

Mags readied her equipment, as did the others. Hooks—repurposed from other equipment, for the most part, bent tire irons and metal brackets and such—hung from coils of hemp rope barely exceeding ten feet in length. These weren't much more than last-ditch safety systems, only marginally more effective than wishing hard. *If* someone missed the jump, *if* they survived the fall to earth at speed, *if* they managed to retain their hold on the rope and weren't too injured, then maybe they could climb aboard before being left behind or dragged to death.

All in all, Mags figured she'd be a lot happier if she never needed to test it.

Five ropes flew, five hooks fastened themselves against the edges of the breach left by the shattered plastics. It was a sizeable opening, but not nearly broad enough for them to attempt the leap as a group.

"Kenshi and Panagakis!" Dwayne ordered. Largest and smallest; made sense. Nestor's strength was more than enough to clear the gap, while Roberta's lissome form seemed almost to soar.

Mags glanced sidelong through the window to the cab. Though she couldn't see Sharon's face, the knuckles clenched around the creaking steering wheel were ample evidence of her struggle to keep the ride steady.

"Rose and Suarez!"

Huh. Much as she still despised him personally, her respect for Dwayne as a field commander went up a bit. The longer this took, the greater the chances of Sharon losing control, yet he'd chosen to be last off the vehicle. Mags nodded approvingly and tensed, ready to jump.

Several rounds slammed into the bed of the truck, fired by one of the drones above. Mags yelped and dropped prone, arms covering her head, Dwayne and Trevor landing beside her.

One of the bullets lay not a foot from her, smashed flat against the metal bed.

Lead, she couldn't help but note. *They're back to lead.* Must have figured out that the silver myth was just that: myth.

Something swirled overhead, a *lot* of something, and the drone ceased firing.

Dwayne didn't have to repeat the order. Mags and Trevor rose, braced, and leapt.

She was caught in a storm, wind whipping around her, tearing at her. Its grip tightened, struggling to haul her away with the rest of the debris, then loosened once more.

The floor rushed up to greet her with painful enthusiasm. Waves of pain shot through her shoulder and she couldn't quite catch her breath. Nonetheless, she rolled to her feet, unslinging the shotgun strapped to her back.

"It's all right," Nestor told her. "Car's clear."

Indeed, only a single humanoid bot seemed to have been present, and its mangled chassis suggested that he and Roberta had prevailed in that confrontation.

Aided, no doubt, by the very large guns—nothing compared to the machine gun Nestor had left behind, but heavy enough—they carried.

"What about—"? Roberta began to ask, then stopped as every one of them flinched back from the window. A torrent of fire spread through the sky, illuminating the night. Magdalena's eyes began to sting at the first waft of gasoline fumes.

Silver might have been a bust, but clearly the machines

weren't done with the notion of flamethrowers. Mags hoped none of the vampires had been caught in that hellish torrent.

Roberta coughed, rubbed at the corner of one eye, then tried again. "What about—?"

Dwayne slammed into the opening, only half in, grasping for purchase and finding none. Mags and Trevor grabbed him— she by the wrist, he by the collar—and fell back, dragging him the rest of the way inside.

"Ow," he said.

"Never mind," Roberta added.

"I'm guessing," Mags said, rising, "that the ride got a little bumpier?"

"Ow," Dwayne repeated.

Magdalena examined the room, shotgun at the ready. It was plain, open, very much like the train cars in which the 13936 had ridden to and from the city center roughly two and a half lifetimes ago. As it made little sense that the machines would leave so much space unused, she figured that the bots, or whatever had been in here, were currently active elsewhere on the train. "So where to?"

"I—" Dwayne's jaw clamped shut at the burst of gunfire, nigh deafening, from the next car over. "That way," he finished.

Nestor checked the breach on his weapon, working the slide. "Is anyone else bothered that we've been here for two minutes and our plans have already deteriorated to 'Run *toward* the gunshots?'"

The others grinned and converged on the door. She hadn't meant it, but Mags found herself beside her hulking friend, at the rear of the group.

And they *were* about to dive headlong into a firefight.

"Nest," she began, haltingly, unable to look at him, "I... About before, I'm..."

Meaty fingers closed, tight but gentle, on her collarbone. "I know."

A flicker of a smile, and then they were all business, readying themselves as Trevor yanked the sliding door aside, leaving a clear path—of ingress or fire—for his companions. They burst through, spreading out, weapons raised and shooting at the nearest bots before they'd even consciously recognized the machines for what they were. Her earlier distractions shoved fully aside, Mags knew she was damn well ready for anything.

Except, of course, she wasn't. None of them were even remotely ready.

Not, up close and personal, to watch a vampire die.

Chapter Twenty-Two

A humanoid bot and a pair of drones collapsed beneath the withering barrage of gunfire Dwayne, Mags, and the others unleashed as they poured into the cargo car. So, too, did several wooden crates, spraying splinters, spilling coiled wires and shaped-plastic actuators across the rattling floor. Dodging the disintegrating boxes, Mags scrambled atop the next small stack—they were scattered throughout the car, those crates—hoping to secure a better vantage and to clear her companions' line of fire. She heard Trevor clambering up beside her, saw Roberta drop prone to shelter behind the fallen bot. Where Nest and Dwayne had ended up, she wasn't sure, but she heard the big man grunt and the creak of wood, so at least he was still up and moving.

It was from her perch, atop those crates, that she saw it happen.

At the far end of the lengthy car, a large wolf crushed a drone in its jaws before reverting to human form, fists flying, revealing itself as Zach. Other drones, five or so, swirled and flitted about him, diving and veering off, nervous hornets of plastic and metal. They couldn't see him, of course—more than one drone actually careened off him, its flight wobbly, its rotors having done the vampire precious little damage—but they showed some vague sense of where he was. Still, none of the drones fired, preferring instead to swoop from wall to wall. The result was nothing more than easy pickings for Zach, who knocked first one of the tiny bots, and then a second, to the floor in crumpled heaps.

Beyond them, crouched by the opposite door, another

humanoid bot had taken shelter. It carried a heavy assault rifle in its gleaming digits, but made no move to fire, and though it had no head, it gave the distinct impression of watching the drones struggle.

Was there something in here they were protecting, some reason they couldn't risk opening fire? Or...?

A third punch sent a drone wobbling, though failing to bring it down completely, and Mags suddenly knew *precisely* what the bots were doing.

"Zach!" She opened up on the crouching machine, which merely scooted farther back into the doorway until she had no clear target. Still she fired, blast after blast, hoping to keep it pinned. She shouted over the cacophony, trusting undead senses to hear her where a human could not. "Zach, they're hounds! They're pinpointing you for the—!"

One of the drones spun its axis and fired on her, forcing her to drop behind the highest crates. Wood crackled and snapped as bullets dug into it, and she grunted as something too mild and shallow to be bullet, probably a splinter, opened a gash near her right temple.

A quick swipe cleared the worst of the leaking blood from her eyes, leaving a miniature tire-track of crimson across the back of her hand. Trevor seemed unscathed, so far as the briefest glance back could tell her. Mags skittered aside to the next crate, clasped her shotgun tight, ready to pop up and, with any luck, take down the drone before it could do the same to her.

Except the drone wasn't firing any longer. Rather than the lone *pop* of the small machine's onboard weaponry, the room echoed with a burst of heavier and far more rapid shots.

And then it shook with the vampire's scream.

Wincing against the tumult, Mags poked her head up. Her warning had come an instant too late. The humanoid bot had stepped from the doorway while the drone had her pinned and emptied a clip into Zach.

A clip of incendiary rounds.

The machine reloaded, swapping magazines seemingly as fast as the bullets flew, but now it only stood, watching, waiting.

Zach thrashed and flailed, shrieking; the holes in his body blackened, some glowing with embers, the burns spreading and shrinking, spreading and shrinking, as flame and supernatural flesh waged battle.

It was hideously hypnotic, in its way, enough so that Mags did not immediately fire on either the drone or the larger bot. The drone, too, seemed focused on the vampire.

Of course. They can detect him, now. Thermal sensors.

A loud *twang*, seemingly from nowhere, and Zach's thrashing ceased. His cries even higher pitched, a banshee keening, he— and Mags, and the others—stared down at the wooden bolt in his chest. Thick, viscous gobbets and wobbling streamers began to fall from around the wound. Mags choked when she realized she was seeing his flesh rotting and sliding from his ribs.

The stake, unlike the silver, was clearly no mere myth.

Whether the wood through his heart would have ultimately been fatal or only crippling, however, was a moot point.

From the other side of the car, where more of the crates had blocked Magdalena's line of sight, a second humanoid machine emerged. It had already tossed aside whatever weapon had launched the bolt, most probably a crossbow or spear gun. In one hand it carried a makeshift sword: a simple steel pipe, half of which had been heated, hammered flat, and filed sharp. In the other, it held a large plastic canister.

The bot's emergence finally spurred Mags and the others back into action, but again, too late. The drones and the rifle-armed machine opened fire, forcing them to drop back behind the crates once again. Incendiary bullets slammed into and through wooden planks, spraying not merely splinters, now, but flaming shrapnel. Mags rolled, bouncing painfully off a lower crate, and then tackled Trevor to the floor, beating with one hand at a smoldering spot on his back.

She heard the swish and the following thumps, one light, the next heavy, a sequence of sounds that finally silenced Zach's ongoing shriek. That, in turn, was followed by a strong waft of kerosene and the rush of a growing flame.

Mags, after making sure Trevor wasn't himself about to ignite, leaned over to peer around the stack, struggling neither to cough in the thickening smoke nor to flinch at the ache where her fall had bruised ribs.

Zach was little more than a pair of fires, the smaller blaze that was his decapitated head lying several feet from the larger.

The stench of burning flesh couldn't hide the growing miasma of rot. And even *that* wasn't the worst of it.

The vampire's jaw still quivered, opening and closing in silent torment. The limbs of his body still flailed, limp and useless as landed eels. She wondered, in rapt horror, how much Zach would have to endure before his undead body finally gave in.

She discovered she was clenching the shotgun to her chest, dangerously tight; glanced across the aisle and saw Nestor doing much the same with his own weapon. She nodded to him, then extended a single finger.

Then two.

And three.

In unison they leaned from cover and fired. The machine, which had last seen them atop the stacked crates, reacted fast, but not quite fast enough. Even as the assault rifle swiveled toward them, slugs tore into the steel chassis. It staggered, straightened, and finally collapsed, sparking.

Which left one more that they couldn't see from where they were, as well as at least two drones that had survived their encounter with Zach. Still, there were five of them, they might *just* be able to manage—

The door to the next car groaned, buckled, and burst inward, ripping completely from its track. An abyss-black torrent poured through, spreading and screeching. Furiously the bats circled and swooped, and though Mags couldn't see a bit of what was happening, she heard the crunch and squeal of rending metal.

The flapping creatures slammed together in perfect concert, an explosion in reverse. Lacusta's feet struck the floor at the same moment as the mangled drones, but Mags barely registered his presence before he darted forward, leaping over the burning corpse and vanishing once more from sight.

More crunching metal, and then he reappeared, the bot's sword gripped in one tight fist. For a long moment, he gazed at the remains of his "child." Then, with an inhuman snarl, snapped the blade over his knee.

"I trust you could have done nothing to prevent this," Lacusta said, and though he made no effort to look their way, couldn't possibly have seen them, Mags had no doubt he spoke to everyone present. "Should I ever learn otherwise, I promise you a truly unpleasant outcome."

Well, fuck you, too.

What Mags said aloud, though, as she slung her weapon over her shoulder and stepped into sight, was, "We tried. They had us pinned until it was too late."

Various sounds of assent from the others, all save Dwayne, whose glare was sharper than the weapon Lacusta had just destroyed. It only later occurred to Mags that he was probably pissed because she'd spoken up first, rather than waiting for him, as team leader.

"So be it." Just like that, the vampire was all business. "We've cleared all detectable threats from the third carriage to the ninth. The second team is still working their way up from the rear of the train. I am headed there now. Mister McAllister, you will need to split your people. Your path to the main objective should be clear. Start gathering them together, try to have them somewhat organized by the time team two and I arrive. I also require you to send someone forward, toward the engine. I dispatched several of my children that way. They'll need assistants to deal with any annoyances they missed and collect any salvageable equipment."

Mags wondered briefly why Lacusta and the others hadn't taken solid form in the engine itself and then worked their way back, rather than starting at her team's breaching point and splitting up.

Don't be stupid. She swore she heard the thoughts in Jonas's voice, as he'd often sounded during training. She realized she missed him, or at least the man she'd believed him to be. *If they hadn't started in the third car, thinned them out for you ASAP, you'd probably have run into a whole damn wall of machines and been nicely chewed up.*

"I knew that," she muttered absently.

"Knew what?" Dwayne asked.

She mentally shook herself, and only then realized Lacusta had already vanished. "Ah, nothing. Just thinking out loud."

"Well, good. While you're at it," he said through just the faintest smirk, "who do you *think* gets to wander forward and start gathering shit up?"

Mags chose not to waste so much as a facial expression on him. She simply pivoted and began walking, not even waiting to see who, if anyone, Dwayne would assign to go with her.

"This seems awfully familiar," Mags groused, crouched behind a pallet of crates containing who-knew-what.

"You said that already!" Trevor said, ducking his head like a turtle as a bullet crunched into their makeshift shelter.

"Well, see? There you go. Familiar."

Lacusta had told them that he and his progeny had cleared the train from the third car back. So, of course, it was in car two—actually the *third* segment of the train, as he had apparently not been counting the engine—that they found themselves once again pinned down. Bits of wreckage suggested that the vampires had been efficient, tearing apart more than a handful of machines large and small, but clearly they'd missed one.

Although it lacked the pile of crates behind which Mags and Trevor had taken cover, it had grabbed another cargo pallet, this one empty, hauled it onto its side, and sheltered behind it. The result was a temporary stalemate, each side occasionally leaning out and exchanging fire with the other. It would almost have been funny, Mags thought, if it hadn't involved being shot at by a homicidal robot.

"One of us could hop out, draw its fire until the other has a shot," Trevor suggested.

"And get really, *exceptionally* killed in the process!"

"Well, shit, if you're gonna wait around for a *good* idea..."

More bullets. More ricochets. More cringing.

Then, "Did you hear something?" Mags asked.

"Uh, there might've been a gunshot or two!"

"I'm serious! Someone crying or screaming, maybe."

Trevor shook his head, stuck his gun over the crate and fired twice. "I didn't—"

"*Mags?*" The shout squeezed through from the next car, slipping past the door and ducking around the next salvo, only barely reaching her ears. "*Mags, is that you?*"

Ian.

In the dustiest, gloomiest cellar of Magdalena's thoughts, the hollows of her mind where she never willingly set foot, a tiny ember of satisfaction glowed. The pain in Ian's voice warmed a patch of her soul that she hadn't realized had cooled.

She quashed it as soon as she recognized it for what it was, bitterly chastising herself.

What the fuck is wrong with you? You love him. He loves you! He just needs you to give him time. If you can't even do that...

"Can you busy this thing for a few minutes?"

To judge by Trevor's stare, she might as well have been speaking some other language. Some *very* other language; Rabbit or Bear, perhaps. "What are you talking about?"

"I'll be right back! Just keep the damn bot pinned!"

"I don't—"

"Now!"

Grunting obscenities, Trevor peered over the crate and began firing, again and again—not *too* rapidly, just enough to convince the machine to stay down. Mags backpedaled toward the far door, shotgun blasting. The two of them together must have been convincing, since the enemy made no attempt to return fire.

Mags felt the door at her back, yanked it aside, and fell as much as stepped through. She found herself briefly outside, between cars, and noted that the only wind was the night's own breeze; the train had finally drifted to a complete halt. The second door was already open, and a good thing. Had it not been, she'd never have heard Ian's call.

She hauled the first one shut again behind her, in case Trevor couldn't keep the machine occupied and it took a shot in her direction, and leapt into the next car, gun at the ready.

"Oh, *gah!*" She'd taken punches in her time, even some nasty falls, that hadn't hit her as hard as this did. Her eyes burned, watering enough to drown a rat; her throat and nostrils went raw, enflamed, so even simple breathing became an effort.

Even if she hadn't been distracted by the discomfort, though, she'd have needed some time to recognize the scent. She'd come across it only occasionally, in a few otherwise unused corners of the camp gardens.

Garlic. Someone had gassed the chamber in a thick cloud of atomized essence of garlic.

She staggered back to the outside platform, inhaling deeply. A quick splash of canteen water in her eyes, a strip of cloth tied around her mouth and nose. Not much protection, but the best she could do. Then, steeling herself and squinting, she ducked back inside.

It wasn't quite as bad, now that she was prepared and expecting it. Quite.

"Mags?"

She found him slumped against one wall, amidst the wreckage of several bots. His skin chapped, rough as lips in a dry winter, and he wept blackened, clotted blood. It flowed slowly, a viscous sludge, with an occasional bubble and pop as she watched.

Garlic, another of their legendary banes, might not be lethal to the undead, but it obviously wasn't harmless.

"Here." She coughed, painfully, then sank down beside him. His skin felt rough as an old onion's. "I'm right here."

"Hurts. Can't see..."

"Come on." She stood halfway, paused to let a brief wave of dizziness pass, and then tugged. "Up." She hefted him as he staggered, wrapping his arm around her shoulder. "Why not just change into mist?"

No answer. Perhaps he couldn't, for whatever reason—the pain?—and was too ashamed to say. Perhaps, in his agony, he simply hadn't thought of it, which would also be rather embarrassing to admit. Whatever the reason, Mags didn't push the issue.

A step. Another. A stumble. A step.

The feel of the floor changed beneath her boots, and they

were standing again in the gap between cars. Mags turned and slammed the door behind them, cutting them off from the pungent fume.

She might as well have flipped a switch or cranked some dormant engine. No recovery time, no healing process. Ian's skin smoothed out beneath her fingers, and his shoulders straightened. He took his arm from around her, wiping the rotted gunk from his face to reveal a clear and uninjured gaze.

"Glad to see you're feeling better."

Ian cocked his head, as if listening and sniffing the air at once. "Who came with you?"

"Trevor. Trevor Rose."

"Ah. He's dead now."

It was the casual tone, as much as what he said, that shook her, shocked her. "What...?"

"Hold that thought."

The door before them opened hard enough to buckle the frame, and Ian swept through the opening. Mags heard shots and tearing metal, blinked twice to clear the last of the blur from her vision, and by then it was already over.

Ian stood between the crates and the overturned pallet, clutching a handful of wires and cables. The bot sprawled before him, unmoving.

But the vampire's swift victory had not been entirely one-sided. A ragged chunk of his right shoulder was missing, and he seemed unsteady again. Before her eyes, the wound began to close, the muscle and tissue and skin to regenerate, but it was a strangely awkward process, advancing in fits and starts.

"I need to feed."

Mags blanched and retreated. "Ian, no."

"Wouldn't want to make you weak, not while we're on mission. Help me find another option while I still have the choice."

A rough swallow, a desperate nod, and then she forced herself to move into the car, to look behind the crates.

Trevor was, as Ian had sensed, quite dead. The machine's high-caliber weapon had all but ground him into paste from neck to belly.

"Could you...?" she tried to ask, sick that the thought had even occurred to her.

"No. Blood of the dead is useless."

"But he *just* died!"

"Doesn't matter. It's not science, it just *is*."

Mags tried to turn away and couldn't make herself. "He should have been fine. We were at a standoff. What happened?"

"Without two of you taking turns," Ian mused, "it wouldn't be difficult for the bot to maintain fire, keep Trevor pinned, long enough to cover the distance. Once it was close, he wouldn't have stood a chance."

"Then," her voice cracked, "if I hadn't left him..."

"It's okay, Mags." She almost wept at his touch, began to cast him a grateful smile.

It didn't last.

"There's absolutely no reason," he continued, "anyone has to know this was your fault."

Chapter Twenty-Three

Magdalena huddled in the farthest corner of the barracks, ratty blanket wrapped tight about her shoulders, and tried to wish the world away.

Oh, she'd never have admitted to it. Had anyone asked her, she would have claimed, and possibly even believed, that she was keeping out of the way. The new arrivals—the "objective" when they'd hit the train, multiple teams of workers traveling into the region to restock the work camps, to replace the men and women Lacusta had already liberated—were only just settling in. Many were more than eager to take up arms against the machines, were enraptured by the vampires. Quite a few others, however, appeared lost, dazed, unsure of what had just happened, still trying to process the massive change in their world.

The mines grew crowded, stifling, redolent of dirty sweat with just a touch of refuse. The barracks finally ran out of space, so Lacusta directed workers to clean and fortify several of the chambers in the central of the three mine shafts, rather than focusing solely on this one. They'd have more than sufficient room once that was done, but it meant days of cramped and uncomfortable conditions until the new spaces were ready.

Thankfully, none of the participants of the train raid were expected to help yet, having been given the day to rest and recover. Those who had survived, anyway. While Trevor wasn't the mission's only casualty, he *was* the only loss from Magdalena's squad. She could only hope it was pure grief over that loss, and not blame, that had kept Roberta, Dwayne, and Sharon from speaking with her during the long walk home.

Well, Roberta and Sharon. She didn't really care why Dwayne wouldn't speak to her and considered it a gift.

Despite the flurry of activity throughout the mine—*mines, now,* she corrected herself—the barracks chamber remained silent but for shallow breathing and a few snores. Everyone else who'd attacked the train, or rather everyone human, was either deep in slumber or out working off the lingering adrenaline. Only Mags, of all of them, huddled on her stopgap mattress without falling asleep.

Why? Pick a reason. Disgust. Guilt.

"Hello, Mags."

Fear.

"What are you doing here, Ian?"

He smiled down at her, almost bashful. "I just wanted to thank you. If you hadn't stopped me, who knows what punishment I might have faced. Or if any of the newcomers could *ever* have trusted us."

Mags lacked the emotional wherewithal even for a full frown; it came out a mildly irritated moue, instead. When they'd reached the workers on the train, it had been all she could do—arguing that they *were* trying to make allies of these people, that Lacusta would be furious if Ian disrupted that—to hold him back from a feeding frenzy that would have left heaps of emptied husks behind. And even with that argument, she'd delayed him for only a couple of minutes. Had Lacusta not arrived when he did...

"You're, uh, you're welcome." He sounded sincere, his expression seemed earnest. Her heart fluttered like a hopeful sparrow. Still, her exhaustion, and her memory of that *other* expression, the one he'd cast her way when she'd gotten between him and his intended prey, kept her from any more fervent response.

He lowered himself gracefully to the floor. "I need you, Mags."

Another little flutter. "I need you, too, Ian." She reached for his cheek, then froze as his own hand rose to clasp her firmly about the wrist.

"I need you," he repeated, and this time there was something else behind the words, something hungry.

"No! Let *go*!" Her abrupt yank caught Ian by surprise; it was the only way she could possibly have pulled free of his inhuman grip.

Ian let his own hand drop, then glanced around at the slumbering forms and raised a finger to his lips. "Do you want to wake everyone?" he hissed.

"Ian..."

"I hurt, Mags. I've been hurting for hours, since the train. Since the shots I took for you!"

She flinched, but only a bit. It wasn't as though she'd *asked* him to go barging through the door and into the machine's sights. "I thought you had people for that," she accused, clutching her aching wrist with the other hand. "The prisoners. Your 'herd.'"

"I'm not the only one who returned needing to feed," he said. "Every one of the prisoners has already lost blood tonight. I don't know if I can control myself enough not to kill one of them. Not as much as I hurt, not with them already weakened. Someone healthy is, well, safer.

"Besides," he continued, scooting forward so their knees touched, "it doesn't have to be just about feeding. It can be amazing, Mags! Intimate. I know I was out of it, last time, but just picture it! My lips on your skin, our *lives* mingling, intertwining, yours healing mine, soothing..."

It *did* sound sensual, phrased that way, but that hadn't been experience the first time. "This isn't like sex. Your new idea of 'penetration' *hurts*."

"So did sex, the first time."

"I don't want—"

"I *helped* you! I chose not to feed on the newbies, to stay hurting, *for you*!"

"I helped you, too, you know! Or did you already forget that garlic shit you were choking on? That's what friends and teammates and lovers *do*! And you didn't hold off feeding for me, you were just scared of what Lacusta would do!"

It was Ian, this time, who recoiled. "Is that what you think of me?" he whispered.

"Ian..."

"No, you're right. You're tired." His voice rose as he did, not by any means into a shout, but loud enough that he no longer seemed to care if the others awoke. And indeed, as he spoke, several sleepers blinked and struggled to focus. "I should let you sleep. Besides, look at the harm you caused the *last* time you tried to help me."

Mags swallowed a whimper, gaze flitting around the room, wondering if anyone knew what he meant. She didn't know what to do, what she felt. Couldn't think, for the pounding that shook her head and made debris of her thoughts. She was just so *tired*.

"I'm sure I can find someone willing to help," he assured her. "That's what friends and teammates and lov—" He stopped with an audible hitch. "That's what friends and teammates do." He turned away, picking his path across the barracks.

"Wait." Mags struggled to her feet, thrashing a bit to free her limbs from the clinging net of blanket. "Wait, Ian. It's okay, I can do it."

"No, you should sleep. We'll discuss this tomorrow."

"No!" Again she reached out for him, this time imploring. She loathed herself for it, loathed herself for ever having refused him, and couldn't begin to tell which was worse, or even where one ended and the other began. It would be so much easier if she was like him, if they were equals again... "You're right. It's what lovers do. You don't need to go look for anyone else."

He gazed at her, unblinking, weighing, judging.

"I didn't mean to make you feel unwanted," she continued. "I'm sorry."

He came to her, smiling again, taking her in his arms. Together they sank down on her blanket, his mouth working its way down her shoulder, her arm, the inside of her elbow. Already her wrist tingled, aching in fearful anticipation, and it took everything she had to keep her breathing calm.

Maybe he's right. Maybe it'll be better the second time, more intimate, more—

When it came, though, the pain was even worse than she remembered. Sharp. Unnatural. Unclean. Another whimper surfaced from deep within, and this one she couldn't suppress.

All she could do was shut her eyes. She knew some of the others were fully awake, now. She knew that they watched.

She just couldn't bear to *see* that they watched.

Chapter Twenty-Four

Like pooling blood beneath an open wound, Lacusta's army expanded.

With four new detachments behind him, the vampire struck a foundry halfway around the Scatters. Distant from their prior attacks, and seemingly of low value—it held few supplies the ragtag militia would find useful, only raw ores and alloys—it had proved poorly guarded. Sabotaging the place, dramatically slowing production, was almost easy.

Using information offered by the men and women from the train, Lacusta then pinpointed the camp from which they'd come, a camp of which Mags and the others had been completely ignorant. Figuring that the machines would *expect* him to act on that knowledge, the vampire instead returned to liberate the camp from which the 13936 had escaped, so many weeks ago. A significant number of the workers didn't survive, for the machines turned their weapons on *them* when the camp was breached, but enough survived to swell the ranks ever further.

Another equipment depot, which they emptied and burned. Another train, which—after determining it carried no human cargo—they simply blew up, along with a quarter mile of track. Another camp liberated.

At every turn, they seemed to catch the machines unprepared, the bulk of Eyes' resources elsewhere, guarding more easily anticipated targets. Victories mounted, casualties were few.

Until, as the days grew colder and the nights longer, the occasional oily rain turning to occasional greasy snow, Lacusta decided his people were ready to hit a *real* target.

Mags had never seen so much metal in her life. She stared, enraptured, and she was hardly that the only one.

It loomed in teetering stacks of crushed cars and mashed appliances, over twice her height. Those heaps creaked in the wind, shed flurries of flaking rust that warred with the constellations of drifting snow. A thin skin of earth atop the mud cracked with every step, having long since absorbed the variety of fluids bled from old and rotting engines.

She had also spotted the tracks, and on occasion heard the distant yips and growls, of what she'd at first assumed to be coyotes, though she'd not yet seen one and couldn't imagine what would move the creatures to haunt this sort of place.

"Not coyotes," Sankar—whose presence in the field was but one of this mission's abnormalities—told her when she mentioned it. "Wild dogs. Used to be just about every junkyard had dogs. It's their descendants grumbling and grousing at us, I'd think."

Junkyard. That these corroding hulks had once been all but worthless was a notion she could scarcely credit. And this, again according to Sankar, was nothing! A tiny fraction of what this place would once have held. This was only the very worst of it, the stuff substantially more rust than metal, that the machines hadn't yet gotten around to using.

So much metal, some of the most precious substances existing in a post-Pacification world, but ultimately worthless to a ragged resistance movement that lacked the capability or the facilities to manufacture anything from it.

Worthless, except as cover.

Mags leaned around one of the stacks, paranoid about brushing against the jagged and potentially unstable detritus, and again raised the night-vision goggles.

"I said you could use those for a *minute!*" Dwayne bitched at her.

"Shut it. Looking."

It was far larger, and far more advanced, than any prior installation she'd seen. Rectangular quadrants of varying dimensions linked one to the next, forming a single structure.

Although the stone façade appeared primitive, enormous metal tubes and heavily reinforced cables ran in neat rows across the walls and the roof. Smokestacks belched steam and other fumes, powering what must have been multiple generators. Smaller, squatter rooftop structures might have been heat vents, maintenance access, or, well, just about anything. Several antennae bristled here and there, high-tech saplings that hadn't yet grown into larger protrusions.

Visible means of ingress were limited to a handful of doors, ranging from human-scale to a segmented garage door that could have swallowed the entire vehicle pool of Magdalena's old camp, driving abreast. All of them, large and small, were currently sealed tight.

Even from here, Mags could hear—could feel, in her gut, her bones—the overlapping rumble of the many mechanisms and processes running within. One in particular, a deep and nigh inaudible *thrum*, rattled her enough to make the goggles quiver. She couldn't imagine what needed *that* much power.

She knew the purpose, though, if not of each specific process, then in the aggregate. They all did. The vampires had scouted, spied, even communed with the local predators and scavengers, to confirm this facility was what they believed it to be.

Here, machines constructed machines. It was nursery and enemy camp and weapons depot in one. The birthplace of many of the region's bots.

A "real" target.

And one the machines apparently *recognized* would be a target, though the manner of defense they'd chosen was odd indeed.

"...diverted the flow from a nearby river," Lacusta was noting. He stood not far from Magdalena's position, with the detachment leaders and several other vampires gathered loosely around him. "With the sorts of earth-moving devices I've observed since I awoke, I imagine digging even an entire tributary would not prove difficult."

"How deep you think it is?" The question came from one of the human workers; Mags couldn't tell for sure which.

Without benefit of any tools such as the night-vision scope in

Magdalena's fist, Lacusta peered over the intervening darkness, through the curtain of shadow and dust, studying the circular stream—an old-fashioned moat, really—surrounding the plant. "It hardly matters," he observed finally. "The salient point is, it's *flowing*."

Running water. Mags nodded to herself, casting her mind back again to Sankar's tales. The machines had finally gotten around to trying that one.

"How big a problem is it?" she asked without really thinking about it. She *felt* Dwayne's scowl before she saw it, but if Lacusta even remembered that she wasn't technically a commander anymore, he didn't seem to care.

"An inconvenience, Miss Suarez. My children and I can circumvent it, but we shall have to fly at substantial height. Crossing may prove difficult for the rest of you as well, should you come under attack at the time. It limits our options for approach, but I do not believe it should prove an insurmountable obstacle."

"What's wrong, Mags?" Cassie mocked, leering openly. "You want to give up and go home? You still 'sick,' poor baby?"

Mags flushed to the roots of her hair. On more than one morning she'd arrived at breakfast wan and pale, weak and distracted, and people had noticed. Her claim that she was struggling with an ongoing virus didn't appear to be convincing anyone.

"I'm good, how's the shoulder?" Mags snapped back. She didn't have to see Cassie's expression. She all but heard the redhead's smile fall from her face. Several of the other vampires snickered.

It had been during the last camp liberation. Cassie had been showing off, luxuriating in her powers, ignoring the tiny drones with their tiny guns, all but incapable of seriously hurting her.

Until she'd learned, the hard way, that the machines were testing a new form of ammunition: gel-capped hollow points containing garlic oil.

It proved only a moderately effective weapon; the gaseous form they'd used on Ian was far more debilitating. Lacking an active circulatory system, nothing inside Cassie's body caused the caustic substance to spread. The agony remained confined to the point of impact, barely even slowing her down.

It had taken her a moment, however, to recognize that fact. A moment in which she'd shrieked to shame a frightened kitten, injured for the first time since her transformation, convinced she'd been hit by some sort of devastating explosive round. Although half the other vampires would doubtless have reacted the same way, they'd taunted her mercilessly about it since.

"Enough of this," Lacusta declared. "It is time. Warren!"

"Yes, sir?" the young vampire responded, standing notably straighter. Mags nearly snickered at him.

"Make one final flight around the structure, so we can be certain they've made no last-minute changes. Try to determine if there's an extendable bridge or other method for crossing the moat. The machines must have *some* such."

Warren erupted, disintegrating into a geyser of small owls. Dozens of wings fluttered in unison, speaking a sinister whisper that Mags thought she could almost understand.

Upward, ever upward, a rising column becoming a graceful spiral. Some several dozen feet in the air, invisible if not for her night-vision goggles, they sharply turned, arrowing straight for the installation. At the very edge of the moat, however, they pulled back, thrashing and shrieking, as though some incomprehensible horror rendered them unwilling or unable to cross.

"Higher." Lacusta spoke softly but, whether through his inhuman hearing or some far more subtle connection to his maker, the distant Warren understood.

Again the flock rose, circling as if following the path of some forgotten twister. A hundred feet, two hundred, even more, and then the vampire attempted once again to cross the artificial stream.

So far as Mags could observe, this time the water exerted no effect on him at all.

Well, good. Now it should just be a matter of—

A squat protrusion on the factory roof split open, a clumsy flower revealing a framework with three disturbingly large barrels. It spun, rotating to bring its weapons to bear with a high-pitched and somehow menacing whine of servos.

The narrowest of the triple barrels spat fire. Torrents of flame lit the sky, reflecting off the water, forcing Mags to flinch away, goggles falling unheeded to the foul earth. It swept back and forth, painting the world in shades of conflagration.

Every one of the owls cried out in unison, and every one of those cries was Warren's voice. And just as swiftly, the scream stopped, and there was only the roar of the flame until it, too, went dark and silent.

Mags thought the great and ancient Lacusta had never appeared as bewildered, as startled, as he did now. And she completely understood why. It wasn't just the loss of one of his "children," though she knew that troubled him far more than the death of any human.

No, he had seen what she had, both before and during those brief moments of hellish light. The turret—presumably guided by the same mechanical intelligence that the other bots possessed, an intelligence that *should have been unable to see Warren at all*—had meticulously turned and tracked the vampiric swarm before it opened fire.

Chapter Twenty-Five

The floodgates opened.

Every visible door in the structure slid wide, save for the massive garage, and from within poured a rising tide of machines. Drones flitted up and out of sight. Humanoid bots marched into view, armed with blades in addition to their more advanced weaponry. Multiple spiders clambered out onto the grounds, the smaller, more general-purpose types and the larger combat models, both. Through the night-vision scope she'd scrambled to retrieve, Mags could see that some of the latter had been modified, or perhaps even built from scratch, with vampires in mind. Their turrets boasted protrusions that appeared more flamethrower than firearm, and the inhuman manipulators that served the model as hands had been replaced with far more brutal instruments: racing chainsaw blades on some, thick shafts of hardwood that pumped and pulsed like jackhammers on others.

Panels fell away with a series of ringing clangs as the other blocky protrusions on the roof revealed their own multi-weapon batteries. They, and the combat units below, swiveled to face the automotive cemetery in which Lacusta's forces hid. Barrels flashed like artificial fireflies as those machines armed with long-range weapons opened fire. Mags heard not only the gunshots, but the far more terrifying *spark-thud* of electromagnetic accelerators. One of the stacks of rusted husks shuddered as a rail-fired projectile passed cleanly through it.

"Cover!" The cry came from a dozen voices at once as men, women, even vampires dove to the crusty mud. The clatter of bullets on the remains of cars was a violent, hellish hailstorm.

"Cover?" someone else—Dwayne, maybe? Mags wasn't sure—repeated incredulously. "We need to get the fuck out of here!"

"*No!*" Lacusta came to life as rapidly as he'd seized up, shock and confusion replaced by fury. "No, there will be no retreat! If you carry a weapon equal to the distance, return fire!"

The humans complied, if hesitantly, but it proved little more than a defiant gesture. Only a fraction carried rifles capable of any accuracy at such range, and not all who did were expert enough to take full advantage.

"I, uh, don't intend to question you," Cassie began hesitantly, "but if they can see us—"

"That is precisely why we stay!" the ancient creature snapped. "We must know *how* they've done this!" Then, scowling, "Miss Suarez! Bring me Mister Rao."

"I'm not sure where... He took cover somewhere!"

"*Then find him!*"

She ran. Keeping low, dodging in random zigs, she raced between the stacks. Bullets whined overhead, splattered her with mud, sang as they ricocheted from steel. One of the newer soldiers stepped halfway into the open, firing back at the machines, trying to cover her run. The back of his head opened, spraying bullet fragments, blood, and worse in Magdalena's wake. By the time she found Sankar, huddled in a hollow between two mashed cars, she was crawling on her belly to avoid incoming rounds.

From above came the sound of a dozen rotors, perhaps more, as the drones closed in. More shots split the night, smaller and softer but still deadly. Eight people fell before anyone realized the flying machines were there, let alone begun to fire back.

Mags and the old man were both coated in stinging, chemical-scented muck, and very near to hyperventilating, by the time they'd wiggled their way back to Lacusta's position. Mags slumped to one side, gasping, as the vampire began interrogating Sankar.

Something was gnawing at her, something she'd noticed— or perhaps *almost* noticed—on the crawl back. If her chest would just stop burning and her head stop ringing long enough to think!

"...believe they were anywhere *close* to a camera that could see you," Sankar was saying in answer to the vampire's question. "Near as I could tell, they hadn't so much as the first guess as to *why* you're invisible to them. *I* certainly can't bloody explain it!"

"They seek a scientific answer," Lacusta mused, "where none exists. So long as they do so, they'll continue to fail. But if they cannot see us, then how—"

"How many vampires been shot?" Mags asked between gulps of air.

"I beg your pardon?" How the hell Lacusta could manage a polite and urbane growl, Mags couldn't begin to imagine, but that's what emerged.

"Since the bots started shooting. Since the drones got close."

"None." He sounded thoughtful, now.

"Perhaps they haven't got any undead-appropriate ammunition," Sankar suggested.

"Uh-uh." Mags shook her head. "Saw them petty clearly through the scope. These fuckers are ready and waiting.

"Look at what happened to Warren." As Lacusta's face darkened once more, she hastened to add, "They didn't attack until he crossed the water. The flamethrower was spraying back and forth, has to have used at least twice as much fuel as it needed to!"

"You don't believe they *can* see us," Lacusta concluded.

"No. I think they found a way, at short range, to tell *kind of* where you are."

"Sonics," Sankar declared. "Or precise sensors for picking up subtle shifts in wind and temperature when the air moves around you."

The vampire looked as though he'd bitten into a rotten, well, corpse. "Could such a thing sense us as we ride the mists?"

"Definitely not if it's sound-based. If it's environmental? *Probably* not, but I couldn't offer any assurances."

"And if they can, it means they could easily prepare to attack us the instant we materialized."

Sankar and Mags nodded in unison.

"Either way, our speed in such a form is limited. It would

take some time to travel high enough to cross the moat.

"Very well. What we will do is this..."

Ian shouted something Mags couldn't make out over the roar of the massive engine, the wind across the open door, or the adrenaline-spiked pounding in her own head.

"What?"

"I said, just like old times, yeah?"

Mags snorted and wrestled with the shaking wheel, struggling to keep the truck steady over uneven ground. "Yeah, if you're remembering all the times we were fucking idiots!"

The vampire, who was not inside the truck but running alongside despite the vehicle's speed, chuckled at her. He jogged at a slight crouch behind the open door, which provided a modicum of cover to both Ian himself and the other vampires in line behind him. Mags had actually been relieved when an errant round blew out the window in that door. No matter that Sankar's myths and Lacusta's own words had warned her to expect it, no matter that she'd experienced it many times over the past weeks, it had still disturbed the hell out of her every time she'd glanced over to see Ian beside her, but *not* reflected in the glass mere inches away.

Swallowing the last of his amusement, Ian tossed something overhand. It sailed over the door, tumbled end over end in a high arc, cleared the moat, and plummeted amidst the gathering machines.

Not really meant for hurling, these explosives, but then, Ian threw a lot harder than normal folk. The package hadn't *quite* hit the earth when the timer reached zero. Dirt and pieces of bot flew far and wide—then even farther and wider as other vampires followed Ian's cue with their own makeshift ordnance.

From behind them, far enough to one side that they'd not risk hitting the truck, Nestor and several others let rip with the .50s, thinning out the edges of the target zone while the bombardment of explosives cleared the interior. More of Lacusta's soldiers advanced on the moat from other directions, keeping low, presenting just enough of a threat that the bots could not focus solely on the incoming vehicle. They inflicted few casualties; the machines were too quick, too rugged. But at least the truck wasn't taking as much fire as it otherwise might.

Which didn't mean *none*.

"Gah!"

Mags flinched as the windshield exploded inward, a cluster of rounds whipping past within inches of her head. More bullets tore through both doors. Ian and the lead vampire on the passenger side both stumbled, nearly falling. Their wounds might not have been lethal or even debilitating, but the rounds still packed a punch.

"I don't think we're getting much closer in one piece!" Mags screamed at him. "Will this do?"

"It'll have to!"

Mags nodded and hit the big orange button on her radio: one of many connected to a shielded network they'd constructed weeks back with materials salvaged from various raids. "Bail, bail, bail!"

A handful of soldiers, braced for what would be a great deal of pain, leapt from the rear of the truck. That had been their entire purpose, to sit there so the machines could detect them.

Had the truck been mostly empty of life, they might have given themselves away.

Mags propped a tire iron between seat and accelerator, took a deep breath and rolled from the cab, tucking to take the impact as best she could and hoping to avoid being trampled by the vampires running alongside.

She felt Ian's hand close on her belt, yanking her along for a fraction of a second before letting her drop. She screamed, more in surprise than pain, and then found herself tumbling over the sod.

He'd slowed her drop, just a bit, saved her some of the bruising and battering—and possibly worse—the others suffered. Even as she bounced and flailed, she found herself grinning. She ached when she finally came to a stop, ached a lot, but everything still functioned.

Despite the stiffness in her neck, Mags raised her head to watch. No *way* she was missing this! Although, oddly, she couldn't help but think, *we're going to have either a long walk or a crowded ride home, now.*

According to both Sankar's myths and Lacusta's boasts, each vampire possessed the strength of ten to twenty men. Around the truck were eight of them, barreling along at thirty miles per hour.

Most of the machines ceased firing on the vehicle, turning their attentions elsewhere. It appeared to them abandoned, a runaway that could only plunge into the moat and sink.

The vampires, in concert, reached down to grip the frame and *heaved.*

The lumbering vehicle left the ground, engine roaring, tires racing, chassis shrieking, popping, squealing. It didn't so much soar as simply bull forward and *upward*, ignoring gravity and daring gravity to say a word about it.

The truck began to plummet soon enough; not even the vampires had the strength to send it aloft for long. Its abortive flight, though, was sufficient.

It plunged nose-down on the far side of the moat with an ear- and earth-rending crash, digging a broad furrow, spilling fluids and shedding scraps. Swiftly it skidded to a halt, teetering for a breath or two, creaking painfully, before toppling onto its roof.

"Boom," Mags whispered, dropping her face to the dirt and crossing her arms over her head. Right on cue, someone back in the junkyard hit the detonator.

The collection of explosives the rebels had brought with them, spread throughout their various vehicles, had been intended to take down the bulk of the factory. Now, roughly nine-tenths of that stockpile went up in a single massive blast.

Magdalena's body quivered and roiled as the shockwave raced over her; she felt the searing kiss of heat on her skin. Ears ringing and stomach heaving, she raised her head once more.

The truck was gone, save for bits of scattered, twisted metal. A hundred small fires flickered where grass had ignited, puddles of fuel burned off, or various bots had been blasted apart. One wall of the installation was blackened and cracked, and this side of the structure was all but cleared of machines.

Not for long—already drones swept toward them, multi-legged bots skittered around from the back—but long enough.

From where they had circled high above, Lacusta and the remainder of his children descended, crossing the stream as bird or bat and then transforming before the defensive batteries could lock on. Streams of mist and plumes of dust drifted downward, making for the center of the devastation where no bots awaited them, and where the detonation and the crackling fires had most likely blinded any special sensors the machines might possess.

Nor were Lacusta's schemes done, not by far. The machines understood by now how the vampires preferred to fight, so the vampires would show them something new.

A second truck rumbled over at speed, following in the tracks of the first. Again Magdalena's teammates fired on the machines from all directions, slowing their advance, occupying their attentions. The vehicle neared the moat, breaking and slewing sideways as it reached the waiting vampires. Ian and his seven companions sidestepped, allowing the truck to fishtail to a halt between them.

Mags swore, over the lingering scents of the explosion, that she could smell the gun oil.

From the rear of the vehicle, Nestor and the other burliest soldiers began hefting weapons. Really, obscenely *big* weapons. The pair of belt-fed machineguns; a massive automatic shotgun; and a wide variety of only slightly smaller firearms. The absolute heaviest of the army's heavy weaponry.

The humans passed them to the vampires, and the vampires, in turn, sent them spinning high over the moat.

It was a dance, choreographed, graceful. Mags could liken it to nothing else. The weapons spun, firelight winking off cold steel barrels, began to slow, to plummet.

Lacusta and the others appeared around them, solidifying from the fog and the dust, materializing yards above the debris-strewn earth. Pale hands whipped out, fastening on grips and triggers that they could never have carried in their less tangible forms.

Boots struck the ground, the vampires landing in twin rows,

back to back. Even from here, Mags saw the ancient vampire grin as he raised the .50-caliber weapon—raised in one hand, as if it were a pistol, a gun that Nestor could not accurately aim without a bipod—and fired.

The others followed suit. Cassie cackled as she blasted away with the giant shotgun, and her fellow vampires seemed equally delighted. The two lines advanced on the enemy to either side, ripping apart machines that had anticipated, and armed themselves for, close combat.

Ian and the remaining vampires on this side of the moat took to the air, owls and bats climbing high, seeking the sweet spot at which they could pass across the water to join their brethren.

Mags groaned to her feet and set off toward the moat, and the others began falling into place around her. She still didn't know if they would have to wade or swim, but at least she could be fairly sure that they'd make it. The machines—what was left of them—had more pressing matters to attend to.

"That," Mags grumbled, peering up at the ever-shifting electric lights recessed into the ceiling, "is getting *really* annoying."

After expending their ammunition and reverting to proven techniques of fists and shape-shifting, the vampires had moved from the grounds into the factory itself. There they'd encountered additional resistance, judging by the sounds, but Mags had no idea precisely what. She knew only that when she and the other humans had entered, they'd faced no enemies but the occasional drone and a single spider of the smaller variety.

She would very much have liked to see the massive machinery, the automated assembly, the artificial womb from which the tyrannical machines were birthed. That, however, was not her job. Along with a pair of relative newcomers—she knew them only by their last names, Reese and Little—she watched Sankar's back while the old man searched. He carried a small computer, one with which he hoped to access information from the facility network; indeed, that was why he'd come along on this mission at all. He appeared to need a particular variety of interface, however, and Mags was about ready to scream in frustration before he finally found one, tucked away behind a large bin of spare parts.

Now they waited, watching for trouble as Sankar alternately cursed at and argued with the computer, pounding on keys and occasionally jiggling the connecting cable in frustration.

And those damn lights kept shifting hue just as Mags grew accustomed to the last!

"The hell is all that shit about anyway?" Little finally demanded, aiming a pistol in what Mags hoped was an *idle* threat to shoot out the nearest electrics.

"Machines trying to zero in on what it is about sunlight that weakens the undead, I'd wager," Sankar answered without turning from the monitor.

"You think they're gonna figure out that they can't any time soon?" Mags asked.

"I tend to doubt it. They're looking for a specific wavelength, but I'm fairly sure it's another 'no scientific explanation' thing. The Eyes seem reluctant to accept those, though."

"Whatever," Reese said. As always when he spoke, Mags had to battle the urge to wince at his obnoxiously high voice. "You almost done?"

"No, I am bloody well not almost done!" Sankar smacked the terminal with an open palm. "This damn thing was never intended to interface with anything a human being can interact with, and I'm not exactly conversationally fluent in the machine code! I'm getting what I can, as fast as I can, and you hounding me about it *is just one more bloody distraction*, isn't it?"

"Um, sorry?"

"Damn right." Another moment of key-punching, and, "Reese, Little, take a quick look around. Make sure nobody's creeping up on us."

"Uh..."

"I'll be fine. Magdalena will stay with me."

Reluctantly, they shuffled off.

"All right, Sankar, that was about as subtle as the truck bomb. What's up?"

Still the old man kept his attentions fixed on the keyboard. "I'm worried about you."

"That's kind of expected in a combat zone, isn't it?" *Don't say it, don't say it...*

"That's not what I mean. I've seen you in the mornings. It's regular now. Every few days."

A familiar ache across her neck and shoulders, a familiar pang in her gut, all the offspring of a familiar tension. "Sankar, don't."

"Magdalena, I sympathize, I do. I know you love him, but—" *God dammit.*

"Now? Now?! Really?!" She wanted to haul off and hit him, wanted to run away and huddle in the corner, wanted to go quiet, wanted to cry. She settled for indignation. "This feel like a good time to chat, to you?"

"Since I know that Ian's not going to overhear us in this chaos, yes, rather."

"Unbelievable. Un-God damn-fucking believable!" She yanked him by one bony shoulder, spinning him to face her. "It's not enough I have Nestor riding me about things that are none of his business? You're gonna give me shit, too?"

"He's hurting you."

"It's not his fault! He's getting better! God, he saved me from a bad fall just a few minutes ago!"

"That's because he wants to keep using you."

"First, I am *trying* to prove myself to them! And second, he loves me!"

Sankar gently pried her fingers off him. "We know he's feeding on you, Magdalena. Often. *Too* often. We all know."

Later, Mags would wonder what expression she must have worn, to make the old man recoil as he did. Much later. For now, through a jaw that felt as rusted as any of the junked cars outside, she said only, "Do your damn job."

And that, until long after he'd downloaded everything he could, after the team had sabotaged every piece of machinery and fled the installation, was *all* she intended to say to him.

Chapter Twenty-Six

"Missed you at breakfast," Nestor chided gently.

His voice didn't precisely echo, but it had assumed a hollow quaver. Most sounds did, in this chamber. Branching off the central mineshaft, it had been put aside for storage and use of the computers, radios, and other electronic equipment acquired over the course of the war. A small generator sat in the corner, humming contentedly, a bristling sea urchin of cables and attachments. The glare of Sankar's monitor shone across the room, despite the lights glowing above.

Mags and Ian stepped into the room, his arm around her shoulders, her head tilted to lean against him. He appeared happy enough, even smug. She, however, could muster only the faintest smile of pallid lips for her friend's greeting.

"Wasn't hungry," she told him weakly.

"Ah." Nestor looked away, perhaps hiding an expression he couldn't suppress. In near synchronicity, Sankar turned from the monitor to direct a sad, shallow smile of his own Magdalena's way. The others present—Roberta, Sharon, and Dwayne, all adding up to a gathering rather larger than was customary for the electronics room—peered this way or that, whatever didn't require what had suddenly become awkward eye contact.

"So." Ian gave Magdalena a gentle but obvious squeeze. "What are we all doing here? Not exactly the social center of our little family."

Nestor made a sound somewhat akin to a dog choking on an overripe radish.

"I was here working," Sankar explained, before Ian could react. "Nestor came to me for some counsel on a… personal matter. The others showed up during that conversation."

"Oh, uh, yeah." Dwayne clumsily picked up the thread. "Yeah, just, Sankar knows the machines better'n anyone, and Nest's got a pretty good tactical mind. I just wanted to get their opinion on the drone situation."

"Drone situation?" It was Mags who asked, but Dwayne's attention shifted, or so it appeared, to Ian.

The vampire scowled but nodded. "It's getting harder to avoid the Eyes', um, eyes. They try to track us—well, you; humans—after every operation. They've got search patterns going all the damn time. The dust and cloud cover help, but only so much."

"To this point," Dwayne said, "the vampires have been able to take down or warn us away from any scouts. But not even you guys can be everywhere at night, and of course during the day..." His hands fluttered in the lower half of a shrug.

"It's been too easy," Sankar muttered, then seemed startled at everyone's sudden attention.

Ian's scowl deepened, flashing just a hint of fang. "The hell are you talking about, old man?"

"I just, well, all of it. A whole swathe of drones, but I'd have expected more. As heavily as most of our targets have been defended, we've taken remarkably few casualties. We've *never* been routed without accomplishing at least part of our objective."

"They don't know how to deal with us," the vampire insisted. "We're too much for them, and we've got a lot more people than they could ever have expected."

"Maybe." Sankar began clacking beads together in his pocket. "It *has* been decades since Pacification. Perhaps the machines focused on other purposes in the interval and lack the resources for open war."

He didn't point out that, were that the case, the situation would change dramatically once the machines altered production or shipped soldiers in from other territories. Every one of them heard it anyway.

Ian didn't quite scoff, but it was a near thing. "Lacusta will figure something out."

"For all our sakes, you'd better be right." Sankar placed one hand beside the keyboard, prayer beards clasped and still clattering between his fingers, while he typed with the other. After a bit of uncomfortable silence, he began muttering under his breath.

Something jostled Magdalena's head, and she realized Ian was fidgeting. She'd never seen any of the undead do such a thing—the nosferatu lacked such "mortal idiosyncrasies"—but she couldn't doubt it now. He shifted foot to foot, ground his teeth, scratched at his palms with his fist-clenched fingers.

"Would you fucking quit it!" he finally spat.

Mags jumped back in alarm, pulling herself from the half-circle of his arm. The others appeared only marginally less startled.

None of them, however, harbored any doubt who he meant. Ian leaned sharply toward Sankar, much like a leashed hound.

Minus the leash.

"I have no idea what you're talking about," the old man protested.

"Your... You... You're muttering! It's... It's..."

Sankar's stare remained blank.

"Um, so?" Sharon ventured.

Something rolled at the base of Ian's throat, a primordial sound that hadn't fully evolved to a genuine growl. He appeared two steps nearer the doorway before Mags registered that he'd moved.

"You coming?" he barked.

"I want to hear more about this drone thing."

"Fine!" Ian folded inward, almost deflating, and vanished into a streamer of mist that quickly flowed into the hall and away.

"All right, Sankar. Spill."

"Beg pardon?"

Mags leaned against the desk—really just a rough slab of wood, propped on makeshift legs—and began idly picking splinters from the edge. Casual, nonchalant, and perfectly concealing the fact that standing on her own for more than a few minutes was an iffy prospect.

Or she hoped it did.

"Don't 'beg pardon' me. You were praying. You *wanted* to make him uncomfortable."

"Was I? I suppose between my nervousness over the drones and trying to concentrate on this bloody machine code, I hadn't realized—"

"Sure you didn't. I know this'll come as a terrible shock, but I'm not buying it."

"Mags," Nestor began hesitantly, "about Ian…"

"I'm out of here."

"Wait." Sankar's hand closed on her sleeve. "Please. Nestor, Magdalena has made it clear she doesn't care to discuss that topic with us. We should respect her wishes."

Nestor mumbled something at his feet. Mags felt a fist of pure guilt form in her gut and begun pummeling her from within.

She swallowed hard, twice, perhaps hoping to drown it. "So what *did* you want to talk to me about?"

"Even if I were attempting to shoo Ian from the room, how do you know I'm not simply unfond of his presence?"

"Sankar."

"Yes, right. While we *were* discussing the drones, that wasn't why this lot came to see me."

"Hang on," Dwayne interrupted. "I'm not sure we can trust her."

"*What?*" Mags shot from the desk, anger lending her strength. "God dammit, Dwayne, I know you don't like me much—"

"It's not about *liking* you, it's about you fucking a vampire!"

Just that quickly, a wave of dizziness washed her newfound strength away. "I… We haven't! Not since… Since Ian…"

Why am I defending myself to this shithead?

"I'm quite sure," Sankar said, standing to put himself between them, "that whatever Magdalena's personal relationships, she can be trusted to keep a secret for her friends. Can't you?"

"Of course I can." She leaned over to glower at Dwayne around Sankar. "And him, too, if I have to."

"Ah, fuck it." Dwayne folded his arms over his chest. "If she gets us killed, it's on you, old man."

"A burden I'll endeavor to bear."

"Uh-huh. All right, look, I... One of you want to do this?" he asked, turning toward Sharon and Roberta. "This was your deal to begin with."

Sharon fiddled with the cuff of her sleeve. "We're not sure of anything."

"*She's* not sure of anything," Roberta insisted. "*I'm* sure!"

"You can't be!"

"You bet your ass I can!"

"Hey!" Mags snapped. "*I'm* sure I have no clue what you're talking about and it's getting irritating!"

Roberta stood, tried to pace, and realized she lacked the room for it. All but bouncing in place, she said, "How many vampires are there now, do you think?"

"Uh?" Whatever Mags had been anticipating, that was far from it. "I'm not sure. A dozen, now, give or take?"

"Closer to twenty. Maybe more."

"Really?"

Sharon, Roberta, Dwayne, and even Sankar—who remained focused on the screen, and appeared to be half-listening at best, nodded in unison as though they'd rehearsed it.

"Every time we get a new detachment joining up with us," Dwayne said, "Lacusta and the others pick a few of them out for, uh, remaking."

And yet I'm still not worthy. Ian was, almost immediately, but me... "All right. I'm not thrilled about that, but—?"

"What do you think they're eating?" Sharon asked.

Mags blinked.

Dwayne picked up the narrative again. "With each new liberation, fewer and fewer people turn down Lacusta's offer. Word of us is spreading, and the machines have gotten even harsher since we've been poking at them. The vampires' *herd...*" The shiver that ran through him at that word earned him a few points of respect. *Not a complete shithead, then.* "...isn't expanding at the same rate the vampires are. And, well, look, don't throw another shit-fit, but not a whole lot of us are willing to let ourselves be fed off of on a regular basis."

"And," Roberta said, saving Mags the trouble of deciding

whether to take offense, "we haven't captured a lot of scrips alive, either. So, where are they feeding?"

"You have a theory, I take it?" Mags asked.

"Yes," said Sharon.

"It's not a theory," said Roberta.

"We *think*," Sharon continued with a quick side-eye at her friend, "that some of our people who didn't make it back from our recent missions? Were lost *after* the shooting stopped."

"*What?* That's ridic..." Come to think of it, had she seen Reese since the factory? Suddenly she wasn't sure. Not that it would prove anything if she hadn't, but, "You think the vampires are killing our own people?"

"When they need to," Roberta confirmed, "on the battlefield. But Mags, I think they're also bringing some of them back alive and throwing them in the cell with the other 'cattle.'"

"They wouldn't!" This new surge of nausea had nothing to do with Ian's most recent feeding. "I—I mean, it'd be too easy for us to find them out!"

"Mags," Nestor said softly, "they've added a latch to the cell door, to hold the bar in place. A length of metal piping from one of the raids. You can only slide the bar open if you're strong enough to bend pipe out of the way. And there's no way any of us—hell, any *three* of us—could manage it."

"Mortals keep out," Roberta spat. "Undead only."

Slowly, clumsily, Magdalena sagged back against the desk where she'd begun the conversation. "It's not proof. But..."

"Yeah," Sharon said. "But."

"So what do we do?"

Roberta snorted. "I know what *I'm* doing. I'm waiting for my shot, and then getting the fuck out of here. Anyone smart'll be coming with me. I didn't sign on to be lunch!"

"You should wait until we're sure," Sharon protested, "before you start spreading stories or planning some crazy escape."

"I *am* sure!"

"*I* think," Sankar said, his back popping sharply as he stood and stretched, "that it's going to take me days, if not weeks, to sift anything useful from this code, assuming I can manage it at all. I think that, while there will doubtless be smaller operations in the interim, Lacusta is unlikely to initiate anything major until I'm done. I think you'd be well advised to take advantage of that time, learn what you can, and avoid doing anything, let's say, *imprudent*.

"And I think, until then, you could all do much worse than to sleep lightly and watch one another's backs."

Chapter Twenty-Seven

"What if they're tracking us?" Nestor asked for what must surely have been the ninety-seventh time.

Mags groaned and hauled on the wheel, circling around a tree that, though quite dead, could still do the truck some real damage. The dim headlights, barely bright enough to prevent her from running into such obstacles, or off a cliff, gleamed briefly on bare patches in the bark.

"That's why we went out of our way," she explained, for what must *also* have been the ninety-seventh time, "to pass through the assigned rendezvous point. So we could—"

"We could pick up a vampire escort to make certain the skies are clear of drones and nobody's following our trail, yeah, yeah, I know."

"Then why do you keep worrying over it?"

"Do you see any vampires? *I* don't see any vampires! I *haven't* seen any—"

"Nest, love you to death, but I'm about to tape your mouth shut and toss you in back with the others. See if Monique or Colbie or someone wanna keep me company up here instead."

"Mags—"

"The whole point is for them *not* to be seen!"

Nestor shifted in his seat, a motion that wobbled the entire cab. "We were a whole day late!"

"Missions aren't predictable. They'd have waited or come back."

"You don't *know* that! We could be leading the machines right back home!"

"Fine!" The truck rattled to a halt, squealing and hissing. She couldn't help but wrinkle her nose at the sharp stench of burning oil. "We'll just sit here until one of the vampires drops down and asks us why the fuck we've stopped." She reached out, clicked a button on the radio. "Just a brief delay, guys. Sit tight back there."

Nobody bothered to talk back, but a quick banging on the partition between cab and cargo confirmed that they'd heard.

"Got any dice?" she asked.

"This is serious, Mags."

"Okay. Got any *serious* dice?"

Silence, then, save for the faint creaking as the truck settled, and eventually a distant chorus of crickets.

"Look," Nestor said finally, "I just don't have as much faith in the vampires as you do."

"Faith? I don't have… Oh, God dammit, Nest!"

"This isn't about Ian!" he protested with a defensiveness that screamed *This is entirely abut Ian!* "I don't know if we can count on them as much as you do, is all."

"I trust them to act in their best—"

"Hey!"

Mags and Nestor both jumped violently, the latter hard enough to smack his head on the roof, at the call and hard tapping on the glass. Out her side window, Mags could just make out enough to recognize the figure as Kelso Li, one of Lacusta's newer progeny.

"Why the fuck are you just sitting here?"

"You know, I knew you'd ask almost exactly that." She smiled prettily. "Just a personal matter. Biological issues I don't think you have to deal with anymore. You know how it is."

The fang-filled expression she received in return was very much *not* a smile. "Just get your ass moving. They've been cruising higher these days. Longer you're here jacking off, better the chances of one of them slipping by us."

"Wish I'd thought of that. Only thing that occurred to me was a game of dice." Mags cranked the ignition and got them underway as soon as the behemoth roared back to life.

"Okay," Nestor conceded a bit later, his voice rattling with the bumpy terrain. "I was wrong."

"Hey, it happens. And it wasn't a *bad* worry." Mags chuckled. "Anyway, you've had my back when I've made a mistake, so I owe you a pass."

"If *that's* how we're counting, you owe me about a hundred."

Magdalena's giggling ruined the effect of the glower she aimed Nestor's way.

They won their race against the dawn, though it was a near thing. Mags had just steered the truck under the rocky overhang, after a frustratingly long spiral down and around the quarry sides, when the sun peeked over the horizon, removing any undead cover they might have had.

For a long moment, she and Nestor sat, confused. The activity schedule in and around the mines had always been odd, given the vampires' general unwillingness to go outdoors during the day, but right now far more people scurried about on far more errands than was normal for early morning. Other vehicles had been driven from the third mine, which served now as a vehicle pool, and were undergoing detailed inspection and maintenance. Workers schlepped all manner of supplies, and several smaller groups sparred with one another at the far end of the outcropping.

"Well, *something's* up," the big guy muttered.

"I was just coming to that conclusion," Mags said, before popping open the door. "Supervise the others and get the truck unloaded, will you? I'm going to see what's going on."

"But..."

"I'll fill you in, Nest, you know that."

A loud, resonant sigh. "Fine, but you owe me."

"According to you, I already did."

The clatter of tools, the soft rumble of conversation, the thumping of feet, all combined to become more of a shock, as she hopped from the cab, than the early morning chill. She shook herself, rubbed her hands together, and set off in search of anyone she knew better than "in passing."

God, there's a lot of us now.

Still, it didn't take her long. Just inside the mouth of the third mine, she spotted Dwayne and Sharon overseeing a vehicle work-team. The former stood, shouting orders and gesticulating like a drunken caterpillar. The latter sat on a stack of tires, a small slab balanced on her lap, scribbling figures in chalk.

"Hey, guys!"

Sharon looked up from her notes with a broad grin. Dwayne, though rather less overly delighted to see her, offered a polite nod.

"Had us worried, Mags," Sharon said as she slid from the tires, stumbled awkwardly, and then righted herself.

"Sorry about that. We had to hunker in for a while to avoid a search pattern. Once we were sure they'd gone, it was too late to make the rendezvous point before dawn, so we were basically stuck for the day. All good, though."

They shared a brief welcome-home hug, but Mags couldn't help noticing that Sharon had wrapped only her right arm around her. The left hung stiffly, though if it was injured, her sleeve hid any evidence of it.

"You okay? How did the liberation go?" While Mags and her team had been raiding another supply depot, some of the others had accompanied a few vampires to liberate the last of the nearby work camps.

Sharon's face fell, as did Dwayne's. "Bad," he said. "Real bad."

"I guess..." Sharon took a deep, ragged breath. "I guess the machines got tired of losing people to us."

Magdalena's tongue turned to sandpaper. "You don't mean they—"

Dwayne swallowed and nodded. "Soon as they realized they had a vampire problem, they turned their weapons... Shit. By the time we trashed the last bot, less than a quarter of the fucking camp survived."

"God." Mags leaned in, hugging Sharon a second time, then even walked over to lay a hand, however briefly, on Dwayne's arm. "I'm sorry."

"Yeah. We all... Yeah. Thanks."

"So what's all this about?" Mags asked, sweeping an arm to encompass the ongoing activity and, not incidentally, changing the subject.

"Not actually sure," he admitted, his tone firming.

"Yesterday, Lacusta announced that everyone was supposed to start getting all our shit in order for a major op. Wouldn't say what or when. We're supposed to let him know when the last mission team returns, though, so maybe he's planning a briefing then."

"Makes sense. Who's the last team still out?"

"Oh, uh, you were."

"Oh."

A pause. A trio of blank stares.

"I, uh, should probably let him know we're back," Mags said finally.

Sharon poked absently at the tires with her left hand, then winced at whatever injury she'd picked up. "That, uh, would have been the wise thing for *one* of us to do, when you walked up," she admitted.

Dwayne's contribution was, more or less, "Um."

With that scintillating exchange of ideas, Mags wandered off to find one of the last people she wanted to see.

Lacusta's army had grown so large that the mess hall could no longer host a general assembly. They gathered, instead, in the massive open chamber of the third mine, where the vehicles were normally stored. The mixed atmosphere of gas fumes, antifreeze, sweat, and breath was a congealed film coating Magdalena's throat. It made her lightheaded and heavy-stomached.

Worse still were the memories, an avalanche that crashed down on her at each and every one of these gatherings. Images of the first assembly, echoes of her growing desperation, mounting panic, as she struggled and failed to find Ian. Memories of all that happened afterward.

One of the smaller trucks still within the chamber creaked as Lacusta appeared from nowhere, standing within the bed. Heads turned, and mouths shut, so that he had the entire room's attention within seconds.

"Some of you are aware," he began without preamble, "that, during our assault on the production facility some weeks ago, we copied a substantial amount of information from their archives. Two nights gone by, Mister Rao and his assistants finally succeeded in interpreting something useful from the code."

His affection for Sankar is just dripping *from that sentence.*

"In brief," the vampire continued, "the machines are constructing a new manufacturing facility, and have been for some weeks. It is intended to construct additional warrior models and new weapons for use by models already extant.

"Said machines and said weapons being designed *specifically* for battle against my children and me."

Mags was surprised at the murmurs and whispers that rolled through the assembly, since all she could think was, *Yeah, that makes sense.*

Lacusta remained stiff and silent for a moment, and Mags wondered if he wasn't struggling to keep his fangs hidden, if his anger burned far hotter than he was willing to reveal. "Every technique, every instrument, that they have determined to be effective against nosferatu is to be mass produced. As are the heightened sensors that permit them, at times, to detect us. We—You have something to add, Mister Panagakis?"

Nestor nervously lowered his hand as the entire room's attention crashed down on him. "I, um…" He coughed once. "I was just wondering if we figured out yet whether they were using sonics or air movement."

Apparently, Lacusta decided it was a point worth addressing, as a sliver of the ice had melted from his voice when he spoke again. "It appears to be both. Sometimes separately, sometimes in concert. We can avoid such methods in our insubstantial forms, and it should sometimes be possible to call flocks of wildlife to us, to confuse their instrumentation. Nonetheless, it remains a distinct problem. We cannot stop them from utilizing such techniques, but we can and will make it a slow, difficult process for them.

"Ready yourselves and be certain to rest. We mobilize the evening after tomorrow. No infiltration. No theft of supplies. Nothing intricate. We will visit this new facility, and we will depart only when ash and powdered rock are all that remain."

"Don't get me wrong," Mags said to Sankar as they wandered toward the far mine, just part of the dissipating crowd. "I understand how important it is to protect any advantage we have. I just..."

"You're not entirely opposed to the vampires feeling a tiny sliver of the worry we live with every day," he finished for her.

"Uh, yeah." Her grin somehow found what should have been a nonexistent middle ground between mischievous and sheepish. "Pretty much."

Sankar chuckled. "I sincerely doubt you're the only one. I shouldn't be surprised if—"

"Mags?"

They both watched as Dwayne slipped around another knot of conversation to stand beside them.

"Um, yeah? What?"

"I, um." The newcomer lowered his voice, until even Mags could scarcely hear it for the people around them. "I was wondering if you could, uh, maybe help me with something."

Magdalena honestly wondered if she'd heard correctly. "You want *my* help?"

"Yeah." With a feigned nonchalance, he led Mags to one side of the large hall. Sankar tagged along behind, and while Dwayne looked less than thrilled at his presence, he never objected aloud.

"Look, I wouldn't ask for myself, but something's wrong with Sharon."

"What? What do you mean? You and I both just spoke to her a few hours ago!"

"No, I don't mean something just happened. She's been kinda weird. Since *before* we left for that God damn work camp."

Mags waited while Dwayne stared at nothing in particular, and then cleared her throat. "Want to be a tad more specific?"

"Forgetful. Tired. Listless. Just generally not well, and not herself. And she *will not* fucking talk to me about it! I thought, well, it might be a girl thing."

Girl thing. Mags couldn't help but giggle, then giggle even harder at the offended twitch that crossed Dwayne's face.

"Why Magdalena?" Sankar inquired. "Surely you have

women from your own detachment who know Sharon better than she?"

"Yeah, but Sharon and I both trust her—you—on certain topics that, well, my people haven't proven themselves with, yet."

Something stomped on Magdalena's giggles, crushing them flat. "You think," she began slowly, "that if it's not a 'girl thing'..."

"It might be a vampire thing. Yeah."

"You think just because I—"

"This isn't about you and Ian. She's been worse than you ever were, that I saw. I know that you'll keep secrets from the vamps, and Sharon's your friend. That's all. Promise."

"All right. I... Wait a minute! Why not Roberta? She kept our little suspicion secret, too—hell, it was hers to start with!—and she's known Sharon a lot longer than I have."

Dwayne's sudden distress, and Sankar's equally sudden sympathy, could only mean one thing. "Oh, no."

The younger man spoke around a quivering lip. "Roberta never made it back from the camp raid, Mags. And I... I can't find a single person who knows for sure how she died."

Chapter Twenty-Eight

"Y es."

"Uh?" Mags wasn't entirely sure how to take that. Sharon, again perched on that same stack of tires and again making notes of the repairs and maintenance continuing before her, hadn't even waited for her to speak.

"You really think I didn't see Dwayne jumping in place waiting to talk to you after the briefing?" Putting her weight on her right arm only, Sharon scooted around, squeaking faintly against the thick rubber, so they could keep their voices low. "He's all buttsore because he thinks there's something wrong, and I won't tell him what it is, so he sent you to ask if I'm okay. I figured I'd save you the trouble. Yes, I'm fine. I'm just... You heard about Roberta?"

She sounded down, yes, but not as distraught as Mags would have expected. "I did. I'm sorry, Shar. Do you believe she died in the firefight? Or do you think, maybe...?"

"Trying not to think about it right now. In either case, Dwayne's worried over nothing. We've all lost people before. I'll get over it."

Well, that *was abrupt*. "Sure. It's just, Dwayne said you were off *before* the camp raid."

"Was I?" Sharon tapped the chalk against her leg, leaving a powdery smudge. "I caught something a little while ago, wasn't feeling too well for a few days. That's probably it."

"I don't—"

"I'm *fine*, dammit!"

A tiny worm of doubt began burrowing into Magdalena's thoughts. Not doubt of Sharon, but of herself.

Is this how I sound to everyone?

"What about your wrist?" she challenged.

Sharon stopped in the middle of reaching for the small slate to resume her calculations. "Huh? What about it?"

"How did you hurt it?"

"Hurt? Oh." She held up her arm, examining it as if it'd suddenly dropped by unannounced. "Don't remember. Probably scraped it against something at the camp."

"Can I see?"

"Mags..."

"Look," Mags offered through a smile she didn't remotely feel, "You let me take a quick peek, I can go back to Dwayne and tell him truthfully that nothing's wrong, and that it's sweet of him to worry, but shut it already. All right?"

Sharon grumbled something, sighed heavily, and pulled up her sleeve.

"There. See? Just a scrape."

"And you really don't remember where you picked it up?"

"I really don't. Hell, might've been working on the damn truck, for all I know."

Mags faked another smile, muttered some vague farewell, and wandered aimlessly from the vehicle pool. The thing was, she believed Sharon. She harbored no doubt at all that her friend really *didn't* remember.

She wasn't supposed to. She'd been told not to. But Mags knew. She sure as all hell recognized the bite of the undead when she saw it.

Which wasn't even the worst of it.

Of this, of course, she could *not* be certain. The wound was rough, ragged. The vampire's fangs might be precise, but the jagged teeth surrounding them were far messier.

But between its location on the soft underskin of the left wrist, and its general shape, Magdalena swore she recognized not merely *what* had bitten Sharon, but *who*.

"What the hell are you accusing me of?!" Although they sat in the cab of one of the trucks—it had seemed to offer the most privacy—Ian's shout was audible throughout the garage.

Mags flinched, smacking lightly against the door. "I'm not accusing you of anything, I promise! I just wanted to know if you knew how Sharon—"

"You just don't trust me, is what."

"I don't just let you feed on me for the fun of it, you know! I'm trying to prove something to Lacusta, to you! If it's such a meaningless act, maybe I won't bother anymore!"

"That's not all, and you know it. You think I don't see what this is?" His voice was thunder, a pressure thickening the air in the cab. "Shit, I don't *have* to see it! I can *smell* the jealousy! It's *dripping* from you, like sweat."

It took everything Mags had not to flee the vehicle, but then, her hands shook enough that she might not have been able to operate the door handle anyway.

Yeah, I'm jealous, Ian. And I hate *myself for it. You* hurt *her! You hurt someone, like you've been hurting me, and I'm* jealous *over it.*

"God, what the hell have I let you *do* to me?" Lost, plaintive, a lament she'd no idea she'd whispered aloud until she heard it.

"Or maybe," he hammered at her, "you're just trying to deflect your own guilt!"

"I—what?"

"Don't imagine for one *second* that I haven't noticed how much time you're spending with that old fuck!"

"What do you… *Sankar*? God, he's like family! And he's *old*!"

"Oh, family? Do you let most of your 'family' put their—"

"It's not like that!" Mags felt sick, though she couldn't begin to unravel what had pushed her to that point. "How could you even think that?"

"Show me, Mags." He leaned toward her, equal parts intimate and intimidating. "Prove to me I'm wrong, and I promise I'll drop it."

He'll drop it? Didn't I start all this? "How… how would I do that?"

"Just stop spending so much time with him. Keep away from him when you're not working on something mission-related."

"Oh, is that all? And the fact that you've never liked him, and he gives every one of you the shivers, that's got *nothing* to do with it. You're so full of shit."

This time it was Ian who recoiled, startling Magdalena more than any further outburst could have. "I was right," he breathed. "You *don't* trust me."

She started to reach out, stopped, began again, and ultimately just left her hand sort of hanging between them. "It's not like you're giving me a lot of reasons to lately."

"I know." He took her hand in one of his own, placed the other on her knee. "Mags, I'm not doing as well with this as I thought. It's hard, sometimes, for me to remember who I'm supposed to be. If I'm being over-protective of your attention, it's just… I don't want to lose you. I need you."

"I'm right here, Ian. I'm not planning on going anywhere."

"Good." He gave her hand and knee each a gentle squeeze, but Mags couldn't help but feel something was just a tiny bit off, a tiny bit reptilian, in his smile. "I'm counting on it."

"What? What'd you—I mean, say again?"

Mags crouched low and tight behind the broken concrete pillar, pressing her finger to one ear and the clunky old radio to the other. With the former, she hoped to block out the worst of the pounding gunshots and tunelessly singing ricochets, the shouted orders and cries of pain. Against the crumpled-paper crackling in the radio itself, she had no options whatsoever.

Still, it could have been worse. Up until about ten minutes earlier, it'd been sleeting.

"… uck is wrong … th you … oddamn hearing?" Ian's words came back to her, or at least some of them did, surfing the waves of static.

"The hell do you want me to say?" she shouted back. "I've told the machines we're trying to talk, but they keep right on shooting! It's *rude.*"

She winced, trying to retract her head entirely into her torso, as something *spang*ed off the concrete, shaking the pillar and showering her with cement dust, all followed immediately by a prolonged burst of return fire from Nestor's machine gun. She couldn't tell if Ian had responded at all in the midst of that, let alone what he might have said.

Mags twisted around the column, craning her neck to see if the situation had changed at all. From here, and other partial buildings, the mortal men and women of Lacusta's army traded fire with a thick but slowly draining sea of bots. In the center of that field of steel rose their target, an installation far newer than any other they'd besieged. They'd found the place easier than the machines had anticipated, to judge from the lack of running water or flame-based defensive batteries. Still, the bots were putting up a respectable resistance.

Or they would have been, had the bulk of the vampires not already slipped past them in various forms and entered the facility, through preexisting doorways and a few rocket-launcher-installed openings.

Again she lifted the radio to her cheek, fumbling for the button through thick gloves. "Can you move to one of the openings? We might have less interference that way."

"... 'm *at* th ... ucking openi ...!"

Shit. Some kind of shielding in the walls, maybe? She'd never heard the damn thing this ragged. "Gonna have to try again, then," she shouted into the mouthpiece. "Loud and slow!"

"We need ... r advice! You were alwa ... etter at the Recogniz ... nd Disposal stuff."

If they were calling on her R&D expertise, it meant the vampires had run into something other than the manufacturing facilities they'd expected, something they were unsure how to handle.

"All right! Tell me what you see!"

"Well, all ... uipment here is ... n't appear ... ed."

God dammit! "Say again!"

"The equipment ... ssembly lines and ... ll that don't appear ... been used! There's no ... of the weapons ... posed to be making!"

Okay, that was weird. Could they have caught the machines *that* early? Before the plant was even up and running? "All right! What else?"

"... arge numbers ... metal crates."

"Check them for wires and sensors!" Mags shouted, almost standing upright until a nearby ricochet reminded her of the time and place. "Don't open them until—"

"... elax, Mags. I ... that incompetent. I ... over it through ... fore opening one. There ... inside except a ... oken chunks of metal."

And that was even weirder. Had she even interpreted correctly? "Can you repeat?"

"Nothing ins ... crates except ... of metal, broken ... pieces. We thought mayb ... you ... something we missed?"

She tried, tucking her head down, blocking out the sounds of battle as thoroughly as she could. For the first time in months, she struggled to put herself in that old familiar state: hyper-aware, trying to imagine every angle, knowing that if she failed, and if her failure didn't kill her, the machines definitely would.

Not a broken device or machine of some sort. Even if Ian couldn't tell what it had been, he'd have recognized pieces of some mechanism. Wouldn't have just described "chunks of metal."

Raw materials? No, didn't make sense. The machines wouldn't keep small bits of ore spread out among multiple crates.

Multiple *metal* crates.

On her feet now despite the bullets, slipping and stumbling on the icy ground, Mags pushed herself from the cement column and dashed, hunched and swerving, for the truck. She skidded up beside the vehicle, landed hard on her tailbone as her boots swooshed out from under her, and hauled herself upright on the rear bumper. A deep ache, made worse by winter's chill, radiated through her. She ignored it, practically diving into the equipment, digging like a mole seeking shelter from the cold.

It *had* to be here! Even before her whole world had been flipped on its ear, it'd been well over a year since she'd used it, but it always remained a part of her R&D toolkit. The sort of thing you might never need, but when you did, you *really* did.

There! Mags shoved everything else aside, filling the truck with echoing clatters, and hauled her prize from the bottom of a canvas backpack. Then, keeping the heavy wreckage between her and the incoming fire, she slowly walked back toward her earlier post. In one hand, a wand of electronics she only partly understood; in the other, a blocky device with a numbered meter, connected to the wand by a thick cable.

Even from here, the needle began to jump, the sensor to click.

Mags dropped the wand—it bounced off her foot, and she utterly failed to notice—in her mad scramble for her radio, her desperation to get Ian and the others out of that building.

Now.

Lacusta—who, after several transformations to mist and some strenuous washing, was no longer dangerous to nearby humans—sat at the desk normally occupied by Sankar, seething. Ian and several other vampires, equally "cleansed," and some of the most experienced mortals, sat or stood or leaned throughout the chamber.

"To what end?" he finally demanded, of the room at large, yes, but with particular attention toward Magdalena. Perhaps because it had been she who, with some difficulty, had explained to him the concept of "radiation."

Her "I don't know" was accompanied by half a dozen similar expressions from the people around her. "I think we're all agreed," she continued alone, "that this was a deliberate ruse. Something the machines planted in their code for us to find eventually. But as to why?" She shrugged.

"A test?" Dwayne suggested. "I mean, radiation wasn't really a thing when vampires were around and all the stories spread. Maybe the machines just wanted to know if affects them."

"They could've done that in any battle!" Ian snapped. "Just load up a couple of bots with uranium or cobalt-60 or whatever. They sure as hell weren't going to waste a ruse like this on something that easy. Fucking idiot."

"While his manners may be lacking," Lacusta said with a raised hand—unnecessarily, as it happened, since even Dwayne wasn't likely to mouth off at one of the undead in the ancient's presence—"I believe Ian's point a valid one. The Eyes' thought process is far too orderly, too efficient, to—"

"Found him!" Cassie swept into the room, her hair a crimson halo still weighted down by its recent washing, dragging Sankar along in her wake. The old man looked pale, almost sick, and Mags was halfway to her feet, fury rising, before she realized he hadn't been fed on.

He was *frightened*.

"Mister Rao," Lacusta began, "how good of you to finally—"

"Is it true?"

The vampire bit back a snarl at the interruption. "Is what true?"

"You were dosed with radiation?"

"It is."

Sankar slumped back against the wall, sliding down until he sat, gangly legs jutting out, on the floor. Mags shoved someone out of her path, she wasn't sure who, to crouch beside him.

"It's okay," she began. "We've measured. None of us got anywhere near them until they were safe."

He smiled, then, and cupped Magdalena's chin. She thought she heard Ian growl from across the chamber. "It's not okay," he told her gently. "Not at all. This is what they wanted. This was their plan the whole bloody time."

Ian puffed himself up. "What the fuck is all—"

Another raised hand from Lacusta stopped him. "What is the danger, Mister Rao?"

Sankar sighed deeply. "The satellites I told you about. The few that survived Pacification. Old, damaged, imprecise."

"What of them?"

"A great many satellites of the pre-Pacification age were designed with the ability to detect radiation spikes. And those instruments would *not* be greatly impeded by the dust and cloud cover."

Mags could swear, though she knew it to be impossible, that even the undead paled at the pronouncement.

"Are you suggesting...?" Lacusta began.

"Yes." Sankar, seeming gaunt and feeble, hoisted himself upright against Magdalena's shoulder. "Unless I am very much mistaken, the Eyes now know precisely where to find us."

Chapter Twenty-Nine

"Everything secure and ready here?" Mags asked through her palm, pressed lightly to her mouth and nose to filter the worst of the sawdust and ambient dirt. Wooden stanchions, brand new and freshly secured, braced newborn earthen walls. The tunnel, though partly natural, had been rapidly lengthened and expanded over the past few hours through judicious use of undead strength and meticulously shaped explosives.

Not that she had any real reason, or even the authority, to ask. It just beat sitting around waiting or rechecking the forward fortifications for the ninth time.

"Pretty much." One of the workers wiped from his forehead a sheen of sweat that had accumulated despite the passageway's mild chill. "We still need to reinforce the outer wall a bit, in case a stray round hits it, and we're only half-done rigging the emergency charges, but the tunnel's ready to use. Just needs a small blast or one good vampire punch to open up."

"Huh. Okay." Not that she was even listening, not after the "vampire punch" comment had reminded her just how pissed she actually was.

Months. Lacusta and his offspring had been preparing this emergency tunnel for *months*, almost since the beginning. A naturally occurring corridor that meandered away from the rightmost mine, it had petered out only a few yards from the surface. The vampires had expanded it over time, only now, at what was arguably *beyond* the last minute, bringing in human workers and explosives to hurriedly complete the task and transform it into a viable escape route. They'd left only a flimsy layer of rock, enough to mask the new tunnel from outside detection.

All of which was perfectly fine and dandy, except that Lacusta hadn't bothered to tell the humans about it! Had Sankar's realization not spurred the entire community into a frenzy of activity, had the ancient vampire not realized that the tunnel couldn't be completed in time without more overt methods—not if the machines were bearing down on them even now—it would probably still remain secret.

This despite the fact, Mags fumed, that the vampires didn't *need* the damn tunnel! It was only the living, those who *couldn't* just dissipate into a swirling fog, who depended on such mundane means of escape.

He had, at her indignant squawk, explained the secrecy as a security measure, in case any of the humans should be captured and interrogated by the machines. Mags, for her part, was sure it had just been another way of retaining control over everyone.

"Well." She realized, bemused, that the workers were waiting for her word to resume their tasks. Apparently, simply asking after the job was enough to convince them she was somebody they needed to listen to. "Back to it, then!"

I remember when there were less than a dozen of us. Now we don't even all know each other. I couldn't name one of these bastards to save my life.

As the last bits of pounding and drilling resumed, Mags wandered off in search of some other diversion—and the first blast reverberated through the mine's winding corridors. It was flat, distant, audible only by a quirk of acoustics, but others, louder, closer, would follow soon enough.

Mags sprinted through the passageways, sometimes alongside other people, sometimes pushing past them, as the soldiers of Lacusta's army assumed their assigned positions. She skidded around one corner, bounced off the wall of another, cursed with every other step, and finally slid to a stop by the main entrance.

Granted, it didn't much resemble an entrance anymore. The rocks that had lain heaped beside the gaping mine were now stacked across the opening, carefully fitted and bolstered into a formidable wall. Tiny gaps remained to serve as gun ports and to provide a view of the quarry.

Wooden benches from the mess hall had been placed along either side of the tunnel, allowing access to the higher gaps. From these perches, sentries equipped with rifles could fire out and upward—so far as the stone overhang allowed—at any incoming drones, while the remaining defenders, standing on the floor, aimed larger weapons at ground-bound targets.

They were, in short, prepared to meet anything that dared approach the barricade with a tsunami of bullets.

Nestor grunted at her arrival, stepped aside from his post— and his now-expected .50-caliber death machine—so that Mags might take a quick look from his vantage point. She pressed her face to the cold stone, peering out into the dust.

The quarry was brightly lit, or as brightly as the haze allowed; the machines had taken the obvious precaution of launching their attack in daylight. At the moment, she saw mostly spider-bots—the smaller variety, not the combat models, though even these had been retrofitted with guns in place of tools. Some scampered directly down the cliff-face while others galloped along the winding path. And both occasionally blew up, thanks to the improvised mines the vampires had spread throughout the quarry the prior evening.

A small cluster of the machines reached the quarry floor, the first to do so, and Mags cast a quick glance at her friend. "Hey, Nest, you mind? Just the once?"

He chuckled. "Go for it."

Mags crouched, wrapped her hands around the stock, made sure the weapon swiveled freely on its bipod, and opened fire.

Once, early in her R&D career, Mags had stood up in the back of a truck just as Jonas hit a rough patch. It had taken several minutes for him to realize what had happened, what all the shouting was about, and to come to a halt, minutes in which Mags had clung desperately to the side of the vehicle, feet dragging in the dirt, spurred to herculean efforts by the knowledge that a fall—in addition to being painful no matter what—might just find her beneath the wheels.

This felt similar.

The gun shook, and she shook with it, teeth vibrating in their sockets. Two of the bots danced a bit before folding in on themselves, and then she had to release the weapon and stagger back. At first, she couldn't tell the sound of other weapons firing from the echoes in her own ears.

"You all right, Mags?" Nestor asked.

She stared at him, wide-eyed. "I think it thinks *it's* in charge."

Again he chuckled and then resumed his post, firing short, controlled bursts that, so far as Mags was concerned, were no less supernatural than the undead. Shaking her head clear, she hefted a weapon much more her size, and waited in the second rank, ready to take the place of the next defender wounded or tired.

"You know what this means, right?" she shouted to Nestor during a brief lull. "The bots we're seeing out there?"

He nodded, squeezed off another burst. "They're probing. Seeing what we have to throw at them before they send in the big guns."

"Think we can hold once they do?"

"For a while. They only have the one way in."

"Assuming," Dwayne said as he, Sharon, and several others arrived with crates of ammunition, "they don't just cluster-bomb the whole place."

"I'm so glad you're here to brighten things up," Mags deadpanned. "I was starting to get worried."

"I live to serve."

"They won't do that," Sharon said with a nasty glare at her pessimistic friend. "Not anytime soon, anyway. These mines go deep. They'd want to be sure that—"

"*Coming through!*"

Sankar, of all people, came racing down the corridor, a heavy satchel slung over one shoulder, a pistol strapped to his waist.

"Need passage!" he continued, slowing to an impatient halt. "Quickly!"

"Sankar?" *I'm seeing things, right? That damn gun shook something loose in my brain!* "What the hell are you doing?"

"I need to get out there. Special assignment."

"You're insane! There's already enough machines out there to kill you so hard you'll be dead yesterday, and more on the way!"

"All the more reason I have to get out there *now*! It's important!"

"What could possibly—?!"

Mags came up short at the sound of stone on stone. While most of the sentries remained focused on the outside, and a few more watched the argument in sheer bafflement, Nestor pulled one of the larger rocks aside. It, along with one or two others in each cave mouth, had been meticulously positioned so that moving it wouldn't destabilize the barricade.

That it was intended precisely for any urgent scouts or sorties that might arise, however, didn't mean that Mags was going to let Sankar crawl through it.

"Nest? What are you *doing*?"

"He has to get out there. It's important!"

"But—"

"Don't argue with us, Mags!" the old man shouted.

Growling, she lunged, trying to tug Nestor away from the stone. As absently as he might shrug off a bug, he brushed her aside.

"What's so important?" she demanded. Screeched, really.

"Can't tell you," Sankar said. "Sorry."

"Why does it have to be you?"

"Can't tell you. Sorry."

"Has everyone gone…" *Wait one fucking minute!*

Again she waved a hand between Nestor and the stone he tugged at. Again he brushed her hand away without apparent thought.

And without blinking.

Son of a bitch!

"Sankar, wait. At least, uh, at least pray before you go. For me."

"Pray?"

"Yes!" Mags shoved a hand in his pocket, found nothing, tried the other and felt the string of wooden beads beneath her fingers. Through it all the old man merely stood, bemused.

She pressed the beads into his hand, closing his fist around them. "Please."

"I'm in a hurry."

"It'll be faster to just do it than to argue or try to push me aside."

Slowly he nodded, his lips already moving in a mantra Mags wasn't sure she'd heard before. *"Om gam... gam Ganapataye..."* He struggled, stumbling, hesitant, but already Mags could see his breath speeding, his pupils steadying.

"Lacusta." Mags thought she might choke on the hatred in her own voice. "I can't fucking believe even he would—"

"No." Nestor mumbled, his lips slack, barely able to form the words. "Not Lacusta."

"No." She didn't want to hear what must come next, *refused* to hear it.

Didn't have to hear it. She already knew.

The tunnel tilted beneath her, and for a moment she was amazed the barricade didn't come crashing down, the stones didn't roll away. For one insane moment, she pictured *herself* crawling outside, firing on the machines and laughing in the seconds she had before they took her down.

She did no such thing. Instead, with a snarled "Look after them!" directed at Dwayne and Sharon, she raced back into the depths of the mine.

"What the fuck is wrong with you?!"

Ian bolted upright at Magdalena's shout, as did the other undead lying atop the earthen cairns throughout the sleeping chamber. Fangs protruded, growls and hissing filled the room. Cassie and a couple of the others were already standing, ready to make the insolent mortal suffer.

The "insolent mortal" didn't notice. To her, there was only a single vampire present.

"Are you that scared?" she demanded, striding close enough to shove him by the chest. "That insecure? That—"

"Step aside, Ian," Cassie snarled. "I'm going to finally teach this bitch her place."

"No, you won't." He reached out for Magdalena's hand, scowled as she yanked it away. "Let's take this outside, okay?"

"Why the hell not? You're fond of that notion, aren't you?"

His expression tightening, Ian guided her out into the hall

and around the nearest bend, leaving an enraged chorus behind.

They'd barely turned the corner when she shoved him again. Dirt *poofed* around him in an almost perfect silhouette as he thumped against the packed-earth wall. "You need to stop that," he warned.

It was a warning Mags scarcely heard. "What'd you do?" she demanded. "Catch him by surprise? Grab him while he was asleep? Hook him in the middle of a conversation?"

"I—"

"It's the only way you could've done it, since he'd have just scared you off like a whipped dog if you'd given him even half a second!"

Ian's face twisted, everything down to the bone structure warping with the effort of keeping his temper, and his fangs, in check. He calmed, however, just as swiftly. Even chuckled.

"It wasn't *that* hard," he said. "You stupid humans. Even when you don't trust someone, you let your guard down once you're around them long enough."

"So you *did* hypnotize him!"

"Seems pointless to deny it. Guess I wasn't smooth enough. The whole 'implanted suggestion' thing is harder than you'd think."

"But..." Mags hadn't expected him to just come out and acknowledge it. "And you picked Nest for your tool why?"

"He stuck his nose into our business. Not as bad as the old fuck, but he had to learn. Still does."

"This isn't a joke, you bastard! Sankar would've gotten himself killed!"

"Well, yeah. That was sort of the point."

Mags forgot how to breathe. She noticed only when her lungs began to burn, and even then, she had to consciously force them into action. His admissions—ungrudging, even nonchalant— were far more disturbing than any denial.

"Who *are* you?"

He laughed aloud in the face of her broken whisper. "Ian. Ian Masse. Nice to meet you."

"No. No, you're not. God, you haven't been for—"

"Oh, here's who else I am."

Pain. Stunning, blinding. She found herself sprawled, fetched up against the opposite wall, tongue coated and mouth full of the warm, coppery, slick sheen of blood. Had Ian wanted it to, Mags knew, that backhand could have shattered her jaw, even killed her outright.

She almost wished it had.

"Frankly," the undead shell of the man she'd loved told her, "you've had that coming for a while. Uppity little dog."

Mags rolled, spit to clear her mouth, started to prop herself up. She couldn't even cry, though part of her felt the urge; the white heat of her fury evaporated the tears before they formed.

"I thought you were fighting it!" she accused. "I thought there was some of you left!"

"Oh, puh-lease!" Ian squatted down before her, close enough to reach out and help her up if he wanted to. He didn't. "I'll let you in on a little secret, *my love*. None of us are the same silly, insignificant animals we used to be. None of us care much for any of you. Some just prefer to hide it more than others. I mean, really, what could we possibly see in creatures like you? Other than food, you make for a cute pet, in an irritating sort of way, is all."

"Then why?" No tears, perhaps, but definitely on the verge of vomiting. "Why pretend?"

"You have any idea how much easier it is to have one of the herd just tripping over herself to get bit? That's more than worth a little kissy face and puppy eyes. Just can't do enough to help poor, tortured Ian adapt to these horrible changes, can you? He doesn't *meeeeeeean* it!"

Mags gagged, dry heaved, and, though shaking, started to stand. "Well, *that's* fucking over," she began.

"No, it's not." He cupped her chin, holding her off-balance. "I'm going to get Sankar out of the way, and I'll be a lot more precise about it next time. I'm going to make you fucking miserable. I'm going to hurt you, a lot, because you've started to seriously piss me off. And you're going to keep throwing yourself at me, through all of it."

"And why the hell do you think—?!"

"Do you really think this is the first time you've 'had

enough'"? The first time we've had a conversation like this?" His grip tightened, fingertips digging into the bruise already forming from his earlier blow, forcing her head upward. "You'll keep giving yourself to me for the same reason you always have. Because…"

Oh, God. His eyes. She *felt* them, chewing holes in her mind, peering lasciviously into her most private moments.

"…you're not going to remember…"

God, no. "Ian!" Now she *could* have wept, felt her body shake with unshed tears, except he wouldn't *let* her. He hadn't even left her that. "No, please no! Oh, God, *please*…"

"…any of this," he finished with a sadistic leer.

One single sob escaped her throat and then she was falling, falling away from the world, falling away from Magdalena.

"Get away from her, you fuck!"

It wasn't Nestor's shout that dragged her back to herself, a lifeline she only just snagged before going under, drowned in Ian's unnatural will. Nor was it that shout that drove the vampire off her, snapping and howling, as though he'd been scalded.

No, it was the vaguely familiar litany, a mantra of protection chanted in a voice both wearier yet stronger than Nestor's own, that saved her.

"Om dum Durgayei namaha…"

Ian's leap carried him across the corridor, where he clung just below the ceiling like a squatting beetle or toxic mold. Any semblance of control, of human restraint, had fled. His eyes blazed, his lower lip dribbled a blackened, clotted sludge where a fang, extended in sudden anger, had punctured tissue and flesh.

Pale and sweating but standing tall, Sankar advanced, neither his pace nor his mantra slowing. He drew nearer, ever nearer, and finally Ian broke. With a final, wordless wail, he disappeared down the corridor, his bestial gait leaving finger and foot impressions in the earthen wall.

"We need to go," Sankar said, sucking in deep breaths. He'd lowered his hand, but the beads still *click-click-click*ed beneath his fingers. "He'll be back quick enough."

"Let him." Mags made a shaky grab for the pistol at the old man's belt. Only an awkward side-shuffle prevented her from getting it. "Sankar..."

"No. You know that won't kill him."

"We can put him down long enough to make it permanent!"

"Gunfire in the halls is going to attract attention, yeah? The other vampires aren't going to let—"

Again she lunged for the weapon. This time, it was a pair of tree-trunk-thick arms wrapping around her from behind that kept her from it.

"Come on, Mags," Nestor breathed not ungently in her ear. "This isn't the way, and you know it."

She thrashed, flailed, shouted something she never could remember but was pretty sure she hadn't actually meant. Nevertheless, she'd calmed after they'd gone only a short way down the passage, apologized to Nest and asked to be allowed to walk on her own two feet. Her friends were right, and she knew it. It was just, they couldn't know what Ian had done, was *about* to do, to her. Not really, they couldn't.

Mags reached up to brush a strand of hair from her face. Her hand came away damp.

Try as she might, though, she could not remember at what point, during those last few minutes, she had finally managed to cry.

"We can't stay here, Magdalena," Sankar said. "Not anymore."

Days, even hours ago, the sentiment would have been insanity. Try to survive out *there*? If the wilderness didn't kill them, the machines sure as hell would.

Now? After what had just happened? What *would* have happened? Mags needed zero convincing.

Sankar looked resigned; Nestor angry; Dwayne and Sharon, who had awaited them some short ways down the corridor, troubled. None seemed inclined to argue the point.

"Only what you absolutely need, can carry, and can get *fast*," Mags barked. "Back here in five."

She dashed into the barracks chamber, ignoring the groggy

glares of those who were trying to sleep, resting up for the night shift, and made a beeline for her own mattress. She already had her weapons, so all that remained was to gather her tool belt and shove some clothing and supplies into a rugged nylon backpack.

Still, perhaps she remained shaken, somewhat slowed, by the events of the past half hour. By the time she'd finished, Nestor—who'd been gathering his own gear across the room—waited by the entryway. And by the time they returned to the main hall, all three of their companions were already present.

Arguing.

"Guys, what the hell?"

The other two had to duck to avoid being whipped across the face by Sharon's hair as she spun. "Dwayne thinks he's staying!"

Mags gawped. It made no sense, but she saw that Sharon must be right. Her less-than-favorite detachment leader carried no equipment beyond his weapons and ammunition.

"Are you insane?!" she demanded.

"Probably," Dwayne said seriously. "But I'm going to stay and fight."

"This is hopeless," Sankar said, "Don't you see? Lacusta will fight, because he doesn't want to lose what he's built, but when it all goes pear-shaped, he and the other vampires can just turn into vapor and bugger right on off. He's got nothing to lose by dragging this out.

"But the rest of you lot? There's no winning this. The machines won't stop. You may hold them back a while, but eventually they'll assemble an army big enough to push through any defense—and that's assuming they don't just refit some old missile still lying around and nuke the bloody quarry! You stay here, Dwayne, you're going to die. Come with us."

"Odds aren't much better out there," the younger man argued. "But that's not even the point."

"Then what is?" It was Sharon who asked, but he directed his reply, oddly enough, at Mags.

"Your team," he said softly, genuine sympathy in his voice, "is basically gone. You lost most of them before you even got here, and most of the rest aren't... who they were anymore."

Magdalena's answering nod was stiffened by the lump in her throat.

"Mine's not," he continued. "I've lost people, dead and undead, but only a few. Most of my detachment's still here. Still human. Still fighting.

"Means I need to be here with them, no matter what. I owe them that."

Mags did the only thing she could. She extended a hand, shook his when he clasped it in his own. "You're a surprisingly good guy," she told him. "For a rat-ass bastard, I mean."

Dwayne snorted. "Well, and you know, as raging bitches go..."

He took Sankar's hand, then, and Nestor's in turn. "Trusting you to keep Sharon alive," he told the big guy.

"Of course."

"Hey!" Mags protested. "Why tell him that and not me? She's my friend, too!"

"You're not big enough to take cover behind."

"Huh. Point."

Finally, Dwayne and Sharon clasped all four hands together. Neither spoke aloud, and even had Mags believed she could interpret whatever silently passed between them, she wouldn't have tried. Eventually Sharon nodded once, sniffed once, then turned away.

The others followed, leaving Dwayne standing alone in the corridor behind them.

The rest was almost ludicrously easy.

The emergency escape tunnel was guarded, of course, but given that they couldn't effectively fight outside until after nightfall, it was currently a trio of nosferatu—Suni among them—who'd been given that duty. It had, therefore, been a simple enough matter for Sankar to drive the undead from the corridor, however briefly.

A small charge on a twenty-second delay, a quick huddle around the far corner, and the last thin layer of rock blew aside. (Mags had insisted on the smallest possible charge, and the others agreed. Eager as they were to escape, none of them wanted to leave a hole the defenders couldn't swiftly conceal.)

At a dead run—praying they could get clear before the vampires reacted to the sound of the blast; praying that none of the machines were observing this bit of terrain—they fled into the murky sunlight, broke for the cover of the nearest tree line, slipping and skidding on rough scree.

Once only, Mags looked back. Scarcely visible through the dust and shadow, she saw moving figures, all rushing to stack the hole full of rubble, to hide its presence from scouting drones.

All the figures but one. One that stood, statue still, letting the others work around it as it stared into the wild. A figure, a silhouette that Mags had known for years, just as thoroughly as her own.

Grunting with exertion, she tore her gaze away and focused all her attention on what lay ahead, rather than behind.

Chapter Thirty

Even the winter was lazy that evening.

The wind sighed, running casual fingers over bare, creaking branches, but never mustered itself to blow. A soft snow, flakes wobbling drunkenly in their downward spiral, accumulated only an inch or so, too tired to stack itself any higher.

Magdalena, Sankar, and Nestor huddled on a patch of cold, hard soil kept moderately snow-free by overhanging trees. Shoulder brushing against shoulder, hands clasped together or held over the pitiful, flickering fire. Every few moments, one or the other of them plucked a few small twigs from a heap of carefully selected sticks and fed the infant flame.

"This is stupid," Mags snapped through chattering teeth. "This isn't a real fire. If you stuck a piece of paper in it, this fire would catch on paper, not the other way around."

"Anything larger—" Sankar began in a long-suffering tone.

"I know, I know. Anything bigger, someone might see the smoke. The slightest bit of wet wood, or melting snow, someone might see the smoke. I get all that. I'm sure our frozen-solid corpses will greatly appreciate the steps we took to keep them hidden."

The old man snorted and hauled a few thin strips of jerky from his pouch. He passed one each to Mags and Nestor, keeping a third for himself and putting the fourth aside for Sharon.

"Not exactly filling," Nestor muttered, examining his as though looking for hidden depths.

"Soon as you figure out how we're going to hunt anything without shooting," Mags said, "we can stop rationing."

They'd all agreed on that much. The need to conserve their precious stores of ammunition, to say nothing of the need for *silence*, meant that guns were a last resort. For *anything*. "We could make a bow and arrow, maybe."

"Have you ever shot a bow, Nest? Any idea how to make one beyond tying a string to a branch?"

"Um."

"Exactly. No, I'm thinking our best bet is a snare, somewhere along—"

"Did you hear something?" the big man hissed, jolting in place and trying to stare in all directions at once.

"Yes," Sankar said slowly. "That would be Sharon."

"How do you know?!"

"Because," and now it was Magdalena's turn again, "that's the direction she went."

"Maybe something snuck up on her!"

"And then made enough noise coming after us for *us* to hear it?"

"Um."

Mags leaned, nudging her shoulder against his. "Nest, what's wrong?"

"Just not crazy about the wilds, is all," he admitted, sheepishly focusing on his hands. "Give me a mine or the Scatters any day."

"The mines and the Scatters are crawling with vampires and robots."

A pause, then, *"Almost* any day."

She snickered, he forced a smile in return, and then both stopped as Sankar's only response was to prod the fire with a stick.

More silence, then, save the crackle of burning wood, until he noticed that silence and looked up. "I was thinking. Nestor's not wrong to be concerned. Our situation is, to sum it up, tricky. None of us has had to survive long circumstances like these."

"No, maybe not," Mags said, "but we've all been trained how. And it's not like the camps were all warm and comfy."

"We know how, yes, but we aren't all as well suited. I'm an old man, Magdalena, and the cold is only going to slow me up even worse. Which means *I'm* going to slow *you* lot. I can survive on my own, if I must. I should go, leave the rest of you to—"

"No."

Not a shout, not a request, not an argument. Just a flat declaration. Sankar raised an eyebrow.

"No," Mags said again. "You're not going anywhere without the rest of us. And before you say that I can't make that decision for you, you should know you're outvoted." She cocked her head at Nestor, who nodded.

"Definitely outvoted," he said.

"Unanimously," Sharon added, the crunch of her boots in snow announcing her approach just before she stepped from the dark of the sparse woodland into the dim firelight. Over one shoulder, like a rifle, she carried a large branch bedecked with snow-coated pine needles. She tossed it aside almost absently and knelt beside the fire, pressing up against Nestor like he was a human space heater.

"All taken care of?" Mags asked.

Sharon shrugged, a gesture that faintly rocked all four of them. "I'm not exactly an expert forester. Our tracks don't look like tracks anymore. Whether wiping them away left anything even vaguely natural-looking, I couldn't tell you even in daylight."

"It'll do."

"It'll have to. What's this about Sankar leaving?"

"Nothing," Mags said, her expression daring the old man to contradict her. "Nothing at all."

After a few more moments of struggling to suckle the maximum heat from the sickening fire, she continued, "Sankar's not *entirely* wrong, even if his suggestion is pants-gnawingly stupid. We *do* have to move fast. Gonna be hard enough surviving out here in general. If we're having to dodge machines and the undead constantly, it'll be damn near impossible."

"No, my love, not 'damn near.' *Completely* impossible."

Ian emerged from the shadows without the tread of footsteps or the rustling of brittle branches that had heralded Sharon's arrival. The night simply extruded him, a vile birth or hideous pustule.

Everyone shot to their feet, weapons or prayer beads in hand, scrambling to the opposite side of the tiny fire. Sheer chance kept their scurrying from kicking up enough snow to douse the flame. Ian chuckled and stepped closer, dragging his fingertips over the rime-coated trunk of a tree as he advanced. He left no mark; the frost refused to melt beneath his touch.

"How..." Mags was surprised to see her breath steaming in the cold, considering how hollow she felt inside. "How did you find us so fast?"

"Not 'us.' Just you." His words, a sibilant whisper, rode no such visible plumes, despite the chill. In its own way, it was the most disturbing thing about him. Mags shivered, retreated a step as he continued, "I've tasted you, absorbed the essence of you, so many times. Run to the ends of the Earth, and I'll find you. You're a part of me, Mags. Inside me."

And with that, Magdalena's fear was gone. "So let's get in there and find me!"

Her first shot took Ian in the forehead, just left of center. A regular bullet from a regular gun, it wasn't much more than a sting to the vampire, perhaps more startling than painful.

But Mags didn't fire a single shot. Mags emptied an entire clip into Ian's face.

As did Sharon and Nestor, only a heartbeat behind her.

What flew to splatter on the bole behind him, to spray itself across the snow, was not blood. Between chunks of pale flesh, a clotted, oily sludge quivered in patches atop the frigid slush, and melted not one single flake or crystal.

Ian hit the ground, gurgling a liquid hiss of agony. He turned her way a ragged rim of tissue surrounding a ground mass of dead meat, misshapen maws gaping where eyes and nose and mouth had been. Turned it her way and focused, as though he watched her clearly despite the lack of organs with which to see.

And who knew? Perhaps he did.

Someone gagged behind Mags. She never looked to see who it had been.

Ian struggled to rise, until the arm beneath him collapsed. Struggled again, slowly drawing upright.

Sankar pressed forward, then, prayer beads in one fist, a tiny but visibly burning brand from the fire in the other. The gruesome burble from the ruined mass of the vampire's face dropped in pitch, pain to fury. With that he was gone, a mist drifting away in the winter breeze until it faded into the ambient gray.

"Run," Mags ordered.

Nobody argued.

They did not, however, run long.

"This'll do," Mags panted, hauling herself to a stop. She stood beside another copse of trees, a mix of thriving evergreens and bare wooden skeletons, that bedecked the skirts of a small hill.

"Are we stopping?" Nestor asked, shoulders heaving. "Why are we stopping?"

"I vote *not* stopping," Sharon added.

"How long do we have before Ian comes after us again?" she asked them.

"Uh…" Nestor said.

Sharon's response was a slightly more articulate, but equally unhelpful, "I don't know."

Sankar, doubled over and gasping, just waved a hand in ignorance.

"Exactly," Mags said. "Days? Hours? Maybe minutes. We have no God damn idea how long it takes a vampire to recover from something like that!"

A vampire. He had to be *a vampire* right now. She couldn't afford for him be *Ian.*

"And if he told us the truth about how he found us," the old man said, finally having found the breath to speak, "then running's good for sod-all, anyway."

"So what do we do?" Sharon asked, a nervously tapping foot digging tiny ramps into the snow.

"We," Mags answered, gesturing again at the tree line and hoping her companions would mistake the renewed quiver in her hand as a shiver against the cold, "make him welcome."

"Mags!"

The scream, an animalistic howl, shattered the stillness an hour or so before dawn. Mags scrambled to her feet, heard the others doing the same behind her. Oddly, even as she checked her weapon, ensuring a bullet waited in the chamber, all she could think was, *it's too bad there are no birds. A shout like that should be accompanied by a panicked flock of birds.*

"*Mags, damn you!*"

Then again, as close to panicked flight as *she* felt, perhaps the birds would have been excessive.

He stormed between the trees, face alight with the gleam of his own crimson eyes, burning brighter and bloodier than Mags had ever seen. His face was, indeed, his face once more, but not entirely recovered. It seemed lumpy. Unfinished. A sheath of skin plastered over flesh as yet incomplete, a skull with a few remaining cavities.

As horrid as he appeared, as murderous as he sounded, Mags couldn't quite suppress a sigh of relief. Though they had tried their best—positioning themselves to one side of the copse, where the hillside began, shifting some of the dead underbrush, where they could do so subtly, to form apparently natural paths—still they could not ensure their pursuer would approach from the optimal direction. Not only had he done just that, he had chosen, in his anger, to approach in corporeal form. Mags just needed to be sure he hadn't the time or inclination to change his mind.

And that she didn't, either.

"I hate to be the one to tell you, Ian," she called out, "but you're having serious complexion issues!"

"Really, Mags?" Nestor groaned from behind her as Ian charged.

"It worked, didn't it?" Then, as she truly registered the vampire's speed, "Uh, maybe too well. Sankar?"

The old man prayed, beads clicking one by one through his fingers.

Already the vampire had reached the edge of the trees, and then closer still, a wind wrapped in undead flesh, blowing through the copse. Almost faster than Mags could see, could think, he neared.

Neared, and yanked the thin cord stretched across his path. A sharp *twang*. A huge puff of snow and pine needles as the branch—it had taken Mags and the others so very long to find one in this weather that would bend without snapping—whipped itself around, released from the knots that had held it taut. To the end of that branch was lashed a trio of wooden stakes, thick and sharp.

The branch reached the end of its arc with a quivering thump, the whole tree shuddering with the impact. Slowly, the detritus hurled up by the sudden spring began to settle, and Mags, though unsurprised, couldn't quite repress a disappointed grunt.

Ian stood, arm outstretched, having caught the trap before its wooden talons got anywhere near his chest, his heart. One of the stakes punched through his hand, but his scowl was more annoyance than pain.

"Really, Mags?" he asked, unaware he was echoing Nestor's question. "A Charlie?" He snapped the end off the branch and began advancing again, slowly pulling the thick spike from his palm. "I have the same training you do, silly bitch! I've been disarming those things as long as you have! Did you honestly think—"

The ground beneath him ceased being ground.

Strong as he was, even Nestor could never have dug a pit deep enough in the time they'd had. The hard, winter-frozen soil was far too stubborn. The contour of the hill-adjacent terrain, however, had offered them a head start. Not a hole, per se, but a natural depression in the earth. That, then, had allowed Nestor to complete the task, while the others made a flimsy tarp of snow-covered branches—and an additional set of stakes for the floor.

Unfortunately, while Ian had been distracted enough that he failed to notice the camouflaged pitfall, Mags knew instantly that their second trap had proved no more effective than their first. Even as the nosferatu plummeted in a burst of sticks and snow, she was sure she saw his body falling apart, dissolving into dust.

A belief that Ian confirmed, barely seconds later, as he leapt from within the pit, utterly unharmed, holding the broken ends of a punji stick in each fist. He clucked his tongue, tapped one of the shafts to his lips, and then mimed stabbing himself in the heart while sadly shaking his head.

"What else you got?" he challenged, tossing both stakes away. Again he approached, this time at a slow, deliberate walk. With each step, his leg faded away into mist from the knee down, passing through and around roots, sticks, anything that might hide another hidden trick, before resolidifying just as his foot touched the earth. "Or was that it?"

Mags drew her pistol, nodded for Sankar to resume his protective litanies. She *did* have a trick or two remaining, in addition to the twin defenses of bullets and beads, but whether any of them would be enough…

Well, she'd never know if they would have been enough.

The first round blasted through the canopy and detonated overhead, wiping the world away behind a curtain of blinding light and a burst of mind-shattering thunder. Mags toppled and rolled, with a scream she felt in her throat, but couldn't hear. Her fingers pressed into the skin of her palms, two tight fists, and only then did she know she'd lost her weapon.

Several more shots—not flash-bangs, like the first, but standard ammunition—tore into the branches, the tree trunks, the hillside. Those she heard, if muffled, cottony, distant. Warning shots, had to be. They came in too high to be anything else. Whoever was firing wanted their attention, not their lives.

Whoever or whatever.

When the voice called out, augmented so she and the others could hear it through the ringing in their ears—that flat, inflectionless, inhuman voice—Mags felt sick.

Had they been watching since the fugitives fled the mines? Had they been attracted by the earlier gunfire? Was Ian, perhaps, still radioactive enough for tracking?

She didn't know, and ultimately, it didn't matter. They were here.

<ALL HUMANS AND ANOMALOUS ENTITIES WILL SURRENDER THEMSELVES IMMEDIATELY. ANY ATTEMPT AT RESISTANCE OR ESCAPE WILL RESULT IN

CRIPPLING AND/OR TERMINAL COUNTERMEASURES. NO ADDITIONAL WARNINGS WILL BE OFFERED.>

A quartet of drones dropped from the canopy, rotors ripping snow and leaves from the branches, revolving to keep guns trained on any movement. A pair of the headless humanoid bots crashed into the copse; these models had been modified, each with a polymer container or tank attached to its back. And from atop the hill skittered one of the arachnid machines, a combat model, turret bristling with barrels of differing shapes and sizes.

Had they come solely for the humans, it would've been laughable overkill.

The pair of humanoids converged on Ian. Whether it was indeed leftover radiation or one of the other methods they'd developed, they clearly had some vague sense of where he was. Each raised its hands, outspread. Jets of water, doubtless pumped from the canisters on their backs, blasted outward in a tumultuous rush. The paths of those streams crossed to either side of the vampire, so that he was encased on all sides by either the jets or the bots themselves.

And Ian just laughed. He reached into one of the streams, so that water splashed in all directions, individual drops freezing before they hit the ground. Then casually, even tauntingly, he stepped through the flow.

Again, Mags only had theories, not certainty. Were the streams too thin? Did an artificial spray not count, for whatever reason, as running water? Whatever the cause, the effect was clear. The machines had hoped to trap the vampire in their liquid cage, and they had failed.

At which point, with an echoing *thub*, the spider lobbed a gas bomb at Ian's feet. Mags could smell the garlic even before the vampire screamed.

Ian folded in on himself, trying to huddle away from the burning substance. Mags swore he went briefly transparent, doubtless attempting to escape as mist. Whether it was a property of the garlic itself, however, or an inability to concentrate through the pain, he couldn't pull it off. He rolled over, whimpering, burying his misshapen face in the snow.

The multi-legged machine ran the vampire over, punching massive, ragged holes in his arms and legs with its own pointed limbs--nothing from which Ian wouldn't recover, but temporarily crippling. Finally, as though to be certain, the bot withdrew a capsule from some internal compartment, crushed it in steel digits, and dribbled the viscous contents into Ian's open wounds. The shriek that erupted from beneath the snow was utterly inhuman.

She couldn't be sure, from where she was, not with the air already saturated by that smell, but Mags would've wagered that it was garlic oil.

It turned her way, then, and took two steps, the rotting blood of the undead smeared thick across its legs, slowly drooping off in wobbling, mucous threads. A floodlight snapped on from the front of the chassis, forcing night-adjusted eyes to squint and water. The threat in the bot's posture would have been unmistakable even without the gaping gun barrels.

Sankar was the first to raise his hands above his head. "This way," he said softly, "there's at least a chance. Fighting, we've none at all."

It stung, burned at her exhausted pride as badly as the garlic did Ian, but Mags knew he was right. The spider alone was far more than the four of them could handle.

First she, then Sharon and Nestor, followed Sankar's lead.

<Leiber, Sharon. Panagakis, Nestor. Rao, Sankar. Suarez, Magdalena. You will place all weapons, tools, and utensils on the ground.>

Nothing for it but to obey. If nothing else, Mags was glad to see that Sankar kept his prayer beads, and that the machines made no objection, apparently not considering them a tool of any sort. It would bring him some comfort, if nothing else.

The humanoid pair vanished into the dark and the snow, returning moments later with two halves of a large steel shell. God knew where they'd gotten it from. They must have been carrying the thing along and left it behind when they launched their attack.

As they neared, Mags could see that the inside of the container was lined in a heavy rubber or polymer of some sort.

When fastened together, the tube would be airtight.

Tube? No. *Coffin.* The damn thing was a sealed, steel coffin. And she knew precisely what it had been built for even before the bots crammed Ian inside and began to weld it shut at the seam.

Still, Mags couldn't help but picture other bots, machines torn apart from within by the impossible strength of the nosferatu. "That won't hold him too long." She wasn't sure if she was warning the machines, her friends, or just contemplating aloud.

It was the steel arachnid, however, that replied. <It is not required to.>

Chapter Thirty-One

"Hello, Mags."

It was the first human voice she'd heard in over a day. In silence, the machines had marched the prisoners overland, across broken old roads and rolling fields, until they'd reached the snow-dusted architectural bones of the Scatters. There, another motley-hued, leprous train had awaited them. Mags and her companions had been herded into one car, Ian's coffin-prison dragged into another. The latter, she had noted, contained an excess of transparent plastics in its construction, allowing the dim sunlight to flood every corner of the interior. Mags doubted they'd chosen that car for vampire transport by coincidence.

Just as she was sure the choice to stick the humans in a car that had *no* windows was equally deliberate.

Still, when the vehicle finally shuddered to a halt and the prisoners were herded into a nearby structure, Mags saw enough to know that they stood somewhere in the middle of what had been Pittsburgh, in the heart of the conformed regions. The heart of machine rule in this corner of the globe.

Onward, then, through sliding doors and sterile hallways, passages of unpainted brick or polymer, sharp with the tang of ozone and oils, until they reached what could only be a holding area. Individual cells—the walls between them solid stone, but the sides facing outward a transparent plastic— lined the sides of a larger circular chamber. Most were empty, so far as Mags could see as she was shoved ungently inside, but she spotted one that was already occupied. Who or what lay within, however, she couldn't say. She saw only a shape sprawled beneath ratty blankets on a cot, hooked up to an array of beeping equipment.

The transparent wall of the cell was, itself, the door, sliding up into the ceiling with a pneumatic hiss, and back down with a horribly solid thud once Mags was inside. And then there'd been nothing but to sit on the cot, peer with distaste at the bucket provided for waste, and wait.

The prisoners probably could have spoken with one another. While the stone walls were solid, an array of small holes, probably for airflow, speckled the polymer. Mags was certain, however, the machines were listening, and besides, for now they had little enough to say.

So she'd waited, blank and unfeeling as she could make herself, until she'd slowly drifted off into a restless slumber. A slumber from which that voice had pulled her.

The first voice she'd heard in many hours, and the last she'd expected, or wanted, to ever hear again.

"Hi, Jonas. Fuck off."

He was more worn than she recalled, a bit more gaunt, more ragged, but it was definitely him. He sat before her cell on a stool he must have brought with him, since it certainly hadn't been present when she fell asleep. Behind him loomed one of the arachnid machines. For all Mags knew, it might be the same one that had captured her.

"Look," he said with a loud sigh, "I want to apologize—"

"Apologize?" The next cell over shook as Nestor hurled himself against the polymer door. "Apologize? You fucking bastard, people are dead! *Daniel's* dead! Because of you." A second, smaller thump could only have been a fist pounding on the plastic.

"Not because of me!" Jonas stood so fast it seemed the stool might have bitten him. "Because of *them!*" He aimed a shaking finger at the bot behind him, which truly seemed unable to care less. "Tell me what choice I had!"

"You could have chosen *not* to betray us!" Nestor hollered at him.

Mags, however, was more thoughtful.

"If I'd done that," the overseer said, "the only difference

would have been that I'd be executed along with you. I couldn't *change* anything!"

"You could have warned us to keep quiet about what we'd seen," Mags accused.

"I was told not to. I wasn't to bring it up, no matter what."

"A whisper," she insisted. "One sentence. You could've risked *that* much for us."

<Lang, Jonas, understands his responsibilities,> the machine interjected. <Others are advised to follow his example.>

"Right." Mags leaned back against the wall. "And you've been, what, working here ever since?"

"Or places a lot like this, yeah. It's been harder than I'm used to. They weren't about to put me in charge of another team after what happened."

"Well, shit, I'm sorry. If we'd known how much it would inconvenience you, I'm sure we'd have thought twice about this whole 'trying to survive' nonsense."

Jonas's brow furrowed, so that he appeared older even than Sankar. "I hoped you, at least, might understand."

"When you tell me how to *understand* my teammates back to life, I'll work on it."

"How—how many of you made it?"

"Between the dead and the *un*," she said with just the smallest quiver, "not a lot more than me and Nest."

"I'm sorry." Jonas slumped back onto the stool, hunched and shrunken. "They've taken Ian to facilities better suited to his, um, condition. I'm afraid he's not going to enjoy the upcoming experiences, but at least he's alive. I thought you'd want to—"

"Eh. Kill him. Won't bother me any." Then, at the old man's shocked stare, "The Ian I loved died months ago. What you've captured is a monster wearing a stolen face it's *not worthy of!*" She hadn't meant to shout that last. It just happened. Nor had she meant to lunge from the cot, slapping both palms against the polymer.

As to whether or not she meant any of what she actually *said*, well, Jonas's guess was as good as hers.

"I don't know why you wanted us alive," she said, forcing herself to calm, "but we're not telling you a damn thing."

"I will." From a far cell, Sankar joined the conversation for the first time. "I'll tell you anything you want to know. *If,*" he clarified just before Mags could shout something horribly rude, "you let the others go."

<Rao, Sankar. You have betrayed your position once already. You will be granted no further trust or leeway.>

"Besides," Jonas said, "that's not, uh, exactly why you're here."

He sounded *nervous*. That was worse, Mags decided, than any threat.

"You *could* offer us useful information," the overseer continued. "About the vampires and about the numbers and defenses of your, uh, commune. If one of you does that, or otherwise makes herself useful..." His use of the feminine was not lost on Mags. "...then the machines have promised they'll consider sparing her from the worst of it."

She swallowed once, hard. *Don't ask. Don't ask. You don't want to know, don't ask.*

"Worst of what?" she asked.

Jonas hung his head.

<Examination and classification procedures for the anomalous entities remain flawed,> the bot answered in its flat, implacable tone. <The entities' mesmeric capabilities, methods of feeding, and other traits are comprehensible only in relation to their effects on living humans. Their invisibility to mechanical means of observation has also proven difficult to analyze.>

I'll bet. But what does that have to do with us?

<Thus, the necessity of human experimental subjects.>

Oh. Shit.

"The basic procedures," Jonas said, "are fairly simple. Measurements and readings. Minimally, um, minimally invasive. Usually. That bit, I'm afraid, you're all going to have to live with. But, anyone who makes themselves useful enough? Well, you might be spared phase two."

<Determination of what biological factors allow living beings to observe the anomalous entities,> the machine clarified. <And development of mechanical and/or cybernetic alternatives.>

Mags wasn't entirely certain she followed that, but it didn't sound good.

Apparently, her confusion, and her companions' as well, was enough for the bot to notice. <Observe.> Each leg clicking across the floor with a horrid finality, it approached the door to another cell, the one already occupied when they arrived. The plastic barrier slid upward, the machine reached inside with its elongated grasping digits, and Mags knew, to her core, that she did not want to see what came next.

Not that she could possibly have forced herself to turn away.

The bot dragged a wheeled gurney from the room. Several medical monitors and medicine drips, also on rollers, came with it, pulled by the tubes that bound them to whoever lay beneath the blankets.

<Lang, Jonas.>

He didn't have to ask what he was being ordered to do. With a hesitant shuffle, he approached the gurney, and drew back the concealing fabric.

Magdalena's horrified cry was but one of four.

She didn't think she knew the poor soul, though she frankly couldn't be certain. His left leg, from the calf down, was gangrenous, rotting. Skin puffed, bulged, and split, leaking gruesome substances onto the cot. Several of the medical tubes pumped substances into the man's leg just above the infection, somehow preventing it from spreading without curing it or forcing amputation.

Another, narrower tube plunged into the corrupted flesh, feeding a very slow, sporadic drip of a black and viscous fluid.

Vampire blood, or whatever it was their blood had become. Mags had no idea where the machines had gotten hold of it, but she knew it when she saw it.

Experimental subjects, the damn thing had said.

And God help him, the leg wasn't even the worst of it.

Two hollows gaped in the subject's face, staring emptily, where his eyes should have been.

One appeared to have been removed surgically. The socket was pink, angry, but so far as Mags could see, largely undamaged. But the other?

The other was a massive, ragged ruin, a deformation of torn flesh and broken bone. To all appearances, something foreign—something larger than the socket, and unevenly shaped—had been forcefully inserted in place of the missing eye, and then later removed.

The heaving in her stomach made Mags reconsider her animosity toward the waste bucket.

The machine said nothing further. It departed the holding area, leaving Jonas to slide the sad creature, scarcely less undead than the vampires, back into his cell.

"Why?" Sharon rasped. "Why would they keep him alive after that?"

Jonas stepped back from the doorway, triggering some sort of sensor to close the cell. "Because he still has three limbs and multiple organs that could prove useful for testing. Keeping him alive is more efficient than trying to preserve them all separately.

"Make yourself useful." Somewhere between an order and a plea, one that Mags was certain he'd aimed at her more than the others. "Find a way."

Then he, too, was gone. The door to the main chamber, steel rather than polymer, slammed behind him, leaving four horrified prisoners alone with their fears.

Their fears and, for some, their guilt and grief.

Because now, Mags had both silence and solitude. Silence and solitude meant time to think.

And thinking meant *him*.

How had she been so *stupid*? So *pathetic*? How had she let it all happen?

How—not yesterday, not in the past weeks, but months ago, when she now understood she'd truly lost him—had she failed him so completely?

Magdalena curled up into a ball on the cot, facing the wall, and wondered if the machines could really make her feel any worse, cause her any more pain, than she already felt.

Chapter Thirty-Two

The damn cell didn't even provide enough room for decent pacing. And Mags *needed* to pace.

She needed to lash out. To punch the walls. To curse the machines at the top of her voice, in the most vile language she knew, and to hell with the microphones that Sankar said were assuredly monitoring the whole detention area. She had to work off some of the adrenaline, some of the aggravation.

Some of the intense fear for her friend, which had flooded her from the instant the cries of protest awakened her and had never subsided.

Now and again, a curse or a grunt from the cell next door announced that Nestor, too, remained agitated. Even more infrequently, the acoustics lined up so that Mags heard a snippet or two of Sankar's softly spoken mantras.

Her relief escaped in a sob as much as a sigh when the main door hissed open to reveal Jonas, a pair of the human bots, and—between those mechanical sentries, pale and shaken but seemingly unharmed—Sharon.

The imprisoned trio were shouting greetings and questions at her before the machines had even guided her back to her cell. In the hubbub, she couldn't manage much beyond reassuring them she was okay, which got them to quiet down a bit. The softer sound of her cell door sliding home was barely audible.

Jonas took the opportunity that silence afforded him. "I told you when we came to collect her, Mags," he said gently. "She wasn't to be harmed. For now, they're just doing observational testing."

"Sharon?" Mags called out, seeking confirmation.

Just the slightest pause—Mags wondered if her friend had nodded instinctively, forgetting that her companions could no longer see her—and then Sharon's reply. "Yeah. I'm okay. Just a lot of electrodes and needle sticks and some trippy meds. Didn't feel great, but it wasn't anything awful." A sudden unsteadiness in her speech, however, belied that last bit.

"Sharon?" Magdalena repeated.

The other woman groaned softly. "They had me watching Ian," she explained. "They wanted to monitor my reactions to seeing… what they were doing. It was… It was bad, Mags. Ugly."

"I see." Face all but pressed against the plastic, she turned her attention to Jonas. "Thank you for keeping your word."

The overseer's smile was faint, at best. "It's not exactly my word to keep. When they decide it's time for more, um, thorough procedures, there's nothing I can do. Still, to the best of my ability, I won't lie to you about any of this."

"Thanks," she said again. Jonas bobbed his head once in acknowledgment and followed the departing machines, who were already at the main door.

Just before they stepped into the hall, she called out. "Test me!"

All three of the Eyes' servants halted in their tracks. Jonas and one of the humanoid bots came back her way, while the remaining machine waited where it stood.

"Mags? What are you—?"

<Suarez, Magdalena. Explain.>

"Just what I said," she told them, wondering, as she was sure Nest and Sankar must be, if she'd lost what sliver remained of her mind. "The observations and exams you conducted on Sharon. Test me."

Jonas practically glowed with an incredulous confusion. "That doesn't make any—"

In a startlingly human gesture, the bot raised a hand for silence. <Tell us why we should do this, Magdalena Suarez.>

The shift in phrasing, the sudden variations in inflection, that gesture—she knew immediately what they meant, struggled to keep herself steady.

"I should have figured," she forced herself to say. "Something as important as a firsthand study of the undead? You'd want to participate, not just monitor through the network."

<A logical conclusion,> said the Eye through its mechanical intermediary. Jonas, though he didn't appear shocked, shuffled a few steps away from it. <Also obvious and irrelevant. You will answer the query.>

"Ian and I are..." She coughed once, trying to dislodge whatever had just taken up residence in her throat. "Bound, somehow. He f-fed from me. A lot. We have some sort of link now. It's how he found us in the wild. I don't know what it is. If he can just, I dunno, smell me like a bloodhound or something, or if there's more to it. But my reactions to him might be different than other people's. Might tell you something."

<Unlikely,> the artificial entity mused. <Not impossible, however, and worth investigating. Why, though, would you propose such a thing? The offer is untrustworthy.>

"The more time you spend on these tests," Mags said without hesitation, "the longer before you do something worse to one of us."

<You seek to buy time, either in hopes of escaping or coming up with a use that will encourage us to declare you a non-experimental subject. The latter is improbable. The former is impossible.>

"It's not just that." Mags was glad, now, that Sankar couldn't see her, or rather, that she couldn't see his reaction to her forthcoming words. "You know what Ian was to me," she told Jonas.

"I do."

"I've told you what he's become, but you don't know the worst of it. The half of it. How much he hurt me. I want... If we're to die here anyway, I want to see him suffer first. I want to know he got what's coming to him."

She couldn't tell what was worse, the boiling flood of conflicting emotion or the imagined look on her older companion's face.

Sorry to disappoint you, Sankar. Trust me just a little longer.

<Do you believe Magdalena Suarez, Jonas Lang?>

"It's more vindictive than I've known her to be," he replied after a bit of thought. "But she's been fighting for months, and I *do* know that her feelings for Ian were intense. Yes," he decided. "I believe her."

Mags started breathing again.

<Human inefficiency. Regardless of motivation, however,> the Eye declared, <the possibility raised is worth testing.> The bot gave an imperceptible twitch, and then, in a far flatter voice, said, <Suarez, Magdalena will accompany this unit. Any disobedience or attempted escape will result in immediate and crippling reprisal.>

"I understand."

The door rose into the ceiling, clearing her way.

"Do you know what you've done?" Jonas hissed, falling into step behind her.

"I hope so. Were you talking about something in particular?"

"You just told them that you have a unique connection to the only vampire they have to study! When it *does* come time for the second-phase experiments, who do you think they're going to choose first?"

Of course she'd already thought of that. Nevertheless, she hugged herself to keep from shaking. "I guess we find out when we get there."

And hope to God this works, so I never get there at all!

Through sterile halls and sliding doors, past sterile *rooms* and sliding doors, they'd led her. Only rarely did they encounter other bots, a circumstance that puzzled Mags until she connected it with the siege of the mines, presumably still ongoing. Considering the size of the attacking force, and after all the damage and sabotage of the past few months, there couldn't be that many autonomous machines remaining in the Pittsburgh area. The local Eye had doubtless sent for replacements from other regions, but those couldn't have yet arrived in any great numbers.

She was just as surprised, perhaps even more so, to see the occasional human wandering unescorted, going about this errand or that. Again, though, it made sense. The machines would want scrips available to do the minor jobs, freeing bots up for more important duties. The fact that they could see the vampires where the machines couldn't probably entered into it, too.

An audible rippling from behind one closed door resolved itself, as she neared, into the babbling of a brook or stream, accompanied by the hum of a small generator.

Of course. A constant flow of running water. *How better to imprison a vampire?*

The machines halted before a nearby entryway. <Enter.>

She entered.

Even just walking into the room was an experience. The doorway was broader and taller than average—and "average" was already quite sizable here, to accommodate the various machines—but what astounded Mags was the *depth* of that doorway. The walls were close to two feet thick. She didn't even want to imagine the weight of the steel door hanging over her head as she stepped through the opening.

Whoa.

The chamber was larger than the entire holding area and boasted obscene quantities of refined metals. A floor of slick stainless steel gently sloped toward a sequence of drainage grates. Whole banks of computers and other instrumentation lined the far wall. She saw multiple slots and containers for just about every form of biological sample she could imagine, and a few she wouldn't want to. A small generator hummed loudly in one corner, suggesting that the bulk of the room's equipment could go on operating even if the building, or the entire city, shut down.

Given the hazards of what they worked with in here, Mags understood why.

In the center of the room squatted a massive accumulation of servos and pumps that only vaguely resembled a table. Atop it, strapped down by wrists, ankles, waist, neck, and forehead, lay Ian, not merely stripped naked, but with multiple deep gashes and patches of skin missing. From a framework overhead, a trio of spigots sprayed a constant, fine mist, occasionally strengthening to a more forceful jet. Not only did this prevent the clotted substances of the vampire's innards from building up on table or flesh, but—Mags realized after a moment's observation—it made the vampire easier for the machines to track, by observing the flow of the water.

It didn't sluice away the gore swiftly *enough*, though. A pungent rot, some horrid mix of fresh decay, flourishing molds, and soured stomach acids, thickened the air.

Too much. It was far too much. She wanted to scream, wanted to laugh; to tear him from the table and carry him to safety, to lean in for a better view of his suffering; to beg forgiveness, to taunt and gloat.

She continued, coldly, to study his predicament, and the room around him, because it meant she wasn't doing anything else.

Powerful floodlights in various wavelengths shone down on him, as did the sun itself. The rightmost wall was entirely transparent, and multiple mirrors, positioned around a sequence of tubes in the ceiling, suggested the ability to reflect sunlight directly into the chamber at any time of day. His skin had taken on a filthy cast, as though burned and infected both. Even as she watched, he whimpered—not a human sound, but the cry of a frightened animal—and writhed so far as the restraints permitted. Mags didn't think it was the wounds, awful as they were, that most bothered him.

All right, so that explained how they expected straps, however reinforced, to hold him. He couldn't change shape. Doubtless they always had him back in that other room, behind running water, well before the sun set.

Small spider and humanoid machines skittered about the chamber. Horrifying surgical devices, probes and blades and pincers and contraptions that could serve no sane purpose, hung from the ceiling, sliding along a network of tracks to reach any corner. They seemed to act on their own, guided by some other mechanized awareness. Perhaps the Eye itself?

Other examination tables stood throughout the room, but Mags was fixated on this one. Well, this and the heavy chair, complete with its own set of restraints, that had been set up nearby.

"Guess that's my seat?" she asked weakly.

<Sit.>

"That'd be a yes, then."

"*Mags?*" Ian spasmed, tugging against the restraints at the sound of her voice. He tried to turn his head her way and couldn't even manage that much. "Mags, get... get me out..."

Again, she couldn't begin to determine how much she truly meant, but she had to keep the machines believing. "I'm not sure which makes you more of a shithead: that you think I can do a fucking thing for you, or that you think I would if I could."

The vampire's response was an enraged gurgle, as something wet—Mags decided, for her own well-being, to assume it was the water and not something bursting internally—clogged his throat.

Only as she settled into the metal contraption, facing both Ian's "bed" and the door through which she'd entered, did Mags realize the room also hosted a pair of *human* guards. They were clad in tactical armor of polymers and Kevlar, every inch of skin covered. In addition to full-visored helmets, they even wore collars of chain mail.

Protection from vampire fangs?

Each was armed not only with a brutal heavy pistol, but a wooden stake hanging at the hip like a sword, and a powerful crossbow. Sentries, the only sort who could actually see the prisoner, standing watch just in case the undead should escape confinement.

What the hell did these guys do to earn that sort of trust?

Mags flinched only a little as the bots methodically stripped her from the waist up and began sticking electrodes to her face, her head, her arms, her chest. It didn't take her long to decide she'd rather not know. It'd probably just make her want to kill them.

She winced, crying out once as the machines jammed a few thick needles under her skin, some wired to sensors, others to medicinal drips. Her stomach flipped, making her gag. Whatever they were pumping into her—internal dyes, perception-altering drugs, something else entirely—her body didn't care for it.

She began to mumble under her breath, reciting the specific procedures for breaking down and maintaining her equipment after an R&D mission. Something to keep her focused, to keep her mind off the intruding chemicals that she swore she felt oozing through her veins.

Long probes descended from the ceiling, some red hot, some crackling with electricity, to penetrate Ian's skin. Behind them came blades of various sizes, sharp enough for inhuman precision, heavy enough to dig deep.

Again Ian thrashed, and though he refused to scream, noises far more primal burbled in his throat.

Equipment whined and shrieked and crackled, machines skittered to and fro, observing and recording. Scanners clicked or hummed, analyzing data as it flowed from sensors on the vampire and on the human witness both.

And only when it had reached a crescendo, a numbing cacophony echoing through the steel-and-plastic chamber, did Magdalena's muttering change in tone.

"Ian?" It wasn't even a whisper, a breath only gently molded by lips and tongue. "I know how good vampire ears are. If you can hear me, clench your left fist twice."

Nothing but random thrashing, and Mags despaired. This was her only plan, her only chance...

The fist clenched.

Come on, come on, come on!

And again.

God, I can't take much more of this.

"All right, you hate me, and it's fucking mutual—" *Isn't it?* "—but neither of us wants to go through what the machines are going to do to us. So suck it up and listen to me *real* carefully..."

Chapter Thirty-Three

She scarcely remembered the last hour or so of testing, or the staggering trek—bots to either side of her, Jonas ahead—back to the detention area. Neither her sight nor her hearing quite wanted to focus on anything. Sour sweat dewed her skin, plastering hair and clothing flat. She burned from inside, yet the moderate temperature of the hallway reduced her to violent shivers. She ached from the needles, itched from the electrodes, and what fragments of her awareness hadn't been scrambled by the drugs were numb from watching bits of Ian split open and turned inside out.

Only after she'd been guided into her cell, the barrier sealed behind her, and Jonas and the bots had almost reached the outer door, did she call out. Dramatic, yes, and a clear echo of some hours earlier, but for all that, she hadn't deliberately left it to the last minute. It had just taken her that long to swim through the haze that filled her head and remember what she had to do.

"Jonas!"

His shoulders stiffened. "This can wait for tomorrow," he began.

"Jonas, please."

With a long-suffering sigh, the overseer shuffled back to her cell. "What?"

"I don't..." She glanced sidelong at the wall to her left, and then leaned in close to the breathing holes in the door. Jonas took the hint and leaned in as well. "What I saw in there?" she whispered. "And the guy in that cell? Jonas, I don't want to... You can't let them do that to me! Please!"

"I don't *want* them to!" he hissed back. "But I don't 'let' them do anything! I told you the rules, Mags. If you can make yourself too valuable—"

"I tried!"

"I know you did. But you heard them. Your scans showed nothing different than Sharon's. Whatever link you have with Ian, it has no measurable effect on how you see him."

"But…"

"They don't care about intentions, Mags, just results. You know that." He tensed as though to pull away.

"I can get you the answer," she said miserably.

"What?"

"The answer. Why the machines can't see the vampires. That's really the big question behind all of this, right?"

"So tell me!"

"I don't *know* the answer! I said I can *get it* for you!"

The overseer crossed his arms, scowling. "I'm listening."

"The vampires know. They've talked about it in front of some of us. Ian could tell you."

"Do you think we haven't thought of that? Ian was questioned intently before his first, ah, procedure, and multiple times since. He knows he can escape some of the torment by answering our questions. He swears he doesn't know, and I've seen nothing to suggest he's lying."

"God dammit, Jonas, you don't know those undead fuckers like I do! Were you even watching what happened in there? You think any human being could take that much agony and not go insane? They don't feel pain like we do! It's not as big a deal to them. No matter how much you torture him—sorry, 'examine' him—he's gonna keep quiet for weeks, even months, just out of spite!"

"And you can do better?"

"Yes. You just need to offer him something he wants more than he wants to spite you. Something he… hates more than he hates you."

"Ah. And I suppose you have someone in mind." It wasn't even remotely a question.

"You have no idea." She turned, slumping against the plastic so she could slide to a seat without stepping away from the holes. "No fucking clue how much I loathe what he's become, and how much he—*it*—returns the favor. And that was *before* I sat and watched him suffer for a few hours straight. You wait until he's back in his cell, drag me over there, maybe in cuffs, and make a deal!"

Jonas didn't look remotely convinced.

"Look," Mags begged, "what are you worried about? The machines? They're not gonna care how you got the information, long as you get it! And you know that *he* can't do a damn thing to you, not across running water!"

"Actually, I wasn't sure—"

"Worst that can happen is he refuses. So let's at least give it a try!"

"Uh-uh. I'm not stupid, Mags. You're awfully anxious to go see someone you claim to hate."

"I—"

"I'll see if he's willing to make a bargain, but you're staying right the hell here. *If* he's willing, we'll figure it out from there."

Magdalena bit her lower lip but nodded.

"You realize," Jonas warned, "that the machines just might keep this bargain, if he's willing to make it. Hand you over to him."

"Still better than getting slowly cut up."

The older man grunted something noncommittal, shot his former protégé one final suspicious glance, and was gone.

Mags watched until the outer door slid shut, and then stumbled to her cot and slumped. So very much had to go exactly right for this to work, and so very much was in the hands of the one man—or former man—she trusted least in all the world.

He's taking too long. He's taking too long. Something got screwed up somewhere. We're all fucking dead. He's taking too long. He's taking too—

"Mags?"

She almost fell to one knee as she scrambled up off the cot and stumbled the few short steps to the cell door. There Jonas stood, unfocused and seemingly lost in thought.

"So?" she demanded, unable to keep as calm as she'd have preferred. "How did it go?"

"He said, and I quote, 'Tell Suarez she can bite me.'"

Holy shit, it worked!

That had been the code she'd given Ian in her mutterings: to have Jonas use her last name if the plan could proceed. If Jonas could now be... counted on.

And you know, she had said to the old man, *that he can't do a damn thing to you, not across running water!* A lie bundled up in truth's overcoat. The vampire couldn't *cross* the water, no.

That didn't mean his *gaze* could not. His gaze, and all that entailed.

And the machines wouldn't have seen a thing.

"Dammit!" she cursed aloud, punching at the plastic. "I *know* I can get him to tell you. Will the machines let you give me something to write with? I need to think over everything I've seen, everything I've heard him say, try to come up with something."

"I'll go find out."

He returned only minutes later. The cell door slid open by a few inches, a gap through which Jonas slid a length of colored wax and a white rag.

"What, are they afraid I'm going to stab myself if they give me a pencil?" she groused.

"Maybe."

"Oh, for... Fine. If you'll come back in a bit, I'll tell you what I've come up with."

An affirmative grunt, and Jonas went on his way.

Mags sat cross-legged on the floor, spread the rag on her cot—now a makeshift writing table—and began. Of course, she had no idea how most of this stuff was spelled; hopefully Jonas wouldn't have too much trouble interpreting her best guesses.

Asetallenetorch, the list began, *or equivilent.*

Standard basic R-and-D tool kit.

God, this wax-on-fabric crap was awkward! Already her hand had cramped, and she was barely into the list. She hadn't even *gotten* to the instructions yet!

Also, this would've been a lot easier if she could've just asked for C4 or the like, but while a scrip carrying tools was surely a common sight, she rather doubted the machines were as lax about monitoring their armaments.

Sighing, she forged ahead.

White fumeing nitrec acid...

The alarms were remarkably subtle. No klaxons, no strobing lights, just a ringing buzz, one second on, one off. They'd been sounding for almost a minute before they pulled Mags from her light doze, and a few seconds more before she recognized them for what they were.

Guess that makes sense. The machines don't need *audible alarms, so these are just for the scrips.*

"Any idea what the hell's going on?" Nestor asked from next door. "Sankar?"

"Sorry to disillusion you," the old man answered wryly, "but I fear my knowledge of the machines doesn't extend to actual clairvoyance."

"Whatever it is," Mags said, "just follow my lead. *If* there's any sort of opportunity."

This all would be so much easier if I could've told them the plan. Or that there even is *a plan!*

Four prisoners stood pressed against the polymer, wondering what was happening in the halls beyond, anxiously waiting—though only one of them knew for what.

Until, finally, the outer door slid open and Jonas entered the detention area. He moved, not to any of the cells, but to a panel on the wall. A few moments of juggling screwdrivers and clippers, a few more of fiddling with the wires inside, and every cell in the chamber opened.

"You should hurry," he told them dully, absently. "The alarm's only going to keep the machines occupied for a few moments, until they figure out there are no invisible vampires actually attacking the building."

"Why the *hell* is he helping us?!" Nestor made a beeline for the overseer, fists raised, halting only when Mags stepped between them.

"We need him."

"Oh, come on! You *know* this is a trick!"

"Yes. Mine. Jonas? Look at Nestor, please."

He obeyed, and even enraged as he was, Nest couldn't possibly miss the vacancy in his features. "Holy shit. You? Ian? What?"

"Later. You heard the man. We don't have a lot of..." Her voice dribbled away as something across the room caught her attention.

"But won't the machines hear all of this?" Sharon asked as she stepped into the open. "Didn't we just tell them the alert's a trick?"

Mags only half-heard the question. "Jonas? Explain."

"I faked damage to several internal systems, along with the alarm. Observation is down in this sector of the installation. For minutes only, until they reroute. If we're *really* lucky, maybe an hour."

"Minutes?" Nestor was suspicious once more. "Sankar was able to shut the cameras and shit down for much longer when Mags and Ian—"

"A far less secure installation," Sankar interjected. "I'm rather impressed Jonas managed even this much. I... Mags?"

She had already crossed to the fifth occupied cell, stared down at the mutilated wreck that had once been a whole man. She reached out, clenching and twisting with a deliberateness that was itself almost mechanical, until she'd wound a whole bundle of medical tubes and cables in her fist.

Everyone nodded when she glanced their way. Everyone understood.

Memory washed over her in heavy fumes, almost suffocating. She wasn't in the chamber any longer; she stood, instead, in a newly opened mine, back during her very first mission as field leader for the 13936. Staring down at a member of an excavation team who'd been here before them, who'd triggered a chemical trap, twitching, gurgling, suffering.

Feeling her soul shrivel as she'd unsheathed her utility knife.

Watching as Ian, pale as she would ever see him until the day he died, raised a crowbar and ended the poor soul's suffering so that she wouldn't have to.

Mags wasn't sure what she screamed, then, as she yanked out the connections that kept this man, this stranger, from the peace that the machines denied him. She wasn't even sure *why* she screamed. She knew only that she'd lost something—that she'd had something stolen, ripped from her—she could never reclaim.

She said nothing to anyone as she pushed past them and out into the hallway.

Where she discovered one of the spidery machines awaiting them.

Chapter Thirty-Four

It must have just arrived while Jonas was inside the holding chamber. Mags was unsure how far her secondhand control over the man went, but he'd followed every order, and her instructions had been clear enough. If he'd been aware of the bot outside, he should have warned her.

Not that it made any difference now.

The gun ports on the turret snapped open, reminding Mags, strangely enough, of some wild beast's gaping maw. <You will return to your cell and explain how you gained egress. You have five seconds to comply. This is your only warn—>

"In here!" The scream was Sankar's, and for a fearful moment, Mags hadn't the first idea what else could possibly have gone wrong. "Gods, they're in here! Hurry!"

And then he appeared in the doorway, slowly backing out into the hall, mumbling mantras under his breath between shouts, his prayer beads raised before him.

For a fraction of a heartbeat, Mags didn't get it. She stiffened, expecting one of *them*, perhaps Ian himself, to burst from the chamber.

Almost as quickly, though, she understood, and it was all she could do to swallow a relieved, even maddened cackle. Instead, she pointed back the way she'd come with a finger that she didn't need to force to tremble. "Help us!"

Nestor and Sharon, thank God, also realized, after several confused breaths, what Sankar was doing. Both fled the room as swiftly as they could. Jonas, although clearly bewildered rather than frightened, followed.

So quickly Mags and Sankar barely dodged aside, the

machine lurched through the doorway. There it stopped and opened fire, guns tracking back and forth across the chamber, seeking a target the bot knew it couldn't see.

And wouldn't have, even had that target been real.

"Seal it!" Mags hissed.

Jonas jumped, waving a hand in front of a sensor on the wall. The door slammed shut with a heavy *clang*.

"That door's going to open right back up again as soon as that thing wants it to," the overseer warned. "And there've got to be reinforcements already on—"

Nestor yanked one of the screwdrivers from the old man's belt. With a loud cry he stabbed it into the sensor mechanism until wires snapped and sparks flew.

"That gonna do anything?" Mags asked.

Jonas shrugged. "I have no idea."

"Got it. So, um, run."

After which, since she was the only one other than Jonas who knew their destination, she proceeded to lead by example and tore off down the hallway.

That massive door, the monolithic slab of twenty-inch steel that guarded the medical facility, shuddered in its frame.

From all around the examination chamber, everyone wrist deep in their own assignments paused to stare in horror at the reverberating metal.

"Time's about up, guys," Mags said, weakly and unnecessarily. "Whatever you got left to do, better get it done now!"

Hours. They were trying to do in hours, with only the tools Jonas had been able to smuggle into the room overnight, what should properly require days. Jonas and Sankar, cursing and dodging the occasional spark, had delved into a variety of panels, ensuring that the door would not open and the room's sensors would not function even when the systems Jonas had sabotaged came back online. All five had then gotten to work: moving, opening, disassembling, scavenging, bending, breaking. Metal tubing from within the operating tables and the overhead piping; glycerol and other chemicals from various testing devices; thick copper wire from, oh, everywhere. And, of course, the generator itself.

Theoretically, they had everything they needed.

Practically, with the tools and the time available—well, best to keep thinking theoretically.

Again the door shuddered, making everyone jump, and then flinch in case Sharon had jumped *too* hard.

"Look on the bright side," she said with a shaky grin, sliding a glass cylinder of oily fluid into the nightmarish contraption on which they were working. "If I *do* drop this, you won't care very long."

"This to you is a bright side?" Nestor grunted, double-checking the gap between tube and wiring with a set of calipers.

"Well, it'd be really bright for a second, anyway."

On they labored, skin crawling, muscles tensing, struggling against every tick of the clock. Until, finally, the door shuddered one last time—and then, with an agonizing groan and the cracking of internal mechanisms, began to slide upward. Mags didn't even want to think about how strong the bots outside must be to lift the damn thing!

She dropped into a crouch beside the slapdash device, atop a fresh streak of corrosion where an earlier accident had splashed acid across the floor, and began desperately twisting wires together. "Cover!"

"But—" Sankar and Nestor both began.

"Now, God dammit!"

Against the leftmost wall, the fugitives had constructed a makeshift shelter, using the heavy medical beds, minus a few cannibalized components, to form a thick barrier. Now, at a reluctant shuffle and with many a backward glance, Magdalena's friends moved to huddle behind it.

Mags worked as fast as her aching fingers would permit. They throbbed as she clenched cables between them, struggling to make just these last few connections. She felt her skin open against edges of unfinished metal or beneath the prodding of bare wires; wincing, cursing, she paused only long enough to ensure the blood hadn't made her grip too slick.

Until, finally, the device itself was as ready as they could make it. She turned her attentions to the small box beside it, a simple cube containing an equally simple switch.

"Mags!"

She heard Nestor's warning, heard the sudden clatter of metal limbs against metal flooring, knew the machines had raised the door enough to slip inside. Mags ran, desperate, terrified. She was still in the air, diving over the makeshift barrier, when the first shot sounded. Bullets shook the metal tables as she landed with an agonizing jolt beside her friends.

A jolt that yanked the device in her hand free of the wire connecting it to the generator. Mags wanted to cry.

Instead, even as she snatched up the wire and began struggling to reseat it, she called out, "You come any closer and I'll detonate!"

The guns ceased firing. <Suarez, Magdalena. The chemicals and equipment available to you limit your options. Any explosive device you have constructed is either too weak to do damage beyond this room, or too powerful for you to survive. In either case, your threat is of no consequence. Surrender now or be executed.>

"Yeah, funny thing about that!" She was stalling, and she knew they knew.

Why won't this fucking wire fit?!

"See, you trained me. R&D. You didn't want to mess with the shit you taught me to disable!"

<Redundant and irrelevant input. You are still limited by the available materials. You have five seconds to surrender.>

"Yeah, but..."

Come on, come on, God dammit!

<Four seconds.>

"But, uh, you're assuming..."

<Three seconds.>

"That what I built..."

Yes!

She felt the wire slip into the terminal, a loose connection at best, but that was all she needed.

<Two seconds.>

"Is just a bomb!" she finished.

<One second.>

Everyone else huddled in tight, hands over their ears. Mags pressed her empty hand to one ear, leaned her head against Sankar's shoulder to protect the other as best she could, and flipped the switch.

The blast was more *crack* than *boom*, but still enough to make her head ring, to plunge twin spikes of pain and vertigo through her skull. She felt the pressure in her gut, her limbs. The tables jolted, slamming into them, and thrummed beneath a rain of shrapnel.

The machine had been quite correct, of course. The blast wasn't very big. It couldn't have been, if the humans wanted to survive.

But as Mags had said, the blast wasn't the point.

In the core of the generator, the cylinder of nitroglycerine detonated inside an aluminum tube. A tube, in turn, that expanded to connect with the helix of copper wire surrounding it, wire heavily charged by the generator itself. Oh, there were other modifications, other bits and pieces, other chemicals, but *that* was the heart of it all.

She knew how to disarm devices that made even the machines wary, Mags did. And she knew how to build them.

The electromagnetic pulse ripped through the installation in a fraction of a second, leaving burnt circuits and scrambled electronics in its wake. The lights died. The cameras died.

And the bots died.

All of them? Maybe not. Magdalena had no means of measuring either the precise output of the EMP or the shielding of any given portion of the structure. She might have gotten the whole building, or the entire block, or just a few floors.

Only one way to find out.

"What now?" Sharon asked.

Mags, who could only barely hear her, struggled to her feet, bracing herself on Nestor and a scored and buckled table as she wrestled vertigo into submission.

"Now? Now we get the hell out of here."

She didn't actually add *or die trying*, but she knew the others heard it just the same.

Chapter Thirty-Five

An hour later, they had neither escaped nor died trying. They had, however, learned two critical details.

First, a small but significant minority of the combat-model machines were hardened against electromagnetic pulse, and thus fully functional.

And second, most of these bots had congregated by the facility's only exits.

"So what now?" Nestor's question sounded oddly tinny in the cramped room serving as the fugitives' latest shelter.

"That question," Mags snipped, "hasn't led to a good answer yet. I wish people would stop asking." Then, giving herself a quick shake, "We go up. Try to find a way onto the roof. With any luck, we can climb down or across from there. If not, we can at least get the lay of the land. See if we can figure how far the EMP spread, what sort of presence the machines have on the streets."

Nobody argued. A few quick peeks around the doorframe, to be certain the hallway remained unoccupied, and they were off again, scampering along the walls, jumping at every sound, real or imagined. Jonas, however, reacted to Magdalena's orders more slowly than before, and his expression was no longer quite so slack as she'd have preferred.

Clearly, even as simple a post-hypnotic suggestion as "Obey Magdalena's orders" had a limited lifespan. They needed to figure out what to do with him sooner than later.

Some of the halls through which they crept were empty. A couple were occupied by scrips, and on those occasions, Jonas had proved a useful distraction while the others crept up and hit the guards with very solid tools. They even acquired a few pistols in the bargain.

And some of those halls contained machines.

Most had toppled midstep or teetered in awkward, frozen stances. A few, however, stood upright, perhaps burnt out or perhaps lying in wait. Every time she inched her way around one, Mags was convinced that *this* time it would spring to life, grabbing her or slamming her against the wall with formerly dead limbs. She left streaks of perspiration behind her, to mark the graves of a few more overloaded nerves, and she knew the others were just as on edge.

The stairs they finally located took them up several floors, but not nearly all the way to the roof. From there they'd had to find another flight—relatively nearby and yet still too far for comfort—and from that one, eventually, they were forced to go in search of a third.

Mags knew this floor was different the moment she crept from the stairwell. She couldn't have said *why*, but something was off. A subtle difference in the antiseptic, ozone-kissed atmosphere? Something in the acoustics, too faint to register on a conscious level? No idea, but it was there, and from the way Nest and Sharon carried themselves, they felt it, too.

Sharon darted ahead, belly-crawling to the first intersection and peering around the corner, using a shard of broken mirror from the examination chamber rather than exposing herself. Just as swiftly she scurried back, gesturing with suddenly bloodless hands for the group to hunker down and be quiet.

"Three bots," she whispered between rough breaths, "way down the hall. Combat-models. They weren't moving, so I guess they *could* be fried, but they sure as hell look like they're standing guard."

"Over what?" Sankar asked, fidgeting with his beads.

"Door. *Big* door. Couldn't make out a lot of detail, but I'd guess at least as heavy as the one to the medical bay."

Everyone looked expectantly at Jonas. Then, when he failed to take the hint, "What's in there?" Mags asked.

"Not sure. I know it's heavily reinforced, that sector. Armored."

"Shielded against EMP?"

"Don't know. Could be. No idea what's in it. None of us were ever allowed in. Machines only."

Mags frowned, sketching a map in her head. "Am I crazy," she asked, "or is this mystery room directly above the examination chamber?"

"Is this an either/or question?" Nestor smirked. Then, more seriously, "I think you're right. I mean, not *immediately* above. More than a few floors between. But in a direct line, yeah."

Sankar briefly touched Magdalena's shoulder. "What are you thinking?"

"I'm not sure yet," she admitted. "There's something... I'd really like to know what's in there."

"Oh, sure!" Sharon said. "We'll just go right up and ask! I say we go back down, try to find an alternate stairwell that brings us up elsewhere on this floor."

"Actually," Mags noted thoughtfully, "we *might* be able to walk up and ask."

Again everyone's attention went to the overseer.

"The machines may well have realized he's working with us by now," Sankar warned. "We've no idea what they've seen or recorded from before the pulse. And even if they *haven't* realized it, if this area is as secret as Jonas says, they might not appreciate even a scrip's interruption."

"Only one way to find out," Nestor declared, sounding almost cheerful. He rose from his crouch and, before Mags or the others could quite comprehend what he was doing, hauled Jonas upright by the old man's shirt and all but flung him, staggering and stumbling, around the corner.

At which point every bit of the overseer above the waist—apart from his left forearm, which flopped to the floor, twitching like a landed fish—disintegrated beneath a fusillade of bullets and other projectiles. The wall behind him buckled, as cratered as the face of the moon and coated in a glistening crimson.

The fugitives ran madly at the first sound of gunfire, plunging back down the stairwell and not halting until they'd locked themselves in another small room some two stories down. There they spent endless heartbeats, listening for any sound of activity.

Only then, when all seemed clear, did Mags realize she had Nestor's own shirt in a two-fisted grip, unsure if she was trying to haul him down to her eye level or herself up to his. *"What the fuck was that?!"* She couldn't afford to scream it, but her boiling cauldron of emotion wouldn't let her whisper. She settled for a quiet but grating squeak.

Sweat gleamed on his forehead, his lips had paled, but his words, when he answered, were steady. "For Daniel," he said simply.

She spat something exceedingly rude and released him. Without another word, she led the fugitives back out into the halls, in search of an alternate stairwell.

For all her anger, however, all her other worries, Mags couldn't help but notice, and wonder. Yes, they'd fled instantly. Yes, the bots might not realize that Jonas hadn't come upstairs alone. Still, she thought it odd that, so far as she or the others could tell, the machines hadn't even *tried* to investigate or pursue.

Four fugitives, crawling on their stomachs, peeked over four sides of the roof, scanning the surrounding structures and the streets below, before scurrying back, dodging vents and weapons turrets and antennae, to meet in the middle.

Each carried the same report: The pulse hadn't reached far beyond these walls. Lights and machines still operated only a quarter block away. So far as the night allowed them to see, the machines were slowly converging on the facility from all across Pittsburgh. Steel feet tromped across broken roads, and the dust swirled in the grip of small rotors. High overhead, a far larger form of drone—winged, jet-propelled, armed with God-knew-what—roared past and began to circle.

The walls of the building offered no good options for climbing. A few narrow bridges or thick cables might provide access to neighboring structures, but those buildings were beyond the reach of the EMP and the walkways wide open to attack from above and below.

They were far fewer in number, the machines, than one might expect, thanks to the war and the ongoing siege, but more than numerous enough. For the time being, they hung back from the building, seemingly content to ensure the fugitives made no escape, but nobody doubted they would eventually move in, flooding the structure floor by floor until there was nowhere left to hide.

"What're they waiting for?" Nestor asked in the whisper that had, by this point, become instinctive to all of them.

"Probably making sure we don't have a second EMP," Mags guessed.

Sankar nodded. "I'm sure they realize it's unlikely, but why risk it? They can wait. A lot longer than we can."

"All right. So, options?"

Nothing. Mags scowled.

"Come on, guys. *Options!*"

"Oh!" Nestor half rose and crossed the roof at a crouching jog until he arrived at one of the defensive batteries. He poked head and hands inside for a few moments, withdrew with a grunt, and scrambled back. "So, yeah, all the control mechanisms are toast, but the EMP shouldn't have affected the guns themselves. With the right tools, I can haul one of those suckers out of there."

"Not even you can just carry one of those things around!" Sharon objected.

"No, but I could drag it somewhere. Gives us some options, at least."

"All right." Mags thought a moment. "So far as we've found, there's only the one access port to the roof. And two stairwells that access the top floor. Right?"

Agreement all around.

"So, we block one of them off completely. One of these monster guns at the other stairwell and by the roof hatch should keep anything from getting through. For a good long while, anyway."

"Mags…" Sankar began.

She wouldn't permit him to finish. "I know. All we're doing is buying a little extra time."

"For what?" he asked. Then, at her expression, "I'm not

arguing against it. If buying time is all we can do, I'm all for it. But a solution's not bloody well going to just fall into our lap, and escape's not going to get any easier."

"Believe me, I know. The plan is to hole up and wait."

"Wait for what?"

"Backup."

"Who—?"

"The vampires, obviously." And then, "Would one of you blink or something? You're creeping me."

It was Nestor who started. "Mags?" He cleared his throat. "Are you—?"

"Look, I know I'm the one who wanted nothing more to do with them," she said. "And I've got some damn good reasons for keeping it that way. But I'm firmly set on, you know, surviving, and if that means the undead, well, I'll suck it up. For a while, anyway."

"Even if we had some way of contacting them," he bulled ahead, "Lacusta's not going to come swooping in to rescue us. He doesn't care enough. I doubt he'd even come for Ian, not with everything else he's dealing with right now."

"Of course he won't come for us! He'll come for the Eye!"

"Oh," she continued, shrinking beneath the weight of their combined and accusing disbelief. "Yeah, uh, one of the Eyes is actually here, physically, in the building. Didn't I mention that?"

Chapter Thirty-Six

"Look," Mags told them once they'd returned to the floor below, "it's simple. You just have to put it together."

Silent glares.

"So, uh, maybe I'll put it together for you."

"Do that," Sankar suggested.

"Okay, so, the secure sector where we, uh, lost Jonas. Let's think about what's in there."

"Could be just about anything," Sharon objected.

"It's something important," Mags insisted. "Very. It's heavily armored. Heavily shielded, probably even against EMP. More so than any other part of the building, more than any part of *any* machine installation we've seen. Right?

"It's *so* important that, even though there are only a handful of bots still active in the building, at least three of them are standing guard instead of searching for us or watching the exits."

Sharon still wasn't convinced, and the others seemed to agree with her. "It's something important, sure. But an Eye? That's a big leap, Mags. It could be—"

"Could be what? Just a database or server farm for the machine network? I don't think so. There are about a bajillion of those scattered all over, so any one of them's just a backup. Not that vital. Besides, would trusted scrips be forbidden from even knowing about one of those, let alone approaching it?"

Sankar shook his head, contemplative and far away.

"It's not some super-secret factory," she continued inexorably. "It's not big enough, and they're not going to store a few dozen tons of equipment on an *upper* floor."

"Weapons or computer development," Nest said.

"Not impossible," Mags admitted, "but I don't think so. Again, why keep it on an upper floor? It doesn't require the equipment or raw materials of a production line, but it still takes a lot. Why not just attach something like that to a factory?"

Still gazing into nothing, Sankar added, "To my knowledge, the machines do just that. I've never heard of a developmental setup in the middle of a facility such as this one."

"But why?" At this point, Mags had no clue if Sharon still truly objected or was just playing devil's advocate. "Vampires are the only thing that's really threatened the Eyes since Pacification. Why would it risk getting this close to one?"

"What's going to offer more heavily secured chambers, a better place to imprison a vampire, than a building where an Eye already, uh, 'lives'? And hell, maybe it wants to be close? Maybe it thinks it can learn something through direct observation that it can't from a distance. Maybe it wants to see if it can see the vampires, because it's at least *kind of* alive, where other machines can't. We already know one of them's personally watching from *somewhere*.

"Point is, I don't know. I don't think like a machine. I'm just guessing. But there *are* possible motives."

Sharon and Nestor still looked dubious. "It's a solid theory," Sankar said, sounding only a bit less doubtful. "But it's only a theory. I concede that it's possible, but I'm not remotely convinced."

"That's fine," Mags said brightly. "We don't have to *tell* Lacusta it's just a theory." Then, "Yes, I know. But we're dead if we don't convince him to come, so I'd call it worth the risk."

"How?" Nestor challenged. "Even if we agreed this was a good idea, we've fried any gear we could use to send a message!"

"Actually…" She snickered a bit at the expressions of horror brought on by that word, and by the grin she offered with it. "Not *all* the gear."

"Hello, Ian."

The "vampire prison" was impressive indeed. In the center of a large chamber, an artificial stream—of unknown depth and fifteen feet wide if it was an inch—flowed through a grate in the wall. There it split, one branch flowing out through an opposite grate, the other forming a loop so that the water fed back into itself. The result was a small island, surrounded on all sides. Water that, despite the electromagnetic pulse, still flowed. Either it was driven by gravity, slopes and angles somewhere in the system that carried the liquid to this chamber, or the flow was powered by a generator shielded from, or outside the radius of, the EMP.

"Well. And here I was starting to think you'd been killed. Or decided not to honor our deal."

"I wouldn't do that. I'm not you." Mags approached until she'd reached the water's edge, careful to keep her gaze downcast. Look at the stream, look at the floor, look at his feet, whatever.

Just don't meet his eyes.

No matter how much she wanted to. No matter that part of her felt she deserved whatever he might do. Maybe new-Ian was her penance for failing the old one.

"Aw, Mags, you don't trust me? I did exactly as you asked with Jonas."

"Because you want to get out of here. You need me, much as I need you. And right now..." She paused as Ian—or at least his calves down—stepped through her line of sight. His skin glistened wetly, and now that she was near, she smelled something sharp poking at her nose.

Very carefully she gazed at the rightmost wall, looked up, and only then turned back to the vampire's island, or rather the ceiling above. There she saw an array of mirrors similar to those in the examination room. Were it not the middle of the night, they'd doubtless be blazing with sunlight. She also spotted an array of spigots that had stopped functioning, though they still dripped now and again. Those, too, were familiar.

"Clever," she mused. "A spray? Fine mist, like when they were working on you? To help pinpoint you?"

Ian muttered something unintelligible.

"But it's not water, is it?" Mags sniffed again. *Kerosene.* Well, *that* was blatant enough as threats go. "They had you pretty well pinned and controlled, didn't they?"

"You were telling me you needed something?" he growled. "Right."

Keep it cool, stay focused on business.

"I need the modem and other networking peripherals from inside one of the bots. One still functional. Not much chance the four of us could take one down, and if we did, we'd probably have to damage it so much it'd be useless. But *you*, you can manage it."

"I can. When the machines took me out of here during the day, for my—exams—they brought in a heavy plastic sheet to cover the grate, stop the flow. If you can find that—"

"Oh, I'm not letting you out of there, Ian. I'm not stupid."

"*What?*"

"You get out of there, you can just go. Poof. Mist. Leaving us here for the machines. Or else hypnotize us or kill us yourself."

"We're on the same side! We're working together!"

"Sorry, no. Don't trust you. I have a plan to lure the bots to you."

"Nope. Not going to do it. You let me out, or I'm done helping."

"All right." Mags headed for the door. "The rest of us are just going to die here. I do *not* want to imagine what they're going to do to you in the next few days. Weeks. Months."

She had one foot in the hall before he called after her. "All right, dammit! All right."

"See? I knew you'd be reasonable."

"Bitch. You know I'm not at my best, right? I haven't been… eating."

"You'll do. Unless you know where I can find *another* vampire?"

"Bitch," he said again. "What's the plan, and how much am I going to hate it?"

"Scale of one to ten? A lot."

Between the chemicals they found in various storage rooms near the medical bay, and the ammunition they salvaged from the deactivated bots, Mags and the others had more than they needed to construct a proper-sized bomb.

"You'll want to catch this," she warned the vampire once she'd returned with the device. "It's *really* unstable."

"Wait, what do—?!"

Still very careful where she allowed her gaze to land, she tossed it across the water to Ian. She heard a quick scramble of skin on the floor, followed by a faint *thump* and some not-so-faint cursing.

"I suggest you turn into something hazy," she said. "The EMP may have shut down the sprayers, but you still smell awfully flammable to me."

He was still cursing when his voice faded away along with the rest of him.

After that, it was... well, not *easy*, but certainly simple. Mags retreated to the doorway, ducked behind it, and fired a few shots until one of them struck the volatile admixture. The blast was sharp, deafening, and ignited the kerosene still evaporating in puddles across the island. Even with the building's systems down, she'd no doubt that some of the bots would hear the detonation.

She waited in a room across the hall. In her fist, she held her pistol; at her feet was a second, far more stable explosive on a four-second timer. Her hope was that, given their depleted numbers, the machines would only send a single bot to investigate, but should a second appear, she hoped she could take it down with the bomb before it interfered.

Fortunately, she didn't have to. It was, indeed, a single spider—probably from the band guarding the main entrance, if she had to guess—that responded. Mags heard it coming, the rapid clop of steel appendages, and ducked back into the room until it had scuttled into Ian's cell.

There, she knew what it would see. An island that appeared empty, not merely to sight but to any other sensors the machine might possess, and a hole blasted into the floor. That the hole did not penetrate down to the next level was something that, from this side of the room, the bot could *not* see.

And of course, once it fired a heavy barrage across the island—presumably to drop any undead it couldn't detect—and leapt across the stream so that it *could* examine the hole, it was all over. A ribbon of mist poured in through the gun ports, and Ian tore it open from within.

"Yes," he snapped as Mags ran into the room, "I was careful about what I broke in there."

"Good. Toss the whole thing over, and I'll find what I need."

"Um, you heard what I said about not being at my best right now?"

"I suggest you dig deep and find the strength, unless you'd rather wait for *them* to dig for you. And do it quick, before any more bots come calling."

In the end, by ripping the legs and the heaviest guns from the thing—the scream of rending metal had Mags grinding her teeth almost flat—Ian lightened it enough to heft across the water. She, in turn, immediately set about salvaging the necessary components. She couldn't send any sort of signal, not with this equipment alone, but the parts should be enough for her to jury-rig repairs to one of the broadcast antennae on the roof. As each piece emerged, she dumped it into a sack she'd improvised from one of the dead scrips' coats.

"You want to tell me what your plan is, now?" Ian asked.

"Nope." Mags rose, hefted the bag over one shoulder, and moved to leave.

"Come on, Mags. Let me out of here. I'm not going to interfere with whatever you're doing."

"Remember that bit about how I'm not stupid? Not a chance, Ian. When we're ready to go, not before."

"You can't just leave me here for the machines!"

"They're not likely to kill you, not once they realized you're still trapped. You're too valuable to them."

"What if you're wrong?"

"Uh, well, then they *will* kill you. Obviously."

Ian took a deep breath, a blatantly artificial gesture given his undead physiology. "Look, sweetheart, I can help. I'm sorry I cursed at you earlier. I'm sorry about what I said in the mine. I'm... I'm not myself. I can't handle this, not alone. I need you. I love—"

Mags halted in her tracks. Slowly, carefully, she set the bag of electronics down beside her. At her belt hung several of the tools that Jonas had provided; from amongst them she pulled a small butane torch and pressed the trigger. A tongue of blue flame erupted from the nozzle, and only then—keeping her gaze down, of course—did she face Ian once more. Although she stood clear across the room, he retreated a step from the water's edge, growling and hissing. Parts of him grew faintly transparent as he hovered on the verge of changing shape.

"I should fucking cremate you." She spoke in a raw whisper, knowing he heard her clearly enough. "I owe you a few dozen deaths, you bastard. And I could. It's almost dawn, you know. I just have to wait for a few minutes, for the sunlight, so you can't turn into mist, and then light you the fuck up."

"You wouldn't! We have a deal!"

"Because you've never lied to me? Broken your word? Because I owe you so much honesty?"

"No. Mags, please!"

"Please? I remember saying that to you, more than once. I remember *pleading* with you. I—Oh, look, Ian. It's later than I thought. The first mirror's already brightening a little."

"Oh, God…"

Mags burst out laughing, a harsh, bitter guffaw. "God? You're calling on…?" She all but choked getting herself under control. And then she released the switch, shutting off the flame, and tossed the torch aside.

"I *did* make a deal with you. Plus, I owe you, for—a long time ago. And I'll honor that, because I'm *not* you. You want to pray, you can offer thanks for that.

"But I want you to remember this, Ian. Forever. You *lost*. The big, scary nosferatu *begged*. Begged *me*. After everything you did to me, you only survived because I decided to *let* you."

Ian was still gawping, struggling for words, as Mags hefted the bag and stormed out.

It wouldn't be until later—much, much later—that Mags would learn what transpired in that room after she left.

"You're looking rather poorly, Ian." Sankar gestured at the mirrors overhead. "Doesn't take much sunlight, does it? Not in the shape you're in."

"The hell do you want, old man? If you're here for your girlfriend, you just missed her, so you can get lost."

"I wasn't trying to meet up with Magdalena." Sankar paused, wandered over to the discarded butane torch, and began idly rolling it between his fingers. "Though I *am* here for her."

"You're lucky. Not a lot of people these days live long enough to go senile. You know you're making no damn sense, right?"

"Magdalena has a good heart, even after all you've done to poison it. Not a lot of people these days have that, either. It's worth protecting."

"What are you talking about, you crazy—?"

Sankar raised his prayer beads in one fist and, chanting, advanced to the edge of the stream. Ian cringed back, whimpering, in no condition to take advantage of either Sankar's proximity, or his eye contact.

"I'm talking," the old man said, "about doing for her what she's in no state to do—what she shouldn't *have* to do—for herself."

Between the reflected light of morning, the running water, and Sankar's faith, Ian had nowhere to go, nothing to do but shriek in beyond-mortal terror, as Sankar thumbed the torch back on and hurled it at the vampire's kerosene-coated body.

Chapter Thirty-Seven

"We should have enough nitric acid," Sharon reported dubiously, having quickly inventoried the chemical storage room from which Jonas had acquired the earlier batch. "But it'll be a near thing. And Mags, that's all of it. We do this and wind up needing more nitroglycerine later, we're good and screwed."

"Hmm." Mags leaned back against the stairs on which they currently huddled, popping her back with what sounded not unlike a small caliber shot. "And you're sure they'd move it out by train?"

"I am," Sankar replied. "The Eyes are sizable entities. If they weren't, I imagine they would just install themselves in their own robot bodies. The mobility would be useful. But their systems are mechanically complex, far ahead of the technology that built them. Barring a very large truck or helicopter, both of which should take some time to get here, the train's its only means. If we want to ensure the Eye's still here when Lacusta arrives, the tracks are our best target."

He didn't say *Assuming the bloody thing's even here in the first place*, but he didn't have to. Mags felt the message radiating from his every posture and expression.

And since he *didn't* utter the words aloud, she didn't feel the need to address them. "Antenna?" she asked instead.

"Far as I can tell," Nestor said, "it should just take a few minutes to hook up the transmitter. The connections are pretty straightforward."

Another "Hmm." Then, "All right. I haven't been able to test the transmitter I put together, but it *should* work. I also have no idea how long we're gonna get out of the bot's aux power cell. We might only have a few minutes of broadcast time."

"Less, if the machines interrupt," Sankar reminded them. "Which I think we all know they will."

"In other words, we have to do an afternoon's worth of stuff, simultaneously, in about five minutes. Typical."

"All right," Mags concluded with a sigh. "Let's build another bomb."

The most difficult part, as it turned out, was finding a container large enough to carry the quantity of liquid explosive they concocted, but still readily portable. Finally, though, Sharon had located a steel cask used for transporting hazardous chemicals. When loaded up with the nitroglycerine, Nestor could carry it himself with difficulty, or alongside a partner without much trouble at all.

Now they had wrestled it, and the jury-rigged mess that was Magdalena's transmitter, up into the final stairwell. Above them, glowing with dust-filtered sunlight, was the rooftop hatch.

"Anything?" Mags asked.

Sharon, who had popped up to take a look, shook her head. "The streets are swarming, but they're still keeping their distance. Worried about EMP, or maybe waiting for reinforcements?"

Sankar's beads *click-click-click*ed. "Whatever their reasons, they'll change fast enough."

Mags, amazed the others couldn't hear the machinegun-pounding of her pulse, took a deep breath. "Sankar, you're with me. Nest, Sharon, the rails. Um, don't miss."

"We're on track," Nestor told her. And then, at her glower, "Sorry."

"Uh-huh." Another breath. "Go."

Mags and Sankar lunged through the hatch, sprinting toward, and then dropping to their knees beside, the nearest broadcast antenna. They had already pried open the panel and begun digging in the wiring when the other two lumbered past, cask clutched between them.

"Here!" Mags roughly stripped the insulation from a stretch of wire with a small blade. "Tie in the main output here!" Sankar began coiling and twisting, fingers working as fast as they would go.

Across the roof, Mags heard "Three!" followed by twin grunts of exertion. Then, from below, an explosive *crack!*

Enough, she hoped, prayed, to mangle a short length of track, if not tear it apart.

"Transmitter engaged!" Sankar's shout brought her back to her own task. Swiftly as she could with shaking hands, she activated the power cell. Frequency was already set to the resistance's network, gain was already as high as she could pump it. Either the signal would make it, or it wouldn't.

"This is Suarez! Ian and the rest of us are cornered in a facility near the center of Pittsburgh. Lacusta, if you're listening, one of the Eyes is here! Repeat, one of the Eyes is *here!* The building's along the main rail line, in the southwest section of the conformed—!"

"They're moving!" Nestor cried out from the rooftop's edge. "They're converging on the building!"

"...the conformed regions!" Mags continued desperately. "The rooftop is packed with defensive batteries, some camouflaged as exhaust vents! The structure has multiple levels, all rectangular, but some off-center from the—"

"Inbound!" Sankar shouted, pointing.

High above, scarcely visible against the murk, one of the massive winged drones dropped from the clouds. And while Magdalena might have only just been able to see it, she knew what the sudden flash beneath the bot's left wing meant.

"Get off the roof!" She was already sprinting as she cried out, then dove through the hatch, leaping the stairs five or six at a time.

The four fugitives were spread out, between one and a half to three stories down, when the rooftop vanished in thunder and fire.

It couldn't have been an especially powerful missile, Mags decided, as her thoughts began to connect to one another again around the vertigo and the constant ringing, a jigsaw puzzle only slowly coming together. And that made sense; the bots wouldn't have risked taking out any significant chunk of the installation, not while the Eye itself remained.

If it was even—No. Don't start that. It's here. It has to be.

Probably why she survived. That was the good news. The bad was, she didn't know if anyone else did.

And if that weren't enough, the building no longer resembled the target she'd described to Lacusta. From up close, sure, he'd be able to tell that the roof had been bombed, but from a distance? Mags had no clue how obvious the wreckage might be.

If he was coming. If he believed her. If the broadcast reached him at all. She thought she'd have minutes, not mere seconds. She'd thought they'd have more of a chance.

Groans and gasps and shifting rubble penetrated the haze around her. Mags staggered upright, choking on dust and bitter smoke. Happy to have something else to think about besides their probable failure, she moved to assist her friends.

None were too badly off, thankfully, but neither was anyone in great shape. Worn and tattered clothing revealed blackened skin, burnt by embers or waves of heat where it wasn't bleeding from uncountable lacerations. Sharon winced with every limp, blatantly favoring her right leg. Nestor struggled to find a scrap of cloth or bandage clean enough to press against a ragged wound across his ribs. Sankar just seemed slow and shaken, perhaps approaching the limit of what he could handle at his age, no matter how good his condition.

"Well," Mags offered weakly, gesturing with her chin at the heap of settling rubble where the upper flight of stairs used to be, "we don't have to worry about them coming at us from the roof anymore."

Only Nestor managed to fake a grin.

"All right. Um, we salvaged two of the guns from up top this morning, right?"

Nest and Sharon both offered weary nods.

"Okay." Here she pointed at the doorway off a landing just a few steps down. "This seems to be the uppermost floor that hasn't more or less collapsed. So we'll hole up in the stairwell there. That gives us two lines of approach to cover, and *possibly* a line of retreat if they only come at us from one direction."

Which they won't, of course.

"And then?" Sharon wondered aloud.

"Then we pray the ammo lasts, and we don't get overrun, before help arrives."

"The machines," Sankar said, his words almost ponderous, "aren't going to charge straight up here. They'll search the lower levels and work their way up, in case we try to sneak out behind them. We should take advantage of whatever time we have, get some sleep."

"Shifts of two," Mags said. "Twenty minutes. I know, it's not much, but…" She shrugged helplessly.

They didn't exactly have room to get comfortable, but once they'd dragged the weapons up from where they'd stashed them—and Nest had shown everyone how to use bits of rubble to brace and fire the things without shattering bones or losing control—the big guy and Sharon curled up on the steps and dropped into a light, unsettled doze.

Mags and Sankar sat angled shoulder to shoulder, leaning on each other, each staring off into the distance over the barrel of a ridiculously huge gun.

"We're not going to make it, you know," she said just above a whisper.

She felt the old man tense against her back. "I realize the odds are against us, but—"

"Sankar, assuming they don't just gas the place… Actually, why *haven't* they?"

"At a guess? If they were storing or constructing such weapons at all, it was in one of the facilities we've destroyed. Otherwise, I imagine they'd have used gas or chemical devices at the mines."

"Oh. Yeah." A pause. "But it's not going to take them long to build new facilities, now that they're devoting full resources to the war, is it?"

"No. No, I'm afraid not."

"We'd already be dead if they'd been remotely anticipating

and equipped for a revolt, wouldn't we?"

"Several times over, I'm afraid."

"Lovely." Another pause, and then she continued, "But even if they don't gas us, how long can we last? We've got a good position, and we can obliterate anything that comes into view for a while, but they *are* going to overrun us, sooner or later."

Now she felt his head shaking. "Maybe not, if the vampires reach us first."

"You really think my transmission got through?"

"It's possible. Have faith."

"I can't. Even if it did, even if they decide to come..." She shuddered at the thought of seeing the undead again. "They're not going to head out until nightfall. No way they'd try to sneak past the bots in the sunlight, without their powers. Which means even if they fly, and fast, we're looking at hours after sundown."

It was, at that moment, mid-afternoon so far as Mags could determine.

"Do you really have *faith*," she asked him bitterly, "that we can hold out that long?"

She felt one of his rough hands reach back to take hers. "Magdalena? It's not your parents' religion, but would you permit me to teach you a few mantras?"

"Come on, I don't..." She stopped, sniffled, pondered her slumbering friends. "Yeah. Yeah, I think I'd like that."

She had no idea how long they were at it, or how long Sharon and Nest had been awake. She knew only, sometime later, that her two friends joined them, seated side by side. And for a time, whether in genuine belief or simple solidarity with one another, all four of them prayed.

For almost an hour, until the machines finally came for them.

Chapter Thirty-Eight

Only a few at a time, initially. Scouts, no doubt, making a quick sweep of what was now the uppermost floor, their fellows moments behind.

They appeared in the stairwell below, the steps ringing with each steel footfall. Spider-bots of the smaller variety, accompanied by a rotary drone here, a humanoid chassis there. The machines that had gathered from elsewhere in the city, in response to the EMP, were obviously participating in the search.

Mags and the others had no way to hide, not hunkered down in that same stairwell. So instead, using one of the rooftop batteries, they made the first squad go away.

Even with earplugs improvised from torn bits of tunic, the sound was beyond deafening; it was skull-battering. These were weapons designed for taking down small aircraft, their rate of fire only marginally slower than the .50s Nestor preferred, each round nearly half again as large.

If by some miracle a means of retreat *did* open itself to the fugitives, they sure as hell weren't taking the guns with them. It'd been hard enough to lug the things into position.

The second wave, equally small, came from the corridor: a swarm of drones, flitting and shifting in a constant dance. Using a chunk of blasted wall as a pivot and his own prodigious strength to its limits, Nestor angled the second weapon high enough, for long enough, to take those down as well.

Gagging on rock dust, the quartet collected additional bits of rubble, anything they could free from the mass above without bringing it down on their heads. These they stacked in low makeshift walls, enough to provide a tiny modicum of cover while they lay flat on their bellies, firing the massive guns.

It might buy them a few extra minutes, catch a few bullets, before crumbling.

They didn't anticipate explosives, figured the machines would worry that the rooftop bombing might have destabilized the building. If they were wrong, though? If the machines *did* launch a rocket or lob a grenade?

Then they were probably all dead.

Those pleasant thoughts expanding to occupy every inch of her mind, a growing fear and an even more frightening numbness creeping through her limbs, Mags checked the ammo feed on the weapon Sharon currently operated and peered down the stairwell for the next wave.

Bullets smacked into the stone barricades, into the stairwell walls, but far larger bullets fired back, and another small group of bots was scrap metal.

"If they keep throwing themselves at us in such convenient portions," Sharon said, "this is going to be easier than we thought."

"They'll do no such thing," Sankar assured her, massaging his temples. "They're feeling us out, making us burn ammunition while they gather into larger groups to overrun us.

Mags squinted at him. "Ever the optimist."

"I'm just saying—"

Nestor called out a warning and opened fire, supported by Magdalena's and Sankar's stolen pistols, and a trio of spiders collapsed in the corridor. Two more scuttled over those and also went down.

Then, from around the nearest corner, yet another spider and a pair of humanoid machines carrying automatic weapons darted into the hallway and dropped prone. There they returned fire, using their own fallen brethren as cover.

It didn't take long for the massive guns to tear through the fallen chassis, and then through the active bots, but the message was clear, and the reprieve would be short. The machines were coming in numbers, now, and they had no intention of just charging mindlessly into rivers of bullets.

Each time, there were a few more of them. Each time, the

humans flinched from more near misses, bled from more flying fragments of metal and stone. Each time, the layers of fallen bots grew thicker, tougher to shoot through. And each time, the machines drew closer.

During one brief ebb, Mags wiped powder-thickened sweat from her face. "Anybody got any idea of the time?"

"Best guess," Sharon said, "I'm thinking an hour after dark, maybe ninety minutes."

"Which means," Nest added grimly, "if Lacusta left the minute the sun went down and flew the whole way, he's still a couple hours out. Even if we could possibly keep from being overrun, we don't have the ammo."

Sankar pointed with a finger that seemed to be aging by the minute. "The undead are not the only ones who might have come from the mine."

Following his gesture, Mags noticed several spidery limbs jutting from the growing wreckage—limbs coated with dried mud, too thick to have been picked up in the conformed regions.

"It could have come from the Scatters," she protested, but her heart wasn't in it. If the Eye had recalled a portion of the besieging force when it first realized the danger? Well, their odds of survival had already been about zero. Now, they could take out every bot in the building, every bot in the block, and it wouldn't matter.

"Here they come again!" Sharon warned. Indeed, the stairwell below sounded like the maw of some steel-toothed monster, so heavy were the clang and grind of metal. Bots already reduced to scrap began to twitch and even climb the steps, pushed from below to form a moving shield. In the corridor, the same, a new tide of bots pushing the "dead" before them. On the stairs, on the floor, even clinging to the walls, the machines came, guns blazing.

Mags dropped to her knees beside Sharon, Sankar beside Nest, both to check the belt-feeders one last time. This was the final push, and they all knew it.

"Guys, I…" Mags tried to fight the quaver in her voice, and then wondered why she bothered. "We tried. We mattered. I love all of—"

"Look!"

She jumped at Nestor's cry, adrenaline spiking through her—and sobbed, unashamed, when she saw what he'd spotted.

In the hall and in the stairwell, several oncoming bots vented a familiar mist. Thick and fluid and just slightly *off*, it accumulated around the robots' feet, growing ever more solid.

One of the vampires, however, lacked the patience to wait. Rather than emerge as the others had—perhaps to get the lay of the land? Surely they couldn't see much from inside their artificial enemies—he instead burst the machine apart from inside, appearing, laughing and triumphant, in a heap of ravaged metal.

Three of the bots around him, who might not be able to see him but surely knew what the sudden unexplained rending of their counterpart meant, spun and bathed the fallen machine in fire. The vampire, who Mags hadn't seen for long enough to identify, was ash and ember before he could scream.

"Flamethrowers!" Mags shouted, unsure it would do any good, but screaming at the top of her lungs all the same. She'd no idea what the vampires could see, could hear, in their nonsolid forms, nor how many might yet remain inside any machines. "They've got flamethrowers!"

The mists ceased swirling, slowly settling along the floor, very much like a natural fog on a winding stream. They did nothing more, and the bots, though far more cautious now, kept coming.

"Maybe warning them," Nest grumbled, "wasn't the best idea."

"*I* didn't know they were just going to stop—!"

The machines halted in their tracks, some turning around to face back the way they'd come. Only then, over everything else, did the humans hear it.

Buzzing. Fluttering. Screeching. *Droning.*

From the stairwell below rose a swarm—no, not a swarm, a *tide*, a cresting tsunami—of the night's flying creatures. Birds and bats, but above all, insects. So many, so very many of them. They were a wall, a solid front of darkness choking off all light, all sight. The stench was somehow alien and familiar at once, a prime ingredient of rot.

Mags might have been embarrassed by her own shriek, had her three companions not also cried out. Huddled, eyes and lips squeezed tight, she swatted frantically about her head and shoulders.

She needn't have bothered. Not a single creature alighted on the weary humans. Driven by an intelligence far more advanced than their own, they split into two thick clouds, clogging hall and stairwell both.

They could not obscure every one of the machines' cameras and sensors, but they interfered with many. Nor could they block much in the way of weaponry or projectiles, but even the tiniest deviation of a bullet or the slightest delay of the fuel spewing from a flamethrower was, for the alert vampire, an opportunity.

"Legend says they command the beasts of the night," Sankar rasped, shuddering in revulsion. "But bugs... I didn't know..."

In the midst of the swarm, the vampires rose. Beside the machines, beneath the machines, *within* the machines, unnatural mist became unnatural flesh. Fists closed or struck with impossible strength, and steel snapped like plywood.

And before the exhausted, scarcely comprehending fugitives, one final figure emerged through a column of mist and a wall of vermin. Coat flapping around his ankles, Constantin Lacusta addressed "his" people.

"You left us," he said. Simple, calm, ignoring the chaos around him.

"I had no choice," Magdalena said. "Ian was... He... I had to. And the others were... They saw what he tried to do."

"And I shall want to hear about it, from all of you, and from him. Where is he?"

"Caged by an artificial stream. Five levels down, toward the building center."

"Assuming," Sankar added just a bit quickly, "the machines haven't done anything to him. We've not seen him since before they reoccupied the installation."

"I see." He turned, barked a quick order, and, though Mags could barely see it, one of the vampires burst into a smaller swarm of bats amidst the larger. It flashed overhead, spiraling down the stairs in search of the missing Ian.

Mags watched them—it—go, and then couldn't hold it in any longer. "Not that I'm complaining, but how can you be here?!"

"We heard enough of your message to take your meaning. We had, I confess, some doubt as to the validity of your claim, but within moments of your broadcast the machines began to withdraw. I interpreted that to mean that your transmission, accurate or not, posed some threat to them. One for which they were now preparing.

"They—just as you, it seems—must surely have expected that we would not depart until after nightfall. They failed to consider that the advance units of their attack were near enough to the mine that they stood beneath the shadow of the overhanging ledge."

And with that, she understood. "No direct sunlight! You just misted into them and rode them all the way here!"

"Indeed." Lacusta waved a hand and the massive swarm flooded past them again, pouring down the stairs, leaving almost a dozen vampires and a sea of wreckage behind. "Other machines yet wait below," he told them. "On the intervening floors, and outside in the streets. Some appear occupied in repairing damage to the railroad tracks, but most, I believe, are intended as reinforcements for..." He waved his fingers dismissively at the broken heaps. "Now, we—"

Even faster than it had vanished, the small cloud of bats reappeared. They flapped up the stairwell, circled once in a tight column, and then Cassie stood beside her master, fangs extended and face distended in fury. With a brief, hateful glare at Mags, she leaned in to whisper in Lacusta's ear.

"I see. Well, Miss Suarez, you needn't worry about Ian making any further threat against you. It appears our enemy chose to leave no danger at their backs."

Ian's dead? As in dead *dead?* She rolled the thought around, chewed on it, and wondered why she couldn't put a name to what she felt.

Later. Feel later.

"Let us go and see," Lacusta continued, "if the child's sacrifice was worth it. And Miss Suarez?"

"Uh, yeah?"

"If it turns out you have brought me here in error, or under false pretenses? You'll wish you'd given yourself wholly to Ian."

It took everything she had not to turn to Sankar or Nestor in panic. Instead, holding herself painfully rigid so that she couldn't tremble, she nodded.

"By all means," the ancient nobleman offered with a faint bow, "lead the way."

Another nod—or was it the same one? Was she so preoccupied she'd forgotten to stop?—and Mags began to pick her way down the debris-strewn steps, toward the sentry bots, the shielded door, and the Eye that, dear God, had damn well *better* be behind them.

Chapter Thirty-Nine

It was the first transmission of its kind in decades.

Broadcast via equipment salvaged from multiple stores in the city center, its audio and visual signals were intended for machine input and human senses both. On every achievable frequency, every usable wavelength; to appear on every screen, sound from every radio.

A burst of static, the electronic snow slowly clearing to reveal a table and three chairs, all facing the camera. The wall behind was gray, neutral. It could have stood anywhere.

In the center chair sat a young woman, dusky of skin, dark of hair. To her right, an old man. If any humans watched the broadcast, odds were he was among the oldest they'd ever seen. His hair, too, was black, though whitening at the temples; his complexion even darker than his companion's.

The third chair, to the woman's left, was unoccupied. Or so it appeared.

"While I hope some of my fellow workers are somehow seeing this, this message is directed specifically to the Eyes all across the world. You know who we are." She turned briefly, but meaningfully, to her left. "And you know who else we speak for."

The empty chair slowly turned and rocked back, as though someone unseen took his ease within.

"Yesterday," she continued, "just before midnight, one of the Eyes—one of your own—went offline. No doubt you know this, and no doubt you learned, before you lost contact, that its home facility was under attack.

"We have it."

The both of them leaned in over the table, toward the camera.

"It has not been harmed," her older companion said. "It's still fully functional, still... alive. We've simply moved it and cut off all means of communication to the network."

The woman picked up the thread again. "We know there aren't many of you. We know that new AIs are currently impossible, the resources to construct another life-modeled system unavailable. We know that one Eye is worth any number of humans, any quantity of resources, to you.

"So here's what's going to happen. What was once Pittsburgh is now a free city. A human city."

"Demeter," the other chimed in abruptly. "The free city of Demeter."

She started, clearly taken by surprise. The other chair also shifted, if only slightly. Then, visibly dismissing her bewilderment, she continued. "You will withdraw from Pitts—Demeter, completely. Every last trace of Eye or machine presence. You will come no closer than thirty miles from the outermost reaches of the Scatters. You will surrender all claim to anyone living in, or who successfully makes it into, the free city.

"In return, we'll keep to ourselves. We won't cause any further trouble for you beyond our borders. The rest of your world can remain as orderly and efficient as you want. And your 'brother' will remain unharmed."

Again it was the old man's turn, and his expression went hard, unwavering. "Make no mistake. We're prepared against any attack, so don't even think about trying to just wipe us out. The Eye is under guard by humans and vampires both, at all times. Their orders are to destroy it at the first sign of any hostilities.

"You know how difficult the vampires are to kill. You know that very few weapons, few explosives, are guaranteed to take them down with any speed. And any that could? Would undoubtedly obliterate your 'brother' along with them.

"Do not respond to this broadcast," the woman concluded. "Signal your agreement to our terms by ordering your machines to depart this city by dawn.

"For all our sakes, I hope you make the right choice."

In the uppermost story of a facility half a block from where Mags and her friends had been held prisoner, Lacusta cast a final glance at the now inactive camera, then leaned back in his chair with a soft chuckle. "Demeter, Mister Rao?"

"I don't get it," Mags complained.

Sankar raised a hand in a half shrug. "A goddess from ancient mythology. Greek. She symbolizes the harvest, rebirth. It seemed appropriate."

"Greek mythology, yes," the vampire said. "But the name appears in other literature as well. I *did* read Stoker's ludicrous fictions. You have a sense of humor I'd not suspected."

"It seemed appropriate," Sankar repeated. Mags decided not to ask.

She had something else to do, anyway.

It wasn't technically a grave. That would have required a body. And the seared *bits*, the encrusted smears she'd found when she'd finally had the chance to examine the "island," did not remotely qualify.

At the time, she'd had nothing left. Exhaustion, confusion, had numbed her completely.

Now? Now she stood in a tiny patch of winter-hardened soil behind one of the seemingly endless buildings, a rare spot in the conformed regions where, come spring, something might actually grow.

She hadn't had the strength, especially not with a small spade as her only tool, to dig deep. But then, all she had to bury was a tattered shirt. Ian's, one of the few personal belongings he'd brought along from the camp where they'd lived as the 13936. His favorite, while he'd been alive. She'd recovered it when vampires located the weapons and belongings the machines had confiscated from their experimental subjects.

Nothing but the uneven heap of dirt under which she'd buried it marked its location now, and Mags hoped weather and growth would soon hide that, too. Nobody needed to know this spot. Nobody but her.

Now that she was here, though, Mags found herself grasping, unsure what to say. She knew only that she had to say *something*.

"It's silly, isn't it? I mean, I should have been thinking about this for months. You've been gone, really, for... But it doesn't feel like it, Ian. It feels like days."

Days which, thus far, had proven far too short for Mags to figure out how she was supposed to feel. Relieved that the monster wearing her lover's face was gone, certainly. But so very much more had gone with it.

"I should have done more. Months ago, I mean. When you were still... I could have made you understand what you were asking for. I shouldn't have let you... let you die.

"But I did. You did. And I couldn't accept it. I shouldn't have let you do what you did to me. I—we—shouldn't have soured your memory like that. I just wasn't strong enough to stop you."

The ground blurred, her cheeks grew chill, but she refused to wipe the tears away.

"I guess... I guess what I should say is: I'm sorry, Ian. I'm sorry I let you down. I'm sorry I believed for one minute that *thing* was you.

"And I'm sorry I can't... I can't promise to remember you only for what you were, not what you were made into. But I promise I'll try.

"I love you."

Some little while later she stood atop a short structure, on the border between the conformed regions and the Scatters. It was an old edifice, only recently reinforced by the machines and not yet put to much use. For her, however, it was a watchtower. Bathed in the glow of floodlights from other buildings where, no doubt, other men and women watched, the bots filed slowly through the old streets, looking somehow sullen despite lack of either emotion or expression.

"They're leaving." She didn't turn to Sankar, hadn't even acknowledged that she knew he stood behind her until she spoke. "Somehow, even after everything, I never thought they would."

He stepped forward, wrapped an arm around her shoulders. "It won't last, you know. All this is temporary."

"Way to celebrate the moment, Sankar."

"I—"

"No, you're right. I know. The machines won't let this stand forever. They'll find a way to attack us, or trick us, or maybe they'll decide someday that their brother's life is worth the sacrifice. But we have time. Maybe a long time. We can prepare."

"All true," he said softly, "but not what I meant."

Mags tilted her head against his shoulder. "I *do* want to see the machines gone eventually. Everywhere, not just here. But you don't mean that either, do you?"

"No."

"Lacusta, then."

"He's a monster and a born dictator, Magdalena. Once he's sure his rule is secure, it'll get harder. A lot harder. And there will be more of his ilk, too.

"What will they eat? For now, they have a few scrips as 'stock,' and gods help them, but eventually? What? Mandated 'volunteer' schedules for the citizenry? A police state with assignment to the larder for any infraction? Maybe he'll abandon the charade completely, and a few people dying every night will just become the new status quo."

"You've given this a lot of thought."

"I have. There's a harsh road ahead, and the people are going to look to you for guidance."

"*Me?*" Mags pulled herself from his friendly embrace. "Sankar, I agreed to do the broadcast, but..."

"You agreed to do the broadcast because everyone *wanted* you to. They all know you made the transmission to Lacusta. You're the hero who showed them the Eyes weren't invulnerable. You're the reason they have a new home."

"No." It was all she could muster.

"Why do you suppose Lacusta never changed you? Always insisted you were unworthy? I think you threaten him. You stood up to him, even as a 'mere' human. You're a leader, Magdalena. People *want* to follow you."

"Well, I don't want them to! I can't—!"

He reached out, took her hands in his—and when he pulled back, she felt something wrapped around her wrist.

She stared, uncomprehending, at the string of prayer beads.

Then, and only then, did she notice the backpack, stuffed to bursting, lying at his feet.

"Sankar? No!" *Not you, too!*

"We both know I'm dead if I stay, Magdalena. Lacusta's put up with me until now, so as not to look weak, but in a city under his rule? My faith is a virus to him. He knows it might spread. He won't allow that."

"But out there?" She sniffled once. "Alone?"

"I'm not decrepit yet! Besides, there's a pretty wide band between us and the machines. Between that slice of wilderness and the Scatters, I'll make do. And I do have this." He reached into the sack, removed one of the team's radios, then rattled off a frequency. "We can't afford to talk often. I could be tracked. But we can check in." He grinned broadly. "And you can come running when I need you."

Magdalena threw her arms around him, nearly knocking them both from their feet. "Your gods better watch out for you there."

"And you," he whispered. "My gods, your parents' God, yourself, your friends. It doesn't matter. It's not our gods that frighten them, it's our faith. So *have* faith."

A soft kiss atop her head, a grunt as he hefted his pack from the rooftop, and Sankar walked away.

Mags was still there when Nestor, Sharon, and Dwayne emerged onto the rooftop to watch the last of the machines withdraw.

"So what now, Mags?" Nest finally asked after a long silence. "Do any of us really know how to run our own lives if we're not enslaved or at war?"

Her fingers slackened, allowing the prayer beads to dangle from her fist with a series of rapid clicks. "Now we learn how. And we learn everything we can, and I mean *everything*, about the vampires. And about Lacusta."

She nearly quailed beneath the growing devotion in their eyes, the weight of their expectation. She didn't want this, didn't want to be responsible for so much. For *them*.

But this wasn't about what she wanted. It never had been.

"'Cause we're *not* running our own lives," she continued.

"We traded one master for another. But the undead aren't all over, all-seeing. Not like the Eyes. We need them to free ourselves of the machines, but after? It'll be time to free ourselves of them, too. *Then* we'll be running our own lives. Like we're supposed to."

"You really believe we're gonna get there?" Dwayne asked, dubious.

Mags looked up, outward. There, in the Scatters, against the very first light of dawn, she swore she saw a lone figure. Maybe Sankar. Maybe one of the humanoid bots, a final straggler. She couldn't tell, and she supposed it didn't matter.

"I do," she finally answered.

"Why?"

"I have faith."

She watched the distant traveler as it crested a small rise and faded into the gleam of the rising sun.

About the Author

When Ari Marmell has free time left over between feeding cats and posting on social media, he writes a little bit. He's been a storyteller since childhood, something he did frequently in lieu of schoolwork. His professional endeavors include novels, scripts, short stories, role-playing games, video games, and the occasional dirty limerick. He's worked with publishers such as Del Rey, Pyr Books, Wizards of the Coast, Titan Books, Aconyte, and now Crossroad Press.

Ari currently resides in Austin, Texas. He lives in a clutter that has a moderate amount of apartment in it, along with George—his wife—and the aforementioned cats, who probably want something.

You can find Ari online, if you're not careful.

Website: mouseferatu.com

Twitter: @mouseferatu

Facebook: facebook.com/mouseferatu/

Curious about other Crossroad Press books?
Stop by our site:
www.crossroadpress.com
We offer quality writing
in digital, audio, and print formats.

Made in the USA
Middletown, DE
19 March 2024

51234041R00217